Wood You Rather?

Lovewell Lumberjacks
Book 3

Daphne Elliot

Melody Publishing, LLC

Published by Melody Publishing, LLC

Editing by Beth Lawton at VB Proofreads

Cover design by Erica Connors

 Created with Vellum

To the anxious control freaks and the over preparers: never change, the world needs us.

Chapter 1
Parker

I put my feet up on my old metal desk and slammed my laptop shut. Billing, tracking expenses, and responding to unhinged emails from clients were far from my favorite tasks.

But they were my reality now.

I leaned back in the old chair and took a big sip of my iced coffee. Things weren't bad. Despite my dad's best efforts, I had clients, and my business was growing. But it turned out that working for myself wasn't as satisfying as I had imagined.

I tipped back another inch or so, the chair squeaking loudly. One of the armrests was constructed entirely out of duct tape, and the cushion was so worn it offered no padding, but I wasn't the prissy type. It was a chair. It did its job.

Until it didn't. Because in one instant, I was sipping my coffee and channeling all the positivity I possessed, and in the next, I was plummeting to the ground. I hit the linoleum floor with a thud, and the cold rush of iced coffee hit my neck and chest.

Fuck. My. Life.

I picked my head up and surveyed my surroundings. The chair was in pieces, several looking sharp enough to do real damage. I was wearing my coffee, and I had no doubt that by morning, I would be covered in bruises. My hip throbbed, and there was already a twinge in my shoulder. Motherfucking old-ass chair. Why hadn't I driven my ass to Staples and bought a new one?

Comfortable chairs are a human right, not an outrageous luxury. When would I stop punishing myself?

I stood slowly, cringing as the coffee seeped through my bra. It was one of my favorites, pearl pink lace, and it would likely never be the same.

Before I could fully recover, there was a loud knock on the door. And I hadn't even steadied myself on my feet before it opened.

I was brushing the ice cubes off my pants when I saw him.

Fire coursed through my veins, and my spine snapped straight. What the fuck was he doing here?

I crossed my arms over my chest, fully aware that my silk shell was probably transparent.

"Can I help you?" My voice shook slightly, and I cursed myself for not being more self-possessed.

"Good to see you, Sergeant Harding."

"It's just Parker now," I gritted, mustering as much dignity as I could, given the circumstances.

He nodded. The fucker knew I wasn't with the force anymore. Why else would he be standing here? Also, why *was* he standing here?

I hadn't responded to his emails or his calls. Still had no clue what he wanted, but I sure as hell wasn't doing business with the man responsible for the death of my career.

"What do you want, Gagnon?"

He smirked. That fucker smirked at me. "I'm here to hire you."

I laughed. Fancy corporate assholes like Pascal Gagnon did not hire lowly PIs like me, no matter how prestigious my background.

"Leave. I've got real work to do."

He took a step closer, taking in my old desk and the broken chair.

"Of course. I wouldn't want to keep you from all your vital work. If the location of your office is anything to go by, you're clearly wildly successful. Doesn't get more professional than the back room of a tattoo shop." He scanned my pathetic space for emphasis.

Miraculously, I resisted the urge to pick up my stapler and throw it at his head. With my luck, it would pull a boomerang move and wind up injuring me instead.

"This is an adjacent gathering space," I said, lifting my chin. "Not a back room. I rent this office and use it for my business. As you could see by the sign on the door." I waved him toward the door and plastered a fake smile to my face. "Take a look on your way out."

"You didn't return my calls."

"I'm busy."

He grabbed a folding chair from the stack in the corner, flipped it open, turned it around, and straddled it in a matter of seconds.

Whoa. He did *not* seem like the sit backward in a folding chair type.

But now his thick forearms were draped over the back of it, and his eyes were dark and serious.

"Parker." His voice was deep and gravelly, and I really hated the way my body naturally leaned forward in response.

"I want to hire you. I—well, my family—we need your help."

I sighed. Today had already been a shit show. And here I was, wearing my coffee and distracted by the light dusting of dark hair on his tanned forearms. Those were the forearms of a working man, not an entitled number cruncher like this dude. And the expensive dress shirt with its sleeves rolled perfectly to the elbow and the crisp white fabric highlighting his golden skin didn't help either.

"Not interested," I said, picking up a stack of papers on my desk in an effort to look busy. "First of all, my business is here, in Portland. I can't drop everything and head up to East Bumfuck." I piled things neatly, actively avoiding his steady gaze. "And second, I'm not going to work for an entitled asshole I actively dislike."

He let out a deep chuckle. "Aw. And all this time I thought you hated me."

I pinned him with a glare. *Dammit.* Twin dimples teased me from beneath the thick stubble. "Nah, that takes too much energy. All I can muster up for you is moderate irritation and mild disdain."

"I'm wounded."

"You should be. Get the fuck out of my office. I'm trying to build a business here."

And I *was* building a business. It wasn't the business I'd hoped for, but it was mine.

"Huh." He steepled his fingers on the back of the damn chair. "Catching cheating husbands? Tracking down deadbeat dads? Running background checks? Is that the kind of work you live and breathe for?"

Ass. We couldn't all be finance douches with MBAs and

Beamers. Maybe my job wasn't glamorous, but it was honest work, and I was helping people. Most of the time.

"Fuck off. I've got things to do."

But the jerk didn't budge. He stayed planted in that chair, looking all rich and powerful and handsome. After the shit hit the fan, he lost his job, but that was all I knew. Clearly, he'd landed on his feet if he was sitting in my office wearing those fancy shoes.

I had met many versions of this guy over the years. Conducting financial investigations usually meant coming face to face with privileged rich dudes who believed it was their right to lie, cheat, and steal their way through life. Whose families and prep schools and country clubs insulated them from the consequences of their actions.

"Please. After everything that happened, you owe me."

I scoffed and balled my fists at my sides. I wasn't huge, but I was strong as fuck and had spent years training. I could have him pinned to the floor and crying for his mama in seconds. And part of me really enjoyed the thought of that scenario. I'd have to unpack that later.

"Puh-lease. I don't owe you shit. If anything, you owe me. If you hadn't fucked up my investigation, I wouldn't have left the state police."

"You left. I got fired. Big difference. My entire career? Down the drain. My name is mud in the private equity world now."

"Oh no, what will you do? The other privileged frat bros don't want you to play in their tequila and roofie-laced sandbox? They'll make deals and move money around to evade taxes without you?" I teased. "Get me a tissue. I can barely contain my empathetic sobs."

"I forgot how mouthy you are," he growled.

My thighs involuntarily clenched at the sound. Dammit.

"Please don't make that sound sexy. You repulse me," I said, pressing my arms tighter to my chest to conceal the nipples that were trying to escape my fanciest bra.

He ran his hands through his hair, and for half a second, the façade fell. The dark circles under his eyes were more pronounced, the gray hairs at his temples highlighted by the overhead lights, and the slump shoulders heavier.

"Please listen for one minute. And then I'll leave."

I nodded. Rolling my lips in frustration.

"My father died two years ago."

Okay, this time my empathy really did kick in. "I'm very sorry for your loss."

"He was murdered."

I froze. That was the last thing I'd expected him to say. "Oh shit."

"At the time, it was ruled an accident. Driver error. But we have new evidence."

I nodded. I had been in this situation before. As a detective, I couldn't count how many times people came to me with theories and "evidence," hoping to make sense of the senseless. It was the shitty part of the job. Watching people fall apart in real time, and being forced to stand by while they searched for answers they would probably never get. Because terrible shit happened every day. And most of the time, there was no rhyme or reason for it.

I went to the wall and snagged a folding chair for myself.

"Tell me more," I said, setting it up behind my desk.

"My sister," he murmured, studying his hands, "she's an engineer. And she manages our equipment. She found evidence that the brakes had been tampered with. This part called the slack adjuster. I have photos on my phone." He dug into his pocket and pulled out the device.

I held up a hand. I had no idea how brakes worked, so photos would do us no good. "Did you contact the police?"

"Of course. The police, the FBI, the safety inspectors. The forestry commission." His voice cracked in frustration on the last word.

"And because they closed the case two years ago, no one wants to reopen it," I guessed, keeping my voice soft.

He looked up, his eyes—eyes that just a few minutes ago had been cold and calculating—swam with sadness. "Yes. And that's not it. Last year, my brother Henri was in a serious accident. Same cause." He rubbed the back of his neck. "Something big is going on."

All my senses tingled. I had so many questions. The familiar whirring of my brain activated, ready for a problem to solve. A puzzle to put together piece by tiny piece.

But before I could ask any follow-ups, the door swung open.

"Is this guy bothering you, Parker?" Tex was standing in the doorway, his large, tattooed arms folded across his expansive chest. He was technically my landlord, since he owned the building and the tattoo parlor, but he was also my friend.

I gave him a smile. His drawl was adorable, as was his huge heart.

We'd fooled around a couple of times when I was in a bad spot the previous year, but there wasn't any chemistry. He was a big, burly, tattooed biker, but a total softie on the inside. I let him down easy, and he'd been an excellent friend every day since.

He eyed Pascal up and down, one side of his mouth hitched up, making it clear he was not impressed. Tex was objectively terrifying, but Pascal didn't seem bothered. My ex-boyfriend Bryce, despite being a federal agent, would have shit his pants if a guy like Tex had glared at him.

But instead, Pascal looked annoyed.

He gave Tex a dismissive smile. "We're discussing business. Could you give us some privacy? As I'm sure you understand, Ms. Harding's business requires the utmost discretion."

Tex grunted in response and watched me, waiting for direction.

"It's business," I said, raising a brow, silently signaling that he should leave.

Turning slowly, he said, "I'll be outside if you need me, sugar."

When he was gone, Pascal narrowed his eyes on me. "Is that your boyfriend?"

"Maybe," I said flippantly, annoyed with the interruption and also with his prying. "Why do you care?"

"I don't. Just trying to determine whether you're actually capable of doing this job."

"Says the man begging me to take it."

"I don't beg," he grumbled, his voice deep and smooth. He tugged on the collar of his dress shirt like it didn't fit properly. But from where I sat, it looked like it was custom made for his body. On further inspection, I realized that, though his suit was expensive, as well as his shoes—and despite the haughty air he put on—he was restless. Uncomfortable in his own skin. It was fascinating.

He clearly put a lot of time and effort into cultivating this veneer of confidence and professionalism. But there were cracks in that armor. Though most people probably didn't see them.

But I wasn't most people.

I was trained to ignore the pretense and the exterior and look deeply.

And looking into those deep brown eyes, I saw a man who was scared.

And fuck me, I felt that familiar tug in my gut. The one that told me I should help. That I could help. I could find answers to unanswerable questions. Give him closure. That feeling was what had pushed me into law enforcement in the first place.

"Listen, I need someone I can trust. That my family can trust. We need to do this right."

I closed my eyes and took a breath. This was becoming more and more difficult to walk away from. It was like he knew just how to activate my hero complex. "And you trust me?" I asked, twirling the end of my ponytail, a tell that I couldn't control. "Because I sure as shit don't trust you."

"I don't trust you," he said, holding my gaze for a moment longer than necessary. "Yet. But I think I could. You're smart."

"No shit," I replied.

"And determined."

Twirl, twirl. I could not stop touching my hair around him. "Naturally."

"And," he said, placing his large, masculine hands on the table and leaning toward me. "You don't give up. Those are all terrible qualities for a person who wants to move up in a backward boys' club bureaucracy like the state police, but in this line of work, it's gold."

I was taken aback. He had a read on me, that was for sure. "You're not wrong," I hedged.

"You don't like me. And you blame me. I get that. But we both know your days with the state police were numbered.

Because mouthy women who are always right are not the ones who get promoted."

"Hey!"

He held up one hand. "I didn't create the patriarchy. I'm merely offering an observation about the world we live in. And hopefully helping you see that as much as you want to blame me, maybe there was more to it."

This fucker had a point, and I was not here for it. He was getting under my skin, saying the quiet things out loud. Things I knew but pushed down so I could let my anger and resentment flourish. I wanted him out of my office.

"Name your price. And I'll supply anything you need if you'll come up to Lovewell and take your time. Follow the leads. We have evidence to get you started. There are so many threads to tug on. That's why we need you, someone with the brains to put it all together."

He paused and inspected me, clearly gauging my reaction.

My stupid lack of a poker face was obviously betraying me, because he smiled. Then he went on. "It will get you out of this place, and if this goes as deep as I think it does, it could put you on the map. Get you bigger jobs, more connections. Help grow your business."

I tried to school my expression, though my curiosity was getting the best of me. Dozens of questions were already swirling around in my brain. It wasn't about money. No, this was about the cold trail of evidence begging for me to follow it.

"I have a lot going on right now," I said lamely.

"Think about it," he said, sitting straighter and tugging on his collar again. "I'll be in the city for a few days."

He slid a thick business card across my old desk.

"Call me when you want to talk. I can give you more details."

With that, he stood, making my tiny office feel even smaller, and strode out the door without a backward glance.

It was only then that I glanced down at my coffee-stained shirt and noticed that not only was my pink bra visible, but so were my very attentive nipples. *Motherfucker.*

Chapter 2
Parker

I rolled over and stared at the ceiling. It was an old home, and not in that charming, vintage way. The original plaster moldings, once beautiful, were now peeling. And the wide-plank floors were scuffed into oblivion.

But the federalist style brick mansion possessed a certain grandeur. A history. Gravitas. Nestled in the Old Port District, it was in the heart of the old city, where a history lesson could be found on every corner. The British had burned this entire area to the ground during the revolutionary war.

The house belonged to Liv, my best friend, who had inherited it from her great-aunt. Since college, a group of us had moved in and out at random. It had seven bedrooms, so there was always space, and while she had done a damn good job of fixing it up over the years, most of the money had been sunk into very unsexy things like upgrading the wiring and replacing the roof.

Thus, my room featured ancient peeling mint green wallpaper with climbing roses all over it and a window that wouldn't open.

But Liv loved this house, and always, she generously opened it up to friends and family who needed a place to stay. It had a massive library, where she wrote, and several rescue animals that warmed the place up. At any given time, visitors filled the extra rooms, and the home was filled with lots of laughter and music every weekend.

At the moment, the house was fairly empty. Marc, a writer friend of Liv's from Warsaw, was staying for a few months while he workshopped his new book.

And then there was me.

I had done more than a few stints on Pearl Street. Liv and my old room always welcomed me back with open arms. It'd been several years since I'd bunked here last, and for a time, I really thought I'd never come back.

But life had a funny way of boomeranging a person around when they least expected it.

Even after resigning from the state police and losing my paycheck, benefits, and future pension, I optimistically thought I could swing it. But ultimately, I'd had to sell my condo. The mortgage and taxes put me in too much of a pinch when I started my business. I'd wanted to get away from that life and those goals anyway. It had been a soulless place. New construction, beige walls, the same shitty granite countertops in every unit.

I'd purchased it because it felt like the right thing to do. But in the end, it became one more thing dragging me down, shackling me to a life and a version of myself I didn't like.

So I'd sold it, made a tiny profit, and moved back in here. The rent was cheap, my best friend was here, and there was always Diet Coke in the fridge. One of her rescue cats had taken a liking to me. His name was Chris Hemsworth, and he came up most nights for a quick snuggle before tiring of me and wandering off. Those moments alone were filled with more affection than I'd gotten in the last few years. Or for the entirety of my childhood.

"Are you going to tell me why you're lying in bed fully clothed at"—Liv checked her watch—"5:18p.m.?" She sauntered through the open door, her dirty blond hair was pulled up in a wild knot on top of her head, and she was wearing a camisole and a hot pink silk shawl.

"Did I interrupt your sprints?" I asked.

"Nope. Hit my word count for the day. Was gonna make gnocchi tonight. You game?"

A smile spread across my face, and I nodded. Liv was a fantastic cook. She claimed that it was an effective procrastination strategy. When her characters weren't talking to her, she would make beef Wellington or baked Alaska or any number of complicated, time-consuming meals.

Her dinner parties were legendary, both because of her cooking and because, when she inherited this crumbling old mansion, she also inherited its fully stocked wine cellar. Back when we were broke twentysomethings, we'd uncork five-hundred-dollar bottles of wine to pair with our ramen noodles.

"I've got to work late tonight. Thought I'd rest for a bit. I had a weird day."

She flopped to the mattress beside me and surveyed the crumbling medallion in the ceiling. "Another stakeout? This fucker is too slippery."

She was right. I had been chasing this guy for the last two weeks, desperate to get the evidence my client needed. Which meant lots of cold nights in my car, bored out of my skull.

I was working a matter for Diana Gainsborough, a society lady and woman about town. She was married to Dr. Gainsborough, who was a member of one of Portland's old shipping families and a close friend of my father's. They had four kids, two houses, and dozens of marital problems.

Diana had hired me to find evidence of her husband's infidelity in order to nullify their prenup. Along the way, I had discovered he was hiding assets from his soon to be ex-wife. I'd also stumbled upon some fun insider trading. I'd be sure to tip off the DA once I got what I needed for my client.

Gainsborough was a scumbag. I had him at strip clubs and I had him bribing city officials, but so far, I hadn't been able to snag photographic evidence of him banging his mistress. He was crafty and evasive. He wasn't particularly secretive, but I was still working to understand his patterns. Sometimes he'd drive himself to their trysts, and other times, he'd use a ride share.

But despite all the tailing I'd done, I had a hunch that I hadn't dug up all I wanted. And I wanted it all so I could nail him to the wall. Diana would be fine regardless. She was wealthy and well connected in her own right. But there was something satisfying about sticking it to a terrible man.

"This guy came to see me today. Pascal Gagnon."

She rolled over, snagging one of my pillows and hugging it to her chest. "That name sounds familiar."

I scrolled through Instagram on my phone, looking for a photo of him I had found earlier. He didn't have social media as far as I could tell, but his youngest brother did. He was a professional athlete of some sort and had shots of his family on his profile.

Perhaps I had spent the afternoon stalking Pascal Gagnon online. I'd gathered as much information as I could about his family's lumber business and the death of his father, Frank Gagnon, two years prior. It was what I did. I dug and dug until all the answers were revealed.

"Here." I held up my phone.

"Hmm." She took the device and held it out over her head, using two fingers to zoom in on the photo. "I don't know him, but *damn*," she said, handing it back to me. "How do you know him? He ask you out?"

I snagged a throw pillow from above my head and swatted her with it. "Jesus. No. He was an informant in a case I worked a couple of years back."

She sat up, eyes wide. "A case or *the* case?"

I bit my lip. There was no use dodging the question. When she got that look, she was like a dog with a bone. "*The* case," I mumbled, rolling over and pressing a pillow to my face, which Liv promptly pulled off.

I stared at the wall, studying the old wallpaper until my eyes lost focus. The case. The one that had ruined my career. The investigation that had gotten fucked six ways from Sunday.

The one that ruined my life.

And it was his fault. Pascal Gagnon was a slick suit who was too smart for his own good. And like all finance bros, he possessed the kind of unearned self-confidence that led others to make mistakes and overlook details.

"It was him," I breathed out after a long silence. "He sent the wrong files and blew the whole investigation."

Liv slung her arm around me and dropped her head on my shoulder. "Didn't he get fired?"

"Yeah. And you know what happened to me."

"Yup," she said into my hair. "Scapegoated."

"Not sure that's a verb."

"I'm a writer. I know these things."

I hit her with the pillow. "Not just a writer. An amazon top one hundred author."

She lifted one shoulder. "For a few hours."

"It counts," I insisted. "Maybe you're not a millionaire yet, but L.T. Shipman is on the verge of blowing up. Especially with the new series."

"The first book was your idea."

"Nah." I shook my head. "I only helped you with the murder details."

Liv self-published suspense novels. She was crazy talented and had a very loyal following all over the world. Her fans loved the unique way she combined psychological thriller, horror, and romance. "The rest was all you and your dark, dark mind."

She laughed. "I suppose you're right. You'll never meet another person as nuts as I am. Don't forget your promise."

With a grin, I nodded. If anything ever happened to Liv, I had been instructed to clear her search history, delete the contents of her Kindle, and dispose of her vibrators.

She sat up and crossed her legs, pinning me with a look. "Stop deflecting. What's the deal?"

"He thinks his father was murdered," I said.

The look on his face when he told me, the fear and the sadness, flashed through my mind. In that moment, he looked nothing like the guy I'd known a few years before.

He was older, wearier, with gray hairs peppering his temples. His patented *my shit don't stink* sparkle had been snuffed out. He had been the type to buy rounds for everyone at the club. That alone had made him a valuable law enforcement asset. His dickwad clients loved to tell him their dirty secrets over drinks.

"Shit. Really?" Liv asked, clutching her shawl closed.

I nodded. "It's intense. Trucking accident on a remote logging road. Police and safety inspectors ruled it an accident two years ago. But the family recently uncovered evidence that suggests tampering."

I had always put stock in the work of my colleagues. Investigators usually did their jobs, and despite what most people thought, most of the work was pretty black and white. But as Paz had shared the details, the hairs on my arms stood up. I couldn't shake the feeling that he was right and there was way more to this story. So despite the black and white, I couldn't ignore my gut.

"He and his siblings want to hire me to find the truth."

She got up and paced from the door to the window and back again, pursing her lips as the wheels in her mind turned. "You should do it. You're so talented."

I sat up, hugging my pillow. "I don't know."

"As long as the pay is good, I say go for it. This is the kind of work you've been looking for. This is so much more than catching cheating husbands and running employee background checks. Get away from the network of cronies who have blacklisted you and make a name for yourself."

Liv was rarely wrong. My father was a classic abusive narcissist. He had been furious when I left the state police, and he'd done what he could to make my life difficult. It had always been this way. Even when I was a kid, if I did what he wanted, if I made him look good, then he'd shower me with love, affection, and praise. If I didn't do exactly as told, he'd manipulate, lie, and interfere until I was forced to do it his way.

After a lifetime of emotional abuse and several years of therapy, I'd learned to say no. I'd drawn boundaries, and I was standing on my own two feet. That meant leaving the force and going out on my own as a private investigator. It wouldn't have been my first choice, but when I found myself miserable, fed up, and facing years of traffic duty after the case that shall not be named, it felt like the right choice.

Sadly, my father didn't agree. He'd used his power, influence, and connections to make sure no decent client in New England wanted to hire me.

"I think you should go. Head up to wherever the fuck it is. Canada?"

I laughed. A quick google search had revealed that Lovewell Maine was a tiny logging town situated hours from anything, smack dab in an enormous state. "No, but close."

She tapped her chin. "Okay, head up to the great north, where people fuck moose for fun and subsist solely on potatoes and expired Moxie. Go up there; have an adventure." She was dancing around now, clearly inspired by my disastrous day. With my luck, a loose version of this situation would appear in her next book. "You'll solve the mystery. Because you're freaking brilliant. You'll uncover what the cops missed." She shuffled to the bed, tilted forward, and cupped my face. "And then you'll come home a hero, with experience and confidence and a plan."

"When you put it like that," I said, rolling my eyes.

She bopped me on the nose. "Parker Harding, we both know you're bored out of your skull. This is the challenge you need. It'll get you out of this room and back into the world of the living."

As always, her enthusiasm was infectious. The more she talked, the more I wanted to do this. To work this case, unearth all the small-town secrets, and help this family get the closure they needed. Bringing bad guys to justice would be a nice perk too.

"Plus, you can have a hot fling with a lumberjack."

"I seriously doubt that. If I want to repair my reputation

and get the experience I need to prove to the people here that I can and will help, then I need to stay focused. And let's face it, in a tiny logging town, the pickings will be more than slim."

She reached out, and when I put my hand in hers, she pulled me up off the bed. "You're definitely not getting laid with that kind of attitude. Now come downstairs so I can feed you before you head out on your super boring stakeout."

I slumped in the front seat of my car, rolling my shoulders, in search of relief. I had been here for three hours, and so far, nothing.

Stakeouts were the worst. Movies and TV made them look glamorous, but sitting in my car until my legs went numb, hoping for a sliver of evidence, was pure misery.

My phone dinged from the cupholder. Without taking my eye off the house I was watching, I snagged it and held it out in front of me.

Paz. Ugh, I should have known he would be persistent. His brand of alpha asshole wasn't used to hearing the word no.

You're thinking about the case, aren't you?

He wasn't wrong. It had only been about twelve hours since he showed up in my office, but I'd already mentally planned out the information-gathering stage of my investigation. Records, maps, financial filings. Starting with the paperwork would give me a feel for things.

I think you'd really like Lovewell.

A photo came through. Naturally, it was an image of a massive moose.

> This is Clive. He's one of many moose up here. He may seem out of your league, but I promise, you could enjoy a vibrant social life up here.

I laughed, despite myself. Maybe the soulless corporate bastard did have a sense of humor.

Keeping the window of the luxury townhouse in my periphery, I responded quickly.

> I'm going to need you to walk me through all the evidence. I don't have months to waste on half-baked theories.

I brought my phone to my lap and focused on the task at hand again. But naturally, another chime sounded almost immediately.

> Done. Dinner. Tomorrow night at Fore Street. 7 pm.

Was he high? There was no way I'd meet him at a fancy, romantic restaurant like that. How could we talk about evidence and records and truck brakes over candlelight and vintage wine? Nope. For a guy like him, reservations at Fore Street were probably like going to Chipotle for the rest of us, but no thank you.

> No. Meet me at my office at 4. Bring everything you have. I'll look it over and think about it.

Sorry. I'm the client. Your office is depressing, and the mussels at Fore Street are life changing.

I'm not meeting you at one of the fanciest restaurants in town.

My treat. I live in the boonies now. Can't pass up an opportunity for fine dining.

I hated to break it to him, but that wasn't how I did business. What should be a quick informational meeting under the flickering fluorescent lights of my dingy office would, if he got his way, become a meal that lasted half the night. And I'd have to share it with a man who infuriated me to no end.

Choosing not to respond, I returned my attention to the stakeout. Closing this case would not only mean a paycheck, but it would also free up my evenings and alleviate my lower back pain.

Pascal could sweat. Despite my utter lack of interest in the suggestion, I would meet him. He was the client, after all. But I wouldn't go willingly, and I'd be vigilant. I'd force him to remain professional and stick to discussing business only. That would work, right?

My phone flashed again.

Wear something sexy.

Talk like that and I'll be wearing my sidearm.

hot.

Chapter 3
Pascal

I stood up when she strode through the small restaurant like she owned the place. She had her dark hair slicked back into a ponytail that hung down her back. And she was wearing a dress. I had never considered Parker as the kind of woman who wore dresses, but shit, she looked amazing.

Granted, I didn't know her well. Our paths had crossed a couple of years ago when my career went to shit, and aside from her slightly annoying personality and professional skills I couldn't help but respect, she hadn't made much of an impression.

But after months of searching for an investigator, I wound up in her office. And I used that term loosely. It was wild that someone with a résumé like hers would be working out of a glorified utility closet in the back of a tattoo shop. But what did I know? The past few years had certainly not been what I had expected.

So my job tonight was simple. Pull out all the stops. Do whatever it took to convince her to take the case. Because my family needed her considerable talent in order to help us finally understand what had happened to my father.

Because the unknown was becoming suffocating. It was a heavy rock that rested on my chest every moment of every day. Since Adele had shown us those brakes, I hadn't been able to take a single deep breath. Something horrific had happened. Twice. And if we didn't solve this, it could happen again. We could lose another person we loved.

My life had gone to shit, and that was an understatement. But I had one job these days—protect my family. And I would use every dollar I had and all my connections to keep them safe and secure.

Even if the price was an evening with this woman.

As she made her way through the crowded space, I had to remind myself that I disliked her. Because the sight of her was scrambling my brain.

It was probably the dress. Definitely.

It was black. The top was conservative, with a high neck and long sleeves. But the skirt was short. So short that my traitorous eyes drank in every inch of her long legs.

Parker Harding was not a tall woman, but she was athletic and carried herself like she could take on the world.

As she approached, I was momentarily stunned by her glossy lips and her thick eyelashes.

I pulled out her chair, ignoring the grimace she gave me as she sat.

This would be even harder than I thought. Because I was here, in a Michelin-starred restaurant with flickering candles on the table, seated across from a complete bombshell.

It had been years since I'd shared a meal with a gorgeous woman.

My sex life had certainly slowed when I moved up north,

though I still had plenty of fun. But I didn't date. Sipping wine and verbally sparring and soaking up the delicious tension for hours with a woman I ached to get naked? Hadn't realized I missed it until this very moment.

Not that I wanted to get Parker naked, of course. She was pretty, sure, but my response was purely biological. I was a man, after all. And she was wearing a sexy dress.

Though the look of annoyed boredom on her face helped. Because it left my dick confused as hell.

"This isn't a date, Gagnon. Stop looking at me like you want to eat me for dinner," she snapped, placing her napkin on her lap in a prim way that juxtaposed her fiery words.

I froze. Dammit. Looked like my cock liked the sass. Those words, that tone, would be my undoing.

She was tough and rough around the edges but sleek and pretty and mouthy all at the same time. Shit, it was a turn-on. She was probably the type who would insult my technique in bed. And I'd love every fucking second of it.

I shook the thought away and urged my dick to knock it off. Because I was desperate. My siblings were counting on me to find a PI who would go above and beyond to help us. None of the folks in Boston I'd called had any interest in schlepping up to Northern Maine. And frankly, outsiders would have a hard time getting information from the locals.

And while there were some very well-regarded people doing investigative work in and around Portland, so many were connected to the logging industry. Given the stakes, we couldn't risk compromising the investigation we'd started.

Law enforcement had been no help. Even after my brother Remy and his wife Hazel were literally chased by drug traffickers through logging territory this summer.

It was all related. Dad's death, Henri's accident, the cache of pills and guns Remy and Hazel had stumbled upon.

"Can we hurry this along?" She smoothed the front of her dress. "I've got someplace to be."

My stomach clenched. Did she have a date? I had invited her to dinner. It would take as long as it took. Did she seriously plan to meet up with some dude after I bought her an over-priced gourmet meal?

"We have business to discuss," I said coolly, dropping one forearm to the table and sitting back in my chair.

Her mouth turned up in a sardonic smile. "I promised to hear you out. I did not promise to stay for dinner or take the job."

There was no way in hell she was leaving here looking like that. I would keep her fine ass in that chair until she agreed to take the damn job. Then I'd insist she go straight home to start working on it.

I gave the waiter a confident smile. "I'd like a bottle of the Evenstad pinot noir to start."

"Water for me." Parker huffed.

The waiter, likely a local college kid, looked uncomfortable.

"Two glasses." I held up my fingers. "And oysters."

"Very good, sir," he said, scurrying away.

"Are you shitting me?"

I leaned back in my chair again and folded my arms. "Nope. Do you have any idea what the culinary options are like where I live? I'm going to relish every second of this meal. Even if the company is subpar."

She sat silently for a moment, with her hard eyes fixed on me. I took the opportunity to unabashedly study her face. High cheekbones, square jawline, and a thick and undoubtedly bitable bottom lip. She was using some sort of cop trick on me.

Sit silently so the opposition gets uncomfortable, thus securing the upper hand.

I'd love to say it wasn't working, but my collar felt tight and desperation coursed through me. I needed her.

I scratched my beard. Or whatever this was on my face. I had lost a bet with my baby brother, Remy. He'd competed in the National Timbersport Championships last summer. And I told him if he won, I'd grow a beard.

The bastard placed fifth overall, but won the speed climbing event, setting a record in the process. Here I thought I was the smart one of the bunch, but I'd neglected to clarify whether winning a single event counted. So my siblings voted, and I was forced into growing a beard.

I'd always been a clean-shaven guy. Beards were the standard in Northern Maine; it was far more distinctive to show the world my jaw.

I'd never been a country boy like either of my brothers. Sure, I was born and raised in Lovewell, but my heart had always been elsewhere. Or maybe it was my head. Not sure I'd ever had much of a heart, really. If I ever did, it was nonexistent these days.

I had to fight the urge to pick up my phone and check my email again. I had been gone two days, but I had been checking in on operations back in Lovewell every few hours. Things were finally picking up. We were looking at a really strong upcoming season, and the work I had been doing to clean up the finances was finally falling into place.

My fingers itched as I eyed the device in its crushproof rubber case. It was an impulse I struggled to control. The constant need to check on everyone and everything. Texting my mom every morning to make sure she was alive. Though I never voiced my concerns so blatantly. That would be crazy.

Instead, I'd send her a funny meme or random quote or my Wordle score, just to get her to respond.

Other times, I would stop by my brother's house to talk to his kids about how school had gone that week. Then there were the daily calls to Richard at camp. Those allowed me to verify that our guys were safe and that things were proceeding according to plan. There were so many variables in the woods. So many things that could go wrong. It only made sense to keep on top of things.

I took a deep breath and forced my mind to focus on the task at hand, convincing Parker to take the case.

"Let me walk you through some of the background," I said, breaking what could only be described as a torturously long silence.

She gave me a single nod in response.

I dove into our story, feeling more unnerved by her beauty and backbone by the second.

First, I ran through the basics of the timber industry—how we operate and manage and maintain our roads and land. Then gave her a brief overview of the families and our history. I went into a little more depth about how the logging roads allowed opioid traffickers from Canada to reach the US undetected.

She nodded along thoughtfully. At one point, she opened her massive purse to remove a notebook. I paused while she scribbled notes, considering how I should play this. Go with honesty and tell her how desperate we were? Or play it cool? Option two was my default. Except our brief interactions alone told me she wouldn't be swayed by my bullshit and bluster.

After she'd taken two pages of notes, she set her pen down and lifted her wineglass. She swirled the dark liquid, then brought the glass to her nose and inhaled. With an appreciative look on her face, she took a sip and let out a tiny sigh of pleasure.

That noise, probably imperceptible to most, had my pants tightening. Thank fuck my lower half was hidden beneath the table.

It was intoxicating. Giving Parker pleasure, even if only through my selection of the perfect wine, was a type of rush I had never experienced.

"I can take you through the process, from cut to transport to mill. It's dangerous work. Technically the most dangerous job in the United States. Everyone thinks it's the cutting and the machinery, but our process and safety procedures are top-notch.

"The real danger lies on the road. Narrow mountain roads are hazards year-round, but in the dead of winter, when the majority of cutting happens, they're treacherous."

She tipped her head while she listened, nibbling on the tip of her pen. Those plump, glossy lips were distracting. The way her eyes narrowed and her face scrunched when she was concentrating wasn't just cute. It was sexy as hell.

She interrupted me constantly, asking question after question. "So you think this is related to drug trafficking?"

I paused, taking a sip of wine. "Yes." There was no use beating around the bush. The others I'd spoken to thought I was crazy. But how could it not be? Especially after what had happened to Henri and then to Remy and Hazel. Those incidents weren't coincidental. Bad things were going down in those woods.

"Could your dad have been involved?"

"No," I snapped, my anger getting the best of me. "Sorry." I tugged at my hair. Right now, I wasn't sure what to believe. "Dad hated drugs and always cooperated with law enforcement. He was a real by the book type. And he was invested in our community and helping those who struggled."

She jotted more notes, keeping her head ducked and scribbling furiously.

My heart raced. Could she help us? The more I spoke about this, the more I realized how much I needed answers. How much we all did.

"But," I continued, because I might as well lay all the cards on the table, "I'm beginning to think he knew who was involved. He brought home files." And not only files. Old maps and ledgers and rolls from years back. No one questioned what his interest was. My dad was like that. Always working, always thinking.

"Old files, half of which are in Acadian French. My brother Henri spent months studying them but hasn't found any answers. My sister-in-law Hazel put a few of the pieces together, though. She found reference to a location no one had heard of. Turns out it was a stash house for the traffickers."

"Wow. She's good."

I shrugged. She didn't know the half of it. Hazel was a genius who had discovered more than all four of us Gagnon siblings put together. "I told you; my entire family is invested in getting justice."

We were interrupted when our waiter delivered our entrées.

She brought a bite of her hanger steak to her mouth and slid her fork between her teeth. "Damn," she said softly, closing her eyes and tipping her chin up.

I froze, and my chest constricted. I was captivated by the look of pure pleasure on her face. Parker was an enigma. She was all hard edges and badass attitude, but with a softer side that came out in these *blink and you'll miss it* moments.

We ate in a comfortable silence for a few minutes. The food was too good and the conversation too heavy to continue.

And I enjoyed it. After a few minutes, we made small talk about the food. We sipped really good wine and simply existed in one another's presence.

Even though our reason for meeting was a devastating one, I felt a little like myself. Not exactly carefree, but engaged. Maybe it was the wine or the fancy restaurant or the pretty girl, but the numbness that had defined so many of my days recently was starting to fade.

But like all good things, it couldn't last.

Because as the tension drained from my shoulders, my phone buzzed. The phone that was face up on the tiny bistro table. And it was a text.

My reflexes were usually fast. But I was momentarily frozen, worried that because I hadn't checked in at work, something had gone wrong.

So instead of immediately grabbing it, I stared down at it for a moment too long. A message popped up. And Parker, paused with a forkful of steak on its way to her mouth, saw it.

It wasn't only a text. There was a selfie too. And while I couldn't make out the identity of the subject of the photo, it was obviously a woman in a very tight dress.

"Freckles?" she asked, her eyes widening at the photo.

I snatched up the phone and unlocked it.

> Hey cutie! Heard a rumor you were in town.
> Text me later if you wanna meet up.

She had thoughtfully sent a selfie as a reminder of her identity. She was making duck lips while squeezing her tits together in a way she probably thought was sexy but was thirsty as hell.

I ignored the text and put the phone facedown on the table, hoping to reengage the conversation about the case.

"What's her name?" Parker was smirking at me.

Fuck, why did that look have to be so sexy?

"Kate," I said with fake conviction, then popped another bite of pork loin into my mouth.

She cocked a brow and pulled her lips to one side, clearly not buying it.

"Okay," I said, putting my fork down in defeat. "It may be Katelyn. But definitely one of those two."

She picked up the phone and swiped up, holding it in front of my face to unlock it.

"You should reply," she said, giggling. "Don't want to leave Freckles hanging."

"I didn't invite you to dinner for commentary on my social life," I gritted out, reaching across the table for my phone.

But her reflexes were too good. She pushed her chair back, scrolling with her mouth agape.

"You call this a social life? Silver dress? Barista? Pink hair? These are your contacts?"

I dropped my focus to my plate, refusing to take her bait. I took enough shit about my sex life from my family. The last person on earth I wanted to discuss it with was the person I was desperate to hire to help my family.

She covered her mouth with her hand. "Botox girl? Jesus."

I shrugged, chewing thoughtfully. After I swallowed, I gave her a smirk. "Her face didn't move. Even, you know. During."

"Gross." She threw her linen napkin at me. "You know this is fucked-up shit, right? Reducing human beings to physical attributes? If you're gonna stick your dick in someone, maybe ask her name when putting her number in your phone."

She was enjoying this entirely too much. "I had no idea the low-rent PI also gave etiquette advice. I'm a lucky man."

She cocked her head and grinned. "You're welcome. Don't charge for it either."

"Please finish your overpriced dinner. I've spent more than enough time in your company already."

She ignored me. She was thoroughly entertained by my pathetic life. "What should I put you in my phone as?" She tapped her chin, and then her face lit up. "Ooh, ooh. I know! Patrick Bateman."

"Very funny."

"Who did you go to first?" she asked, bringing her espresso to her lips.

I hesitated for a second. But given how disastrous this night had been, I didn't have the energy to bluff.

"A few big shops. Some in Boston."

She nodded, saying nothing.

"And Sheerin, Boyd and Marks."

"They turned you down?"

Yes. They did. Most firms weren't interested in investigating what the authorities had already determined was an accident. Some worked for other timber companies and had conflicts of interest.

"They aren't right for this work. I don't want a big agency with lots of wannabe rent-a-cops. I need a dedicated resource. A person who's smart and thoughtful. Not a bunch of kids running google searches all day."

"A lot of PI work is done online," she said. "That's the nature of the job."

I angled closer, lowering my voice. "This isn't just PI work, and you know it. I need someone who can put the pieces together. Understand the broader context. Make sense of all the random pieces that we've pulled together."

Moving closer, she matched my stance. She was interested. Her eyes were bright and her look thoughtful and empathetic.

This was my moment. My chance to close.

"I need you." Shit, that came out wrong. "My family needs you."

"I have a business here. A life here. I can't relocate to rural Maine for an extended period of time."

"Are you really satisfied chasing bail jumpers and cheating husbands?" I asked, giving her a pointed look.

"Not in the fucking least," she hissed. "But my asshole father has blackballed me. I had contracts lined up, and he killed all of them because I dared to defy him."

Whoa. Wasn't expecting that kind of confession. She didn't give off the daddy-issue vibe. Though I supposed I'd been out of the game for a while. There was a lot to unpack there, but I decided flattery was my best play.

I took a thumb drive out of my jacket pocket and slid it across the table.

"Here are the incident reports and interview records, along with a bunch of miscellaneous information."

She reached for it, but I snatched it back.

"This," I said, holding it up, "is your chance. A huge investigation that only you can handle. The average guy couldn't do this work, and you know it."

Her face softened. Clearly this woman wasn't often told how extraordinary she was. "And you won't get in my way?"

"Nope. As much as it pains me to hand this over to anyone, my family deserves answers, and you're our best option."

She took the drive and turned it over in her hand, studying it. Then she directed those keen eyes on me.

"Tell me right now why you want me for this case. What's the real reason?"

I sat up straighter, enjoying the command. Hmm. I'd have to file that away for later.

With a deep inhale, I willed myself not to fuck this up and say the wrong thing. "Parker Louise Harding, you are one of the sharpest people I've ever met. And that's saying a lot. I've worked with some straight-up sharks in my life. And it's obvious you care about justice and doing the right thing.

"So help me. Help me find out what happened to my dad. Not because you have any empathy for me, but because it's a fucking challenge."

A slow smile crept across her face as she squeezed the drive in her fist.

"Wood you rather stay here in Portland and spend your time on work that doesn't challenge you? Or head up north and really test your skills?"

Her shoulders were pulled back, and her chin was tipped high. She was eating it up.

"The thing is—you and me?" She pointed back and forth between us. "We are mutually assured destruction. Any agreement to work together is essentially a suicide pact. Now that I'm working to build a successful second career, I'd like to keep it."

She pressed her lips together and scrutinized me.

I was ready for it. She could drag out the silence as long as she wanted. She wasn't going to turn me down. Chalk it up to confidence or experience, but I negotiated for a living. I knew when to be quiet and let my opponent hand me a win.

"We'd have to work out the details."

I nodded.

"And I'm not cheap."

"Of course not. We're prepared to exceed your standard rate."

"And I'd need a few weeks here to wrap up my cases and prepare."

I stood and held out my hand. She followed suit, sliding her smaller palm against mine.

Her handshake was firm and authoritative—yet another turn-on—and she never broke eye contact.

"I'll take the case. But swear to me that you will stay out of the way and not fuck this up."

"It would be my pleasure."

Chapter 4
Pascal

"This is fantastic." Alice clapped her hands, fussing over the number of snacks she'd set out on the kitchen island.

Henri, who had a protective hand firmly planted on her ass, grunted. That was the equivalent of an effusive thank-you from my grumpy older brother.

"You did good," Adele said, popping an olive into her mouth. She elbowed Henri in the ribs but got no response.

"Use your words, Brawny," Alice admonished.

He grimaced. "You did good. How soon can she get here?"

Alice gave him a peck on the cheek, making a blush creep up from under his beard.

We had gathered at their house to talk about the investigation and Parker.

The house, a massive timber frame on the side of a mountain, was spacious and private, which was essential for any gathering of the Gagnons. For a long time, it had been his fortress of solitude, but in the last year, his girlfriend Alice had moved in, as well as their two foster kids, Goldie and Tucker.

Add two dogs and a kitten Goldie had recently guilted him into, and the once cold and lonely house was filled with constant chaos and love.

My sister, Adele, sat on a plush couch across the room, swirling a glass of red wine, while Remy, my youngest brother, shared an armchair with his wife, Hazel.

Every eye in the room was on me, and the weight of their expectations pressed heavily on my already sore shoulders. My relationship with my siblings was... complicated. They were all close. I was the outsider. The one who'd left.

Since coming back two years ago, I'd worked with them daily, dedicated to getting the business back on track. But in the fifteen years I'd been gone, their relationships with one another had grown and evolved. They had inside jokes I didn't understand, and they trusted each other implicitly. They'd settled into some version of a friendly, competitive adult sibling dynamic I could not begin to understand.

So I owed them. They had been here all along, working with Dad, and with my mom after he died. They were all committed to the business and this way of life. And I was the interloper.

So I had to prove myself. Get this right.

"If she's as good as you say," Adele hedged.

"She is," I said firmly, leaning on the kitchen island. "Prior to becoming a PI, she was a state police detective assigned to the special investigation unit. I've interviewed so many PIs over the past couple of months, and trust me, she's perfect."

Hazel eyed me warily from where she sat perched on Remy's lap. She was not my biggest fan, and she was fiercely protective of my little brother. She was also the one who'd gotten this whole thing going. Digging into Dad's records, scoping things out and putting the pieces together. She and

Remy had been chased through the woods by drug traffickers for her trouble, so she was deeply invested in justice. On top of it all, she was our resident opioid expert and was currently working on her PhD. No one had done more to move this forward than Hazel. I would always be grateful, even if she did despise me.

"Why isn't she police anymore?" she asked as Remy nuzzled her neck. The newlywed phase was still going strong with those two. They were never not touching one another.

"Hates bureaucracy," I said. So what if it was a gross oversimplification? "And her dad is a former colonel with the Staties. When I asked her about it, she said she wanted to do her own thing."

Heads around the room nodded. Fierce independence ran deep with this crowd. That was all I needed to stop any further questions about her qualifications.

"So," Adele said, leaning forward, her dark hair hanging like a curtain on either side of her face, "here's the big question. Can we afford her?"

"Yes." And I left it at that.

The past two years had been difficult for us financially. The business was struggling with increased competition, and my dad, good guy that he was, had entered into some difficult contracts to help other citizens of Lovewell, which made it even harder to turn a profit.

Henri had refused a loan from me. He'd said he didn't want to use my money to bail the company out. That stung. The entire reason I had pushed myself to earn like I did was to take care of my family. But I understood his pride and respected his desire to get the company to a place where it could sustain itself.

But this was an expense Gagnon Lumber could not afford.

So I'd cover the cost. Not that I'd tell my siblings that. They were proud of and deeply invested in the business. And they did not want my money. Every one of them had made that very clear.

But more than a decade of my life had been spent in the pursuit of money. I wasn't a billionaire or anything, but I had enough to take care of my needs as well as my family's.

Hence the house I'd bought for my mother, which she promptly rejected.

Parker was no dummy. She wouldn't pick up and leave her life and business in Portland without the guarantee of a decent paycheck. So I offered her a number she couldn't pass up. Although it didn't put much of a dent in my portfolio, it was sizable enough to draw ire from my siblings if they knew.

But for Dad? For answers surrounding his death? I'd spend my life savings for justice and peace of mind.

An image of Parker materialized in my mind. The shiny hair, the plump lips, the constant curiosity. I smiled. "We need this, guys. We need help. A pro. But someone who can be discreet, fit in and get the right evidence."

Alice snorted. "Fit in? That's gonna be a problem. It took a year for the townsfolk to trust me enough to allow me to order my coffee the way I like it."

Henri pulled her close and kissed the top of her head. A gesture that made me pause. It was so easy, so affectionate, and so unlike my older brother. Alice and the kids had changed him. He was still a grumpy bastard who preferred to communicate using grunts rather than words, but he had softened. He was happy. He had purpose. And for the first time in my adult life, I was jealous of him.

"Alice is right," Remy added. "Lovewell is not a welcoming place to outsiders. Especially outsiders poking around and asking questions. I don't think it's possible to keep this quiet."

Hazel pushed her glasses up her nose. "Agreed," she said from under the protection of the arm Remy had draped over her tiny shoulders. "She needs a cover story. The town gossip will be out of control."

Lovewell was a small town with a proud history that was built on hard work and struggle.

It was a community of survivors. A person did not live this far north without a fierce sense of independence and a dash of crazy.

This town, this region, hell, this state, was built on timber. When the railroads came in, the forests of Maine built all the major east coast cities. Towns like Lovewell sprang up in the middle of the wilderness to support the timber trade, and citizens built their lives around it.

Times had been tough. The population had declined in the last few decades. Businesses had shut down, and towns like ours—where everyone knew everyone else—didn't host many tourists, especially in October, or midwinter, as it was known here. So news of her presence would spread like wildfire through town.

"No one outside this room can know," Henri said. "Not even Mom. We can't do anything to impact the PI's ability to find the truth."

"And we don't know who we can trust," Adele added, her blue eyes steely. Never the warm and fuzzy type, she had become even more withdrawn and angry and distrustful since she'd discovered the tampered brakes.

I gave her a firm nod. I would not let anything get in the way of justice for Dad.

"You know," Alice said, placing an artfully composed charcuterie board on the table and effectively breaking the tense silence, "we could tell everyone she's your girlfriend. Say she's visiting from Portland." She clapped her hands together. "It would be perfect."

I whipped my head around and glared until Henri cleared his throat, garnering my attention. If I wasn't careful, my older brother would kick my ass just for looking at her wrong. Regardless of how batshit crazy her suggestion was.

Remy laughed. "You know, it's not a bad idea. People would talk, of course, but it could give her a good excuse to be here. And the gossip would be centered on your 'relationship.' Plus, people would be a little more welcoming if she was dating a Gagnon."

"No," I gritted out, shaking my head.

At the same time, Henri said, "Yes."

This time *he* was on the receiving end of my glare.

"Think about it," he said. "If she's with us, at work or out at camp, no one will bat an eyelash. If she's chatting with folks and asking questions, she's just your curious girlfriend. It'll work."

"Not necessary." My fingernails were going to leave half-moon shaped scars in the palms of my hands if I clenched any harder. It was a downright terrible idea. A fake relationship? The thought made me nauseated. I was allergic to relationships and had a strong aversion to faking anything. I was a straightforward person who hated bullshit.

My mind spun out, my thoughts racing and looping, sending the same message over and over. *You can't do this. You'll fuck it up. It's too much pressure. A woman like Parker would have no interest in being your fake girlfriend.*

I shook my head, both to signal my opposition and to shake my brain out of its negative thought spiral. It was untenable.

And though I didn't know Parker well, I had spent enough time in her presence to know that she was professional, and she would absolutely hate nothing more than being attached to me, fake or otherwise.

"It's our best bet. And you have more than enough room at your house."

"Whoa." I held up both hands. "Who said anything about my house?"

Adele gave me a withering look. "Where else would she stay, dipshit? The inn closed, and the closest motel is thirty minutes away and filled with vermin. Human, mammal, *and* insect."

I stood and paced the length of the kitchen, rubbing the back of my neck as my heart raced. "Could she stay at the cabin?"

Henri had a small cabin at the bottom of the hill. He'd lived there before he built the house we were in now. He rented it out frequently. In fact, that was how he met Alice. She had lived in the cabin when she first moved to town.

"It's occupied," Remy snarled. He'd been living there for the past year, and Hazel had joined him once they were married.

Shit. I had forgotten about that.

"You have other rentals," I said to Henri, my desperation growing.

He was a bit of a real estate investor here in town, picking up cottages and cabins and turning them into vacation rentals in the summer when the tourists descended on Maine.

"Most are full. And we need her close. She'll need access to all the evidence we've compiled. It doesn't make sense to put her in a remote cabin when the best place for her is here with you, in town, where she can get to know the locals and come to the office and access any records she might need."

My stomach churned. No. My house was my safe space.

It hadn't started out like that. I had actually bought the new construction farmhouse for my mom after my dad was killed.

Her grief was all-consuming. She'd been staying at Henri's house for weeks because it was too difficult to be in the home they'd built together, where they'd raised their kids. The place they'd planned to enjoy retirement together.

At the time, I had recently returned. I was devoted, confused, and desperate to help.

Henri, Adele, and Remy had banded together and had held each other up. They'd taken care of Mom and the funeral and everything else necessary. And I sat on the sidelines.

The wayward son. The one who'd left. I was an outsider to their grief.

So I did the only thing I could do. I threw money at the problem.

This big, luxurious house had been built on a five-acre piece of land that was close to town. I thought it was perfect. A fresh start. Apple trees and a wraparound porch. The very type of house my mom had always loved. Lots of millwork, a massive kitchen, and a fieldstone fireplace.

She hated it.

She didn't say that, of course. But she burst into tears, and not the happy kind, Adele told me later. After that, she went back to her house. She refused to get rid of my dad's stuff. And night after night, she slept on her side of the bed like she'd wake up one morning and find him there.

And I was left with a vacant four-bedroom farmhouse. So I sold my condo in Portland and moved in. And I'd been living there for almost two years.

It was quiet and bright, and other than the lawn—which I paid my teenage neighbor to do for me—it was low-maintenance. I didn't need the space, and most of it remained empty, but it suited me.

My guest rooms had no furniture, though that was an easy fix. What was truly filling me with dread was having to share my space and my solitude. With Parker Harding, of all people. She probably talked nonstop and watched trashy TV.

"This won't work," I said, unwilling to give in to the acceptance leveled at me from every direction. They'd already decided that this was my new reality.

"You're a terrible actor," Remy said. "But even you can pull this off. You're a hermit, so you won't have to worry about being seen in public more than occasionally. All you gotta do is give her a room and let her work."

I braced my hands on the kitchen island, racking my brain for a logical argument. But how else could she investigate for several weeks without stirring up suspicion? Especially when we didn't know who we could trust.

I looked around at my siblings. Every one of them was desperate and hopeful. I was doing this for them. So they could have answers. So that my mom could heal.

I was dead inside. No amount of justice would take away my guilt or grief. I was a lost cause. But my family? They had beautiful lives ahead of them. Henri had kids now, and Remy had just gotten married. I had to do this for them. Give them closure and healing so they could have a chance at something better than I'd ever deserve.

"Okay. I'll do it."

Chapter 5
Parker

"Please explain," I said, adjusting my AirPods as I walked briskly along the bayside trail. The sun was coming up, and the cool autumn wind made my lungs burn. It was my morning ritual. Before coffee, before emails, before the bullshit of my day. Just me and the sky and the ocean.

My body, as well as my mind, needed exercise. Usually, it was lifting weights. But on nice days I ran or walked along the ocean. Whatever felt right in the moment. And today, as I was wrapping up and feeling my morning Zen, I received a call from my neediest client.

Pascal Gagnon.

Suit-wearing pain in my ass.

"We're getting ready for your arrival. And, well, I'm not sure how to explain this."

"Get to the point, Gagnon. It's 6:45 and I'm uncaffeinated."

"My siblings came up with an idea that'll help explain your presence." His words were choppy, hesitant, so unlike the cocky asshole businessman I had encountered three weeks back.

The way his eyes roved over me at dinner, as if he was studying every inch of my body and soul and finding me lacking, had consumed me. What was his problem? And why was I so eager to help him?

"They think we should introduce you to the town as my girlfriend."

I turned down Congress Street, toward the old mansion, mentally computing how much time I had before I had to start my workday. I was headed up to Lovewell this weekend, so I was wrapping up as many loose ends as I could.

"Okay," I said, digging the ancient keys out of that annoying tiny pocket in the back of my leggings.

"Huh. I thought you'd put up a fight."

I threw my hip into the sticky door, then headed directly for the kitchen. It was huge and bright and thoroughly out of date. However, Liv had invested in a fancy robot coffee machine that could be programmed using a smart phone app. That meant my espresso was ready and waiting for me when I walked through the door.

"Listen, I'm a professional. A good cover is necessary for any investigation. It'll be fun. It's been a while since I had to do deep cover."

"This isn't deep cover. Jesus. It's a white lie that'll keep the investigation a secret."

I took my first sip and did my best to suppress the small moan that came out of my mouth. I wasn't particularly fancy. There was no collection of designer purses or obsession with the state of my nails. No expensive laser facials for me or Egyptian cotton sheets. I had one luxury. One thing I needed.

Coffee. Good stuff, prepared correctly, consumed at regular intervals throughout the day.

"You okay over there?" he asked, his voice strained.

I ignored him, closing my eyes and visualizing the caffeine hitting my bloodstream. "I'm fine. And think about it. Lovewell is a small town, yes?"

"The fucking smallest," he replied.

"And rumor has it you northerners don't love outsiders. Especially ones from the city. Me poking around for weeks. Asking questions and showing up everywhere. That's going to arouse suspicion."

"Certainly."

"And my ability to gather evidence would be impeded by that. We could blow this whole thing if it gets out that I'm a PI investigating your dad's murder. Which, by the way, the town thinks was an accident."

I gave it a moment to sink in. Did I want to play fake girlfriend? Of course not. But it would ultimately make me more effective at my job.

Plus, Pascal Gagnon was distractingly handsome. I could fake it for a couple of weeks for the sake of justice.

"If I start walking around asking questions, people will be suspicious. I don't know much about small towns, but I assume someone new would raise eyebrows. I realize you have a low opinion of your hometown, but surely the people aren't complete morons."

"No. Not at all. You're right. If any suspicion arises, the whole community will know your blood type within a few hours."

In the last two weeks, I'd finally caught my cheater, and I'd closed out a few other cases. Now I was ready to put everything I had into Lovewell. Not only because it was the most interesting and challenging case I'd been offered since going out on my own, but because I empathized with the Gagnons.

What I had learned about Frank Gagnon had made me even more determined to find out what had happened to him. By all accounts, he was generous, kind, and deeply involved in his community. He coached sports and volunteered, and he was active in his church.

All while single-handedly running a multi-generational family timber business.

I wanted this. Not just to satisfy my own curiosity and desire for justice, but to help the family and the community that had been devastated by this loss.

I put him on speaker as I jogged up the stairs, peeled off my sweaty shirt, and rifled through my closet.

How many layers would I need up north?

"I poked around at housing and came up empty. There are no open short-term rentals available at the moment. And if we're doing this fake relationship thing, it makes sense for you to stay at my house."

That was a curveball, and it had my mind and my body halting. Although I guessed it made sense on paper. I wasn't sure how I'd handle sharing space with Mr. Uptight Maine 2023, but I had lived through far worse.

"I have guest rooms. I'll make sure you have office space too."

I hummed in agreement as I sifted through the clothes hanging on the rod. I needed to focus, or I'd freeze my ass off up there.

"Are you really sure?" he asked. "You aren't upset? Confused? You're not going to quit on us, right?"

"Um..." I said, holding up a down parka I had bought years ago for a ski trip, "wasn't planning on it."

He exhaled. "Okay, good. It was my sister-in-law's idea. I didn't think you'd go for it."

"It's a great idea." I tossed the parka onto the *yes* pile on the bed. "I can't wait to meet your sister-in-law. She sounds a lot smarter than you."

He groaned in response, and I had to bite back a laugh. He made it too easy sometimes.

"Hopefully the ruse won't require much," he said, his tone businesslike again. "A few public appearances and some chatting with the gossipy locals, and then everyone should leave you alone. I'll make sure we keep a low profile to avoid suspicion."

"I'll be fine. And I'm a great actor. I'm sure you have experience with this. Girls faking it with you?"

"You get a lot wrong. You know that?"

"Sorry, must have gotten you confused with another soulless finance bro I know."

"I can't wait to show you how wrong you are about me."

"Goody!" I said in a fake cheerleader voice. "Just think, we'll have so much time to get to know each other. You can teach me all about your favorite cryptocurrency and regale me with the minutia of your golf game."

"You really think I'm boring, don't you?"

"What gave it away?" I threw a few more sweaters onto the bed, then reached for a fleece hoody in the back. "Ooh," I said, almost dropping the phone. "We need pet names to really sell the ruse. What do you think about Schmoopy?"

Silence.

"Pookie? Sweetums? Muffin? Yeah, not feeling it. Oh, okay, I got it! Stud muffin. Yup, that's the winner."

"Are you done?" he growled, his annoyance traveling through the phone, bouncing off a satellite, and landing in my ear.

"I'm just getting started. This is gonna be such fun."

"What the fuck is this?" Liv asked, holding up an oversized woolen sweater. It was a sad oatmeal color but really thick. My aunt had given it to me for Christmas eight or nine years ago, and it was just the type of thing I'd need up north.

"This needs to be burned. Or turned into a kitty blanket for Chris Hemsworth. And these?" She held up a pair of waffle-knit long undies from L.L. Bean. "You can't be serious."

"I'm headed up north for weeks, Liv."

"It's October. This is Maine. Not Antarctica." She shuffled over to my closet and pulled out several dresses and three pairs of heels. "Plus, you've got to look good."

"There is literally no reason for me to look good. I've got a job to do. And I need to finish packing so I can wrap up the last of my cases and get moving on my preliminary research. The logging industry has a lot of moving parts. I'm trying to familiarize myself."

"Do you have a cover story? How are you going to explain randomly showing up in East Podunk, USA, wearing the world's ugliest clothes?"

"He called me this morning after my run. We actually figured out how we're gonna play it."

"Hit me."

"Fake relationship," I said, snagging the backless black dress from the bed.

"Solid choice," she said as I hung the dress in the closet again. "One of my fave tropes, actually. Beware. The lines get blurry really quickly."

"Yes, in romance novels. Not in real life. This is a job. A good cover story is essential."

She rubbed her hands together. Shit. That meant she was mentally working on a list of scenarios.

"Okay. Let's work through this. Your backstory, your motivation." She held up a sequined halter top I wore when we'd scored last-minute tickets to see Beyoncé four years ago.

"My motivation," I said, grabbing the hanger out of her hand, "is to solve a crime and get paid and come back here to hang out with your overdramatic ass."

She paced to the window, tapping her chin. "So you're his long-distance girlfriend. How did you meet?"

"I dunno. We'll figure all that out eventually."

She pressed her fingers to her temples. "You are literally killing me right now. This is what I do."

"You write thrillers that involve grisly murders."

"But I include romance. Sometimes."

I rolled my eyes. "Could have fooled me. Was it romance when the heroine in your last book fucked the killer on the hood of his car?"

"*Yes.* That was hot. And she eventually caught and killed him."

"Not real life. And not this situation."

"Okay, okay, okay. Give me a minute." She paced back to the door, taking her hair down. She stopped by the bed and shook it out before arranging it artfully in a messy bun that on her looked artistic and chic, but on me would look unwashed and crazy. "You met years ago. In passing. You got stuck somewhere—an elevator?" She tapped her chin again. "Ooh, a boat. You were on a boat together."

"A boat?"

"Yes, go with it. And you parted, never exchanging phone

numbers. He spent years tracking you down, and after he went to a psychic who saw your initials in a crystal ball, he found you." At this point, she was jumping up and down excitedly.

"That sounds batshit crazy."

She scratched her head. "Not my best work, but first drafts always suck. You know that. I'll keep working on it."

I pulled up my Taylor Swift playlist, hit Play, and dropped my phone onto the mattress.

Liv generously helped me fold sweaters and jeans, and only once did I have to pull out a lace bodysuit she had hidden between cardigans.

"I've got it!" she exclaimed after several minutes of uncharacteristic silence. Not total silence, of course. Naturally, when "Anti-Hero" came on, we both sang along.

"You should be me. Tell everyone you are Amazon bestselling novelist L.T. Shipman. You're researching your next book series, which is set in the wild Maine wilderness."

"I can't impersonate you, Liv."

"You totally can. I've never shown my face. Gotta keep the readers wondering. And it's my pen name. Pretend it's *your* pen name. You help with research, and you've read all my books. It'll be easy."

I shook my head. I loved Liv, but she was known for her ideas. Mostly because they were rooted less in reality and more in the wild fantasies that lived in her head. An amazing quality in an author, but less so for solving mundane, everyday problems.

"That way no one will even blink when you ask intrusive questions. Everyone knows writers are nosey assholes who're always looking to take people's lives and turn them into stories."

"Huh. You actually have a point."

"Um. Of course I do. It's perfect. You know what goes into

researching and writing books. And people are always psyched to overshare when I tell them I'm an author."

She wasn't wrong about that. And book research was no joke. She spent months figuring out details and planning every book.

Could I do it? It would certainly make a plausible cover story. And since the world didn't know what L.T. Shipman looked like, the folks of Lovewell would be none the wiser.

I was contemplating how to make this work when Liv held up a tiny yellow bikini.

"What are you doing? I don't need that."

"Of course you do!" She shook it in front of her. "What if there's a hot tub scenario?"

"This is not a smutty book! This is my job. And my life."

Pointedly ignoring me, she folded it and put it in the suitcase. "What about lingerie?" She held up a delicate pink lace demi bra. "This is way too gorgeous to waste. Wear this shit."

"That is not a backwoods PI work bra."

She fished the matching panties out of my underwear drawer—apparently, we needed to work on boundaries—and folded them gently. "You are not just a PI. You are a sexy goddess, hell-bent on bringing bad guys to justice. A sweet bra is part of the package. If you feel good, you'll do an even better job. And who knows? Maybe you'll spot a lumberjack hottie or two up there."

"I'm already spoken for, remember? I have a fake boyfriend."

"Even better." She grinned wickedly. "You can torture him with your hotness."

"You are impossible."

"You love me. Also, you hate leaving the city. So how did he finally convince you to take the case? I was sure you'd say no."

I looked at my oldest friend and sighed. "Honestly? By being vulnerable."

Her eyes widened, and I rushed to explain. "He's this slick, cocky dude. Finance guy who refers to his conquests by their body parts when saving their numbers in his phone. But he's clearly carrying around a lot of loss and trauma."

Liv shook her head so vigorously she'd no doubt give herself a headache.

"He laid it out. How much he and his family needed my help. It was honest and earnest, and I really want to help them."

She threw her hands up. "*No*! Flag on the play. Red fucking flag, Parker."

"It's not like that," I said, wishing I had kept my mouth shut.

"I am invoking my best friend privileges right now. You love to fix broken guys. It's basically a hobby. You minored in it in college."

"Not anymore. I'm done with that. Never again. Especially after Bryce."

She groaned. "He was the fucking worst. Thought that shiny FBI badge could make up for his tiny dick and terrible personality."

I smiled. Liv never held back. Bryce, the selfish prick, had been my last serious relationship. We'd ended things more than a year ago, and I was not even remotely interested in getting involved with anyone anytime soon. Aside from my brief fling with Tex, I had been resolutely single and avoiding men. "I have zero interest in him. This is a job. A difficult job that's gonna push me and make me work my ass off."

It would be difficult. And probably emotionally draining. But ultimately, a family would get answers. And hopefully justice. Providing that kind of peace was why I did this. It was my purpose.

Liv scooped up an armful of lacy bras, panties, and nighties from the top dresser drawer. "I want the record to show that I logged my objection. But if you're going to shack up with an emotionally unavailable lumbersuit hottie with a damaged soul, then you need to pack *all* the lingerie."

Chapter 6
Pascal

I canted forward, resting my forearms on the metal worktable and waiting patiently for my sister to acknowledge me. Next to me, Adele was flat on her back on a creeper, yelling at an engine.

When she emerged, I pushed the coffee cup toward her, which she took and sipped.

"Thank you," she grunted, bringing it to her lips again. "I've been here since five trying to get this motherfucker to run again."

She kicked the metal piece at the bottom—I had no idea what any of this shit was called—and swore under her breath.

Adele was wearing her usual uniform—dark coveralls over a white T-shirt—and she had her hair scraped back into a ponytail.

Safety goggles sat on top of her head like a headband, and her work boots were bright pink. My sister was a conundrum.

She was tall and strong and feminine. She spent all her time working on machines or working out—hell, her biceps made *me* jealous—but she always had freshly manicured nails, and she had a thing for jewelry. Today she was wearing a pendant necklace and gold hoop earrings.

Never a slouch, she was a fierce competitor on the local lumberjack competition circuit and an accomplished gardener. Her tiny cottage was surrounded by perfectly maintained flower gardens rarely seen in Northern Maine.

Because my sister lived up to no one's expectations but her own.

I scanned the shop, marveling at how efficient and organized it was. One wall was covered with whiteboards, and every task for the day and week was laid out with assignments, parts needed, and time estimates.

She had four employees here and two who rotated up at camp, and she was known for running a tight ship.

All tools were stored carefully and labeled and inventoried in complex spreadsheets she spent her weekends obsessing over.

This was her kingdom, and she was the queen. Every employee at Gagnon Lumber knew better than to get in her way. Occasionally, I came down here and made a coffee so I could inquire about orders or repair costs or replacing tire treads.

If it was a big conversation, like end-of-year budgets, I brought donuts. Feeding her crew usually softened her up.

I stood off to the side, checking my emails. I knew better than to interrupt. She ignored me as she walked the space, sipping her latte while she chatted with Tony and Amelia and helped them inventory parts.

When she finally returned, she gestured for me to enter her office.

Unlike the shop, it was pure chaos. Paper everywhere, random chargers on the floor, and a long-dead plant on the windowsill.

On her desk was a framed photo of her and Dad at her college graduation from U Maine. They were both beaming, matching slightly crooked Gagnon smiles on full display.

Adele and I had always gotten along. Maybe because we were the two in the middle, but from an early age, we understood one another.

Henri was the responsible, honorable son who'd spent every waking moment of his life with my dad before he passed away. Remy was fun and charming, and even at thirty, he was still my mom's baby.

Adele and I, we were sort of stuck in the middle, but we were there together.

She was smart and prickly and had never tolerated bullshit.

And I would have liked to think I was similar.

"Are you here to yell at me about expenses again?" she asked, sitting in her desk chair and tipping back.

"No. Actually, you've been keeping your expensive taste in check recently."

She threw a pencil at me. "You told me to cut back on the expensive tools. You're Mr. Business over there with your fancy shoes and expense reports. I'm a grease monkey."

I threw the pencil back at her. "You are an accomplished electrical and mechanical engineer. Or did you forget? Miss Phi Beta Kappa?" I pointed to the graduation photo.

She shrugged. "Whatever. Tell me what you want and let me get back to work."

I half turned and kicked the door closed. "Parker arrives tomorrow. I wanted you to know. In a day or two, once she's settled, I figure we can all meet with her."

She closed her eyes and savored her coffee before responding. "I was really impressed with her during our phone call. She's sharp. Knows her stuff."

I raised my coffee cup in a mock salute.

"I'm going to say this once, then I'll drop it. I'm not stupid. I can't imagine what she actually costs, and I know you're paying her bills, so thank you. Henri may be too proud to accept the help, but this is too important to let pride get in the way. Hopefully one day I can repay you."

Her words hit me like a blow to the chest. It wasn't often that my siblings opened up like this, and Adele, of all people, was not one to express her gratitude so openly.

Unsure of how to respond, I settled on a tense nod. It meant the world to me that she saw what I was doing, how hard I was working, and appreciated it. Finding Parker, convincing her to take the case, and now getting her here, letting her live in my house, pretending to be her boyfriend, was a lot. And I was scared shitless.

She held up one finger. "You're not gonna like what I say next. But it needs to be said out loud."

I braced myself.

She thinks I can't do it. That I'll fuck it up. I'll blow it, and we'll never know what happened to Dad.

Where my family was concerned, I was a perpetual disappointment.

"Paz, I respect you. Especially what you've done for the business."

"But," I said, waiting for the other shoe to drop.

"But..." she hedged. "Please. Please, do not sleep with her."

I slammed my coffee cup down on the desk so hard liquid splashed up through the lid. "Are you shitting me, Adele?"

She gave me a pitying look that somehow made this exchange even more insulting. "I will never mention this again.

But we both know you'll screw anything with boobs and two legs. We also know that most women are morons who can't resist your asshole charm."

I looked down at my hands, now covered in lukewarm coffee. "That's harsh."

"I'm sorry. But this is huge. I know it's been hard for you to be back here. I know you miss your big, exciting life in Portland. It must be lonely. And..."

"Let me stop you right there. You've got it all wrong. First, things have definitely slowed down in the bedroom department since I moved back. Second, yes, I enjoy the company of women. But only casually, usually for a night, and with no strings. This is clearly not that scenario."

"Yes. But—"

I held up a coffee-soaked hand. "I haven't gotten to where I am by being unprofessional. And I'm certainly not going to sleep with the woman I hired to solve Dad's murder. Please give me some fucking credit."

I glared at her, all kinds of shitty feelings flowing through me. Of course she thought the worst of me. Hell, I thought the worst of me. And while I was making a bit of a show of being offended by her suggestion, the truth was, I'd thought about it. Though I wouldn't tell my little sister that I had spent quite a bit of time thinking about having sex with Parker. In several scenarios and in various rooms in my house, to be exact.

Parker was smart and sexy, and she really disliked me.

If she was as good at her job as I thought she was, there was no way in hell I wouldn't be actively fantasizing about her all the time.

The thought of her striding through that restaurant in that dress had me instantly sporting a semi.

But there was a big difference between thinking and acting.

And it cut right to the bone that my sister, who I respected so much, thought I couldn't keep my dick in my pants for the sake of my dad.

"You're right." She opened her desk drawer and handed me a stack of paper napkins. "I shouldn't have said that. You're an absolute pro. And you're the best person to handle all this."

"Thank you."

"Everything is so scary right now. Not knowing who we can trust. Being targeted. It feels like everything is slipping away. I guess I envisioned the beautiful, smart PI living in your house with you and jumped to the wrong conclusion."

I couldn't fault her there. My track record was terrible, and I was known to be an Olympic-level self-saboteur.

Adele was probably even less likely than Henri to express fear. So for her to be so openly vulnerable meant she was deeply rattled. Since she'd discovered the evidence of tampering on the brake mechanism on Dad's truck, and since she'd found similar evidence on the truck Henri was driving last year when he'd almost been killed, she had been consumed by guilt and fear. She took total responsibility for every truck in our fleet and took every single flat tire personally. But the thought that someone was actively trying to hurt our family? It was eating her up.

She had withdrawn, and when she wasn't working nonstop or at the gym, she was in Orano with some guy Remy claimed was a professor. My sister sure had a type, but I wasn't even sure about that anymore. Like the rest of us, she wasn't okay. Looking at her, seeing the fear in her eyes mixed with the hope that Parker could solve this, activated every protective instinct in my body.

If only this was the type of problem I could throw money

at. Because seeing my sister scared gutted me. And soon my own fear was bubbling up, threatening to consume me.

"I'm scared too," I said after a lengthy silence. "This is so important. There's a reason Henri runs the business and you run the shop. I'm the money guy. I like spreadsheets and certainty. Now I have to fake a relationship with the PI we hired to find our dad's killer? All while running our business, getting her access to possible records and employees, *and* keeping it all a secret?"

I ran my hands through my hair, resisting the urge to pull it out in frustration.

"You are so dense." She leaned forward, putting her elbows on the desk. "You're smart and worldly. You're the one who got out, traveled all over the world making your deals and meeting all kinds of people. I don't know why you can't get it through your skull that you're the right person for this job."

"But Henri—"

"Stop. Even if Henri was single, have you met him? Thank God Alice came around, but he could never do what you've already accomplished."

"He always puts the business first."

She gave me an exaggerated eye roll. "You and your perverse guilt! So you went and lived your life. There's nothing wrong with that. Do you know how jealous I am?"

Her words had me reeling back in my seat. Sure, I had always suspected she was jealous that I'd left Lovewell. Paved my own path away from the Gagnon name and the family business. But she'd never said the words out loud.

She'd come visit when I was in Boston and also when I was in Portland. The rest of my family never did. We'd go out for nice meals and sometimes to a play and I always enjoyed our time together.

Adele never made me feel bad for my choice to leave. On the contrary; she got it, my need to escape. The need to get the fuck away from my family and all the expectations and baggage that came with it.

Because even loving families could be stifling. Even good people could put a person into a tiny box, cast them in a role, and never give them a chance to grow.

I thought she'd be next. Potential and drive had never been problems for Adele. She was the smartest of us all, taking advanced courses and earning scholarships. When she earned a full ride to U Maine to study engineering, I figured her next step would be to get even farther away and build rockets.

Never did I think she'd come right back to Lovewell and dive headfirst into the family business.

For the most part, she played the role of contented employee, showing up every day with a smile on her face, though Adele had never been the happy type.

She *was* satisfied with her shop and her role and her team.

Henri gave her complete control, and she took pride in her work. She mentored mechanics and techs and encouraged more women and girls to learn the trade.

But every once in a while, I saw it. The wistful way she walked down the cobblestone streets of Portland. I'd catch the sighs that would escape when we took the ferry to Martha's Vineyard for a weekend with friends.

She was stuck.

Not that she would ever say it out loud. She'd probably punch me for even suggesting it. But I knew my sister. And for her, something was missing.

She'd turned down a dozen or more job offers, though she'd never told me why. And she'd never explained why, after getting her master's, she didn't go for the PhD she was more than capable of achieving.

Maybe Dad knew.

The two of them were tight, and at the time, I was busy in Boston, more worried about myself than any of my siblings or my parents.

But here she was, running her side of the business, overseeing the employees she hand-picked and trained, doing the thing she was really fucking good at every day.

I was the jealous one in this scenario. Because she was settled. Content.

She had built a life for herself here. She had friends and colleagues and a home she loved.

And now that I was hitting my midthirties, I could see her wisdom for what it was.

If only she would stop dating pompous assholes who treated her like shit.

"When you put in an effort, you are charming as hell. This is going to be difficult, but since when do you let that stop you?" She raised one eyebrow in challenge.

I nodded. She was right, as usual. I could do this.

"And," she continued, "if she's a brilliant as you say she is, then all you have to do is pretend to date her when you go out in public and stay out of her way the rest of the time."

"You make it sound easy."

"Maybe because it is."

For her, maybe. But she didn't live with a brain like mine. The kind that always made things harder. That obsessively reviewed every bad outcome over and over until I was either too tired to keep my eyes open or too wired to think straight. She didn't see all the scenarios in which I could let everyone down. But how could I tell her that? How could I explain?

I shrugged. "I'm an asshole."

"Yes, you definitely are. But you're a smart, hardworking, loyal asshole."

I smiled. My sister certainly had a way with words. "I'm just an asshole who's trying to do the right thing."

"And maybe that's good enough for now."

"Wow, you give one hell of a pep talk, sis."

"Get the fuck out of my shop. I've got work to do."

Chapter 7
Parker

Lovewell was a three-hour drive from Portland. I started up the coast, then inland. After a pit stop in Augusta, our state capital, I headed north.

Massive mountains loomed ahead, and large swaths of farmland were chopped up by rivers and streams. The farther I got from Portland, the more spacious and wild the land became. I passed dozens of farms, watching fields of blueberry bushes disappear into the horizon.

And it felt different. Good, really. Kelly Clarkson sang through the car's speakers; she was a wonderful road trip companion, and I had a couple of true crime podcasts bookmarked on my phone. Liv had packed a road trip survival kit filled with peanut butter M&M's (the best kind, period), flavored seltzer, and heart-shaped plastic sunglasses. She said they would fit right in up in Lovewell.

It was like the first day of college all over again. Leaving home, embarking on a new endeavor, and being forced to live with a roommate I hadn't chosen. It would all be strange and different. I wasn't an eighteen-year-old kid with no clue this time around. No, I was a thirty-four-year-old grown-ass woman who *still* didn't have a clue. But I'd picked up a few skills over the years.

I arrived at Paz's home right on schedule. I hadn't seen much of the town on the way in. I'd have to do some exploring later. The wide driveway was paved, and it led me to a large white farmhouse with crisply painted black shutters.

It had a wraparound porch and a giant picture window right smack dab in the middle. The front lawn was large and well-manicured, with native wildflowers and artistically pruned shrubbery.

I supposed the *American Psycho* style penthouse was clearly out of the question up here in the woods, but the last thing I'd expected was this bright, cheerful family home.

Tacky columns, a collection of imported sports cars, a golden toilet? Perhaps. Details that would add to my list of reasons to hate the guy and all that he stood for? Absolutely.

But this? There were matching rocking chairs on the porch, for Christ's sake. Had I stumbled into some kind of Norman Rockwell horror movie? God, if Liv was here, she'd be whispering furiously into the dictation app on her phone, plotting out her next bestseller.

I parked next to a familiar blue BMW and eased out of the driver's seat, stretching and taking a big breath of mountain air.

The front door opened, and Paz jogged down the stairs to meet me. The last time we met, he'd worn a perfectly tailored dark suit. Not today.

Nope, the man had the audacity to wear a flannel shirt and jeans. Both were clearly expensive, and both molded to his thick, strong physique. Like this, he looked less douchey finance bro and more grumpy lumberjack who could cut down trees and build fires and possibly make me orgasm with a quirk of his brow.

I took a step back toward my car. This transformation was uncalled for. I had placed this guy in a nice box in my mind labeled "rich asshole." But the damn plaid shirt was prying the lid off that box and making my brain run wild—straight toward thoughts of the lingerie Liv had forced me to pack.

He walked closer, giving me a small wave. His face was still serious, thank God. I wasn't sure if I could handle a plaid, bearded smile in my current state of semi-swoon.

"Parker," he said, holding out a hand and giving me a firm shake. "Good to see you. I hope you had an easy ride up."

I nodded. "It's a nice drive. And thank you."

"Why don't you come inside? I'll give you a tour."

Quickly, I gathered my purse and followed him up the porch stairs.

"You live here alone?" I asked, as we stepped into a bright foyer.

"Yeah. It's too big for me, but choices here are limited. Not much of a booming real estate market. Snagged this from the developer."

I shook my head, still trying to understand how someone like him inhabited this exquisite family home.

But then he led me deeper into the house.

There were windows everywhere and gleaming dark hardwood floors. But not much else.

The blank walls were painted a non-offensive gray-beige color. The kitchen looked fully stocked. There were two small stools at the island and an empty space where a large dining table should be.

The living room was also bare, except for a baby grand piano and a massive leather couch. There were no photos, no decorations, no throw pillows, no area rugs.

The open space was vast, and the view of the mountains was spectacular from the living area. "Did you just move in?" I asked, attempting to be polite.

He shook his head.

"Are you a minimalist? Don't like furniture?" Who buys this kind of real estate just to sit in an empty house?

He shrugged. "I don't know. Haven't bought any."

"Because...?" I ran my hand along the back of the cognac leather couch. Yup, it was basically butter. Not surprising.

He turned and pinned me with an annoyed glare. Great, I'd been here for seven minutes, and the bickering was beginning.

"Because it's not necessary. I'm not staying here. This house is an investment and temporary lodging. I don't need a lot of stuff."

I could understand that, to a point. "Where's your TV?"

"I don't have one."

"Sorry, what?"

"I don't watch TV."

My eye twitched. Doesn't watch TV? "But—"

He folded his arms. Shit, the flannel shirt looked even sexier now. "It's perfectly normal," he groused.

I scrunched up my nose. "If you say so. Let's get it out in the open now, though. Are you a serial killer? If we're gonna be roommates, I need to know whether you keep body parts in the freezer. Is this a *Silence of the Lambs* thing? Because I'm not an actual cop anymore."

"Are you done?" he growled. "I'm not storing body parts anywhere. And I'm not a serial killer. Though your endless chatter certainly makes me see the appeal."

"Hilarious. Inability to take a joke—isn't that one of the top traits on serial killer psychological profiles? Either way, it's a great movie. We could watch it if you had a TV. Have you seen young Anthony Hopkins? Mmm. He could get it."

He picked up his pace, headed toward a large set of stairs. "While I'm happy that we've cleared that up, how about I show you your room before you get started on the rundown of which real or fictional serial killers you would sleep with?"

"Fine," I grumbled, following him up the stairs, doing my best to avoid looking at the way his ass filled out his jeans. On the landing, he pointed to the right. "My bedroom, bathroom, and office are down there." He turned left and started down a long hallway. "The guest rooms are this way. There are three up here and another one on the third floor. Each has its own en suite."

I gaped as we passed empty room after empty room. He pushed open a door at the end of the hall and held out his arm, gesturing for me to enter. "I ordered some stuff."

The bedroom was enormous. It had to be bigger than the condo I'd lived in while I was with the state police. The windows were giant, and the view of the mountains was spectacular. Settled along the middle of one wall was a king-size bed on a wrought-iron frame. It was covered with the kind of fluffy white bedspread luxury hotels used and dozens of pillows. A plush armchair with matching ottoman was in one corner, and an ornate dresser with a large mirror was anchored to the opposite wall.

"The door to the left is the walk-in closet," he said, "and to the right is the bathroom."

"This is amazing," I said softly, feeling bad about how I had teased him. The rest of the house was a barren wasteland, but the windows in here were fitted with expensive drapes, and a blue striped area rug warmed the room. That chair looked like the perfect place to curl up and read.

"I'll order a TV for in here," he grumbled, wearing an annoyed scowl. "I should have known you'd be one of those women who sits at home alone watching murder shows on Netflix."

I wheeled around to face him, hands on my hips. "Nope, you're wrong."

"Really?" He quirked one eyebrow.

I hated how sexy it made him look.

"Yes. I watch *Housewives*. Like a fucking lady."

I spent the next few hours unpacking, FaceTiming Liv so she could see my room, and trying to get my bearings. My thoughts and feelings were all so confusing. I was here to work. I was a professional. But when I was near Paz, I transformed into a hormonal teenage girl who wanted nothing more than to tease and annoy my crush.

I made my way downstairs, hoping to talk strategy and reestablish myself as a cool, competent professional.

But that went out the window when I stepped foot inside the kitchen. There was a wok on the large professional-grade stove, and he was throwing chopped up vegetables into it. Classical music played from what was probably a very expensive sound system, and his shirtsleeves were rolled up.

A totally normal thing, right? Sleeves certainly did get in the way at times. But then he was chopping, and his forearms were flexing and covered with dark hair. It was the exact kind of detail I'd never get out of my mind.

"Hungry?" he asked, never taking his eyes off the zucchini he was cutting into uniform chunks.

"Can I help?"

He tipped his chin. "Plates are in the cabinet next to the fridge. I don't have a table, but we can eat at the island. There's wine if you'd like some."

I *would* like some, more than some actually, but rather than overindulging, I needed to settle my nerves and get to work.

Generally, I took pride in my ability to read people. To understand what made them tick. I had double majored in criminology and psychology in college, and the learning continued beyond that because so much of my police training had been related to predicting behavior and responses.

But standing in his home, I felt like maybe I had read Pascal Gagnon all wrong.

Was he the suited-up city playboy? A guy who made millions playing with other people's money and livelihoods and banged everything that moved?

Or was he an anxious hermit who lived in a massive family home alone with his piano? A man so consumed by grief that he welcomed a stranger into his home in pursuit of answers surrounding his father's death?

Maybe he was both.

Was I losing my touch?

Was it because he was hot? More than hot, really. Especially standing in front of a gleaming stove wearing that damn flannel that hugged his thick chest and biceps in all the right ways.

He clearly splurged on expensive haircuts, and his hair was styled with the perfect amount of product. Yet it was wild, like he had been pulling at it subconsciously. And his nails were short and ragged, like he'd never outgrown the habit of biting them when he was anxious.

What other secrets was he hiding in this empty house?

Because he worked really hard at being an asshole. Likely to conceal, I gathered now that I'd gotten a peek into his life, an abundance of vulnerability and hurt beneath the shiny, hardened exterior.

I set the plates next to the stove and the forks and napkins on the island. Then I filled two water glasses. When I'd completed those tasks, I tried to be helpful by wiping down counters and putting things in the dishwasher.

He was quiet. Not unfriendly, just quiet. I was grateful for it. If either of us spoke, we'd probably only insult each other. And if this was going to work, we would have to move beyond our differences.

Finally, he set two plates of stir-fry down, sending a sweet, spicy aroma wafting my way.

"This smells amazing," I said, attempting what I hoped was a friendly smile.

"Thanks. I wasn't sure what you'd like. I picked up a ton of groceries. Help yourself."

We chatted about the house as we ate. The conversation was a bit awkward, but nothing about this situation was straightforward.

"I was hoping we could talk about our plan."

He nodded. "I agree. My siblings insisted on this fake relationship arrangement, and I'm willing to do whatever it takes for your investigation to be successful."

"Great. I've been working on my cover story and background as well." I explained Liv's idea for me to pose as a writer so I could conduct interviews and ask questions without arousing suspicion.

"We can really sell this," he said quietly, smiling. "And people will probably be happy to talk to you all about the town and the timber industry." He shook his head, chewing a piece of chicken. "Wow. That's a really good idea."

I was taken aback by his easy agreement and approval. Perhaps this could work. We were on the same team. I'd have to keep reminding myself of that fact.

"Can you tell me about her books? If we're going to sell the dating thing, I should know the details. I'll text my siblings later and let them know so they don't get caught off guard. Tomorrow morning, we can head to the diner."

I shot him a confused look. My plan for the following day was to dig into the files I'd brought with me and map out what I needed to accomplish this week. Maybe scope out a place where I could get in a much-needed workout.

"Trust me, the diner is the center of life in Lovewell. If we go there and chat with a few people, by lunch, the entire town will know every detail we feed them. Then we can focus on the investigation."

I admired his efficiency, but anxiety pressed against my ribcage. "I thought I'd have a few days to get settled before we had to take our fake relationship out for a spin."

"We don't have time to waste," he asserted. "So we should probably spend some time getting to know one another." He frowned like it was the last thing he wanted to do.

"I'm an open book, Gagnon. What do you want to know? Fears? Dreams? Favorite sexual position?"

His cheeks flushed pink. "Let's stick with the standard-issue dating stuff."

"Hmm..." I tapped my chin. "Okay, I'm thirty-four and an Aries. I love coffee and dark chocolate. Growing up, I played tennis competitively and the flute badly. My parents are divorced. I'm an only child. My mother lives in North Carolina now, and my dad is an asshole, whom I avoid as much as possible."

"Okay..."

I shrugged. He wanted an info dump, so an info dump I gave him.

"And I suffer from migraines. They come on and sometimes last for a day or two. With medication, they're mostly under control. But stress makes them worse."

"I'm sorry."

I cleared my plate, enjoying how wide his eyes got while I rambled. If we were going to sell this "relationship," he needed to do his part to get to know me.

"I manage. Let's see, what else? I love Indian food, and I'll argue until my dying day that *Die Hard* is a Christmas movie. I'm really good at Scrabble and never wear thongs because they feel like a nonstop wedgie. I like to lift weights, but I run too. Even if it's boring. And when I'm feeling sad, I usually buy shoes online." I turned from where I had been loading the dishwasher. "Anything else?"

He shifted on his bar stool and grimaced. "No, that seems like quite enough for now."

"Great. Do I get to hear all your deep, dark secrets?"

He pinned me with his signature glare. "No. I assume you've done your research on my family and me. As for personal things, I work a lot, and I occasionally do lumberjack competitions with my brothers."

I smirked. Oh yes. Liv and I had found the photos. Two words: drool-worthy.

"I like to read and hike, and in my twenties, I traveled a lot."

"The piano?" I asked, gesturing to where it stood in the empty living area. "Do you play?"

"Yes. Started when I was five. It's important to me..." His voice trailed off, and he ducked his head, focusing on the surface of the island in front of him. "Helps with stress."

"Give me some more details. What's your favorite food? Movie? Band?"

I snagged the cooled wok from the stovetop and got to work scrubbing, staying half-turned toward him as he put his elbows on the countertop and gripped the ends of his hair.

After a long moment, he looked up at me. "My mom's banana bread is my favorite food. But after that, probably sushi. Not that there's a single place to get sushi within a one-hundred-mile radius. I always liked *Terminator*. And all the superhero movies too. Not sure I have a favorite band, but I minored in music in college and listen to a lot of classical."

Okay, I could work with this. Sure, his life was fairly boring, but that meant I probably wouldn't have to worry about major fake boyfriend curveballs. We could make this work for a few weeks.

I got the last of the dinner dishes loaded into the dishwasher and filled up my water bottle. "Okay, then. I'll be up bright and early, ready to be the best fake girlfriend you've ever had."

"Do you have everything you need? Is the house okay?"

"Yes. I was surprised when I saw it. It's lovely. Not what I expected."

"What did you expect?"

"I don't know, the Batcave? Maybe a Patrick Bateman–style penthouse with glass and stone? You know, good surfaces for cleaning up blood."

He shook his head, clearly weary of my antics.

"But in all seriousness, everything is great." I took a step closer to him. "Thanks for letting me stay."

"I didn't have a choice," he grumbled. "My siblings forced me. Trust me when I say this is the last thing I wanted."

I blinked. "Wow. You really know how to make a girl feel welcome."

Chapter 8
Parker

Small wasn't quite the word I would have used to describe Lovewell, Maine.

Minute? Itty bitty? Either was more fitting.

Main Street, the center of town, ran alongside the river and housed all the things one would expect it to. Post office, town hall, diner, grocery store, and a bakery. Trees lined the sidewalk at regular intervals, and across from town hall was a large green area with park benches.

Across the small valley were clusters of small, tidy homes that got farther apart the higher they sat in the mountains.

The scenery was nothing like Portland, where I'd grown up.

The minute I climbed out of the passenger door of Paz's BMW, heads were turning my way. I was wearing jeans and a Patagonia fleece, so I couldn't attribute the attention to my ravishing beauty. No, each glance was more curious than the last. I was an outsider, and in stereotypical fashion, that meant I garnered immediate attention as I walked along the sidewalk beside Paz.

As the bell over the door rang, another dozen people picked their heads up to see who had come in, and the confusion on their faces when they were greeted by my unfamiliar presence hinted at just how hard this job would be.

I focused on watching Paz. He wore a mask of contentment, yet his posture was ramrod straight.

After we were seated, I reached across the table and took his hand in mine. It felt like the right gesture, regardless of the people who were staring.

Across the table, his brown eyes widened on me as his large, warm hand enveloped mine. And for the briefest moment, it was as if we were sitting here alone. We were two people trying to figure one another out rather than a sideshow in a small-town diner.

While we were touching, he didn't feel like an adversary. All the animosity and snarky remarks faded away. In their place was a man who was deeply uncomfortable but pushing through it for his family. And as much as he annoyed me, I respected his commitment to them.

Maybe it was because my own family was so broken. Or maybe because I'd never experienced that kind of sibling love. Either way, it made me want to help him that much more.

So, under the scrutiny of every eye in the place, I did something rash. I leaned over that diner table and kissed him on the cheek.

It was only a peck, but his skin turned pink, and his mouth dropped open. His eyes were full of a mix of confusion and fear and maybe a little awe.

"This place smells amazing!" I said with faux enthusiasm. "What's your favorite thing on the menu, stud muffin?"

In an instant, his blush turned into a glare. "No stud muffin," he growled under his breath.

Ignoring him and the stares of every other patron here, I picked up the menu. Perusing it would give me a minute to center myself and decide on how best to play this. Before long, an older woman with winged eyeliner and a frilly blue apron came out of the swinging kitchen door with a pot of coffee in one hand and headed straight for us.

"Pascal," she said, wrinkling her nose. "I feed your siblings almost every day, but you never come to see me."

Another flush creeped up his neck and into his cheeks. "Watching my figure," he said, patting his flat stomach. "You know I can't resist your blueberry pie."

She rolled her eyes. "Louie makes veggie omelets for Remy when he's training. That's no excuse."

She turned her gaze in my direction. "And who is this young lady?" She raised one drawn-on eyebrow in my direction.

I gave her my most *aw shucks* small-town smile. "I'm Parker," I said, offering her my hand.

She didn't take it. She was too busy sizing me up, and no inch of me was safe from her inspection.

"Parker is my girlfriend," Paz said calmly. "I told her how incredible the pancakes are here, so she begged me to bring her."

Bernice's expression softened a bit. She wasn't smiling, but the scowl was gone. From her apron pocket, she pulled a notepad out and looked at me expectantly.

"Yes," I said, trying to win points. "I would kill for chocolate chip pancakes."

As the words were coming out of my mouth, it hit me that I'd made a grave error. Bernice's eye twitched, and those lips turned down once again.

Paz interrupted before either of us could speak again.

"She's kidding. We'll both have the blueberry pancakes with the house-made blueberry syrup and coffee, please."

Without another word, Bernice gave me a withering look and walked off with our menus.

Paz glowered at me. "This is Northern Maine. Everything has fucking blueberries. Beer, sausages, even soup. When in doubt, always order blueberry shit."

"Noted," I snarked, annoyed at being deprived of chocolate chips.

He angled closer, giving me a whiff of his undoubtedly expensive, annoyingly delicious cologne. "See how everyone is staring?" He scanned the restaurant. "Over there is Mayor Renee and his wife. Father Marcel is in the back with a few members of the garden club." He gave a polite wave in their direction. "This is easy. We show up and eat our pancakes. Then the town rumor mill will take over. We won't have to go out in public too much."

Bernice returned with a coffeepot and filled our cups silently. Before I could request milk, she walked away. Apparently black coffee was all I was getting.

I took a sip of the scalding liquid and slyly studied the crowd.

"Ready for a brief history of the town?"

I held up a hand. "No need. I've done my research. Logging town. Grew rapidly in the first half of the twentieth century. Global competition and resources hit hard, jobs were lost, employers left, population dwindled. Crime and drug use rose."

I didn't mean to sound like a pretentious Wikipedia entry, but did this guy think I'd come in cold? Like a fucking amateur? This was my job, and I took great pride in doing it well.

He nodded. "Sure. But there's more to it."

I didn't doubt that, but I was hungry, and it was my first day on the job.

I took another sip of coffee and set it on the table again, ready to warn him that I'd need a full belly before I was ready for an elaboration on that comment, but the chime on the door pulled his attention from me.

His face fell. Instead of his charming smile, or even his ambivalent disinterest, he wore an expression of pure rage.

In my periphery, a tall, blond man, probably in his late fifties, strode through the diner with the kind of attitude and bravado I found instantly repugnant. He wore an expensive looking blazer over his pressed jeans, looking far too formal for a quaint diner like this. On his way through, he stopped and said hello to several people, but his smile never reached his eyes.

"Who is that?" I whispered.

Paz dropped his forearms to the table, still tracking the older man as he walked across the diner, smiling and shaking hands with everyone as he passed.

"Mitch Hebert."

A cloud had passed over his face. Paz wasn't a happy kind of guy, but in place of his usual smirk was a hatred more potent than any emotion I'd seen from him so far.

He waited until the man was settled on the other side and talking loudly before continuing.

"I hate that motherfucker and his entire shit family," he spat.

I was taken aback. Paz wasn't the friendliest guy, but he was always the polished professional.

"That seems a bit extreme."

He shook his head and took a sip of coffee. "Trust me, Gagnons and Heberts hate each other. Have for generations.

We've controlled adjacent sections of the forest for years. Our families have worked near and with one another for decades. And they have always been lying, cheating bastards who'll do anything to get ahead."

I clutched my mug and scooted forward. "Ooh, this is juicy. Tell me more."

The smirk he shot me made my stomach flutter.

"My grandfather hit some hard times in the '70s when fuel costs skyrocketed and cheap foreign lumber flooded the market. So he took on investors. Hebert tried to buy out those investors and stage a hostile takeover of Gagnon Lumber.

"Took years and thousands upon thousands in legal fees to sort out. But my family kept control."

"Oh shit." That was some seriously bad blood.

"That's what matters most to us," Paz said. "The family business and legacy. They threatened it."

"And up here, that's grounds for a blood feud," I finished.

He gave me a weary look. "Sort of."

I rubbed my hands together. "Ooh, I cannot wait to dig into this guy. This is some Hatfields and McCoys shit. The perfect kind of small-town insanity to keep things interesting."

"We're not violent or anything. We hate each other and keep our distance. He runs their business; Henri runs ours. We only interact when necessary. He's got five sons, all dumbasses, and for the most part, they're not even involved in the business. Just Mitch the asshole and his dumbass brother."

I snuck another look at Mitch, who was holding court with a handful of townspeople like some kind of redneck royalty. His forehead was suspiciously smooth, and he wore large, garish rings on his fingers.

"The timber business is life up here. The jobs, the community, it's how people survive. No amount of online research can show you the soul of a place. Trees sustain this place, but so does fierce independence.

"Maybe it sounds silly—hell, I thought it was absurd for most of my life—but to the people here, it's meaningful."

"My father understood it, though. It's not about jobs or the local economy. Although those are more important than ever these days. It's about pride and independence and an identity that was founded on the principles of our ancestors. The folks who came here and made this unforgiving wilderness their home."

Taken aback, I grasped my coffee mug with both hands. His words were poetic. The meaning deeper than what I could have imagined coming from someone like Paz.

But as I looked around at the diner patrons, I felt it.

This place had its own strong identity. Its own secrets. And I wanted to unlock them all.

After stuffing my face with shockingly delicious pancakes and tolerating my black coffee, I headed to the ladies' room, aware of the attention I garnered as I made my way across the room. A few well-meaning townsfolk had stopped by to say hello. Each time, Paz had introduced me as his girlfriend, the author who was visiting for a few weeks.

I was washing my hands in the small sink when the door behind me opened and Bernice shuffled in.

Sliding up closer to the sink, I made room for her to pass, but instead, she stood, blocking my exit. "He's a good boy, you know. Doesn't always show it, but he has a good heart. Just like his dad."

I nodded politely, not sure of what to make of this

interaction.

"When our walk-in refrigerator broke last year, we had to shut down for a few days. Lost all our perishables. We couldn't find an affordable one secondhand, and we weren't sure we could reopen. But two days later, a brand-new one showed up. Top of the line and everything."

I smiled, pleased that despite his penchant for evil, Paz could use his resources for good once in a while.

"He's a caretaker. He doesn't want anyone to know it."

"I've noticed," I said. I'd already witnessed how much he supported his family and employees.

"Good. Don't let him act like an ass and push you away. From what I can tell, you've got a good head on your shoulders. So when he tries his usual bullshit, don't budge. Show him that you'll stick." So far, this woman had been nothing but intimidating. But now, here she was, brow furrowed in concern, sticking up for Paz like she cared deeply for him.

"Um... sure." I stuttered. This was day one of our fake relationship. I didn't even know when his birthday was. There was no way I was going deep with this stranger in a diner bathroom.

I nodded and smiled, going for smitten.

"He's a keeper, for sure," I said, tugging a paper towel from the dispenser. "I won't let him go."

"Good girl. Those Gagnons all deserve good things." With that, she stepped aside so I could pass.

I headed back to the table, forcing myself to smile through the anxiety coursing through me as I slid back into the booth. It was happening already. I was getting invested. Not just in the case but in Paz and the Gagnon family. And probably this weird ass little town as well.

Because that was my weakness. What made me a liability as a cop. I cared. Too much. And it could be my downfall.

Chapter 9
Parker

The hardest part of any investigation was getting started. The first steps could make all the difference, or they'd send an investigator on a wild goose chase. Since I couldn't jump into blatantly interrogating people about the accidents, I had to get a read on the community and the industry.

The timber business was complex, but luckily, the Gagnons were giving me full access.

It wasn't that far-fetched to believe that Frank Gagnon's death was related to the rampant drug trafficking happening on the logging roads. Rural areas like Lovewell had been decimated by the opioid crisis. Maine, as a whole, had suffered tremendous losses. Many of my investigations with the state police involved opioids, so I had more than enough background to get started.

So I continued on my mission: getting to know the town, both the pleasant exterior and the unpleasant underbelly. But first, I needed a workout.

Forest Fitness was nothing like I expected and everything I

could have ever wanted. The gym lacked any kind of frills and was set up in an old warehouse filled with weights and people minding their own business. Perfection.

It was cheap and none of their equipment was state-of-the-art, but it was clean. It was off the highway about ten minutes outside of town, near a collection of shady-looking storage facilities.

I'd been in town for less than forty-eight hours, but already, I needed a break from that house. It was gorgeous, with far more amenities than I was used to, of course. But Paz Gagnon was too surly and moody for his own good. The air inside was thick with tension and anxiety so stifling that I had to escape, at least for a little while.

The town wasn't much better, honestly. I was social by nature, and I was here to gather information, but the nosiness was off the charts. People were already dropping by or even stopping me on the sidewalk. This morning, I'd walked to the pharmacy to get toothpaste—Paz only had the weird natural kind—and several people openly stared at me while whispering. Though a bit rude, I preferred it to the way others stopped me and asked intrusive questions. Alice was right. It was tough to be new in this town.

So the internet led me to this place. There were racks of weights to lift and things to punch. That was all I really needed. Liv had tried to get me into Pilates over the years, but I'd found it epically boring. Ditto with yoga and all the other trendy workouts.

Hip-hop cardio and bootcamp and all those other things.

At the academy, I started lifting weights. And it had changed my life. I could be strong and badass and still get in a good workout. Strengthen my heart and bones while not running to nowhere on a treadmill—though I'd stick with the bare minimum of cardio for the endurance, I supposed. And a few yoga poses here and there to get my muscles warmed up. I could blast music and work out all the frustration and anger that came with the job.

After signing in and paying a bored teenager at the front desk, I headed to the weight area.

I snagged a yoga mat from a bin against the wall and laid it out to stretch.

Headphones in, I prepped myself to work through a few yoga sequences to warm myself up. But instead of cuing up my gym playlist, I tuned into the conversation going on between two young guys near the weight racks.

They were in their twenties, covered in bad ink, and rocking homemade tank tops. Meathead One had on a backward hat, and Meathead Two hadn't even bothered to tie his shoes. After thoroughly checking me out, they returned to their conversation and bicep curls.

I stretched and foam rolled while they debated video games. I had almost given up on these dolts when one of them mentioned getting "lit" the other night.

"Fuck, bro. Stinger really came through. That ox beat the hell out of the homemade crank," Meathead Two said, racking his dumbbells.

My ears perked up, but I kept my expression neutral and focused on stretching, praying these idiots could give me some helpful details.

"Yeah, dawg. That shit was epic. Got me so fucked up. That guy's a dick, but he's got the hookups. And his bike? Fuck me."

"He's friends with Knuckles, right?"

"Yeah. They're always drinking at the Hanger."

"Maybe he'll hook us up with a discount. So we can impress those girls."

They fist-bumped like the meathead douches they were and loaded the bar secured above the weight bench.

I hung around, hoping for a few more tidbits. Hanger, Stinger, and oxy. Good start. I considered discreetly taking photos of them in hopes of putting names with the faces but decided against it. It'd be difficult to do it here without setting off red flags. Instead, I continued to observe and listen for any more tidbits of info that could help me get this investigation started.

But after listening to them talk about college football for a solid fifteen minutes, I was giving up hope. I'd decided to move on to a little weightlifting of my own and was working through my last set of stretches when Adele Gagnon walked in. I had only met her once, but like the rest of her siblings, she was hard to miss. We made eye contact, and she gave me a friendly smile. I was mid-wave when her face fell and her body tensed.

It was as if all the air had rushed out of the room. A man walked through the front door, and immediately, Adele turned her back to him, pulled her phone from the side pocket of her leggings, and put her head down.

From my position on my mat, I attempted not to stare. But it was a challenge, because this man was easily six and a half feet tall and built like a goddamn Viking. He had a full sleeve of tattoos up one arm, and his dark blond hair was shaved except for a man bun on top of his head.

"Adele," he said, his voice several octaves deeper than the human ear could hear.

She glanced up from her phone and gave him a bored look. "Stretch."

They stood for a moment, facing one another, tension

radiating off them both. Who was this guy? Were they former lovers? And why were they looking at one another like that?

Odds were they were going to kiss or claw each other's eyes out. Either way, I was invested. I couldn't look away.

Adele was tall and gorgeous, with the kind of body seen on female Olympians. Lean and strong and muscular. And she certainly wasn't afraid to show it. She was rocking tight leggings and a crop top today.

Mr. Viking McManBun took a long look at her ass as he walked away. Not that I could blame him. That woman clearly did a lot of squats.

I needed to befriend her. Not only for the workout tips, but also because I wanted to know what the hell was going on there.

Shit. Was I already becoming a small-town gossip? Had Lovewell converted me already?

When Viking Man headed to the treadmills, Adele's posture relaxed. Given that she was technically my employer and possessed a ton of vital information—not to mention the serious girl crush I was nursing—I decided to buddy up to her the best way I knew how. Compliments and weights.

After I'd wiped down my mat and returned it to the bin, I deserted my useless meatheads and headed over, walking slowly and casually so as not to seem too eager. In case she was anything like her brother, I decided to ease into things slowly. If she was skittish, laying it on too thick would only make things harder.

"Good to see you. Do you think you could spot me?" I asked, gesturing to the bench I had loaded with weight.

She nodded and headed over.

"I'm impressed," she said, helping me hoist up the bar so it was parallel with my chest. "But I suppose you were a cop. Gotta stay in shape, huh?"

I finished my set, racked the weight, and shook out my hands as I sat up. "Yes. I started for that reason. As a woman in law enforcement, you can never be too strong. But now it's more about my mental health. Feeling good and powerful."

"Amen, sister." She gave me a genuine smile. "I come here every morning. A good lift—especially a good deadlift—makes the rest of the day that much better."

Looked like we'd already established common ground. "Good for you. You probably need the serotonin boost having to deal with your brothers all day."

She laughed, adjusting her ponytail. "Yes. They drive me insane. Thankfully, Henri knows that it's best to leave me alone."

"And Paz?"

"Has not learned that lesson. Too much of a control freak."

"I've noticed."

"Tell me he at least got you some furniture. The empty house is eerie."

I felt protective of my fake boyfriend and roommate. Yes, the place was sparse, but he made sure I had everything I needed. "Yes. He's been a wonderful host, actually."

"Good. Anything you need, let me know. We're really grateful to have your help." Her eyes swam with a thick mix of pain and fear and guilt. It was another reminder of how high the stakes were.

"I could really use your help," I explained. "I need to understand how the brakes work, see them, maybe talk to the manufacturer."

She nodded. "No problem. I'll block off a full day to go over it all."

"Thank you. I know it's difficult."

She held up a hand. "It's not. I'll do anything to help. I'll take apart an entire brake system and rebuild it for you if it helps. No doubt you'll be easier to teach than my numbskull brothers."

I gave her a nod. Paz was right. Adele was carrying the weight of far too much responsibility and grief. I had to solve this.

We ran through our workouts near one another, chatting between sets. Adele was a huge *Schitt's Creek* fan, and we spent more of our rest time dropping our favorite lines than doing anything else. She also gave me the scoop on a local nail salon and how to get Bernice to supply milk for my coffee. At first sight, she had a hard edge, but it hadn't taken long to work my way through it.

"Do you know those guys?" I asked, jutting my chin in the direction of Tweedle Dee and Tweedle Dum in the corner.

She shook her head. "Not sure. For the most part, this place attracts people who want to keep to themselves. But they could be from Heartsborough. It's a few miles down the road."

"I overheard them mention a place called Ape Hanger?"

She laughed. "Ape Hangers are the giant handlebars people put on their motorcycles."

"Ahh," I said, swallowing my embarrassment. I should have known that. We had investigated a biker gang or two for money laundering while I was with the state police. "That makes sense."

"It's also a bar not far from here."

Bingo. I made a mental note to check it out. See who hung out there and whether there was any drug activity. Though I'd learned long ago not to generalize, bikers and opioids were a pretty common combination.

Wiping down the bench, I dipped my chin, gathering my courage. "What about that guy?" I asked, darting a look at the large man who'd spoken to her when she first arrived. "The Viking dude."

She dragged her attention over to where he was running on a treadmill, his muscles gleaming. I swore her pupils dilated right then and there. Not that I blamed her; the guy was walking testosterone.

"He's a Hebert." She scowled, as if the words tasted bitter in her mouth. "Their timber company is our biggest rival, and every one of them is the human equivalent of horrible period cramps."

I let out a giggle, only to slap my hand over my mouth abruptly when I saw the fury in her eyes.

"There's a lot of bad blood between our families. Going way back. Thankfully, I don't have to deal with them often. Henri does, though. We share the roads up north with them. They're experts at not pulling their own weight while simultaneously taking credit for everything." She was seething while angrily spraying disinfectant over a weight bench.

I watched her every move, studying her body language, the things she wasn't saying, trying to peel back the layers of her anger.

She rounded on me quickly, narrowing her eyes. "They should be at the top of your list. I don't trust those slimy fuckers. Your first task should be to dig through their lives like a raccoon in a trash can."

"I will," I said, schooling my features to keep from laughing at her poetic metaphor.

Physically exhausted but mentally energized, I headed back to Paz's house. The visit to the gym had given me a handful of threads to pull on, and I was itching to get to my laptop and start digging.

What sort of shit were the Heberts into if the bad blood went back generations? And could I get close enough to figure it out?

Paz was in the kitchen when I toed off my sneakers and headed to the sink to refill my empty water bottle.

He had files spread out on the countertop, and he was wearing only a white undershirt and sweatpants. Yowza.

I took a moment, just a quick one, to admire the way the sleeves of the shirt stretched over his arms and shoulders. He could attempt to hide behind the European car and fancy watches, but those shoulders gave him away. He had strong, capable country boy written all over him, despite his best efforts to pretend otherwise.

But why was he working so hard to hide it? The town, the business, the rural lifestyle. What was it that had made him resent it all so much?

And then he opened his mouth, reminding me that those delicious shoulders came with an obnoxious personality. "You're back," he said, voice dripping with condescension. He didn't even look up from his paperwork.

I threw my bag onto the counter, making him startle in his seat. "Whatcha working on? Calculating the balance of your 401(k)?"

He finally looked up and gave me a withering glare. Too bad it took a lot more to push me away.

If there was any justice in this world, Pascal Gagnon would be short and bald, and he'd probably have a massive goiter. Instead, he was tall, dark, and handsome. The most confusing and tantalizing combination of polished suit daddy and rugged lumbersnack rolled into one.

He was a suit, in personality and spirit, but that body—the broad shoulders, the barrel chest, thick thighs—was 100 percent axe-wielding lumberjack.

And I was a connoisseur of the lumbersnack. This was Maine. Even in a city as big as Portland, there were plenty of pretenders. Yuppies in flannel and guys who didn't remove their wool beanies in July.

But this man? He was the real thing.

How did I know this? Because I *may* have done some light internet research and stumbled upon a YouTube video of Paz and his brothers at a timbersports competition. It was impossible not to be mesmerized by the way he wielded a chainsaw while wearing a tank top.

Did I rewatch it a few dozen times?

Yes. But I was an investigator. It was my job to look carefully and study all the details.

Like the veins in his forearms, the tight bubble butt practically bursting the seams of his jeans, the set of his jaw, and the determined look in his eyes when he wielded a massive blade.

He was an enigma.

One that made my thighs clench every time he turned that glare in my direction, but an enigma nonetheless.

And I would figure him out eventually.

"My mom dropped by when you were out," he said, not looking up from his laptop. "She's furious."

"Let me guess. You didn't bother telling her you had a fake girlfriend."

"Yeah." He ran his hands through his hair, his favorite nervous habit. "I should have thought that through. The minute we walked into the diner yesterday, her phone was blowing up."

"Did you tell her the truth?"

"No. She can't know." He scrutinized me for a moment, as if waiting for me to argue. "It's complicated, but it's best if we keep her in the dark until we have more concrete answers."

I wanted to question it. She could have critical information about her husband's last days that her kids weren't privy to. But the sadness that lingered behind his cocky attitude reminded me to keep my mouth shut. Those pieces of the puzzle would come together eventually.

"She brought that for you," he said, pointing to a platter on the island.

"This looks delicious," I said, already rummaging for a knife to cut myself a piece of the golden banana bread.

"Yeah, it's her specialty. She's perfected it over the years. It's really good."

I nodded, shoving a chunk into my mouth. The second the flavor registered on my tongue, a moan slipped from between my lips.

I wasn't often treated to homemade baked goods, and this in particular immediately made me think of my own mother. She had always loved to bake for me and my friends. She'd whip up oatmeal raisin cookies and brownies like it was nothing so that when I had friends over, we'd have a special treat.

I made a mental note to call her later. We hadn't spoken in a while, and I missed her.

"Oh. My God. This is amazing. Do you want some?" I asked, eyes wide. How rude of me to dig in like that without offering him a piece.

He shook his head. "Nah, she made that special loaf over there for me."

"Sorry. I didn't mean to rub the deliciousness in your face. What are you allergic to? Gluten? Dairy?"

He ran a yellow highlighter over a line on the paper before him, then focused on me.

"No. I don't like chocolate chips, so she leaves them out of mine."

I froze with a chunk halfway to my mouth. "Hold up. You don't like chocolate chips in your banana bread?"

"No. I hate chocolate."

I brushed my hands together to get rid of the crumbs. "That's it. I'm searching the basement. You are clearly some kind of deviant."

He gave me one of those exasperated hot-guy looks. "It's not a big deal."

I gripped the countertop with one hand and fanned myself with the other, pretending I was on the verge of fainting. "You can't be serious. This fake relationship will not work. We're going to have to break up. Have you been tested?"

"For what?" He was working hard to look annoyed, but the corner of his mouth quirked for a fraction of a second. There had to be some silliness beneath the serious facade, and I wanted to see how far I could push him.

"For insanity!" I exclaimed, shoving another piece into my mouth.

"It's not that weird. Lots of people don't like chocolate."

"Not normal ones."

"Yeah, yeah. I know. I suck. I'm a shitty son and a shitty brother and a nutcase who doesn't like chocolate."

My heart sank. He was usually so polished and sharp, but from here, now that I was looking closer, he looked defeated. I guess that earful from his mother hurt him more than he'd let on.

Instead of taking my treats back to my room so I could shower and get some work done, I stayed. For some reason, I had a nagging urge to make him feel better.

"Hey!" I said with mock indignation. "Do not talk about my fake boyfriend like that. I have decent taste. You could at least try to live up to my standards, even if this is fake." I popped the bite into my mouth and smiled.

His eyes danced at that. This man could not resist the opportunity to banter. "You have high standards?" He shook his head. "Sorry. I was remembering your tatted up bodyguard."

"That's Tex, and we're friends."

"Really? Because the way he looked at you made him look like a lost puppy, which was really disturbing, considering the rest of him looks like a murderous felon."

"First of all, he's a gentle giant. Don't let the tats fool you. And second, we had a brief fling. We weren't compatible. But he's a good, kind, decent human who has been an excellent friend. So stop being such a judgmental ass."

"Hmm. So that's your type? Burly guys who look like felons?" If I didn't know better, I'd say he sounded a little jealous.

"I'm not superficial, unlike some people. I'm more interested in personality and character than looks. And his character is top-notch. You should be so lucky as to be compared to Tex."

Now he was pissing me off. What had started as an attempt to cheer him up had devolved into a conversation I was not prepared for. "In your world, being shiny and perfect is a currency. But down here on Planet Earth, where the regular folk live, who you are as a person is more important than how much money you make or your stock portfolio."

He cocked his head and inspected me without speaking. It was unnerving. "You really think I'm that bad?" he asked softly.

I shrugged. "I don't know. I've only been here a few days, but already, it's obvious that you're miserable."

"Because I'm stuck here."

"Oh, please. You're not stuck," I said, wandering closer to where he sat. "That's the story you tell yourself. If you wanted to go back to Portland, your family would be fine."

He narrowed his eyes, and that hint of vulnerability evaporated. "You don't understand. We're getting the business back on track."

"I'm sure they can do it. Or they could hire someone. Hell, you could consult remotely. You're the number cruncher, right? These biceps don't cut down the trees." I squeezed his arm.

Damn, it was thick and strong. He flexed, the shameless asshole, and my face went hot.

I should have stepped away. Unhanded him and preserved my dignity, but instead my fingers lingered, unable to separate from him.

"These biceps do just fine," he said, his voice deep and husky.

I avoided his eye and finally took a step back, putting some space between us. "Those are gym biceps," I teased, rounding the island so I was a safe distance away from his muscles. "Those are not lumberjack biceps."

His eyes flashed as he stood and pulled himself up to his full height. "Are you saying I'm not a lumberjack?"

"You have an MBA, you drive a Beamer, and you create excel spreadsheets for fun. You are many wonderful things, but a lumberjack you are certainly not."

He glowered, though the angry mask couldn't hide the hurt. My words cut him deeply. "You really know how to hit a guy. Sorry to disappoint you, Nancy Drew, but I come from a long line of lumberjacks. It's in my damn DNA." He puffed up his chest, and I was embarrassed about how much I liked it. "I'm the CFO of a multigenerational timber company, and I compete in lumberjack competitions, for Christ's sake."

"I thought that was Remy?"

"Remy is going pro, but every one of us has competed since we were kids. I can climb trees and chop wood and throw axes, babe. And while I enjoy the gym, most of my workouts these days are in the woods with my brothers. We run and chop and train with Remy to keep him motivated. He needs reminding that he's the runt of the litter."

"That's a terrible thing to say about your little brother."

"You didn't grow up in a family full of feral wilderness kids."

Fair enough. I was an only child caught between an abusive parent and his victim, desperate for siblings to commiserate with.

Was it wrong that I liked him like this? All riled up and defending his manhood?

Maybe it was the years-long dry spell or the loneliness of the woods getting to me, but I was finding it harder and harder to deny my attraction to my fake boyfriend.

Chapter 10
Parker

Gagnon Lumber was nothing like I expected. Not that my expectations were realistic. I had prepared for this job the way I always did—with copious amounts of internet research. But in this case, my research had been supplemented with far too many hours in front of the TV, watching shows about people who cut down trees. Sadly, those hours, while giving me ample time to knit, had not yielded a lot of helpful information.

But the employees represented the bulk of my initial targets. I had already ruled out several people, but there were dozens more to vet. Usually, the start of a new investigation was a rush. The endless possibilities, the leads to be followed. But this time the stakes were high, and my attachment to this family and this town was growing every day.

The headquarters was housed in a big, ugly building on the outskirts of town, with several industrial garages and an endlessly large parking lot filled with massive machinery.

But inside, it looked like any other office. Paper, coffee makers, people on the phone.

This was where I did my best work. Peeling back layers and digging under the surface to find what was really going on.

The first floor was busy and open. A series of giant whiteboards held tables and lists of deliveries, weights, and quotas, as well as the weekly transport schedule.

Several administrative types were set up behind large desks. They took phone calls, updated the schedules and weights, and handed out assignments to employees as they came in.

Every person we passed greeted us, but Paz didn't stop to chat. Instead, he gave them tight smiles as he led me through the busy area and up the stairs to a catwalk that looked over the first floor. There were several offices up here. Each was small and beige. Henri was at the end. His office was cluttered with his dad's photos and memorabilia, and there were several crayon masterpieces taped to his walls. One featured him riding a moose with *Daddy and Clive* in crude handwriting below it. I wasn't sure what that meant, but Liv's comment about moose fucking popped into my head, making me chuckle and destroying my professional demeanor.

"Have a seat," Henri said, gesturing to the folding chair. He wore a plaid shirt and jeans. His physique was gruff and rugged, but he had kind eyes and a gentle manner. He was probably a great dad.

"I don't want to draw too much attention to myself." I smoothed my skirt and sank into the chair.

"Too late," growled Paz, peering over his shoulder and looking down onto the main floor. "Everyone is already gossiping about you."

"It's not a problem," Henri said. "They're curious. And it's not your fault, Parker. My brother has a certain reputation.

And coupled with his shitty attitude, it means the appearance of a girlfriend is cause for chatter."

"What my brother is trying to say is that Paz is a man whore with a bad personality," came from behind me.

Turning, I found Remy in the doorway, eating a plump red apple. He was all long limbs and grace, and a lopsided grin split his handsome face. His jeans were ripped, and his T-shirt was rumpled, but it worked for him. Though their facial features were similar, he couldn't be more different from Paz, who was bulky and strong, with perfect posture and designer clothes.

Paz glared at him with a look so rage-filled, tension blanketed the room.

Not wanting this meeting to go off the rails and feeling the need to defend my fake boyfriend's honor, I interrupted. "I'm aware. Thank you. I am his temporary fake girlfriend, after all," I said primly, "but he's a reformed man, and he makes me very happy."

Henri snorted and Paz rolled his eyes.

"Love you, stud muffin," I said, blowing him a kiss.

Watching him squirm was one of my new favorite hobbies, and the look on Henri's face was priceless. Clearly, they enjoyed messing with him too. The man had it coming. He was pathologically uptight. Constantly trying to control the world around him and the people in it. It had to get exhausting after a while.

"I like her," Henri said, opening a drawer to retrieve a thick red accordion-style folder. "Too bad you're not really dating. She'd whip your ass into shape fast."

"Like Alice did with you?" Paz quipped.

Henri grinned behind his beard, the look almost frightening. "Yup. And I couldn't be happier about it."

Remy tossed his apple core into the trash can from across the room, then sauntered over and sat on the edge of the desk.

"We want to be helpful," Henri said, nodding at his brothers. "But not too obvious. You have free rein of the office. You can go anywhere, chat with anyone. The admins will give you any files you ask for. Feel free to take as many photos and videos as you want."

I nodded. "Thank you."

"We let it slip this morning that you're an author doing research. It's probably already made its way around the office and back, so you should be covered," Remy added.

"Any questions, come to me," Paz added, still standing in my periphery with his arms crossed. "No one should give you any trouble, but people here can be a little closed-off about newcomers."

I reached for the folder on Henri's desk, excited to dig in. "It'll be fine. My plan for today is to introduce myself and build rapport. I've got tons of records to keep me busy, but I want to make sure I know who does what here and who can answer which questions. Who's the person who knows all the dirt? Every office has one."

The brothers looked among themselves for a second. "Ellen," they said in unison.

Ellen was a petite woman in her early sixties with a neat bob. She wore a hot pink sweater set and pearls, and she smelled like roses.

"Let me hug you, dear. We're so delighted to meet you." She pulled me in close. The woman was deceptively strong.

"I've known this one since he was in diapers, and he's never brought a girl around."

Paz shifted uncomfortably, clearly hating the scrutiny his love life was garnering. "Ellen has worked here for decades."

She patted his cheek. "I was Mr. Gagnon's secretary back when we were allowed to use that term."

"She's our comptroller now. Couldn't run the place without her." His voice was full of esteem. It was something I had noticed about the Gagnons, and Paz in particular. The pride and belief they had in creating jobs for their community. It wasn't the sort of thing I would have expected of a money-hungry shark like Paz, but perhaps he had grown beyond his private equity roots.

"I told you I'm only giving you two more years. I wanna retire and play pickle ball in Florida. You'll have to replace me eventually."

Paz cringed in response, making her laugh.

Leaning forward, she lowered her voice. "Everyone always gossips about this one. Calling him a womanizer and all that silliness. But I knew better. He only needed the right girl to come along."

I smiled, enjoying how Paz's face turned purple.

"And you're perfect. An author? So smart and ambitious. He's handsome, but a handful. Seems like you've got the backbone to handle him."

Taking advantage of Paz's embarrassment, I pulled him closer and popped up on my tiptoes to give him a peck on the cheek. His beard was softer than it looked. "He's one in a million," I gushed.

"You must tell me how you met."

I shot him a saucy look, enjoying his reddening cheeks. It

was his tell. Despite his cool demeanor, they gave him away every time.

"I'd love to," I told her, using her chattiness to my advantage. "Are you free for lunch? I have a whole bunch of questions about how this place works, and it seems like you're the woman to talk to."

Her face lit up. "Lovely. I'll take you to the diner and we can talk shop. But only after girl talk." She giggled. "I want to know how this one managed to land you."

As expected, Ellen was a wealth of information. She gave me the full history and job description of every single Gagnon Lumber employee for the past five years. As well as all the personal gossip. She was hilarious, and we made plans to get mani-pedis in the coming weeks.

Chatting with her, though, made my heart ache a little. I missed my mother. We had never been able to bond in this low-stakes kind of way. Things were always so fraught, so tense, because of my father. Even after the divorce, I think I reminded her too much of what she had gone through.

She was happy now. And safe. Remarried to a wonderful man who treated her like a princess. Every time we spoke, I could tell how happy she was. But I missed her presence more than I'd realized.

After everyone else had headed home, Paz and I sat in his office. I was looking at a massive framed map of the north woods, which detailed all the logging roads and the claims of all four logging families.

"The main roads are privately owned?" I asked, tracing the massive trails along the map.

He didn't even look up from his laptop. "Yes. There are four main timber companies. We share ownership of the Golden Road and several of the connecting roads. We all use them to transport south to the mill or north to Canada."

"But you're not in business together?"

"Fuck no. It's a partnership for transport, that's it. The Clarks and LeBlancs do their own thing. And those Hebert fuckers are the last people I'd ever do business with."

I shoved my pencil into my messy bun as I studied how the land had been carved up. "Why do the Heberts have so much more land?"

"They bought out smaller companies decades ago. Engaged in all kinds of shady tactics to force out competitors. We held on, but there were some hard times." His head was still bent over his work, but he continued. "We're competitors, but we work together on the roads. Because without roads, we can't get the trees out of the woods and to the mill."

I traced the lines with my fingertip as millions of questions swirled around in my mind. "So we suspect the other families?" It was clear the Gagnons trusted no one.

"Yes. Don't be fooled by the fake harmony. This is a cutthroat business involving multiple generations of each of our families. Shit has happened. Grudges are held."

"Bad blood isn't hard evidence," I said softly.

He looked at me finally, pinning me with his intense stare. But those cold eyes were full of the perpetual sadness he carried around. He wasn't half as good at hiding it as he thought he was. Those eyes gave him away every time.

"While the rest of us have scraped by, especially with the market being so volatile in the last decade or so, the Heberts are somehow thriving. They have more trucks than any of us, sure, but no one knows what they're doing."

"So you think they're trafficking drugs."

He shrugged, looking up at the map. "Can you ever really know what's going on in that much wilderness? That's why the stash house Hazel and Remy found stayed secret for so long. We can't possibly keep track of all the activity. My dad knew it was happening and fought hard to stop it."

I met his eyes, hoping to convey my understanding silently. His dad had been murdered because of what he knew. But what did he know? And how?

"You done?" he bit out. And with that, our moment of connection was over. "I've got some things to do before we head home."

I sat down again, my mind spinning with ideas, and jotted down notes. A few theories were taking shape in my head, and I needed to air them out, let them breathe before I dug deeper. Spending time in the office and learning about the business had unlocked so many questions.

"Must you type so loud?" he snapped after more than an hour of silent work.

I was transcribing notes and organizing files on my laptop. I was in the zone, and I hadn't registered his annoyance. With more humor than I'm sure he expected, I looked up and stuck my tongue out at him.

"It's like you're trying to break the keyboard. What did the alphabet ever do to you?"

I carefully removed my headphones. "I'd give you a nasty look, but you make enough of them for the both of us."

His frown deepened.

"And sorry my typing volume is a problem for you. Is this better?" With one finger, I employed an exaggerated hunt-and-peck strategy. "Does this please King Pascal?"

He shook his head and turned his attention back to his laptop. "You better be good at your job."

"I could be," I snapped back, "if you'd stop interrupting and let me fucking work."

Chapter 11
Pascal

Why did she have to be pretty?

The first time I saw Parker Harding, she was striding through my office in a black pantsuit. She and a bunch of other cops were meeting with management at my private equity firm, Atlantic Partners.

Her dark hair was pulled back in a slick ponytail, and her crimson-painted lips were mesmerizing.

She wasn't tall, but she carried herself like a confident warrior as she strutted through the open space in sensible heels.

I did a double take from my office, leaving a colleague in Hong Kong hanging for a few moments while I drank in the sight of her.

At that time, I didn't know she would become the architect of my professional ruin. Or the dark angel that haunted my dreams.

I didn't know that cool, professional exterior hid a fiery temper and claws as sharp as a goddamn wolverine's. Now, despite my best efforts, no matter how hard I worked to dislike her mouthiness or to be offended by her general disdain for me, things had changed. We were living together, and I was subjected to watching her dance around and smear peanut butter on every possible food. I was confronted by a bra hanging from every hook and every knob. Yet I could no longer access the dislike I'd been holding tight to. Slowly, this woman was breaking me.

Shit.

But how could it be possible? I was the master of my feelings. Or so I'd thought.

Watching the light dance across her face as she chatted with Adele on the far side of the bonfire, I realized that no amount of willpower would keep me from being attracted to her.

She was so much more than the sum of her parts. It wasn't the shiny hair or the mischievous eyes.

Or the curves. Jesus, the curves.

It was the laughing and the chatting. The way she moved through the town, curious and kind, making people feel seen and heard.

It was the last thing I needed. Getting attached wasn't in my makeup. Women were complications I did not have the bandwidth to deal with. But like it or not, Parker was my roommate and my fake girlfriend, and against my better judgment, we were becoming friends.

And so we were at the fall bonfire together. I never showed up for this shit. I hated town events. But this one was not so bad. Mainly because my brothers were here, and Tucker and Goldie, of course. I slipped them each a twenty so they could buy as much junk food as they wanted, and I savored the giant hugs I got in return.

Those kids sometimes made me question my conviction that fatherhood was absolutely not for me.

Generally, I needed fewer things to worry about, not more. But adding Goldie and Tucker to my list wasn't difficult at all.

The fall bonfire was an annual tradition and an opportunity for the town to get together to burn shit and drink. Which, up here, was the highlight of the season. I would have preferred to be home, in front of my fireplace, sipping a glass of scotch and listening to Mahler, but this wasn't quite as terrible as I had imagined.

Eventually, I found my way over to Parker, who'd moved on to chatting with Henri and Alice. He had an arm draped around Alice's shoulders protectively, as if he would kill anyone who dared to touch her.

As we chatted, Parker laced her fingers with mine. It had been a long time since I'd gotten excited about hand holding. But the way her small, smooth hand fit perfectly in mine had my heartbeat kicking up a notch while it somehow simultaneously made a contented warmth spread through me. Being physically linked to her was surprisingly soothing. Her hand was a calming anchor as we made our way through a sea of small-town socialization.

Parker held court, keeping the conversation going with Henri and Alice, while my mind wandered.

"You'll be at the wedding, right?" Alice asked, pursing her lips like she was worried.

Alice was a sunny, kind person, and even though my brother could be a surly asshole, I could see the pull he felt to soothe away all her worries. It was no surprise Henri had taken one look at her and fallen madly in love. She had done so much for our little town in a short time, and she'd completely changed my brother's life in the process. Despite the sweet disposition, though, she had one hell of a backbone. She had to, because keeping a Gagnon man in line was no easy feat.

"It's all so last-minute."

Henri pulled her closer and kissed the top of her head. I was used to their endless affection, but Parker stiffened next to me. The reaction was subtle, but discomfort wafted off her. Maybe, like me, she sometimes felt that desperate desire in her veins to have someone of her own. Most of the time, I was perfectly content. But once in a while, when my guard was down, the ache of loneliness took over and threatened to consume me.

Part of me wanted to ask her later, but that would be crossing a line. We were forging a grudging friendship, sure, but that was a bridge too far.

"Parker, you have to come." Alice turned and looked at me, stricken. "Paz, she has to come!"

"She'll be there," I said, putting my arm around Parker and liking the way she fit perfectly next to me.

"Excellent!" Alice cried, grabbing Parker's hands. "It's going to be super low key, but we would love to have you there."

Parker gave her a tight smile. "I wouldn't miss it."

"I'm gonna be the flower girl," Goldie cheered, darting toward us with sticky hands and chocolate smeared on her cheek.

Parker crouched and gave my niece a bright smile. "Will you wear a special dress?"

Goldie engaged Parker in a lengthy conversation about her dress and her shoes and her hair while I stood by and listened. And dammit if a warm sensation didn't spread through my chest.

"Tucker is walking me down the aisle," Alice murmured, putting her arm around her son, who, at almost thirteen, was growing like a weed and wearing a grimace laced with embarrassment at the physical affection his mom was showering on him. "I don't have the best relationship with my dad," she explained, "and Tucker is so important to me."

He puffed up a bit at that.

"It's gonna be fun," my brother said, ruffling Tucker's hair. "We'll have food and drinks and music. You know, wedding stuff—" His train of thought derailed when Alice elbowed him and pointed across the bonfire. And with that, they were making their way over to chat with a group of teachers from the primary school.

I looped my arm with Parker's and led her toward the fire, ignoring how natural it felt to pull her close. "Let's do a lap. I'll introduce you, and you can get the full Lovewell experience." And this way I wouldn't be alone with her. If I was, I didn't think I could resist doing something stupid like kissing her. Because the image of her lush lips, which were almost always painted red, lived rent free in my brain. Those lips could break a man, but I had to remain strong.

We stopped by the various booths, sampled snacks, and chatted with the locals. Parker was friendly, and she engaged with everyone she met. I admired that about her. At home, she mostly ignored me or danced around while working.

But here, she was laser-focused and processing every single detail.

It was a turn-on, watching someone as smart and capable as her work. I could see the wheels turn when she was preparing to ask a follow-up question, and I'd caught on to the hint of a squint that would appear when she suspected someone wasn't telling the truth.

I wanted to talk to her, keep her all to myself. This funny feeling, was it jealousy? Watching her turn that gorgeous smile on one person after another was slowly gutting me.

Bernice's pies had sold out in minutes, but we'd stopped by her table to say hi. As we were leaving, we were approached by another local.

"Linda," I said warmly, letting the small woman pull me into a strong hug.

"Sweetheart. It's been a while."

"Did you get the updated spreadsheets I sent you?"

She patted my hand. "Yes, dear. Everything went right to the accountant. I'm so glad you helped me clean things up."

Linda was a spry woman in her sixties, and she was the heart and soul behind the Lovewell Food Pantry. She had been running it and fighting the good fight against food insecurity since I was a kid.

I made brief introductions, and Linda's eyes lit up.

"Oh, I'm so thrilled. Paz here is one of the good ones," she proclaimed, beaming at me. "We were scraping by and in danger of closing, but this one swooped in like a superhero and saved the day."

Parker frowned and looked from Linda to me and back again, confused.

"He helped me with everything. The grant applications, cleaning up the books. He even helped us invest and diversify so we can plan for the future." She pulled me down and kissed my cheek. "He's an angel."

If the heat creeping up my neck was any indication, my face had turned crimson. Linda was a friend of my mom's, and I'd helped her with a few small things, just to stabilize the financial end of things. Anybody would have done it.

After Linda found her friends, Parker turned to me. "Aren't you full of surprises, Mr. Superhero?"

I shrugged and put my arm around her, telling myself I had

to play up the relationship. But secretly, I liked it. A lot. "All in a day's work."

"Is your cape at the dry cleaners?" she asked as the smell of her shampoo flooded my senses.

"Of course. It's cashmere. Very fancy."

"I would expect nothing less."

As the night wore on and I had a couple of beers, I became more comfortable with my fake girlfriend. Her touches and handholding and flirty smiles were easier to tolerate, and as we mingled, I pushed away the niggling guilt I carried over our ruse.

But then my mother spotted us.

Loraine Gagnon was out of control. She had channeled her grief after my father's death into a relentless drive to get us all married off. The second Tucker and Goldie came into our lives and she discovered the joys of being a grandmother, there had been no going back. Remy was married now, which meant Adele and I were in her crosshairs.

My sister was smart enough to keep her dating life far from Lovewell, and if my mother even began to pry, Adele shut her down with a ruthless efficiency I admired.

So I knew, from the moment my siblings had talked me into this, that she would lose her mind over Parker.

"Let me look at you!" she exclaimed, grabbing Parker's arms and holding her out. She gave her a thorough examination before pulling her into a tight hug. "Such a pleasure to meet you. I dropped by the other day but missed you." The unspoken commentary was *how dare my son bring home a girlfriend and not tell me first.*

I averted my eyes. I had no doubt Mom was ready to hit me with one of her signature glares. She was of an average height with neatly trimmed gray hair and large brown eyes. She always wore her glasses around her neck on one of many beaded or jeweled chains that matched her outfit perfectly.

After Dad died, she had curled into herself, letting her grief overwhelm her. But things had vastly improved in the last year or so. She had bounced back, recapturing her status as one of those older women who never stopped moving. First by volunteering and gardening, and now by working at the elementary school with Alice. She was constantly on the go, visiting friends, baking banana bread, or engaging in any of a dozen projects.

It felt good to have my mom back but keeping up with her commentary on my love life had been exhausting.

"Have you met my grandchildren? They are the lights of my life." She clutched the pendant around her neck engraved with their initials. They had given her for Mother's Day. "Do you want children?" She wasn't even trying to be cool now.

"Mom!" I looped an arm around Parker's waist and tugged her close. "Please don't interrogate my girlfriend."

She scrunched her nose in a look of disgust. "I'm only having a little fun, Pascal. You've never brought a woman home before. Let a mother dream."

"I'm not offended. Mrs. Gagnon," Parker said in the most goody two shoes tone of voice.

"Please, dear, call me Loraine. You must come over for dinner. How about tomorrow?" She raised one expectant brow at me, daring me to defy her.

"She's on a deadline, Mom," I said gently. "Maybe next weekend."

"Thank you for the banana bread," Parker said sweetly. "It really was the best I've ever had."

Mom was chuffed. "I'll make more this week."

"You are so kind. And we'd love dinner, but I'm so busy with work."

Mom tsked but relented, eventually getting pulled away by one of her friends and giving us some breathing room.

"Sorry," I said, running my hands through my hair. "She can be a lot."

Parker shrugged in what I almost mistook for nonchalance. But on closer inspection, I caught a hint of a frown, and maybe even misty eyes. "She's fun. My mom lives in North Carolina, so I don't have anyone nagging me to get married or to eat veggies. You're lucky."

With that, she continued on, leaving me to catch up while I worked through what she'd just confessed.

What had happened with her family? I knew her dad was a piece of shit, but her mom? Guilt flooded my veins. I *was* lucky. My family, while loud and domineering and all up in my business, loved me. I woke up every day with total certainty that my mother would do anything for me and for my siblings. And while they drove me crazy more often than not, I was beginning to see how rare and special it was to have such a close-knit family.

After another hour or so, we took a break from socializing to grab beers at one of the tents. The wheels were once again turning in her head as she collated all the information we had gathered.

She tapped her chin. "Denise is the retired teacher who works at the library. She was married to Pat, but then they divorced, and he married Karen. She works part time at Gagnon Lumber doing invoicing. Did I get it all right?"

"Yes."

"And her son used to work for you, but he moved down south and got his electrician certification."

"Yes. He always worked hard. Not the brightest, but Dad liked him."

She whipped her phone out and typed in a few notes before putting it back in the pocket of her jeans.

"You are really good at this," I said, genuinely impressed.

She elbowed me in the ribs, making me almost spill my beer. "Stop trying to get in my pants, Gagnon," she said, eyeing me suspiciously.

"I'm not!" I took a step back to preserve my drink and prevent injury. It wasn't a lie. Sure, maybe I was flirting a bit, but I had no intention of going there with her. No matter how irresistible she was proving to be. "Pretty sure if I did, I'd find teeth down there," I quipped.

She popped a hip, giving me her sassiest glare. Damn, I loved the fire inside her.

"Fangs, actually. Good guess."

We studied one another for a moment as waves of heat coursed between us. She was doing something to me. And the sooner I figured it out, the sooner I could fight it and get my sanity back.

Thankfully, my thought spiral was interrupted by my niece and nephew.

"Uncle Paz," Tucker said as Goldie tugged on my arm. "My mom said we can get blueberry ice cream." He raised one eyebrow, confident that I'd say yes, even though there was no way Alice had agreed to it. Not if she'd taken one look at the chocolate smeared all over Goldie's face.

"Isn't it a little cold for ice cream?"

Both kids looked at me in total disbelief. Resistance was futile. Goldie was already dragging me in the direction of the ice cream, so there was no way I could get out of it.

"Okay, fine. I'll take you to the ice cream tent."

"Cool. Miss Parker, do you want some too?" Goldie asked, her curls bouncing.

Parker gave her a big smile. "Of course! It's never too cold for ice cream."

Goldie jumped up and down in excitement as we joined the line. She was heading toward a major sugar crash. I would surely get an angry text from Henri tomorrow morning about buying her too many treats. Even though he was just as bad. The child had more toys than I'd ever seen in my life. He was always coming home with Legos and bikes, and he had recently built a massive swing set in his backyard. Goldie was not the kind of gal who took no for an answer. I only hoped that as she grew up, she would use her powers for good and not evil.

Speaking of evil, Mitch Hebert appeared in my periphery, then, and I had to tamp down the urge to pull the kids closer. He wasn't dangerous. He was just a fucking asshole. I hated the man with every cell in my body. And my protective instincts ran deep.

He cut in front of us and, wearing a lecherous grin, held out a one-hundred-dollar bill to the high school–age girl working the cash register. "Keep the change, cutie," he said, almost bumping into me.

Beside me, Tucker was fuming. He was so much like Henri already. He was obsessed with fairness and nursing a hero complex. I loved the kid, but he sure took on a lot for a sixth grader.

"Hello," Mitch said to Parker, his face a mask of smug satisfaction as he gave her a once-over, blatantly checking her out. "I don't think we've met."

Tightening my grip on her hand, I said, "Parker, this is Mitch Hebert," and left it at that.

She already knew who he was, and I wouldn't give him the

satisfaction of a grand introduction. He was a piece of shit. Though, in a feat of strength, I managed to keep that to myself. I also refrained from throwing a punch. That alone was proof positive that my mother had raised me right.

"Mitch, this is my girlfriend, Parker."

She took his proffered hand and pulled her shoulders back.

"You're the one I've heard about," he said, his beady eyes narrowing. "The writer."

She tilted her head and gave him a smile. "You got me. I'm so fascinated by the timber industry and these small northern towns. Working on a new book series, and everyone here has been so helpful. What a wonderful town Lovewell is!" Every word she spoke was laced with forced pleasantry.

I wrapped my arm around her shoulders, pulling her in close. "Can't wait. My girl is so talented." I planted a kiss on the top of her head. It was dark, but if I hadn't known better, I'd say she blushed a bit.

Mitch watched us, not smiling, only scrutinizing. Like we were an amusing exhibit at the zoo. He dug into his pocket and produced a business card. "I'd be happy to help you with your research." He looked directly at Parker, giving her a smarmy smile that made me want to knock his teeth out. Then he angled in, getting far too close for comfort as he tried to cut me out of the conversation. "My company is *actually* successful." He looked down his nose at me. "And I'd be happy to sit down and give you any information you like."

Instead of drop-kicking him in the nuts, which would have been my preferred response, Parker took the card. "Thanks very much. I'm gonna take you up on that," she said with feigned enthusiasm.

"Smart girl," he said, already walking away.

As soon as he was out of earshot, Parker turned and buried

her face in my chest. The anger I had felt about Mitch dissipated as I savored the feeling of her crushed up against me.

"You okay?" I asked.

She clutched the fabric of my jacket and looked up at me with a sheepish smile. "I couldn't hold it in one more second. What an ass. That cologne. That attitude. The whole 'my company is actually successful.' Fuck that guy."

I wrapped an arm around her, keeping her close as I laughed along with her. "He's horrible."

"And he has no idea what I've got planned for him. He better believe I'll interview him. And I'll dig up every fucking detail of his life. I'll find every single skeleton in his massive closet. That fucker is going down."

A rush of affection filled my veins, and I was overwhelmed with the desire to kiss her. Her evil grin was somehow simultaneously sexy. Her sass and snark drove me crazy every day, but when aimed at my enemies? Shit, that was a turn-on. I needed to step back before I got a visible erection at a town event while standing feet away from my niece and nephew.

This fake relationship suddenly felt real, and it was truly messing with my head. My brain had abandoned all logic and was spinning out with fantasies about Parker that had no right to tempt me. I had a job to do, and so did she.

How the hell had I gotten myself into this mess? And how could I get myself out of it?

Chapter 12
Parker

I wasn't much of a cook, but I managed. And given that Paz was usually the one making dinner, it felt like I should chip in. So I had headed to town for groceries between background checks for one of my clients in Portland, and I'd come home with ingredients for a healthy turkey chili recipe I found online.

I had changed into shorts and a T-shirt and was blasting music when he came home. Trust me, the temptation was irresistible. He had one of those Sonos speaker systems wired throughout the house. It was amazing.

My eyes were tearing from the onion chopping and the simultaneous dancing, but I was having fun.

The grumpy finance bro on the other side of the island couldn't say the same. He had his arms crossed over his chest, and he was wearing a scowl.

"What? No greeting? You could say 'hello, Parker. You look lovely today, as always. Did you have a productive day?'"

"Or I could come home to a quiet, clean house."

"*Boring*. Also. T. Swift is amazing, and this album is *so* good."

"I wouldn't know. Not a big fan."

"Ooh, I'll convert you. Also, found some interesting info today." I snagged my laptop from the corner of the island. After meeting the asshole formally known as Mitch Hebert at the bonfire, I did a little digging. Shockingly, his empire was vast and took up way more of my day than I had anticipated. That guy had more LLCs and corporate filings than I could keep track of, and a ton of random property ownership.

"Have you ever heard of Pattes Holdings?"

He shook his head.

"One of Mitch's filings. Looks like a dog walking company or maybe pet sitting?"

He let out a huff of a laugh. "What the fuck does that mean?"

"No idea. Most of his other stuff seems legit. But this is really out there. It reports earnings in the six figures, but who's walking the dogs? And how many families in Lovewell are in need of a professional walking service?"

"Not many. This isn't really the type of place where people hire dog walkers." He hovered over my shoulder, looking at the screen. "What's the address?"

I pulled up the corporate filing information and plugged the address into Google.

"Looks like a trailer park."

He slid next to me and commandeered the mouse. "That's Mountain Meadows. Local trailer park." He zoomed in on the map and nodded. "Yup. That's a trailer."

"I don't get it. Mitch Hebert lives in a mansion, drives a fancy car, and can't walk down the street without shoving his money in people's faces. Why on earth does he have a random dog walking business running out of a trailer park?"

"No clue." He stood and made his way over to the cabinet. "But it's not because he loves animals." Turning away from me, he filled a glass with water from the dispenser built into the front of the fridge.

"I'm gonna find out. Wanna help me dig up more dirt after dinner?"

He plopped down on one of the stools with his glass. "Nothing would make me happier than to unearth every dirty secret that awful family has."

"Okay. Let me finish up here, and we can figure out what that jackass is up to."

I dumped the diced onions into the pot. They were nowhere near close to uniform in size, but they would do. I moved on to the peppers, keeping an eye on the recipe I had open on my phone.

"Would it kill you to ease up on the mess-making?" he asked, surveying the countertop with his lip curled in disdain.

"I don't see the issue." I scanned the kitchen and shrugged. It wasn't that bad. My laptop, some papers, my coffee mug from this morning, and a half-drunk can of seltzer. He was acting like I had smeared feces on the wall.

He threw his hands up. "My kitchen will never recover."

"You know, you should pull the massive pine tree out of your ass. It would probably help this whole attitude problem you seem to have," I said, gesturing at him with the knife.

"My ass is not your concern," he gritted out. "And I don't remember giving you permission to cook."

"Permission? Oh please. I'm only trying to be a good roommate. And you'll thank me when I'm finished."

"Not likely. I'll probably be chipping whatever you made

off the ceiling, since you seem committed to the art of making a mess at all times."

I paused, knife midair, and contemplated throwing it at him. Sadly, despite all my strength, martial arts training, and firearms skills, my aim wasn't stellar. I blamed my asshole father.

So I'd probably maim him at best and damage the lovely house at worst, and that wasn't a risk I was willing to take.

But while I assessed my lack of knife-throwing prowess, I couldn't help but catch how tired Paz looked. His face, while still stupidly handsome, was pale, and there were dark circles under his eyes. Those broad shoulders were slumped like he'd carried the weight of the world around all day.

That appraisal softened my anger. Though he was prickly on the outside, a chasm of vulnerability welled inside him. Not that he showed signs of it often.

A little loosening up would go a long way. If only it was in his nature. He carried so much with him at all times. His constant vigilance had to be exhausting after a while. And I would know. I had been a cop for a decade. But a person can only keep it up for so long. The thick walls, the endless preparation, and anxiety over every potential outcome. And it seemed to me he had been doing it since he was a kid.

So I resolved to cut him some slack, cook him an amazing dinner, and let him decompress.

When he sauntered up beside me, carefully rolling up the sleeves of another very expensive dress shirt, I softened some more. The sight of those forearms usually helped to soothe my simmering dislike of this man.

But instead of jumping in to help cook, he gathered the random bowls and cutlery. "You've got to clean as you go," he grumbled.

Annoyed, I shot him a glare. "I'll take care of it."

"Sure."

Before he could reach the sink, I elbowed him out of the way and grabbed the faucet nozzle. Replacing my look of annoyance with a wicked grin, I pulled it out and aimed it at him.

"Leave them."

He cocked a brow. "You wouldn't. These pants are Italian wool."

God, he was absurd. "Even more reason to drench you."

"It's ironic. You're willing to spray me with water, but not your dishes." His eyes danced, and the corner of his mouth curled into a smile.

That was it. He was definitely getting it. "Clean this, Gagnon," I said, aiming the nozzle at his chest with one hand and yanking on the faucet with the other. The water burst out in a strong spray, drenching his shirt.

He tossed the dishes into the sink and lunged for me, but I jumped out of the way, narrowly missing his grasp. Sadly, the nozzle reached the end of the hose and tugged me back.

"What the fuck was that for?" he yelled.

"Being so goddamn judgmental and uptight," I countered, aiming for his face.

This time, he was ready, and he bobbed and weaved so the blast missed him, grabbing me at the waist and wrestling me for control of the hose.

I fought him off, but he outmuscled me. He yanked it out of my hand and managed to spray my hip before I took off running.

"Nope," he yelled again. "You're not getting away that easily."

I raced through the empty living room, looping around the

piano, and he was hot on my heels. I shrieked when he reached out for me, but I hurtled over the couch just in time.

His eyes were bright, and his wet shirt clung to his muscular chest in a way that was impossible not to gawk at, even as I ran from him.

Thankfully, the house was huge and had minimal furniture, making it easy to evade him.

I bounded up the stairs and darted for the safety of my bedroom, but his legs were much longer. I was down the hall, almost to the threshold, when a thick arm banded around my waist.

"Gotcha," he growled, slinging me over his shoulder effortlessly. I kicked a bit, laughing as he hoisted me up and stalked down the hall to his room.

Before I could put up a real fight, he was dumping me into his massive walk-in shower and turning on the rain head.

Cold water poured from the ceiling, drenching us both and making me shriek.

"Shit. I should have thought this through." He took a big step back to avoid the frigid spray, but I wrapped my arms around his leg, keeping him close. When he tried to shake me loose, he lost his balance and tumbled to the floor next to me.

He blinked at me, his hair drenched and water dripping down his face, and guffawed once. Then again. Then he erupted into howling laughter that echoed off the tiled walls.

"Shit, Parker," he said, reaching up and adjusting the dial. The water instantly warmed. "This was not how I pictured this evening going."

I pushed my wet hair out of my face and shrugged. "Seems like an improvement over what I can only assume were the world's most boring plans."

He considered me for a moment, his eyes locked on mine.

Then his focus dipped to my lips, making every cell in my body light up.

He had chased me around the house and slung me over his shoulder like a rag doll, and now we were showering together, albeit fully clothed. What was happening?

Because my stomach was fluttering wildly, and my hands were shaking with the urge to run them through his wet hair and pull his face to mine so I could fuse our mouths.

He was studying me with heat and intensity that immediately set my body ablaze. Being the center of his attention was unnerving and thrilling all at once. I felt naked and exposed but also savored, revered. This man, this big, grouchy lumberjack finance bro, was sitting on the tile floor of his shower, watching me like he couldn't help himself. And he was ruining his Italian pants in the process.

And he wasn't mad. Gone was the perma-scowl and the furrowed brow. If anything, his expression was curious. Soft eyes and lips pursed slightly.

I stood up and turned the water off. The shower stall had suddenly become way too small and way too warm.

He stepped out and handed me a neatly folded towel, which I promptly wrapped around myself. Mainly to hide my extremely excited nipples, but also as an added layer of protection from the vulnerability of the moment.

He grabbed a towel for himself. But instead of using it to dry off, he placed it on the edge of the sink and went to work unbuttoning his shirt. It was soaked and plastered to his skin, but he slowly and methodically worked each button from its hole while I tried to busy myself with my wet hair to avoid staring.

In the mirror, he caught my gaze. I wrapped my towel

tighter and watched him in return, not sure how to begin to unpack the vulnerability I was feeling.

He looked at me for an extra moment, raising one eyebrow, then he turned around. "I'll give you some privacy," he said, his usual curt tone returning. With that, he stepped out of the room and shut the door.

I gave him a few minutes before I slipped out and high-tailed it down the hall to my room. Part of me wanted to stay, talk about whatever had happened between us. But nothing good would come from verbalizing what I had just felt.

Because I was a professional. And he was my client. And any fleeting attraction or connection must be avoided at all costs.

Chapter 13
Parker

There were more clothes in the pile on my bed than there were left in the closet at this point. I couldn't decide what to wear. It wasn't an inauguration or a movie premier. No, I was prepping for a night out at the local dive bar, hilariously called Duck, Duck, Moose. No one could accuse the citizens of Lovewell of lacking a sense of humor.

The Gagnons were headed there tonight, along with most of the locals, and I intended to bring my conversational A game. I was feeling the pressure to make a good impression. The longer I stayed in Lovewell, the deeper I was pulled in, and my insecurities were starting to take hold.

Because someone knew. It wasn't Paz's fault. He had been playing the role of doting boyfriend perfectly. I had made a mistake somewhere. A tactical error.

When I left for the gym this morning, I found it. Right on my windshield. A neat manilla envelope tucked behind my wiper.

Inside was a lined piece of notebook paper, the edges jagged from where it had been ripped. Someone had written, in neat block letters, *Go home, pig. Stop sticking your snout where it doesn't belong.*

There was nothing else. My car wasn't vandalized. Nothing was stolen. Only this note.

So someone was on to me. Someone knew. And while I was used to being called every dirty cop word in existence, I hadn't expected it here. I had no social media, no digital footprint whatsoever. My company website didn't even have a headshot. I knew how to fly under the radar.

I racked my brain, trying to figure out where I could have blown my cover. I'd worked nonstop this week. Full of interviews and research and a town bonfire. And I was still working to wrap my mind around the various moving pieces while ensuring I didn't miss any important information. There were levels of complexity to every case, but this was beginning to feel personal. And it worried me. A lot of things were worrying me at the moment.

Especially my outfit. And although it was so unlike me, I wanted to cry. I wasn't under any delusions about my body. It was imperfect, and I was perfectly okay with that. I took care of it, and it took care of me.

But recently, I had felt more self-conscious than I had since I was in my early twenties. More and more often, I found myself wondering if my pants were unflattering, or if I should put on more makeup.

It was infuriating. I had little time for insecurity. I was thirty-four, and I had been through all that shit in my teens and twenties. These days, I was committed to loving myself.

But Paz's gaze was so calculating. As if he was making a mental tally of every one of my flaws when he looked at me. And his physical perfection wasn't helping matters. So my head was fuzzy and confused. And I was suffering through a major bout of impostor syndrome to boot.

I pulled open every drawer of the dresser, hoping to stumble upon something amazing Liv had thrown into my bag when I wasn't looking. And there it was. The pearly pink lace bra. It was almost translucent and had delicate demi cups that enhanced my cleavage and made me feel like a goddess in the process. I shifted my sports bras out of the way and found the matching panties. Of course Liv had packed them. She was a completist like that.

Robed in my finest lingerie like a knight would equip himself with armor, I found a passable denim skirt and a cute off-the-shoulder top and set to putting on my makeup. I'd be damned if I wasn't going to knock this town dead.

Because the clock was ticking. I didn't know how much time I had before my cover was blown and I lost the chance to solve this case.

Though Paz wasn't one for small talk, he was exceptionally quiet on the ride to the bar. When I'd come downstairs ready to go, he had stared for a moment, biting his bottom lip while his eyes roved down my bare legs to my suede ankle boots and then back up to my face. We stood in silence as featherlight flutters erupted low in my abdomen. After a moment, he grunted and held an arm out toward the door.

Things had been really weird since the moment in the shower the other night. He had been keeping his distance. Coming home late and leaving early and generally avoiding being in my presence. I couldn't say I was mad, because the time apart was necessary in order to calm the curiosity that had compounded as we dripped water onto the tile floor while assessing each other that evening. But tonight, we'd have to behave like a couple, and we'd have to do it in a way that convinced the nosy townsfolk of Lovewell. And the thought of diving back into that role made my stomach flip.

I spent the fifteen-minute drive dissecting my feelings and working to categorize them in a way that made sense. His attention, when focused on my body, unnerved me, but there was more to it. Usually, when he looked at me, it was with annoyance or pure judgment. But tonight? He'd practically devoured me from across the room with a kind of hunger I had never experienced before. The curtain had been drawn back during those carefree moments we'd shared, and I had gotten a glimpse of what he was like without artifice or pretense.

And I found myself wanting more.

The Moose was a fascinating spot. Clearly, it aspired to be a dive, but the cleanliness and good lighting betrayed those fantasies, rendering it a charming local watering hole with killer waffle fries. One side was set up with booths and high-top tables, while the other was filled with pool tables and a small stage and dance floor. A massive dark wood bar cut through the middle, giving patrons on either side of the establishment equal access to the alcohol.

Hazel was behind the bar, filling drinks and delivering food, when we arrived. And most of the Gagnons were here, chatting and playing pool.

Remy was sitting on a stool, drinking water and flirting with his wife while she bustled around. "Good to see you, Parker," he said, giving me that easy smile. "What can I get you?"

I peeked over at Paz, who was surrounded by several women who were smiling and flipping their hair at him.

My stomach dropped and my fists involuntarily clenched. What the shit was this? Who were these women fawning all over my man?

Pure jealousy took over. It was one of my worst character

flaws. I was possessive and jealous, and no matter how much I had tried to hide it in past relationships, I always failed. But this wasn't even a real relationship.

It didn't matter. It was the principle. Or at least that's what I told myself.

I turned to Remy with a smile, and idea forming in my evil brain. "I'll take a glass of red wine. And could you ask Hazel to make a strawberry daiquiri for Paz? And really do it up. Whipped cream. Sugar rim. That sort of thing."

Remy gave me an even wider smile. "I knew I liked you. No problem."

When our drinks were ready, I sauntered over to Paz, plastering a giant smile on my face as I approached the group. One of the women, a tiny blonde, had her hand on his forearm, and I briefly contemplated breaking her fingers.

"Here you are, stud muffin," I said, kissing his cheek and handing him the pink daiquiri in a fancy hurricane glass. Hazel had not disappointed. She'd decorated it with an excessive amount of whipped cream and two cocktail umbrellas, and she'd finished it off with a cherry on top.

I even reached around and gave his ass a hard squeeze, making his eyes bulge. With a satisfied smile, I turned back to the women, who were now mumbling into their drinks. Was the ass grab necessary? Probably not. But I had no regrets. Like the rest of him, it was all thick muscle.

He raised one eyebrow. "I didn't take you for the jealous type."

I shrugged, sipping my wine as they walked away. "I don't share."

Our gazes locked, just for a moment, and I could feel the heat in his eyes.

"Keep drinking those, and you'll definitely lose next

month." A man on the shorter side with a friendly smile and dirty blond hair nudged Paz in the ribs, interrupting our stare down.

He held out his hand. "Matt," he said. "I work for these guys."

We chatted briefly about the timber business and his family. Matt was easy to talk to. Since we had arrived, a decent-sized crowd had gathered, so after a moment, I let Paz introduce me to several other Gagnon Lumber employees.

I knew *of* most of them, having pored through employment records and payroll spreadsheets this week, but it was nice to put faces to names. Especially the crews that worked out in the woods. They were the ones I intended to really dig deep into. The information would hopefully give me insight into the accidents. We continued to chat and enjoy the live music while I got a feel for the scene here.

The bar was busy, filled with young singles, couples on date nights, and a very loud and very hilarious group of senior citizens in one corner, who appeared to be on their second bottle of whiskey. Music blared from an old-fashioned jukebox, the upbeat tunes only adding to the celebratory atmosphere.

It only took minutes to confirm that Paz was the most eligible bachelor in Lovewell. Now that his brothers were off the market, the heads of every woman and even a few of the men had turned the moment he walked in. From the looks of it, I wasn't the only one affected by the expensive clothes on that rugged, masculine body.

Because even while his arm was around me, we were fending off glares from women of all ages. I swore some were old enough to be his grandmother.

Though we were playing the part of a happy couple, I could see how the cocky persona he employed worked for him.

Free from his usual anxieties and self-doubt, he could go out, lean on his charm and good looks, and forget about the pressure and the loneliness for a while.

No wonder his phone was full of women's numbers. The guy had no coping mechanisms, no hobbies, and no friends outside his family. The reality of it made my chest ache. He had brains and money and ambition to spare, but no connections. So he had turned to casual sex to fill the void.

Except the more I got to know him, to understand him, to peek behind the façade, the harder it was to truly pinpoint the motivation. There was way more to the story. I'd observed him for days now. His empty house and his sleepless nights and his workaholism. How he itched to constantly check on the business and his mother and his siblings. To reassure everyone and make sure every detail was perfect.

Beside me, he was devastatingly handsome. His beard was perfectly trimmed, his lashes thick and dark. What would it be like? To spend the night with him? To be the woman he chose to take home?

To have all that intensity and pent-up frustration focused on me?

I shivered, despite the warm, crowded bar. Because there was no doubt in my mind he'd be focused. He was not the kind of man who half-assed things. Even casual sex.

Those were dangerous thoughts. I was here to work. Not to psychoanalyze and fall in lust with my employer/roommate/fake boyfriend. Nope. This relationship was already complicated enough. Fuck, it had been so much easier when I thought he was an entitled douche canoe.

Despite the flirty glances from half the female patrons, his attention stayed fixed on the men he was still conversing with. And when it wasn't, it was locked on me. No matter how far I wandered, I could feel his eyes on my skin. It was unnerving and energizing all at once.

The entire population of Lovewell thought I was his girl. And while I usually prickled at the idea of belonging to someone, especially a man, tonight, it gave me a smug satisfaction. Perhaps it was the fake nature of the arrangement, or maybe it was his outwardly flirty smiles.

But the man at my side was in complete juxtaposition to my grouchy roommate. And I was relishing the difference. Maybe a little too much.

As the night wore on, the bar got busier, and I got pulled into one side conversation after another. I switched to water so I could keep my wits about me as I soaked in all the details and categorized them.

As warned, some Lovewell citizens were not super welcoming.

Case in point, my pool opponents. Adele had roped me into playing with her. Unsurprisingly, she was excellent, and she more than made up for my rusty skills. The first game we played, with a duo of friendly Gagnon employees, had been fun.

But then, that smoldering Viking from the gym showed up.

"We'll take winner," he said, putting his large hands on the table.

Adele ignored him and lined up her winning shot. She was seemingly unruffled, even as the intimidating man moved closer, flanked by two other men who were equally large and broad.

When she racked the balls and broke, no one spoke.

"I'm Parker," I said, deciding to go for friendly.

The main Viking offered a large paw and slapped on a terrible impression of a smile. "Finn," he said curtly, never taking his eyes off Adele. He gestured toward the men next to him. "Cole. Jude."

His companions nodded at me in unison, arms crossed. They were smaller versions of the main Viking. Shorter and darker hair, but each had the same piercing blue eyes. One of them had a slightly crooked nose, like it had been broken a few times.

Adele continued to run the table, sinking shot after shot while we stood by awkwardly. The bar had gone quieter, and my cop senses were tingling. But before I could process the scene and put a finger on the cause, a strong arm slid around my shoulders and pulled me close. A strong, clean, familiar scent wafted over me, and a shiver ran up my spine.

"Is there a problem?" Paz said.

Adele looked up, her eyes widening.

"No problem," Finn replied. "Just want to play." The two men glared at each other like they were ready to pull out their dueling pistols. This egregious display of testosterone seemed like overkill for Thursday night at the local dive bar, but that didn't dull my curiosity. I was invested in seeing how this would play out.

Paz's grip on my upper arm tightened. At this rate, I'd have fingertip bruises. "Don't see why. My sister's going to wipe the floor with you. Why don't you head out? Save yourself the embarrassment."

Finn looked from Paz to me and then to Adele, where his focus settled for a moment too long. There was definitely a story there.

Before punches could be thrown or an elaborate dance fight could break out, we were interrupted by a booming voice.

"Boys." An older man was striding toward us. "Don't want

any trouble on my night off. If I have to arrest you, it will interrupt date night with the wife."

Ah. Law enforcement. Though he wore civilian clothing, his posture alone gave it away. The set of this man's shoulders screamed "protect and serve." Despite being in his sixties, he was strong looking with a ruddy face.

"Chief," Paz said, turning toward him, donning a mask of indifference, as if to convey there was nothing to be concerned about. "I was introducing my girlfriend to everyone. This is Parker."

I held out my hand and gave him my most innocent smile.

He took it, giving me a firm shake. "Yes, yes. Heard about the young lady at the diner. A writer? My wife's book club is going to read all your books. I'm sure they'll be coming after you to autograph them." The chief seemed good natured, if not a bit weary. I could imagine his department was understaffed and under resourced. Most were in small towns like Lovewell. He was no doubt stuck trying to right all of society's wrongs for this town.

"That's so kind."

"You need anything while you're in town, don't hesitate to ask." He turned and faced the Viking trio. "Heberts," he said. His mouth was set in a firm line, and the look he gave them, though not hard, was full of authority. With that, he nodded once and headed back to his table.

His warning was implicit. No trouble. And it was clearly heeded. The Heberts headed back to the bar, leaving Paz and me alone while Adele continued to shoot pool by herself. Paz's arm was still around my shoulders, and he gently stroked the bare skin of my arm. It was soothing, despite the tension in the room. He leaned closer, his warm breath making goose bumps erupt along my shoulder and across my chest. "Wanna get outta here, gorgeous?" he murmured into my hair.

Perhaps it was a hormonal reaction to the testosterone showdown I had just witnessed, or simply the sensation of being touched after being alone for so long. But my skin tingled, and my heart raced. And I was pretty sure I'd follow him anywhere.

"Yes," I said, trying to keep a lid on the physical reaction I was experiencing. "Take me home."

Chapter 14
Pascal

All the stress was getting to me. I hadn't been able to sleep all week. And now I was jittery and nervous. I banged out a few sets of pushups in my room, even though I'd put myself through an intense workout this morning. I still had so much physical aggression I needed to work off.

I'd woken up pissed off. After last night, I was confused and frustrated. This woman was everywhere. All over my house and my office and my town.

When I closed my eyes at night, her image was imprinted on the backs of my eyelids. The freckles, the ponytail, the damn bras.

And the questions. So. Many. Questions.

It was her job, of course. A job I had hired her to do. But dear God, I couldn't deal.

Because Parker's questions didn't only pertain to the investigation. She wanted to understand every single detail of each interaction, relationship, event, family, and business that had anything to do with Lovewell. All the time.

And me. She asked far too many personal questions. About my coffee and my workout routine and my car and my clothes.

And it wasn't only surface-level stuff. She dug deep. Evading her constant probing and analysis was getting exhausting. It was like she wanted to understand me on a cellular level. She didn't understand that it wasn't worth her time. I was not that interesting, and she was not going to discover that my soul contained some hidden depths full of meaningful emotions. I was an asshole. And a workaholic. And a pessimist. There wasn't much more to it.

But she persisted. Smiling, laughing, eating meals with me, and teasing me. So I was distracted. Out of sorts.

And none of my usual coping mechanisms were helping. Drinking and obsessive planning and preparation were not doing it anymore. And given that I lived in the world's tiniest town and was in a fake committed relationship, I couldn't fall back on casual sex.

My mother, always concerned about my health and stress levels, had gifted me a basket of fancy tea. She was always on me to relax and de-stress, whatever the fuck that meant. I would relax when the business was thriving. When all my family members were provided for, healthy, and happy. When I could wrap each one of them up in a bubble of protection that only my money, hard work, and planning could provide.

Then I'd fucking relax.

But my father had been murdered and both my brothers had been in danger due to this mess. It was not business as usual right now. Yet it seemed I was the only person who really understood the implications.

I flipped the kettle on. Might as well offer Parker a cup of tea from the basket my mom had delivered. I hadn't seen her all day, and the logical part of my brain screamed to stay away from her, let her work in peace. That she was an added complication I could not manage. But another part of me, the naive, stupid part, overrode that. Choosing to be a good roommate by checking on her and offering her sustenance.

I headed upstairs and followed the sound of loud music. Rather than leading me to her room, it brought me to the tiny guest room she had been using as an office.

Since she'd arrived, I hadn't been in here. I'd wanted to give her some privacy to do her work. Amazon packages had been piling up on the porch for the last week, so she'd obviously been filling the space and doing what she needed to do, but I was not prepared for what I saw when I hovered at the threshold of the room.

Parker, wearing tiny shorts and a tank top. With no bra.

Dancing around to some kind of girl power pop song.

Damn, she was sexy. Not in an obvious, push-up bra and fake eyelashes kind of way. No, her personality created a shield that hid her charms well. Only once a person breached her walls did they see the real her.

She was of medium height, with strong muscles but also soft curves. Full breasts and round hips, but strong shoulders and thighs.

Her quads flexed as she danced across the room. Her face glistened with sweat, and her chest was heaving, drawing even more attention to those braless breasts. I flexed my fingers as my brain pondered how perfectly they would fit in my hands.

I was transfixed. I couldn't look away as she scribbled on a Post-it note, then stuck it on a large whiteboard, all the while bopping her head to the beat.

My body was on high alert, and blood pumped through my veins, urging me to flee this potentially dangerous situation. I lifted one foot, ready to turn on my heel and heed that instinct, but was stopped by the sound of her voice.

"Are you creeping on me, Gagnon?"

I froze, though I ignored her comment. Pulling air deep into my lungs, I stepped forward instead of back and shuffled close to the whiteboard. It was half-full of index cards in different colors, with names, dates, and locations. One side was devoted to the four families—who was related to whom, and who was in charge.

My blood boiled when my focus landed on printed photos of Mitch Hebert and his brother Paul.

"Did you make a murder wall?" I asked, working to decipher her messy handwriting.

She turned the music down and crossed her arms. "What are you talking about?"

"You know. Like in the movies. Conspiracy theorists and killers always have walls covered with photos, scraps of paper, and string."

Shaking her head, she huffed. "This is a visual overview of my investigation and family trees for the Gagnons and the Heberts, as well as the other two logging families. Any resemblance to the paraphernalia of a serial killer is purely coincidental."

"Sure thing, Nancy Drew."

She put her hands on her hips. "Let me walk you through. This side involves people directly involved in the business. We've got Gagnon employees here."

I walked closely, reading all the names and marveling at how she had worked so quickly. Names, addresses, jobs, length of employment—she hadn't missed a single detail.

"And on this side are persons of interest who are not in the business."

I scanned the details. The Maine Marauders. That made sense. Although I didn't know much about them, everyone knew the local motorcycle club was mixed up with the drugs running through the rural areas.

"Chief Souza?"

She shrugged. "I always look at local law enforcement. If things have been happening under their noses for years, you've gotta ask why."

I nodded, feeling uneasy. The chief had been a trusted friend of my dad's, but Parker was right. We had to follow every lead. And I had to hand it to her. She certainly was doing that.

"And the back"—she turned the board around to reveal more names, photos, and Post-its—"is everyone I've eliminated so far."

I tugged on my hair and let out the breath I'd been holding. Seeing everything laid out like this, it was too much for me to process. Was it possible there were this many people on earth who could have wanted to harm my dad? After his death, I had put everything into a neat box in my mind and sealed it shut while working nonstop to save the business and provide for my family.

And now it had been ripped wide open, and all kinds of feelings were taking over. "This is a shit show."

She bumped my hip. "It's my process. It's chaotic and messy, but you don't have to like it."

I pinched the bridge of my nose. "What does this even mean?" I pressed a finger to a receipt, then plucked another item from the board. "Is that a candy wrapper?"

"It's evidence, asshole. Who in their right mind even eats these things? Adele found the wrapper in the shop up at camp after the accident. I'm being thorough." She nudged me out of the way with one shoulder and yanked it out of my hand. It was a bag of Maynard's wine gums. How random. She then secured it back onto the board with a small magnet. "Respect the process."

I seized up. She was close. Too close.

And she smelled sweet and a little spicy.

I wasn't prepared for her to invade my personal space. Especially since she was half-naked and had just been bouncing around my house braless.

The pretending, the deviation from my routine, was getting to me. All the uncertainty and doubt and fear were enough to send me over the edge. And now I was trapped in my own home with a sexy woman driving me absolutely insane.

And the feelings swirling around in my brain were out of control. She was clearly digging, and doing a good job, but the chaos of it all, the unknowns and the risks, overpowered my thinking brain.

So I did what I always did when backed into a corner. I lashed out.

"What is this shit?" I said, waving wildly at a bra hanging from the closet doorknob. "A bra?"

"You're a genius!" The sarcasm dripped from her voice. "Not that it's any of your business, but that's what I do when I come home after a long day. I take off my bra."

My brain short-circuited, and I couldn't keep my eyes from falling to her breasts. Round and bouncy and taunting me. Free from their underwire confines.

"Eyes up here, Gagnon."

My face heated as I lifted my chin and scowled at her.

"You're not entitled to a free show just because I took off my bra."

My eye twitched as I racked my brain for a pithy response.

When all I came up with was nonsense, I snapped. "Wear a fucking bra, then. It's not a big deal."

She crossed her arms, drawing even more attention to the breasts that would be my undoing. "You ever wear a bra?"

What a preposterous question. "Can't say that I have."

"Then reserve your fucking judgment, Gagnon. Because if I want to free my boobs from lingerie prison, then it's my goddamn right."

I focused on the yard outside the window, desperate not to stare. Desperate to rein in my out-of-control thoughts and emotions. This woman was pure human chaos. And I would not survive another day with her in my house.

"Do you think you could maybe wear a bra while you're staying in my house?" I asked, dropping my gaze to my feet, still unable to trust myself to look at her.

It was a simple enough request. And she was supposedly a professional. When I'd told her to make herself at home, I certainly hadn't anticipated those round, perky breasts bouncing around untethered all goddamn day.

"Oh, Gagnon. Are you distracted by my boobs?"

I kept my head lowered, even as my face grew hotter.

"Pascal Gagnon, legendary ladies' man, afraid of a pair of boobs? I like them, but they're not that great."

I bit my tongue to keep from sharing my opinion. Because they were fucking spectacular. I could spend hours exploring them with my tongue.

That, of course, was far from an appropriate response, regardless of our professional relationship.

I took a breath, tried to regain my composure. More than anything, I needed an escape from the topic of breasts and nudity. So I barked out, "Do whatever you want. I've got to go. Henri and I are supposed to help Remy train."

Time with my brothers outside of work was rare, and the longer I'd been back in town, the more I looked forward to it. And since I'd made such an ass out of myself over the past few months, I owed it to them to show up and try to act like a decent human being.

I didn't connect with them in many ways, but sports had always been common ground for us. Especially now that they were busy with their women, and I was feeling even more out of the loop than usual.

Today, more than ever, I needed an outlet for my frustration. Parker had totally taken over my house and my mind. Chopping wood was hard work, especially with my brothers, who tended to take things to athletic extremes. It would be just what I needed to get my head on straight.

Parker took a step closer, her eyes widening. "You guys are going to hulk out and go full lumberjack?" She was hopping around from foot to foot again, wearing a gleeful grin, which would have been cute if her tits weren't bouncing, making it difficult for me to speak in coherent sentences.

"What are you babbling about?"

"You know, axes, plaid, staring off into the distance while you contemplate the meaning of life?" She pressed her palms together in front of her chest and watched me with wide, sparkling eyes.

I huffed and backed out of the room so I could get changed.

"Fighting off existential ennui by attacking trees with bladed instruments?" she continued, following me down the hall.

"You are so strange. Leaving in ten."

"Wait for me. I gotta get some layers. I am so not missing this."

Chapter 15
Parker

Despite my better judgment, I climbed into his passenger seat.

He'd been completely out of line earlier, shouting and carrying on about my investigation. And my bras, of all things.

Just when I was starting to get a read on him, he went and freaked out, giving me way more to consider. Was he stressed about the investigation? Or was he merely a control freak throwing a tantrum because I was a messy, chaotic disruption to his empty house and lonely routine?

Either way, I found myself jumping at the chance to spend more time with him. To see him and his siblings and learn as much as I could. Not only because it was my job, but because I was curious. And curiosity was bad for me. Especially when it revolved around hot guys.

His strong hands gripped the steering wheel perfectly at ten and two as he silently kept his attention on the road in front of him. Like his house, his car was pristinely clean and empty.

No papers or snacks or old water bottles. Instead, the SUV housed a gym bag and a small emergency kit.

"So you boys get together and chop down trees?" I asked.

His eyes never left the road. "Don't forget about Adele. She's frighteningly accurate with an axe."

That didn't surprise me one bit. Adele was one of the most capable humans I had ever met. "I like her," I said, thinking out loud.

"Of course you do. You guys can form a coven and plot the destruction of mankind."

"Don't give me too many ideas. But she's awesome, and maybe if you made an effort to speak to her about things other than this investigation, you'd realize that."

He laughed, throwing his head back. "You don't know Adele. I've tried. Trust me. She went through a breakup last year. I tried to be supportive. Barely left that conversation with my testicles intact. You think I'm a surly asshole? My sister can shoot lasers out of her eyes if she wants to."

"We all can," I said sarcastically. "Haven't you heard? When we get our periods, we develop killer laser eyes."

He kept his focus on the road rather than engaging. "And that's why I'm single," he muttered under his breath.

He was so rigid, so repressed. I wanted to smack him. Tell him to unclench that round, muscular ass and broaden his horizons a bit.

But this was clearly not the moment to get into that. Tension radiated off him. His knuckles were white, and those stupidly delicious forearms were almost as rigid as his jaw.

While I could certainly stand to be a bit neater, I was under no misconception that the reasoning behind his outburst had anything to do with me.

On second thought, maybe it had everything to do with me.

He was impossible to understand. Either way, the fear in his eyes was real. And that was what kept me going. Because hypervigilance took a toll, and this family had been through more danger than most.

After ten minutes of tense silence, we pulled up in front of Henri and Alice's large timber-frame house. It was beautiful and fit in seamlessly with the mountain backdrop.

I wasn't sure I'd ever get tired of the views up here or the cold mountain air. I'd always thought I was an ocean girl. I loved the salty smell of the sea, but I was beginning to love these gorgeous forests and mountains too.

Even stuck in a car with a grumpy lumberjack, I could appreciate the natural beauty of my home state. I would only be here for a few weeks, so I was going to make the most of it.

I got out of the car and let the cool breeze coming off the mountains ground me. The air was crisp, and my cheeks flushed. Remy and Hazel were headed up the hill and waved hello.

"You brought the fuzz?" Remy asked, his eyes bright.

Hazel elbowed him. "She's ex-fuzz."

Draping an arm around his wife's shoulders, he pulled her in tight and kissed the top of her head. "My wife is a genius," he said, beaming with pride.

"She wants to understand the lifestyle," Paz muttered, ignoring their greetings.

I gave them a friendly smile. "Please excuse my fake boyfriend. He's in a mood."

Paz shot me a look, and I stuck my tongue out, then leaned toward Remy and Hazel.

"I made a mess in his house, and he's very upset about it."

Remy laughed. "The fortress of solitude? Oh yes, that's a major crime."

Paz glared at him. "My fake girlfriend is a human hurricane who leaves empty cans and bras in her wake."

"Bras?"

I shrugged. "They're awful."

Hazel offered me a high five. "Amen, sister. The undergarments of Satan."

"Exactly," I said as Alice approached. "He's either offended by their existence or by the sight of them. I can't tell which."

"What did I walk into?" Alice asked with a friendly smile. The woman radiated happiness, and each time I saw her, my desire to befriend her for real got stronger.

"Nothing," Paz said, placing his hand on the small of my back and leading me around the house.

"This is where we train," he said, guiding me to a clearing near the tree line.

There was a small shed with a padlock on it, stacks and stacks of logs, and several pieces of equipment I didn't recognize.

"You're talking to me again?" I asked, hands on my hips.

With a grunt, he unlocked the shed and took a step back. He opened a door, revealing several axes of different sizes, all hung neatly. There were gloves of every size piled on a shelf, what looked like a large saw, and neatly coiled ropes.

"This was Alice's doing," he said. "She organized and labeled everything."

"She seems great," I murmured, studying the various tools.

"She is. Changed Henri's life. Still can't believe that grumpy bastard is getting married. Boggles the mind." He handed me a pair of gloves, and once I'd slipped them on, he held out a pair of safety glasses.

While I had never been inclined to participate, I still respected the institution of marriage. I didn't know Henri and

Alice well, but from our interactions, it was obvious they were madly in love with each other and their kids.

"You don't have to go if you don't want to," Paz said, grabbing a pair of gloves for himself and donning safety glasses.

"I'll go," I said with a shrug, taking the axe he handed me, feeling the weight of it in my hands. "It'd be weird if I didn't."

He frowned and lifted one shoulder, pretty much assuring he'd be the worst wedding date ever. If anything, I had to go. I'd make it my mission to keep him occupied so he didn't accidentally shed his misanthropy all over the happy occasion. I could take him out back and give him an ass-kicking if he was anything less than overjoyed for his brother and sister-in-law.

"You gonna teach her, old man?" Remy asked, wandering toward us, still holding Hazel close. He was the smallest of the Gagnon brothers, and he was lankier, with broad shoulders and a narrow waist.

I had seen clips of him at pro competitions on YouTube. Hazel had mentioned climbing trees. She'd also said that he was a spokesmodel in the lumberjack world. Which made sense. He had the same square-jawed mountain-man appeal as his older brothers. I had no doubt that face could sell some cargo pants.

Paz ignored him. "This," he said, pointing to the thing in my hands, "is a maul."

"I thought it was an axe."

"See the head?" He pointed to the big metal part. "A maul is wider and heavier than an axe, making it easier for splitting wood. The back end can be used like a sledgehammer too."

I nodded, though I didn't really understand the difference.

"How about you let the pro help your girl?" Remy asked, settling on a small log bench nearby with Hazel. He grinned, his eyes dancing. He obviously loved messing with his older brother.

Paz glared at him, then steered me over to an area with large sections of logs cut and stacked.

He took a small piece of wood that had already been split and placed it on top of a large leveled-off stump.

"You want to square your hips with the piece of wood on the chopping block, swing back like this"—he mimed doing it—"and then let gravity bring it over your shoulder while you use your core and legs to drive it through the log."

I took a step back to give him some space.

"Like this." He swung his maul, all grace and precision, and split the wood in half smoothly.

He grabbed another piece from the pile and lined it up for me. "This is pine," he said. "It's soft and should be easy for your first time."

Focusing on the instructions he'd given me, I raised the maul and lined it up properly. I had an audience, which, of course, meant I was worried about missing the wood and looking dumb.

I brought it down like he showed me, but it got stuck. I wiggled it to break it loose, but it wasn't budging. My face flamed in embarrassment, and I dropped my shoulders in defeat.

"Not bad," Paz said. He took the maul from me and, using one foot to hold the half-split wood in place, worked the blade out. "I can't believe I have to tell you of all people this, but you gotta be a bit more aggressive."

I rolled my shoulders back and shook off my abashment while he lined up another piece. Oh, I could show him aggressive.

I brought the maul up and swung as hard as I could. This

time, I missed my target altogether and wedged the blade in the tree stump block instead.

"*Shit,*" I hissed. The embarrassment I'd fended off came back in full force.

Paz stepped up beside me again. "Let me help you with the motion."

He took the maul of out my hands and propped it against the stump. He then stood behind me and put his hands on my shoulders. His warm breath tickled my ear, and I had to resist the urge to shudder. He was close. Really close. And my body was having feelings about this closeness.

It had to have been the chilly weather. It was the only explanation for my rock-hard nipples and the way my leg muscles were clenching.

He moved my arms up and back. "When you swing up, think about making a smooth arc. And when it comes over your shoulder, you have to really use your strength to drive it."

He made the motion with my arms a few times, his large hands gripping my biceps and taking control. Clearly, it had been a while since I'd been touched, because my body lit up like a circuit, and his touch was the electricity coursing through it.

He took a few steps back. "Now try again," he commanded.

I bit my lip. Damn. His deep, masculine voice was even more sexy when he was bossing me around. Thoughts of his incessant nagging about my organization skills and messiness faded away and were replaced with visions of what else that voice could command me to do.

"Parker," he barked again.

I nodded. Okay, it was go time. I was a former cop, for Christ's sake. I could deadlift more than my body weight. There was no reason I couldn't chop wood.

Focusing on re-creating the way it felt when he'd guided my arms, I swung. As the head came over my shoulder, I used my legs to push down as hard as I could while clenching my eyes shut.

At the sound of a low whistle, I cracked one eye open, then the other. Before me, on either side of the log, were two pieces of wood. I had split it clean in two.

In my periphery, the corner of Paz's mouth quirked. It was probably the closest thing to a smile his face was capable of creating. "You did it."

I couldn't contain my excitement. I grinned. "It felt easy. Like slicing through butter."

"Exactly. Because your muscles were cooperating with gravity, and you hit it just right. It's about precision, not brute strength. Try again. This one's thicker."

He lined up another one, giving me an encouraging nod. "This time, keep your eyes open."

And I did it again, cutting it right down the middle.

"She's good," Henri remarked, lumbering toward us with a smile.

"She lifts a lot," Paz said, giving me a nod. "Adele said, and this is a quote, that I should get off my coddled ass and get back in the gym because my girlfriend is a badass."

"Sounds about right," Henri said, planting his hands on his hips and giving me an approving look.

I was already lining up the next piece of wood, addicted to the power and accomplishment coursing through my veins.

After the third piece, I chopped about a dozen more, carefully stacking up the split wood in what was already an impressive pile.

When I was finished, I was sweating and proud and had definitely created new calluses. But I was pretty psyched.

Because I couldn't resist, I took a selfie of myself with my maul and texted it to Liv. She replied instantly.

> Ur a country bitch now. Next stop: tractor pulls and cow tipping.

"You did great," Alice said, carrying a couple of blankets and a bottle of wine. "Henri made me chop wood when I moved here. He caught me lusting after him and made me do it myself."

"That's kind of hot," Hazel said, accepting a blanket.

"Yeah. At the time, I was annoyed. Took me a while to realize it was foreplay." She wiggled her eyebrows and held a thick blanket out to me.

Laughing, I accepted her offering. Though I'd worked up a sweat, the October air was quickly cooling my damp skin.

Alice nodded to a set of large log benches nearby, then led us that way and settled near the end of one. "Hazel doesn't drink, but can I offer you a glass of red?" She held up a bottle that had been resting against the log and a small stack of plastic cups.

"Um... sure."

"Trust me, it will be a while. And this way we can get to know you."

I accepted the wine, and we chatted while the guys talked about axes or whatever counts for conversation in the lumberjack world.

Alice told stories about her kids and her school and her upcoming wedding. Her happiness was so all-consuming it poured out of her like a fountain. "Things were so hard when I first got here." She shook her head. "I was constantly embarrassing myself in front of Henri and the town, but over time, things clicked. And now, a year later, I've got two kids, and I'm about to get married."

Hazel held up her water bottle. "I propose a toast. To Alice, who never gave up on herself, or on love."

We tapped our cups, and Alice wiped away a tear.

"That was so lovely." She put her arm around Hazel's tiny shoulders and gave her a squeeze.

The women were so comfortable with each other, and from this interaction alone, it was clear they were close. Alice was glamorous and curvy, even wearing a down jacket and work boots. And Hazel was petite, with the most gorgeous green eyes and sharp cheekbones.

I felt like a frumpy shrew in comparison. Minimally employed, faking a relationship with a man who could barely tolerate me, and rocking an unwashed ponytail to boot. Not my finest moment. It made me miss Liv fiercely.

But my sadness was interrupted by a very welcome sight. Each of the Gagnon men was holding a massive axe and lining up stumps to chop wood.

I tilted my head. Was I seeing this correctly?

"They do this a lot," Hazel said. "Remy has to train, and his brothers like to push him to work harder."

"This is training?" I asked as the guys stretched and trash-talked one another.

"It's also an unofficial dick measuring competition," Alice said. "Henri does it to keep up with his brothers, but also because I really—and I mean really—enjoy watching."

"It's a Gagnon thing." This from Hazel. "I can't fully understand. Adele sometimes joins too."

I couldn't look away.

Henri, the oldest and tallest, had a thick beard and an air of responsibility.

Remy was thinner, with the build of a pro athlete, all muscle and sinew and mischievous eyes.

And then there was Paz. The thickest and broadest of the brothers. With that neatly trimmed beard and impeccably styled hair, he was an unlikely lumberjack, but lined up next to his brothers like this, it all made sense.

He wasn't just a slick suit or a smooth-talking man whore. He was part of this place and this tradition. He could fight it all he wanted, but he sure as hell looked the part right now.

I sipped my wine, excited about the wood chopping show to begin. But then my mind was completely blown.

One by one, they peeled off their shirts. Fleeces, T-shirts, flannels, all of it. Until they were lined up, shirtless and glaring at one another.

I gasped involuntarily, sloshing my wine and outing myself as the world's biggest perv.

Alice giggled. "We should have warned you. But the look on your face is priceless."

"They each have a stack of logs," Hazel explained, "and the last person to finish chopping has to buy dinner at the Moose."

"It's really a battle for second place," Alice said. "Remy usually wins, because he does this professionally, but once in a while he's tired from a workout earlier in the day and Henri can eke out a win."

I couldn't stop staring. This was the last thing I imagined when he mentioned training with Remy.

"Pick your jaw up off the ground," Hazel said dryly. "Paz might get ideas."

"Right," I uttered, my face already burning.

I'd wanted to see them in action and understand the dynamics of this family. But this far exceeded my expectations.

Those broad, muscular shoulders swinging a giant axe. Or

maul, whatever the fuck it was. With all kinds of power and speed. His thick thighs contracting in his jeans. And my God, the ass on that man. He was definitely the bubble butt of the family, and I was not upset about it. I would have bet my life savings he could balance a tray of margaritas on that ass. Goddamn, he was hot. And strong.

He didn't have the shredded abs that Remy did, but his chest? It was a man's chest. Thick and broad and covered with a dusting of dark hair. Shit, was I into chest hair now?

"Look at Parker," Alice said, nudging Hazel. "She can't believe this is actually happening."

Absentmindedly, because I was too transfixed on the display of raw masculinity in front of us, I accepted more wine from her as the three of us perched on the log bench.

"They do realize they're being ridiculous, right?"

"Oh, sweetie." Alice patted my knee. "It's easier if they get it all out. Plus, we get a free show."

I nodded, taking a gulp of wine. "I figured he'd give me a boring lecture on proper axe maintenance. Not this."

"He probably planned to. But then he had to show off for you. It's the Gagnon way. Be grateful Adele isn't here. She'd be showing them up, and they get all cranky about it. Her trash talk is next level."

I pulled the blanket tighter around me. "It's freezing out."

"They don't care. They gotta beat their chests like alpha gorillas."

I sat there, slack-jawed, as Paz chopped log after log, teasing his brothers between swings. Sweat glistened across his chest, and I could not look away from his shoulders.

The slick suit. The perfectly coiffed hair. The sporty car.

It was all a show.

Because underneath all that material shit, this was who he was.

Raw and masculine and competitive, and holy shit, I had to cross my legs to keep the ache in my core from making me dry hump this tree stump.

What was this sorcery? I was a red-blooded woman. I had needs. But this? This show deactivated my ability to think. Right now, I was nothing but a combination of lizard brain and horny cavewoman.

I looked to my left and my right, and sure enough, Hazel and Alice were drooling over their respective men. It was sweet, if not a little annoying. Because they were definitely getting laid tonight. And I was certainly not.

So I'd have to memorize every move. Because being in the proximity of three sexy lumberjacks chopping wood shirtless in the freezing cold while grunting and sweating was like witnessing Halley's Comet. It required next-level cosmic alignment and a heavy dose of good luck.

I was entranced. By the determination in his eyes and the set of his jaw. And by the contraction of his muscles—even the tiny ones along his ribcage. I'd never wished for a photographic memory before, but right now, I'd give anything to ensure that no inch of hotness could be missed. With any luck, I'd be recounting this story for my drunk old lady friends in the nursing home someday.

And as I sat there, getting tipsy and turned on by my fake boyfriend, I kicked myself for leaving my vibrator back in Portland. Because I wasn't sure my fingers could cut it after this.

Later that night, I lay in bed, my mind racing with all the work I'd been doing. And then there was the persistent ache in my lady parts after my evening with the lumberjack review.

So I called Liv. I missed her terribly. I hadn't been up here that long, but she was such an important day-to-day presence in my life.

She picked up on the second ring. "I miss your face," she said in lieu of a greeting. "You solve the murder yet? I want you to come home."

"Not yet. Slowly chipping away and gathering info. It's not quick or glamorous, as you know."

"Oh, I know. That's why everything is fast-paced and sexy in my books. Readers would hate the reality of investigative work."

"Truth."

"You sound down. What's bothering you? Do I need to come up there and hurt someone?"

I laughed. I couldn't ask for a more supportive friend. "Is it possible to die of horniness?" I asked.

This was not a rhetorical question. After my day of arguing with Paz and then being subjected to a *Magic Mike*–style wood chopping performance, my lady parts were on high alert.

"Probably. But I haven't researched it. Ooh, maybe for my next book."

"Okay, then find something nice to wear to my funeral. Because I can't take it anymore."

"Don't be so dramatic. Besides, I write about murder all day. I own plenty of black."

"No, no." She clearly was not understanding the direness of my situation. "You've gotta slay at my funeral, okay? If I'm dead, then you better be getting laid all the time to celebrate my memory."

"Are you on drugs right now? You want me to pick up dudes at your funeral?" She was laughing so hard she could barely get the words out.

"Yes!" I yelled, also giggling uncontrollably. "More than one, if possible. Go full why choose to manage your grief."

"You've lost your mind. I told you to pack toys. Do you need a vibrator care package?"

"Yes, please. Extra batteries."

"Got it. Now go to bed, you hilarious weirdo."

"Love you too."

Chapter 16
Parker

Another day, another million leads to follow. That morning, Adele was giving me a lesson on brakes. Thankfully, she was extremely patient—despite how emotional this was for her—because engineering and machinery were not in my wheelhouse.

"Why didn't the safety inspector find brake tampering?"

"Because he's a fucking moron," she said under her breath. "Normally, to disrupt a brake system, the brake lines would be cut. That's the most surefire way, and it's relatively easy to do. That way, the brakes simply don't work because the hydraulics will not apply pressure to the brake pads to make the wheels stop turning."

"And this?" I asked, pointing to the diagram she had drawn for me.

"Is different," she explained. "If your brakes aren't functioning, the truck will tell the driver. We have systems in place to prevent this."

She picked up a metal object that was roughly the size and shape of a water bottle. "In this case, the slack adjusters were tampered with. This mechanism automatically adjusts slack on each brake. They get calibrated and checked by a computer system. By law, we do not touch them. But this one"—she held it up and pointed to faint scratches near one end—"someone used a wrench to adjust this. See these scratches?"

I nodded. I could see the evidence of tampering, though I still didn't understand how it had all come together. "So the brakes still work?"

"Yes. The brakes still work, and the driver would not get an alert. But the other slack adjusters are applying evenly when the brakes are engaged. And this one is not. Which creates instability. Over time, it becomes more out of sync, making the likelihood of a roll, skid, or flip higher."

"And if road conditions are bad?" I asked. I was finally making sense of things and connecting the dots. The mountain roads in winter were treacherous, and with unpaved sections and tight turns, even minor instability could be fatal. So the person who did this clearly knew a lot about brake systems and had access to do it without detection.

"Exactly. The brake system did not register an issue, and when the inspectors went over the vehicle, the system was intact, the drums were fine, and the fluid levels were appropriate."

I sat back, chewing on my pen cap. Someone accessed Gagnon trucks not once, but twice, to tamper with the slack adjusters in order to increase the likelihood of an accident.

"I know what you're thinking," Adele said, "but I know my team. You've already interviewed most of them."

"But what about someone who's not a mechanic?"

"I don't allow anyone I don't personally train near my trucks."

"But at camp?"

"Rules at camp have always been strict. And people generally don't hang around storage bays, especially in winter, but it's possible."

"There's no security or cameras or anything like that up there?"

"At a north woods logging camp? Definitely not. We're lucky to have plumbing."

I took a handful of photos of the slack adjuster, making sure to get it from every angle, and measurements, then typed up notes regarding today's discussion while Adele worked. I liked her. In another life, we'd be friends. She was a hell of a gym buddy, and I enjoyed her wry sense of humor.

Sometimes, I thought I might actually miss this place when I was gone.

"Adele." Remy appeared in the doorway, startling us. He was out of breath, and his normally friendly face looked strained. "Get upstairs. The feds are here. There's been an arrest."

I perked up, and my investigative radar whirred to life as I looked between them, not sure whether I should follow. What kind of arrest? As far as I knew, the trail had gone cold after this summer. The organization had gone underground, or it had at least stayed off the police's radar.

He looked over at me. "Paz thought you should probably stay here." He looked a little sheepish as he said it. "Our lawyers are on their way, and we don't want any of our employees to suspect that you're more than his girlfriend."

I nodded, though I was frustrated. If I wasn't privy to the information, how could I help them?

"You can take my office," Adele said, already striding toward the door, her long legs easily keeping up with her brother's.

I paced around for a while, making small talk with some of the mechanics working on the other side of the open area. This place was spotless. Every single tool was hung with precision. Soft music played over speakers mounted in the corners, and a handful of mechanics worked quietly and efficiently.

She was clearly an excellent boss.

Since I was stuck here for the time being, I figured I might as well learn more about the trucks and tools. While I was asking some of the mechanics what amounted to very basic and probably annoying questions, Paz came through the doors. His eyes were red-rimmed, and his shoulders were slumped in exhaustion, but he was as handsome as ever in an expensive dress shirt with the sleeves rolled up.

I jogged over to him and dragged him into Adele's office. "What happened?"

"Drug arrest. Not a major player, but he had enough product on him to entice the feds. They're upstairs finishing up with Henri."

"Any new details?"

He shook his head. "Not that they're sharing. They're heading over to interview Hazel, see if she recognizes him."

I nodded. Hazel had encountered a team of drug traffickers in the woods last summer. She had narrowly escaped, but in typical Hazel fashion, she'd taken photos and had gotten a good look at several of them.

"I need to head home," he breathed. "It's been a hell of a day."

He had probably been expecting so much more from the news. One lousy arrest wasn't going to solve this murder.

"Let me grab my laptop, and I'll meet you in the parking lot."

The sun was starting to set, and it was damn freezing. I had my head ducked and my shoulders pulled up to my ears, and I was cursing myself for not breaking out my winter coat, when a hand wrapped around my bicep.

"What are you doing here?"

I pulled my arm away and spun while taking several steps back so I could put distance between myself and my potential attacker. It took me half a second to recognize him. Fuck. It was Bryce. He looked even more smarmy and entitled than I remembered.

"I was trying to catch a ride home with my boyfriend before you grabbed me."

"Boyfriend? Home? You live in Portland. In that sad, weird house with your weirdo friends. You should not be sniffing around up here, Parker."

I glared at him. He was so pompous.

"I don't want you fucking around. We've been working this drug trafficking operation for months."

"Really?" I said, sarcasm dripping from the word. "Clearly, you haven't accomplished much." I twirled my hair and narrowed my eyes. I wasn't going to let him push me off my case.

"You don't know what you're getting into."

"I'm not getting into anything. I'm just visiting my boyfriend."

Movement in my periphery caught my attention. It was Paz, and he was striding toward us with a look of annoyance on his face.

He didn't stop until he was in my space and pulling me close. When our bodies were pressed together from clavicle to knee, he dropped a chaste kiss on my lips. I stiffened, completely surprised by the gesture, but immediately relaxed, because although it had been a shock, I was desperate for it to happen again.

"Agent Portnoy," he said, his voice deep and serious. "Everything okay here?"

"Only trying to figure out why my ex-girlfriend is sniffing around my case."

Paz pulled me tighter. "Parker? That's... interesting." He gave Bryce a slow once-over, feigning ambivalence, though tension radiated from every inch of him.

Agent Bryce Portnoy wore his hair cropped military short. He had a thin mustache and the sneer of someone who was really, really insecure about his manhood.

"I was just telling Parker to stay the fuck away from my case." Bryce stepped closer, pointing a finger in my face.

Paz dropped my arm and stepped in front of me. Bryce didn't stand a chance. Paz had several inches and probably fifty pounds on him. And his red ears and clenched fists indicated that he was ready for a fight.

"Do not speak to my girlfriend that way. And keep your hands to yourself. Fed or not, I won't tell you again. Stay away from my girl."

Bryce took a step back and sneered. This was always his play. He used intimidation to get past those who stood in his way. With a chuckle, he scratched his chin. "Ooh. Your hick boyfriend is the possessive type." The asshole feigned an exaggerated shiver.

I reached for my back pocket, wondering how long my sentence would be if I tased him. Could be worth it.

Paz pulled his shoulders back and straightened the cuffs of his expensive dress shirt. Sometime between his visit to Adele's office and now, he'd rolled his sleeves down. Probably to endure the cold.

"We prefer hillbilly, actually."

Bryce rolled his eyes and kept his focus trained on me. "Stay away from this investigation. You're in over your head."

"I have no idea what you're talking about," I spat.

"I know you. You're up to some shit. Maybe you've fooled the inbred bumpkins up here, but you and I both know you're a disgraced former cop looking for a big score to make up for the fact that you were shit at your job."

Paz growled. He fucking growled.

I had to intervene. Otherwise, he was likely to commit a felony. There were still feds in the building, and we had come too far to let an asshole like this distract us from solving this case.

So I got in Bryce's face. "Back away. You're on private property. Unless you have a warrant." I raised a brow, but I didn't wait for a response. "Didn't think so. You are a guest of Gagnon Lumber, and I'd hate for the employees here to file harassment complaints against you and your team. So. Get. The. Fuck. Out."

For a moment, Bryce didn't budge. He scrutinized me, his eyes filled with pure hatred, then he pulled his phone from his pocket and held it up to his ear.

"Jenkins," he barked. "Round everyone up. We're leaving."

Without another word, he stomped away. Halfway across the lot, he turned back, wearing a douchy smile.

"I'll have to tell your dad I saw you. Sure he'll be interested in seeing how low you've sunk. We still have coffee every month. In case you were wondering, you're still a complete disappointment." Then he was heading toward his SUV again, leaving me standing in the cold.

Paz pulled me into his car, started the engine, and cranked up the seat warmers.

"Parker, you're shaking. Are you okay?"

I nodded and took the coat he offered. "I hate him," I said softly, my eyes filling with tears as I wrapped myself in expensive wool. "Is there a bear around here that can maul him?"

"Probably, but they generally don't take requests."

Shivering, I buried my face in his coat and breathed in deep, letting the comforting smell of Paz envelop me.

"Thanks for the save out there."

He stroked my hair, his touch so gentle it sent tingles racing down my spine. "My pleasure."

Peering up at him, I said, "He's a federal agent."

"And an asshole. I don't care. You deserve to be treated with respect."

I let out a laugh. "Really? Is that how you've been treating me? Is yelling at me about Post-it notes and stray bras respect?"

He ran his hands through his hair and sank back against the driver's seat. "This whole arrangement has been difficult. I'm sorry I've been a dick. I've got a lot on my mind, and where I was used to going home and relaxing in silence, I've now got you gallivanting around my house in various stages of undress while singing and making snacks at ungodly hours."

And there it was. Vulnerability and honesty. This situation was hard on us all.

Wringing my hands, I tucked my chin and murmured, "I'm sorry. Between running into Bryce and that note, I'm just a bit shaken up. But I promise my head is in the game."

He straightened up. "What note?"

Oh fuck. I hated when my mouth was several steps ahead of my brain. "Nothing," I murmured.

"Parker," he said, his tone angry. "What note?"

I took a deep breath, trying to figure out how best to defuse this situation. "Someone left a note on my windshield. Telling me to back off and calling me a pig."

"When?"

"Four days ago," I replied, shrinking into the passenger seat.

"Four fucking days? Someone threatened you, and you waited four days to tell me?" His face was red, and he was gripping the steering wheel so tightly I thought he might snap it off.

"This is my job," I said firmly. "I deal with shit like this all the time. And yes, I'm terrified that my cover is blown, but in the meantime, I'm going to keep working my ass off to solve this case."

I cannot believe I let it slip. I was clearly losing my touch. Because while PI work was rarely glamorous, it was filled with shady people who generally did not like it when a person was poking around in their business. I'd received far worse threats before.

"We should tell someone."

I laughed. "Who? My asshole ex who belittled me in front of you? Or the local police, who have done nothing about the rampant criminal activity occurring in this town for years and may even be actively involved in it?"

He put his head down until it touched the top of the steering wheel. "You're right."

"I'm sorry you're stuck with me. I've been covering my tracks carefully."

He closed his eyes and pinched the bridge of his nose. "Don't apologize. I'm glad you're here, and I'm glad you're on our team."

"Thanks. I promised you I'd help get justice for your father. And I like being here. You're a pain in my ass, but I like you." I pressed my lips together and turned to him. "You're much smarter than you look."

"Wow, thanks."

I shrugged. "You come off like this total superficial jerk. And that's what you want people to think, isn't it? But you're so much more. You are thoughtful and kind and empathetic."

"Unlike Agent Asshole," he quipped, pinning me with a sharp glare. If I didn't know better, I'd say he was jealous. "That guy sucks."

He wasn't wrong. Bryce was a one-man red flag factory. Every day revealed another layer of his shitty personality. He drove too fast. Like his Ford hatchback was a Lamborghini. His mother would stop by and do his laundry and drop off new containers of protein powder. And in hindsight, it was obvious that since I wasn't a fed, he'd thought he was "dating down." The bastard had broken up with me when my career tanked. Didn't want the stain on his perfect record.

I shouldn't have dated him in the first place, never mind put up with his shit for two years. But it was inertia. He was around, and my father approved. I didn't have to put in any effort. With him or with myself.

That was the crux of it. Doing the work was hard. Thinking and processing and analyzing. Trying to grow and shit. I hated it. When I was with Bryce, I wasn't alone. I didn't have to do the whole midthirties figuring out my life drama. I went to work and came home and saw him when I felt like it.

But now I was committed to growth and evolution. And pushing myself to develop and exceed my own expectations rather than my father's.

"How is that man still in possession of his testicles?" Paz asked, buckling his seat belt. "The Parker I know would have ripped his off for daring to speak to her that way."

"I don't want to do this." I shook my head. "Get into all our baggage and shit."

"Why not? You're well acquainted with mine. Seems only fair I get a peek of yours." He shifted the car into reverse and backed out of his parking space.

I sighed. He was right. He deserved some context for what he had just witnessed. Except I wasn't in the habit of talking about my exes, and the last thing I wanted to do was relive my totally dysfunctional two-year relationship with Bryce.

"You don't know the half of it."

"Let's pick up a pizza, then you can tell me about it," he said, his eyes full of sincerity and his normally stern features soft.

I nodded. Pizza sounded good. Sexy snuggles sounded better, but I'd take what I could get. "He picked my dad over me."

"I guarantee you give better blow jobs."

I paused. "Pascal Gagnon, did you just make a blow job joke?" I punched him in the arm.

He gave me a wink. "I think I did."

I rubbed my hands together. "See? My bad influence is totally rubbing off on you!"

He reached over as he drove out of the parking lot and gave my thigh a possessive squeeze. "You're welcome to rub off on me anytime."

Chapter 17
Pascal

"This is your first stakeout. There are a few rules."

Parker was zipping up a large black backpack and wearing an annoyed scowl. "It will be long and boring. Minutes will feel like hours. You have absolutely no control, and your only job is to observe. For a type-A control freak like you, it will be torture."

"Wow, how fun."

"Stay home, Gagnon."

She wasn't getting away that easily. Not only did I have an all-consuming need to make sure she was safe, but I was curious. Her digging had uncovered so many interesting tidbits, and I wanted to be a part of it.

"Nope. Coming with you. I'm curious. When will I ever have another opportunity to participate in a stakeout?"

She let out a deep sigh. "Fine. But don't make noise and do not draw attention to yourself. We leave in five minutes."

"Okay, I'll go get changed."

I ran upstairs, stripping off my dress shirt as I went. Once

I'd deposited it in the hamper, I went to my closet in search of stakeout clothes, feeling oddly excited and nervous. Maybe it was the desire for information and justice, or maybe it was the thrill of spending time in an enclosed space with Parker that was making my pulse race. Either way, I was in this now.

Downstairs, she had her long hair tied back in its usual ponytail, and she was zipping up her coat.

"Why are you dressed like a cat burglar?" she asked, stifling a laugh.

I looked down at my black sweats, hoodie, and sneakers. "I wanted to look inconspicuous." My gut sank. *I was an idiot.*

"You're one ski mask away from knocking over a liquor store. Get in the car."

It was late, and there were few cars on the road as we headed toward Mountain Meadows.

"To keep this stakeout from being totally miserable, we need to set some goals." Parker looked over at me. "We need to know, up front, what we're seeking to achieve so it's not a waste of four to six hours."

Shit. I hadn't signed up to be here all night. "That long?"

She shrugged. "It takes what it takes."

"Our primary goal," she continued, "is to get eyes on Mitch Hebert and figure out what he's doing. There is no way Pattes Holdings is legit. And I want to see what's going on there."

"Remind me again why you're so obsessed with his random corporate filings?"

I had learned the hard way never to question Parker's methods or process, but I was getting restless. She'd dug into all our employees, inspected the trucks, interviewed the safety inspectors, and reviewed the reports. Hell, Adele had spent the better part of a week teaching her about brake systems. And now we were spending valuable time staking out a trailer park.

"I have eliminated so many potential suspects. And, I've spent days running financials on everyone connected to see if there's any possible connection. Chief Souza, while old and a bit lazy, has no link to any of this. He's got no investments, no expensive real estate. I even checked in the Cayman Islands for potential accounts. He's not dirty. He's not on the take."

That was no surprise. The chief was devoted to this town, and while it was comforting to know he wasn't dirty, it also opened up a lot more questions.

"Your father knew something. His notes and papers sent Hazel directly to the drug and weapons stash house. And all the work I've done to date indicates that there is way more to this story."

I held my breath. Every time we talked about this, the sadness flooded my senses, bringing in a fresh wave of grief I put up shields to keep from feeling.

"I've dug up every ounce of dirt I can find on every person in the operation. The Heberts have a lot of wealth, complicated finances, offshore accounts, and a lumber business that's been declining every year for the past decade. There is more here. And I think it begins with a bogus dog walking business."

"I still don't understand. Dog walking? Of all the fake businesses?"

"It's an on-demand service. There would be a wide range of clients. Record keeping would likely be shoddy, and many people pay in cash. The IRS is not coming to Lovewell to count how many dogs someone walks a day, so it's really an ideal way to launder shady drug money."

"You think Hebert is a drug dealer?" It wasn't hard to believe the asshole could be up to shady shit. Tax fraud? I'm sure. And probably loads of other illegal shit. But a large-scale multinational drug trafficking ring? He was a terrible person, but he was also dumb as a box of rocks. But if it was true, this was big. Huge, really. And made the ache in my stomach even worse. Not only was my family still in danger, but Parker was too. Sure, she'd brushed off that note, but I knew better. She was on to something, and people were scared.

She shrugged. "The dog walking business raised a major red flag. I want to see if he comes to the trailer and what he's up to."

"You think we'll see him tonight?"

"Hope so. I hung out here a couple of days ago. Wanted to get a feel for the place. The trailer was empty and dark. Looks like it's cared for, though. There are a few potted plants out front that are healthy, and the yard is well maintained. I bumped into this sweet old lady. Mrs. Revelle. She's in her eighties and maybe doesn't have the best memory, but she told me no one lives there."

"I think I know her. She's a friend of Bernice's."

"She invited me in for tea and told me how the place has gone downhill. She said every other Wednesday a bunch of men come by, but they don't stay long."

"And it's Mitch."

"She didn't know their names and couldn't really identify them. But she mentioned two white SUVs parked out front."

"Ah. That stupid fucking G-Wagon."

"Bingo. Paul has one too. So I scoped out a few potential vantage points and figured we'd try our luck."

"But what if it's too late? Did she say what time?"

"She said they always arrived during *Chicago Fire*. Not during *Chicago Med*. Said it annoyed her because the engines were loud, and it's her favorite show."

"I don't know what that means."

"It means the poor woman just wants to watch sexy firefighters in peace. But it also means they arrive after nine p.m."

She drove past the entrance to Mountain Meadows and looped around toward the forest. In silence, we continued down the dark, deserted road for another minute or so. Then she slowed and pulled onto the shoulder.

"There," she said, pointing over the dash.

I had to hand it to her. Less than one hundred feet away was the mint green trailer. At this angle, we could see the front area and the small porch that led up to the door.

The country road we were on was desolate and had no streetlights. As long as we were quiet, we'd remain undetectable here.

She reached across me and popped the glove compartment. "What the hell?" she said, leaning over and squinting, giving me a quick peek down her T-shirt. Damn. Naturally, this was the one time she was actually wearing a bra. "What is this stuff?"

"This," I said, holding up a small red pouch, "is a first aid kit. There's also a flashlight and a seat belt cutter."

"Did you clean this out? I want my lip balm."

"I organized it for you and added some safety gear."

She glared at me. "Why?"

"Because you're unprepared for emergencies. This isn't Portland, where you can call AAA and wait thirty minutes to be rescued. You're up in the woods. You need the basics. I also added a collapsible shovel, an emergency blanket, and a box of protein bars to your trunk."

I hadn't thought twice about it. I'd stocked my mom's car with the essentials. My siblings too. For Christmas this year, they were getting top-of-the-line traction tracks for their cars.

That would keep them from getting stuck in snow or mud. Thinking things through, being careful, it was in my DNA. Second nature. I just did it.

And here she was getting worked up over it.

She pinched the bridge of her nose and huffed. "What even is this thing?" she asked, holding up an orange and black tool.

"That's a seat belt cutter. If you're trapped, it will slice through the seat belt." I turned the tool around so she could see the metal point. "This will break a car window."

"All that, and it's the size of a credit card." She turned it around in her hand and studied it.

"A thank-you would be polite."

"I should thank you for breaking into my car, cleaning it, and filling it with random safety gear?"

"Yes. You're welcome. No fake girlfriend of mine will be driving around without emergency gear."

She narrowed her eyes and rummaged through the glove compartment until she located her lip balm. "You really are one of a kind."

"Thanks."

She peered back at me. "It wasn't a compliment."

She applied lip balm, smoothing it all over her full lips. Even in the dim light, it was unbearably sexy. Damn. What would her lips feel like on mine? The thought floated through my mind for what had to be the hundredth time that day. It was an all-consuming obsession lately.

Squeezing my eyes shut, I gave my head a quick shake to clear it. "So now we sit and wait for those fuckers in their tacky ass G-Wagons to show up?"

She pulled a camera from her backpack. "Yup."

"Such an asshole car," I mumbled to myself.

"Says the man who drives a Beamer."

I shot her a glare. "My car is a sensible midsize SUV with good safety ratings. It's not a two hundred-thousand-dollar monstrosity."

She polished the camera's lens with a small cloth and raised an eyebrow at me.

Throwing my hands up, I huffed. "What would you rather I drive? An oversized pickup that gets terrible gas mileage? Is that what Agent Asshole drove?"

She chuckled. "Hell no. He drove a hatchback. How many FBI agents have you met? They're the most practical, boring fuckers on the planet."

She didn't look up as she attached the long-range lens to the camera. "He'd only fuck me in missionary too. Trust me, the blandness is all-consuming with the G-men."

Those words sent my mind straight to the gutter. I would fuck her in every position as often as I could. Parker's body inspired all my filthiest fantasies.

What a fucking chump. How could a guy have such a mouthy, sexy woman on his hands and not give her exactly what she needed?

My pulse quickened as images of her laid out on my bed played like a slideshow in my mind. Suddenly, I was excited about this stakeout. Particularly if it could give me more insight into Parker. Because I was a complete fool who was slowly sliding into obsession with this complicated woman.

"How do you like to be fucked?" I asked in a low voice, shifting in my seat as my pants got tighter.

She didn't move. As if she hadn't heard me. Her gaze was locked on the trailer ahead. After a moment, though, she spoke. "I've never been shy about sex. I've always been the one to initiate it. The men I've dated have always been content to sit back and let me take charge. And that's fine." She shrugged, still facing forward. "But once in a while, it would be nice to be ravaged. Be with someone who wants it as much as I do. Someone I don't have to drag away from TV or work. A man who doesn't see it as an item to check off his list of things to do."

I swallowed, watching her profile. Her lips were down-turned, and her eyes were sad. And I thought, for the first time since I'd met her, that she'd exposed a hint of lingering insecurity.

"I guess I want the kind of need I've read about. Where two people are so into one another they ache to touch. Like they would die if they couldn't have that other person." She turned and looked at me, and I swore the temperature in the car shot up ten degrees. "I know, I know. It's silly and unrealistic..."

"I disagree." I licked my lips, considering my next words so I wouldn't come across as a complete pervert. "It's rare, sure. But not impossible. Sexual chemistry is a real thing. You must have dated the world's worst men, because I cannot imagine a situation where work would be more interesting than fucking you senseless."

Her head snapped in my direction. "I shouldn't have said anything. Isn't this sexual harassment? I'm your employee, after all."

"Technically, you're an independent contractor. Also, I think we're sexually harassing each other at this point."

"Fair enough." She regarded me, holding my gaze for a beat too long. But before she could share all her dirtiest sexual fantasies—because surely that was what came next, right?—the rumbling of an engine pulled our attention to the scene in front of us.

"Slump low," she said, sliding down into her seat.

We were both hunkered down when two identical white Mercedes parked in front of the trailer. Mrs. Revelle was on point. It was 9:38. One would think these idiots would be more discreet, but from here, it was obvious they weren't trying to hide their presence. No, they parked right out front.

Mitch Hebert climbed out of the first SUV. His face was shrouded in darkness, but I'd know that posture and that gait anywhere. He strode toward the porch steps like a man who would do anything to get what he wanted and still woke up thinking the world owed him.

They went inside, and the trailer was immediately lit up.

Beside me, Parker was totally focused, her massive camera lens aimed right at them.

Damn, she was beautiful. The way she bit her lip, the confidence with which she handled every situation. It was hard not to admire her. Maybe she drove me crazy with her chaotic personality and her aversion to bras, but she was damn good at what she did. She followed every lead and tugged on every thread, and she was slowly putting together a full spectrum of information. As frustrating as our lack of leads were, deep down, I knew something big was coming. As long as I could keep my dick in my pants so she could get her work done.

My thoughts were cut off by the deafening roar of motorcycles as three bikes pulled down the street. The two in front were massive Harleys, and the third was a smaller, sportier bike. They came to a stop where they were partially hidden from view by the SUVs. After a moment, the men headed for the trailer, coming into view again.

Next to me, the faint click of the camera shutter sounded over and over.

"They sure as shit aren't walking dogs. Recognize anyone?" she asked, handing me binoculars.

It took me a second to focus them. "No. The faces are in shadow, and I don't know many bikers."

The man leading the way had a long gray beard and a beer belly, while the others looked younger. One had sunglasses on despite it being late at night.

"I'm getting out," she murmured. "I'll be quick, but keep an eye out. If you see anyone come out, whistle."

"Wait." I put a hand on her knee. "You said no getting out of the car."

"I can't see the license plates on the motorcycles from here."

Before I could protest, she slipped out and closed the door softly. She stayed crouched as she moved silently around the hood, slowly heading toward the fence that separated the yard area from the road.

She wasn't far, maybe one hundred feet from me, positioning her camera, when I heard a crunching noise.

My heart rate skyrocketed at the sound. Shit. These guys were probably dangerous, and there was no logical explanation for her to be creeping around with a camera. Fuck.

I was reaching for the door handle, ready to race to her and shield her from whomever was approaching, when I caught sight of a large bull moose ambling out of the woods.

She had chosen this spot because of its vantage point, but the thick pine forest also provided cover to make us less visible. What I hadn't considered when we'd pulled up was the wildlife.

Still gripping the handle, I froze. He would probably walk right by, and with any luck, he would loop back into the woods. Plus, I knew better than to disturb a moose this large.

I lowered the window and let off a soft whistle, as not to draw the moose's attention. Parker, on the other hand, turned around sharply and let out a scream. Shit. It was headed her way.

My mind spinning, I clambered over the center console and into the driver's seat and flipped on the headlights, hoping the blast of light would be enough to scare it away.

That gave me a better view of the creature. And the long scar across its hip. Fucking Clive.

Beyond Clive, Parker was pressed against the chain-link fence, shaking.

"Don't run," I shouted, beeping the horn in hopes that the noise would scare him off since the lights hadn't even fazed him.

Clive yanked his massive head up, condensation flying out of his nostrils. I probably knew less than I should about moose, having grown up in Northern Maine, but he looked mad. I couldn't risk him hitting Parker.

Ramming him with the car would likely do more damage to it and me than it would to him. And running toward Parker, and subsequently, Clive, could put us both in danger.

"Hey," I said, shouting out the window, "stay right there."

I reversed, cutting the wheel hard and hitting the gas so I could whip around Clive and get to where Parker was crouching by the fence before he did. As I pulled up next to her, I hollered, "Jump in," all the while hitting the horn, still trying to scare him away.

Parker dove into the back seat just as a door creaked open nearby.

The lights on the porch illuminated, and several men, one holding a handgun, filed out and scanned the area.

"Drive," Parker shouted, sprawled out along the back seat. She yanked the door shut as I accelerated, dodging Clive by inches and speeding down the road.

I couldn't hear anything over the pounding of my heart, but one peek in the rearview mirror revealed the big grin stretched across Parker's face. The damn woman was laughing.

She climbed into the passenger seat, gasping for breath.

"That was fucking close," she said, tears streaming down her face.

"It's not fucking funny. Jesus, one of the bikers had a gun."

"I swear, Gagnon, this should have been a boring-ass stakeout, but I'm learning that nothing is boring when you're involved."

"Was that a compliment?"

"Yes." She huffed a laugh. "But I know you'll take it as an insult."

I didn't, actually, and as I drove us back into the heart of town, I found I couldn't hold back my own laughter. What the shit had happened? Had Clive the asshole moose blown our cover on a stakeout? Was this my life now?

"You got McDonald's up here?" Parker asked. "After that getaway, I need fries."

"There's a Wendy's two towns over."

She nodded. "Good enough for me."

In the parking lot of the Heartsborough Wendy's, we inhaled fast food, and slowly, my adrenaline wore off.

"Did you at least get photos of the license plates?" I asked.

"Only one of them. But it's a start. I did overhear part of a conversation about a package, and I could hear a whirring sound. Could have been a money counter."

I nodded, digging into my frosty.

"Pretty ace driving, by the way. I gotta say, I didn't expect those kinds of skills."

"Thanks. A few years ago, I was in Germany for a conference and some of my colleagues and I rented these sick cars and drove the Autobahn. Got to take a Ferrari through some mountain passes in the Alps. It was really nuts."

She narrowed her eyes and shook a fry in my face. "Shit. I was feeling so attracted to you after our high-speed moose adventure. But then you went and ruined it by telling that douchebag rich guy story."

Chapter 18
Parker

Cracking open one eyelid, I found Paz looming over me, draping a fluffy blanket over my body. Looked like I'd dozed off on the couch. Working nonstop was finally catching up to me.

"Thanks," I said softly. "But I need to get up."

"You sure?" He was wearing one of those flannel shirts I liked so much. This one was shades of gray and black. I wanted to reach out and touch it. Feel the softness of it against his skin.

He lifted my legs and dropped to the cushion, then positioned my lower half so it draped over his lap.

"Long day?"

I yawned and propped myself up so I could fix my ponytail, feeling self-conscious. "The longest."

He watched me with curiosity, like maybe he wanted to hear about it, so I launched into a story about the clients I'd had to deal with. Today's were the demanding type, and that conversation led me down a rabbit hole to stories about the absurd ones, the unrealistic ones, and, worst of all, the ones who refused to pay my invoices.

His hands ghosted along my calves, setting every cell in my body on fire. Doing my best not to moan, I dropped my head back and closed my eyes. It had been so long since I'd been touched. Not that I'd admit it out loud. But after my ill-advised fling with Tex, I had been setting quite the personal record for dry streaks.

And it had been fine. Until it wasn't. Because moments like these, moments where I was teased with intimacy, with connection, were the worst. They reminded me of just how much I was missing. And they made my brain and my body ache for things I couldn't have.

When I opened my eyes again, he was watching me, giving me a positively flirty smile. After weeks of cohabitating with Paz the grouch, I had almost forgotten what Paz the flirt even looked like. Beard, round dark eyes, long lashes, and those fucking dimples. My panties stood no chance.

Neither did my face, which flushed with pleasure as I bit down hard on my lower lip.

"It seems," he said, effortlessly picking me up and shifting me onto his lap, "that you could use some stress relief."

His fingers made their way up my shoulder blades, pulling a gasp from me. Those strong, capable hands were the stuff of all my filthiest fantasies.

Almost lost in visions of what those hands could accomplish, I was startled by a nudge at my stomach. Straightening, I tucked my chin and came face to face with an impressive bulge straining at his gray sweats. And it was dangerously close to the place I wanted it most.

"That's what you do to me, Parker," he said, gently nipping at my neck. "I'm hard for you all fucking day."

Feeling bold and desperate for more, I ground up against

him, getting a preview of just what kind of equipment he was packing.

"Fuck." I moaned. Damn. Merely brushing against him sent me dangerously close to the edge. What was happening? I wasn't that type of girl. It had always taken a lot of foreplay to get there. A quick dry hump would never suffice.

"Again," he growled, his hands traveling up my T-shirt to palm my bare breasts.

I obeyed. And as I rocked against him, it hit me. A surge of energy and pleasure, making me gasp and groan and—

Bam. My shoulder connected with a hard surface, and my neck snapped back. I threw my arms out, searching for him, but all I found was the cold hardwood floor.

"Parker," he shouted, though his voice sounded muffled through my haze of confusion. "Are you okay?"

Before I knew what was happening, those strong arms were lifting me up and steadying me on my feet.

"Did you hit your head?" His arms were on my shoulders and his brow was furrowed in concern.

"What happened?"

"You rolled off the couch in your sleep. You sure you're okay?"

I shook my head, trying to dislodge the cobwebs. Beside me, my laptop and phone were still spread out on the couch, and there was what looked like a drool spot on one of the throw pillows.

"Yes," I said, taking a step back from him. My shoulder throbbed, and so did my ass. I'd probably have bruises tomorrow. But I was also... turned on.

And I needed space from real-life Paz, who, while broody and sexy just like dream Paz, had not been pleasuring me. No, he'd been watching me drool and fall off his couch.

Not my finest moment. And certainly not my sexiest.

Retreating to my office seemed like the safest bet. A quiet space free from Paz and his brooding. It was late, but my nap and injurious wake-up had left me energized. I'd been pacing for a while, studying the whiteboard I'd been adding to every day, when music wafted up the stairs, calling out to me. Officially, I headed down to the main level to refill my water bottle. Unofficially, I was being nosy and procrastinating.

Halfway down the stairs, I realized Paz didn't have the radio on. No, music from the piano filled the house. It bounced around the empty rooms, making it feel like it was coming through the walls.

I rounded the corner and halted. The grand piano was open, wide and beautiful in all its dark, lacquered glory. His eyes were closed as his fingers flew over the keys. There were several pages of sheet music spread out in front of him, but he was playing from memory. Every few minutes, he'd pause, find his place, and resume.

I leaned against the doorway, in awe of what I was experiencing. He sat, shirtless in sweats, playing the most beautiful music. I watched, mesmerized by the flex of his shoulder muscles while he played.

But the most incredible thing of all? He didn't only play with his fingers. He played with his entire body. He moved rhythmically, and his body swayed as he hit note after dramatic note. The music was coursing through his veins, lighting him up inside.

This was the most alive I had ever seen him.

I was so distracted by him I didn't even hear the music. It

was classical and melancholy, but it was beautiful. I stood, frozen, as the sensations washed over me. The empty room filled with this massive, exquisite instrument, a powerful man, and the most beautiful but sad song I had ever heard.

Like this, focused and passionate and engaged, he was beautiful and vulnerable and real. His love of music had been apparent since I arrived in Lovewell, but this? This type of talent? It thawed some of the frost in my heart. This man was accomplished and gifted and dedicated. He would have had to spend hours upon hours devoted to learning to get where he was now.

Maybe we were more alike than I had been willing to accept. He'd worn armor made of cold detachment for as long as I'd known him.

But this earnestness? This conviction? The desire to dive into the deep end and care about things? That was the kind of stuff that made me tick.

I'd spent the majority of my life being called a try hard. As a child and into my teen years, I'd been made fun of for doing extra credit in school, volunteering for every club and event I could find, and for being "too sensitive" when I was devastated by the soccer loss or the bad grade.

By now, I knew it was because I'd never felt good enough for my father's approval. If I got an A, his response was "why didn't you get an A+?" When the training wheels came off my bike, rather than excitement, he criticized how long it had taken me to get there.

The constant comparisons and the put-downs, combined with little affection or praise, had done a number on me. My therapist and my friends had been counterprogramming me since. It made my brain a really wild place to be these days. I was a work in progress, but that was okay with me.

And now, well into my thirties, I was trying to own it. That wasn't always easy, but it was one of the reasons I'd wanted to be a police officer. Not only because it was my family's legacy, but because I was expected to give 100 percent all the time.

I'd believed that in law enforcement, integrity and fairness were essential. But it didn't take me long to learn that, like in every other aspect of my life, I was too much for it. I cared too much. Fought tooth and nail for justice. I wasn't built to play the political game like my father. Every case was personal, and I'd never figured out how to cultivate the cool detachment necessary to move up in that world.

So while I outwardly blamed the case that must not be named, along with my grouchy roommate, for the demise of my police career, I was beginning to understand that it had never been the right path for me. I needed a job where I could dive in, care as much as I wanted, and do all the things, all the time. And working for myself, as frustrating as it could be sometimes, gave me that.

I closed my eyes as I focused on the notes, feeling the emotion he was emanating. I was so wrapped up I didn't notice that the music had stopped.

"Enjoying the show?" he asked, spinning around on the bench to face me.

There was absolutely no way I could play it cool after that existential experience. Especially was I was now staring straight at his thick, muscled chest. "Yes," I said softly. "That song is so beautiful."

"Puccini." He put his fingers on the keys again and ran through scales. "'Sono Andati' from *La Bohème*."

"Sounds vaguely familiar."

"It's a famous Italian opera. This young woman is on her deathbed, dying of tuberculosis."

"Wow, that's light and fun," I quipped, trying to break the tension and failing.

He shrugged, tapping out a soft melody as I drifted closer. "She's reliving all her happy memories with the man she's fallen in love with. It's happy and joyful and sad and sorrowful, all at once."

I stepped even closer, pulled toward him by an invisible force. In juxtaposition with his usually stiff posture, for once, his shoulders were relaxed. Or maybe that was a sign of resignation, because he wore a soft frown, and sadness swirled in his irises.

"All in one song?"

He nodded. "All in one song. That's why I love opera. It distills human emotion into its most potent form. Every note is meaningful. Every single measure creates feelings and tells a story."

"I've never been to the opera."

He ran his hands through his hair. It was wild and misshapen, so unlike the perfectly styled hair I was used to seeing. He had clearly been doing it for a while tonight. "Not everyone can appreciate the opera. But everyone should experience it once. I'll take you."

An annoying flutter in my chest forced me to move even closer. "Did I miss the opera house when I drove through town?"

"We'd need to go to New York. Once in a while, touring productions come to Boston. But there's nothing like the Met." His tone was soft, wistful, so unlike him.

"You're really talented."

"Come sit. I play modern stuff too." He scooted over, making room for me on the bench.

I sat next to him, my leg pressed to his, and studied the

gorgeous ivory keys. I could feel the heat radiating off his body and tried very hard to focus my eyes on the keys.

"Where did you get this piano?"

"It was my great-grandmother's. During the Depression, her dad bought it from a neighbor who needed money so he could feed his family. She played until her death and then passed it along to my grandfather, who gave it to my father. My mom made us all take lessons as kids, but I was the only one who stuck with it for more than a year or so.

"When I got my first place, I took it with me. After a while, I paid a piano specialist in Boston a small fortune to restore it to its original glory."

I inspected the gleaming surface, still processing his words. His house was still so empty. Obviously, he hadn't brought much with him from Portland. Except this.

He played again, mostly from memory. Some things I recognized, like an Elton John song and "Moonlight Sonata." Beside me, his body moved with the beat, and each note vibrated through me.

"What do you feel like?" He nudged me gently. "What's your favorite song?"

"I like everything. But when I was little, my mom would sing 'Dreamland' to me. By Mary Chapin Carpenter. It was her lullaby."

He shook his head. "Don't know that one. But what about this?" He played the melody to "Blackbird" by the Beatles.

"I love this song."

Naturally, he played it well, and he was warm and strong beside me, as entranced by the music as I was.

When he got to the chorus, he looked over at me, holding my gaze. His eyes were soft and his mouth was parted.

I tilted my head, assenting to something I didn't understand. Slowly, he angled closer, abandoning the keys and cupping my cheek.

"Fuck it." He gasped as his lips found mine in a soft yet firm kiss. It was so much more gentle than I imagined it would be from such a harsh man.

Our tongues tangled in a slow and languid dance as he looped his arms around me and pulled me closer.

I gasped as he deepened the kiss, opening my mouth and giving in to the way my body turned molten. My brain turned to mush, and the only thing that existed was the sensation of him kissing me. My hands found his bare chest, exploring every inch of him

He drew back, his eyes cloudy with lust, and watched me. I held his gaze, afraid to speak, unsure of anything except how badly I needed to kiss him again.

But before I could dive back in, he pulled his arms back and stood abruptly.

"Shit," he said, almost tripping over the piano bench. "Fuck."

Stepping backward, he put more and more distance between us. "Sorry."

"Um." My head was spinning. Was this happening? Did I want it to happen? *That* was a stupid question. My body was vibrating with the power of that kiss. Anything else would probably kill me outright, but it'd be worth it.

I touched my swollen lips. "Was that…?"

He shook his head. "I don't know why I did that. I…" He tugged at his hair, a surefire sign that he was freaking out. "That wasn't good. I shouldn't have done it."

Anguish radiated from him. He wore a pained grimace, and his shoulders were once again rigid.

My stomach dropped. Had kissing me been that terrible?

Hot shame flooded my body. *What had I been thinking?* A sexy dream and a piano concert, and I was ready to throw out all my professionalism, all my boundaries, for a guy I wasn't even sure I liked?

I stood and rolled my shoulders back, mustering all my dignity. "You're right. Terrible idea. I'm going to bed." With that, I turned and stalked out of the room without looking back. If I did, I'd probably slap him in the face. How dare he? He was all vulnerable and approachable, and I let my guard slip.

This was my pattern. I loved a fixer upper. Liv would kill me if I told her I'd kissed him. And she should. God, I was an idiot. When would I learn?

I marched up the stairs to my room and kicked the door closed, then threw myself onto the bed. Paz had turned me inside out and upside down, and I wasn't sure what to think.

My brain spun and my stomach churned. Because what if he wasn't a cold asshole who didn't care about anyone but himself? What if he cared too much? What if he was capable of so much love and concern that he couldn't handle the weight of it all and pushed everyone away for his own sanity?

Stop it. I dragged a pillow over my face and screamed into it. *Stop romanticizing your roommate and focus on why you're here in the first place. You have a job to do.*

Chapter 19
Pascal

"Storm coming," I said to my assembled siblings during our weekly management meeting. Richard was on speakerphone from camp, and Michelle, our bookkeeper, was working from home because her baby was sick.

Snowstorms were as beautiful as they were unpredictable. They were one of very few things that truly brought life to a standstill up here. There was nothing like looking out the window at the snowfall. The sheer power of mother nature was so humbling.

Maine winters were long and challenging, but I went into them prepared. And I was always looking to improve my preparations so things were under control.

But my family was another story.

They didn't understand just how bad things could get. Bangor was a decent size, but we were an hour from there, so even in good weather, it took a while for first responders to arrive.

Every single winter, people died on the roads—in accidents

or frozen in their cars. And others when their heat went out in the night.

And all the information I sent them, the suggestions and reminders, usually fell on deaf ears. If anyone understood what this place was capable of, it was Henri, so I wasn't too concerned there. But Remy and my mom were of the "it'll be fine" mindset, which had me living my life in a perpetually cold sweat.

"Yeah, yeah," Remy said. "We know the drill."

He had returned from a timbersports competition in California last weekend, so he was boasting a tan and feeling a little full of himself after placing third. If things continued to go well for him, I expected he wouldn't be working for Gagnon Lumber for much longer.

I'd miss him, not that I'd ever tell him that. I'd loved seeing my siblings every day. It was what Dad had always wanted for us. The next generation of Gagnon Lumber.

I only wished I could have done this when he was alive.

That it hadn't taken his death to get me back here.

But the sentimentality could wait. A storm was coming. It was early, still October, but that didn't matter to Mother Nature, especially up here. I had been tracking it since it gathered steam over the Great Lakes.

Our position between the mountains always meant snowy winters, but it wasn't even Halloween yet. And that was all the more reason to keep on top of things. My mind was already spinning with tasks that would have to be accomplished before the flurries started. I'd top off my gas tank on the way home from work. The house was stocked with food, but I'd charge up all the electronics, check my generator, and restock the firewood.

"Are you sure?" I asked, cocking a brow. Of the four of us,

Remy was the least detail oriented. The "everything will be fine" attitude had grown old about the time he graduated from high school.

"Can I be excused from the annual Pascal Gagnon 'winter is coming' lecture?" Adele asked, arms crossed over her chest. "I've got dozens of parts to move inside and storage to secure."

"Yes." Since birth, Adele had made it clear that she could take care of herself, and I pitied anyone who told her otherwise.

"You seem especially wound up about a little snow," she said, narrowing her eyes. "What's really bothering you?"

I looked up from my laptop and shot her a glare. "Trying to make sure we're all prepared, individually and as a company. Can't risk losing machinery or productivity."

She smirked. Dammit. She wasn't buying what I was selling. She knew me better than anyone.

Yes, I was fixated on the impending storm. But maybe, just maybe, I was also doing everything I could to avoid thinking about Parker and the kiss and what the hell had happened between us the night before.

Was that so wrong? To put the safety of my family members and employees first?

Because I was not thinking about Parker. And I was not thinking about that kiss. And I was not thinking about what I'd done in the shower after.

Those thoughts were too dangerous. And right now, I had actual physical danger to worry about. Icy roads, equipment damage, pipes bursting. A big storm posed many challenges in an industry like ours, so I'd remain focused on what was important.

Because my roommate slash colleague slash fake girlfriend was nothing but trouble. She dug deep and constantly pushed my buttons, and she was driving me absolutely crazy in the process. But then there were times we had dinner or worked side by side on our computers or sat in front of the fire, and I found myself struck by how funny and smart and pretty she was. And that was far more dangerous. I loved living alone, and I needed my solitude. The last thing on earth I needed was to get attached to her.

Which was why that kiss had been a mistake. Regardless of how good it felt, how right it felt, it was still wrong.

And now there was a storm coming. So once I wrapped things up here, I'd be stuck at home with her for God knew how long.

And I wasn't sure my sanity would survive.

"You can come over to my house and ride out the storm," I said, turning down Main Street.

My mother laughed. "Don't be ridiculous. I'm not leaving. It's just a snowstorm. The first of many this year."

"But they're predicting heavy snowfall and fierce winds. You could lose power, and things could get messy." And this wasn't just a ploy to force her into being an unwitting buffer between Parker and me. My mom was in her sixties, and while she was vibrant and active, she wasn't up for shoveling multiple feet of snow.

"I've lived through more than sixty Maine winters, Pascal. I think I can manage."

I gripped the steering wheel and gritted my teeth in frustration. As usual, Mom was brushing aside my concerns.

"And before you even ask, I've got plenty of food and water and a massive stack of firewood. Not to mention that very expensive whole-house generator you bought me. I probably won't even notice the storm."

"Good." She had fought me, but a generator was necessary up here, and hers was top of the line. I'd even had it hooked up to her natural gas line so she didn't have to worry about fuel. As long as she had food and water, she would be good for a couple of weeks. "Did you fill up your car?"

"I'll gas up after school."

"Do you want me to do it for you? I'm headed out to get gas for my generator."

She sighed in response. Shit. Next would come the lecture.

"I know it's hard, sweetie, but we can't control the weather, or the roads, or anything else. I love you so much for checking on me, but I'll be fine."

"I know I can't control it, but I can make sure you're all prepared."

"Yes, dear. And we are. You've got to respect that we can take care of ourselves, even if our definition of being prepared looks different from yours."

I pinched the bridge of my nose and let out a groan. I'd heard this particular lecture at least a hundred times. *Loosen up. Stop trying to control everything. You can't wrap the world in bubble wrap. Blah, blah.*

"Honey, I'm not sure your obsession with preparedness is healthy."

I snapped. "Healthy? Of course it's healthy. I'm trying to keep everyone alive."

"I know. And I love you so much for it. But what are you trying to avoid in the process, Pascal? What are you pushing away in favor of constant anxiety?"

Leave it to my mom to turn a quick check into a full-on therapy session. She loved therapy, told everyone how amazing it was. She'd recently added meditation to her repertoire and had been raving about it for months. I was thrilled that she had found contentment, but she was constantly on me about growth and mindset and boundaries. It was excruciating.

"I love you, Mom," I said, forcing myself to smile. And I truly did. I couldn't have asked for more loving parents, and I had missed her for all the years I'd been gone. "I gotta pop into the grocery store. I'm going to drop off a junk food care package for Goldie and Tucker."

My house was always well stocked, so I already had the necessities, but if we did end up stuck inside for a few days, I knew Parker wouldn't go for chicken breasts, oatmeal, and frozen veggies for every meal. So I grabbed a couple of frozen pizzas, popcorn, strawberries, which I had recently discovered were her favorite, and a few more cases of bottled water. While my house had a well, the pump was electric, so if we lost power, that would mean no water for a bit. Hooking that up to the generator in the snow wasn't a task I was interested in unless it was absolutely necessary, so I always kept a healthy stock just in case.

By the time I made it home, it had already begun to snow. I carried in the groceries, totally focused on avoiding Parker and mentally reviewing my pre-storm checklist.

After we'd kissed last night, I'd hidden out in my room. Then I'd left early for the gym this morning. I could not risk that happening again.

She was good at her job, and we needed her. I couldn't let my ego or my libido get in the way of finding answers.

But ignoring the way she smiled or chewed on her pens or tapped her foot while she read through endless spreadsheets was getting harder to ignore as the days wore on. She was in my house and in my head, and my damn dick was obsessed with her.

I owed it to Dad and my family to keep my hands off her. This was the one thing I could do for them—give them peace of mind and closure. And in turn, it'd hopefully make everyone's lives safer.

So I went through my list. Plugging in all electronics, including my backup battery bank. Bringing in as much dry firewood as I could to keep the house warm in the event of a power outage. Checking the generator and my backup fuel supply. Checking the barn to make sure the doors were secure. A tiny fizzle of accomplishment rushed through me with every task I checked off. None of them were hard, but each was necessary to ensure we weren't faced with danger or surprises. My family was so absurd. I wasn't avoiding anything. I was only being careful.

Next, I headed to the garage, which was my sanctuary. The barn out back was for machinery, my workbench, and sports equipment, so my garage held only the essentials.

Hooks were mounted along the walls, and a series of racks took up one full side. Everything I needed could be found in here. Tools, shovels, scrapers, oil and gas for the snowblower, and a bin full of manuals for all my outdoor equipment.

I hadn't used my snowblower since last year, and if we were really going to get ten to twelve inches, I had to make sure it would get the job done. So I connected my phone to my portable speaker, clicked on a playlist I liked to listen to while I worked, grabbed my headlamp, and set to replace the spark plugs.

I was in the zone when the air shifted and a shadow moved across the room. Parker stood in the doorway, silhouetted by the light behind her. Her hair was down, which was unusual, and she was wearing her usual leggings and a baggy T-shirt that slipped off one shoulder to reveal her black bra strap. I sent up a thanks to the universe that she was wearing a bra. This entire ordeal would be impossible otherwise.

"Can I help?" she asked, being awkwardly pleasant rather than her usual snarky self.

Shaking my head, I turned down the music. "Nah, I'm almost done. Had to replace the spark plugs and shear pins."

"What's a shear pin?"

I snagged one off the workbench and held it up. "Just a long bolt. If the auger catches on a rock or a chunk of ice or even a frozen newspaper, this pin will snap, forcing the motor to shut off so the entire machine doesn't break."

"So it's a failsafe?"

"Sort of."

She shuffled across the empty garage bay, inspecting all the supplies neatly stored and arranged on the shelves.

"Looks like you're snowstorm ready. I saw all the firewood and groceries and bottled water."

I shrugged and went back to tightening the bolts on the snowblower, consciously avoiding her gaze.

She wandered silently, inspecting every item hanging on the wall like she always did. Like every single detail of my garage fascinated her. It was unnerving.

"I hadn't pegged you as a reclusive mountain man until now. Let me guess: you're preparing for the apocalypse and ready to live off the land after society falls."

"Not exactly."

"You've got enough MREs to last ten years, a high-tech water filtration system, and enough batteries to power a medium-sized city. You're a prepper."

I looked up at her and wished I hadn't. She had that look

on her face. The mischievous, playful one. Like she knew she was pushing my buttons and she loved every second of it. It made me want to throw her over my shoulder and spank her. Fuck.

Shaking my head, I averted my gaze again. "I like to have a plan. To make sure everything is ready. So many terrible things could be avoided if people just thought ahead."

She tapped her chin. "Ah. I get it. You think that if you're prepared enough, you can control the outcome of even the most uncontrollable situations."

"No. I plan ahead. And it's not only about me. My mother lives down the road, alone. And she's elderly."

She let out a sharp laugh. "She'd kneecap you for even saying that word."

"I know. But she's getting older." God. She was right. If my mom had overheard me, I'd never see another loaf of banana bread. "And Henri and Remy are up by the mountains. And the kids."

"What about Adele? Do you stock up her place with food and water?"

"I'm not allowed to annoy her about this stuff."

"Why? I bet there is a story there."

"One time I came over with flashlights and a container of gas, just in case. She said she'd pour it over my Beamer and light a match if I ever insulted her like that again."

Parker threw her head back and guffawed. "Shit. I like her so much. Do you think she'll be my friend? After this is over?"

"Why? You planning on sticking around?" I didn't know why, but the thought made my stomach flip.

"Of course not." She twisted her hands in front of her. She was nervous. She hid it well, but that was one of her tells. "I think it's really nice. How you take care of your family."

Brows raised, I looked up at her, surprised by her sincerity. "Most people think I'm an asshole."

"And I used to be most people. But I've lived with you long enough to know that the asshole exterior is a front. You're deeply protective of the people you love. And I think that scares you. So you end up pushing people away."

For the love of God, she couldn't just give me a compliment. She had to turn it into some kind of indictment of my character. "Please stop psychoanalyzing me."

"I'm not. Think of it as... profiling."

"I'm not a criminal."

"Not a convicted one, at least." She held a hand out and turned in a circle. "But all the tarps, duct tape, and batteries belie that assertion."

Part of me wanted this conversation to end, but the other part relished the idea of sparring with her. So I decided the best thing to do would be to give her a job.

"I need to finish up in here. Can you change the batteries in the flashlights I lined up on the kitchen counter?"

She nodded. "And I'll make dinner. It's the least I can do."

I gave her a firm nod and turned back to the snowblower, but I snuck a quick glance at her ass in those tight leggings as she walked back into the house.

Chapter 20
Parker

The way he stacked wood and got the stove pumping was really hot. It had to be the forearms. Paz's were muscular and thick, with a dusting of dark hair.

He could pretend to be Mr. Businessman all he wanted, but in moments like this, the real him shone through. The broody lumberjack who felt like he didn't belong.

The man stuck somewhere between two worlds, unable to be who he wanted to be in either. I had been trying to play it cool and find my way back to business as usual after our kiss last night.

But I couldn't stop replaying it in my mind. The softness of his touch, the heat of his body, the spark that ignited when our lips touched. And not just that, but the intensity of the moment as I sat beside him while he played the piano with those stupid strong forearms and stupid big hands.

And now, because the universe hated me, I'd likely be trapped here with him for at least twenty-four hours. And while this house was enormous, there was no escaping him.

I was doing everything I could to be on my best behavior.

Hell, I was wearing a bra in the house. But I couldn't stop the desire to be near him, to tease him, to force a reaction from him.

Sitting on the large couch with my feet up on the coffee table, I went through my notes from this weekend. I had finally concluded my initial fact finding and was building connections and flagging issues for follow-up.

Work. That was the best path forward. If I couldn't leave this house, I'd at least be productive.

"I'm working through the org chart," I said, flipping through the files on my laptop. "Can we talk about Richard?"

Standing before the roaring fire, he dusted his hands off and turned to me. "What do you want to know? He's my godfather, and he was my dad's best friend. He's been at Gagnon since he was in high school."

I looked up from my laptop as he padded over. "Haven't been able to meet him yet. Just want to make sure I know everyone who works at camp."

What I wasn't saying was that Richard was a big question mark. He was practically a ghost on the internet. Sixty years old, owned a modest home outside of town, bachelor with no kids. On the surface, he appeared hard working and boring. But that's what made my spidey senses tingle. He was the most senior Gagnon employee who was not a member of the family, and he'd been in the inner circle for decades.

"He's our COO. Couldn't run the business without him. No one is respected more in this business than Richard." His voice was laced with defensiveness. That was the exact reason I'd kept my thoughts to myself. He clearly cared about the man.

But I needed more information to make my own judgment. What I did know was that he was not especially pleasant and that he never socialized with his colleagues. Not that being introverted made a person a criminal. But without a weekly bowling league, golf trips, or even classic car shows to track and verify him, my brain tended to spin out various theories.

"It looks like he was on vacation the day of your dad's accident."

"Yeah. I wasn't working here at the time, but Henri was. I'm pretty sure he was in Florida. His sister lives there. He's always taken care of her and her son, Norman. She had an abusive husband, and Richard stepped up big-time. Helped her get away from him and got her set up on her own. She got sick a few years ago, and he took a couple of months off to take care of her."

That made sense with what I'd found so far. There were a couple of PTO requests from around that time. It looked like he'd taken six or seven weeks total.

Based on the company records, the truck Frank Gagnon was driving had been used for the preceding three days without incident and had been inspected the day before by a mechanic who recorded every detail down to the tire pressure.

"Have you met his nephew?"

He scratched his head. "Norman? Yeah. A couple of times. Think he had some issues. Maybe some petty criminal stuff when he was a kid. Richard straightened him out, got him a job with us. He worked a few seasons, on and off. Wasn't interested in getting certifications for the big machinery, so he never moved up beyond seasonal labor gigs."

I toggled between documents on my computer, adding these additional details to the profile I was building of Richard.

"What happened to him?"

"Not sure. Maybe he moved to Florida too? You can ask Ellen. She probably got his forwarding address so she could send out his final paycheck."

I nodded, letting things spin in my mind. The employment

records I had found had long lists of seasonal laborers for each year. Logging seemed to attract transients and folks who didn't stick around for more than a season. But I'd find Norman and see what I could piece together about him as well.

Because there was no way drug trafficking had become so rampant on those roads without the involvement of someone who worked the forest. Gagnon Lumber kept excellent records. I owed Ellen flowers after she had walked me through the annotation protocols. But despite the attention to detail used when creating them all, quite a bit of information was missing or incomplete.

But I could count on Paz to fill in any blanks he could. He had answered every question and connected me with every potential lead.

The tension between us had finally begun to ease. Eventually, maybe we could get to a place where it felt like that world-altering kiss hadn't happened. Maybe he'd be a helpful roommate who'd happened to hire me to solve his father's murder.

But for now, memories of the kiss still lingered. Especially when he leaned in close to look at my screen, bringing with him a whiff of smoke and pine trees that almost made me need a change of panties. But we could do this. Recover from that incident and move on.

"I overheard some chatter about a place called the Ape Hanger when I was at the gym a couple of weeks ago. Do you know it?"

He had returned to meticulously stacking the wood, which only made it harder to stay focused on work. "It's a shady biker bar off Route 119 near Heartsborough."

My fingers flew over the keyboard, and I found its location in seconds. The Yelp reviews were uniformly terrible, but it was only about twenty minutes from here. "I'll probably head over there next week," I mumbled, typing the address into the spreadsheet I'd created to keep track of businesses and locations.

"No," he said, spinning quickly and almost knocking over the neat stack of wood he'd assembled. "I've heard stories about that place."

His tone was a little too bossy for my liking. What a shock.

"That's great news." I rubbed my hands together. "Means there will be tons of shit for me to dig up there."

He stalked toward me, his eyes sharp. "You're not going. It's not safe."

"Excuse me?" I slammed my laptop shut, itching for a fight. No man, especially a pampered suit like Pascal Gagnon, would lecture me about danger. I shot to my feet, and if I had been wearing earrings, I'd have taken them off. The nerve of this man. "Of course I am. You may recall that I'm a former statie. And I hold not one, but two black belts. And I carry a goddamn sidearm. Sit down, sir."

He prowled even closer, his fists clenching at his sides. "If you go there, I'm going with you."

"So you can blow my cover and offend everyone with your uptight presence? No, thank you. I don't think your Brooks Brothers shirts would blend well there."

Did he honestly think he could tell me what to do?

"It's a shithole filled with grizzled old bikers and criminals."

I threw my arms up. "My kind of people! What does one wear to meet criminals and bikers?" I asked, the words dripping with sarcasm.

His jaw was locked so tight I feared he'd need it surgically opened again. "You can't waltz into dangerous situations with your half-baked theories, stacks of paper, and random Post-its."

Glowering, I contemplated dropping him right on his

round, muscular ass. Instead, I took a breath. "Since you are my client, I'm going to say this nicely. But only once. Get the fuck out of my way. This is my investigation. I'm the one with the training and the experience. I'm the one pounding the pavement for you and your family."

He didn't respond. Instead, he studied me, his eyes narrowed and his face flushed.

"So you can take your judgment and derision and shove them straight up your ass. If there's room, of course, with the large stick you keep wedged up there." I tilted my head and tapped my chin. "Actually, you're a lumberjack. Must be a fucking pine tree. Explains why you're such a dick."

His eyes flashed pure rage, but I swore there was a hint of desire swirling there too. Without a word, he grasped me by the shoulders and kissed me. This time, it was rough and fierce. The opposite of our tender moment by the piano. This was pure anger and lust and desperation.

I pushed him away, confused and more than a little turned on.

"What the fuck, Paz?"

He smirked, still holding my shoulders. "You pissed me off. I had to shut you up somehow."

"You can't just grab a woman and kiss her like that."

He did it again, harder this time, taking my mouth forcefully. So I did what came most naturally.

Gripping his shoulders, I swept his right leg out from under him and dropped him right on his fine ass. Then I pinned him to the floor.

His eyes were wide, and his mouth dropped open in surprise. Despite the violence, I could feel him hardening against his leg while I straddled him on the floor.

We stared at one another for a long moment, and I could feel my pulse quicken.

He broke the silence first. "Sorry. I thought after last night" —he cleared his throat—"I don't know. That you maybe wanted to." He regarded me, his eyes dark and heated.

I bit my lip. I didn't know how to respond. Part of me wanted to lash out in righteous indignation, but another part really enjoyed the thrill of being manhandled by him and equally enjoyed doing the manhandling myself. I didn't want him to get the wrong idea, because the attraction I felt was purely physical. But I couldn't let him think he had taken liberties with an unwilling woman.

"Yeah. Last night was unexpected but nice." I was trying to play it cool, but my face didn't get the memo. A hot flush crept up my neck and into my cheeks, but I refused to break eye contact.

"You kissed me back."

"I did. And if I wasn't so angry at you for criticizing my investigation and barking orders, I probably would have kissed you back a minute ago too."

He rubbed his chin and... was that a smirk? "You're terrible at following instructions."

I straightened my spine and tilted my chin up. "No one tells me what to do."

"Hmm. Bratty. Makes me want to punish you." He quirked a brow.

My legs shook in response. Was he saying what I thought he was saying? Because sirens immediately went off in my head.

I climbed off him, standing up and brushing off my leggings. I needed space between us. "We would never work."

He followed, standing up slowly and never breaking eye contact. "Why not?"

My brain was on overdrive, trying to push down all the feelings that were bubbling up inside me. "Because you drive me insane." I shouted.

He smirked. "You drive me crazy too." He ran a hand through his unruly hair. "I wanted to kiss you last night. I've been thinking about it for so long, and you were there. I was playing, and I couldn't keep a lid on all the things I was feeling."

Huh. That took the wind out of my angry sails really quickly. This was too messy and confusing. I needed clarity. "Who told you to keep a lid on them?" I asked. "Given that we're fake dating and living together, I think we're past that. Just be fucking honest with me."

He looked me dead in the eyes. "Honest? Sure thing. Parker, I'm wildly attracted to you. I spend every minute of every fucking day thinking about you and how badly I want you."

I took a step back. Shit, I needed distance. I'd asked for honesty, and I'd been hit with a heap of it. My heart pounded against my ribs and blood rushed in my ears. What was he saying? That the kiss hadn't been a mistake? That there was more here?

Of course there was. Our chemistry was off the freaking charts, but I wasn't ready to dive into the messy abyss that was our current situation. Clear boundaries were healthy, and he was my employer. But that ship had sailed when I'd moved into his house and started leaving my bras on the doorknobs.

I had to defuse what felt like a massive bomb about to go off.

"It's normal to feel some attraction."

"Some attraction." He threw his hands in the air. "It's a lot more than some. I crave you, Parker. Your touch. Those sassy little looks you give me. I want to possess that smart mouth and make you scream my name."

I gasped. Shit. I wanted that too. I wanted to see what happened when Pascal Gagnon let loose. When he wasn't constrained by expectations and responsibilities. My nipples hardened, and I squeezed my thighs together. Because this man, his presence, his intensity, and his pent-up frustration were the biggest fucking turn-on. No man had ever lit me up inside the way he did, and we hadn't done more than kiss.

He wrapped one arm around me. "I can't keep going on like this. Tell me what you want."

Taking a deep breath in through my nose, I willed my racing heart to slow. But it was a fool's errand. It was too much. All my good judgment flew out the window when I looked into his dark eyes and said, "I want you."

A slow smile spread across his face as he pulled me toward him. He kissed my earlobe and worked his way down the column of my neck. "Good. Because we're going to be stuck in this house for at least twenty-four hours. We may as well find a way to kill the time."

Chapter 21
Pascal

Across the firelit room, her chest rose and fell with her heaving breaths. She wanted me just as much as I wanted her.

It was the small details, how she licked her lips and squeezed her thighs together. How she kept looking away, then taking quick glances back as I prowled closer to her.

Pure fire coursed through my veins. The entire world ceased to exist when I looked at her. Even in a sweatshirt and leggings, she was the sexiest woman I'd ever seen.

And the allure was so much more than physical. It was her attitude. The way she carried herself. It wasn't bluster or bravado with Parker. She was real. Full of honest-to-goodness confidence. A belief in herself that I found equally confounding and intoxicating.

She didn't care about what anyone else thought. No, she pushed through life using her own abilities and convictions.

With her eyes locked on me, she leaned in closer, lighting up every nerve ending in my body. She pushed that dark hair behind her ears, narrowing her dark eyes, daring me to close the space between us.

She seemed to spend a lot of energy trying to hide her soft and feminine parts behind her bluster and edge, but I saw right through her.

Plump lips, long lashes, round hips. The small details that hit me square in the gut.

And the freckles. Lord, the freckles.

"Are you gonna sit there, Gagnon?" she asked, cocking a hip. "Or are you going to come over here like a good boy and make me scream your name?"

I threw my head back and laughed. Parker had no idea how much time I had spent thinking about her. About all the plans I had for her.

"I want you to crawl over here and finally put that mouth of yours to good use."

Her taunting unleashed a primal urge. In a second, I had my hands on her, and I was flipping her onto her back on the couch. I caged her in with my arms. Then, after a deep breath to slow the feral animal that had taken control of my senses, I gently lowered my lips to her ear. "It sounds like you don't believe me."

She shuddered at my words, and I gently thrust against her, letting her feel how serious I was. "Because I meant what I said. Tonight, you're mine. And I take care of what's mine."

I skimmed my lips across her jaw until I found her mouth, then I devoured her. Tongue and teeth and lips taking control while I explored her body with my hands.

She tugged on my hair as I poured weeks of frustration and longing into this kiss. Below me, she moaned and writhed, making me even harder.

I slid one hand under her sweatshirt and stroked the skin of her stomach. She was so warm and soft and perfect.

"Of course you're not wearing a bra," I growled as I crept higher.

She giggled. "You know I hate bras." And then she bit my bottom lip hard. "But I hate panties more."

Fuck, she was going to kill me. My heart felt like it was going to burst in my chest, and my poor dick would probably be imprinted with a zipper pattern for the next decade.

"That's it," I said, pulling back. "Clothes off."

I tugged at the waistband of her leggings, and she lifted her hips, making it easy for me to confirm that she was, in fact, not wearing panties.

I stroked along her hip bones, watching her shudder.

"Shirt too," I ordered.

Without argument about my commanding tone, she sat up and pulled it off, revealing the tits that had haunted me for weeks. Round and full, with pink nipples that were begging for my teeth.

"You are so fucking gorgeous," I gritted, delirious with lust for the woman spread out before me.

She reached for my belt, but I pushed back.

"No. The only thing keeping me from fucking you senseless are these pants. And I need some time to explore."

I heaved myself up so I could position her so she was sitting on the couch.

Then, once I had her where I wanted her, I kneeled and looked up at her. She was watching me with lust swirling in her hooded eyes.

I spread her legs wide, admiring her perfect pussy and fighting back the urge to dive right in.

"You're soaked," I said, kissing along her inner thighs, inhaling the scent of her arousal.

She moaned and arched her back as I teased her, biting the soft flesh of her inner thigh but refusing to give her what she needed.

"You want me to eat this sweet pussy, don't you?" I asked, spreading her legs even wider and gently flicking her clit with the tip of my tongue.

"Yes." She gasped.

"Tell me. Tell me what you want me to do. You're the boss, Parker. I'm the lucky guy who gets to make you feel good."

I pulled back again, my hands still firmly on her thighs.

She looked down at me and licked her lips. "I want to ride your face," she commanded. "I want to come all over your face before you fuck me."

My heart seized in my chest. This woman was a literal dream. How on earth was I going to avoid coming in my pants when she talked to me like that? "Yes. Ride my tongue."

Throwing her thighs over my shoulders, I dove in.

She arched back on the couch, gripping my hair as I devoured her, letting my tongue explore every inch of her.

She bucked against my face, gripping my hair and making me feel more alive than I had in years.

"More," she moaned.

And I obeyed, easing one finger inside her, then another. Fuck, she was already clenching around me. Shit, she was tight. And wet. My dick throbbed as I focused on the task at hand. Worshipping her pussy and driving her over the edge.

She tightened further, screaming and writhing beneath me. "Just like that."

The feel of her clenching around me drove me absolutely wild. This woman was going to kill me, and I would die happily with the taste of her on my tongue.

She writhed and screamed. She was so fucking loud, and I

loved it. We were alone in my house during a blizzard, and there was nothing hotter than her sexy moans and screams.

Completely focused, I kept the pace, enjoying the feel of her climb. And then I felt it. The moment she crested the cliff. Her words became incoherent and her back arched off the couch.

"Yes. Yes. Fuck yes. Good boy."

A bolt of lightning shot through me. Fuck, that felt good. I picked up the pace, determined to give her the best orgasm of her life and truly earn her praise. I doubled down with my fingers, my tongue never letting up on her clit.

And I was rewarded. Because this woman came like a goddamn tsunami. Writhing and screaming and panting for what had to be a solid minute.

I didn't let up. I worked through the aftershocks, feeling quite proud of myself.

When she went limp on the couch, I finally sat back on my knees, admiring my work.

Her head was thrown back, and her legs were spread. Her tits were heaving as she caught her breath.

Fuck. I needed to be inside her. Even if I wasn't sure I'd survive it. The need coursing through my body was scrambling my brain and tunneling my vision.

I stood, stumbling a little before I planted my feet solidly, loving the sight of her sated and quiet. Slowly, she opened her eyes and watched me, biting her lip as I undid my belt.

"It's about time," she said, her eyes bulging as I dropped my pants.

"Think you can handle it?" I asked with a smirk. But the truth was, I wasn't sure *I* could handle *her*. But fuck if I wouldn't die trying.

She sat up on the couch as I loomed over her, scooting

forward to run her fingers down my chest.

"My turn." She licked her lips and pushed the waistband of my boxer briefs down, freeing my aching cock.

"Wow," she whispered, wrapping one hand around it and licking the tip.

My knees almost gave out on contact. The sight of Parker, the sassy, sarcastic pain in my ass, with her lips wrapped around my cock would be tattooed on my brain forever.

This was truly heaven. She looked up at me from under those dark lashes, and a bolt of electricity shocked my heart. The fire in her eyes told me she wanted this as much as I did.

With a hand on each side of her ribcage, I gently pulled her up before she could take me in her mouth. "As much as I love the idea of your smart mouth wrapped around my cock, I've got other plans."

Without a word, she angled closer and gave me one last lick.

"Jesus." I groaned and backed away so I could fish a condom out of my wallet.

"I hope you know how to use that beast," she said.

I rolled the condom on with a smirk, but my mouth dropped open in the next heartbeat.

Because she did the most amazing thing. She turned and kneeled on the couch, then put her hands on the back. That perfect ass faced me, begging for my hands and my cock.

She turned to look at me and raised one eyebrow. "Please?"

How could I deny her? If she wanted a kidney, I'd cut one out with a rusty butter knife right now.

I spread her ass cheeks, admiring how wet she was, then I slowly eased inside her, enjoying her sighs of pleasure. Her pussy was wet, hot perfection, and I had to tip my head back and focus on the ceiling to get control of myself.

"Spread them wide, officer," I said, firmly massaging her ass cheeks. I gave one a gentle smack. "That's for the strawberry daiquiri," I said as she moaned.

"And this," I said, smacking the other cheek harder, "is for making me hard as a fucking pine tree all the time."

She moaned again, and I slid inside her slowly, savoring the feel of her.

She dropped her head forward and moaned loudly. "Fuck, you're thick," she said, already moving against me. "I'm so full."

It would take a miracle for me to last longer than thirty seconds. There was nothing like being inside her, claiming her body, and I had a job to do. I'd make sure this woman never forgot what I could do to her.

Slowly, I thrust, mindful not to hurt her despite every caveman instinct in my brain screaming at me to go wild. As strong as the urge was to rut like an animal, I didn't want this to end.

Curling over her, I palmed a breast, rolling her nipple in my fingers while she moaned even louder.

"You like that?" I asked. "You like being fucked hard, don't you?"

She threw her head back, sending her dark hair cascading over one shoulder. "You call this hard?"

My cock surged. Fuck, she knew how to push my buttons. She was under my skin, and she knew it.

I gripped her hips, slamming into her so hard she had to lock her arms to brace herself against the couch. "This better?"

If not for the filthy sounds of pleasure escaping her, I'd worry about hurting her.

"You want hard? I'll give you hard. You won't be able to sit for a week without thinking about what it feels like to come on my cock."

Now I had to back up those words with action, because tension was already working its way up my legs. But I sucked in a breath and forced down the release creeping up on me. I wouldn't stop until she came again.

I continued to slam into her hard, though I kept my movements steady and controlled. "Rub your clit," I ordered.

At my command, her hand snaked down to where we were joined. Instantly, she tightened around me. I gathered up her hair with one hand, tugging it as she moaned.

Nothing had ever felt this good. This right. This perfect. And I never wanted it to stop.

Her muscles fluttered around me as I strained to hold back, determined to ride out her release and give her everything I possibly could.

But then I felt it, the first wave of her orgasm, and I lost control, pumping with abandon while she moaned and clenched beneath me. Letting loose and crying out until I was totally sated and could barely stand.

I pulled out, disposed of the condom, and collapsed on the couch in record time, unable to form words, never mind walk.

She was sprawled out next to me, naked and sweaty and delicious.

I pulled her into me and cradled her to my chest as we rode the wave of endorphins.

After a few minutes of blissful silence, she peered up at me. "You know, your cock is the least annoying thing about you."

I smiled and closed my eyes as I dropped my head back. "Good. Because as soon as I regain my strength, I'm taking you upstairs. You're gonna ride it, and I'm gonna bite your nipples until you come again."

She snuggled against me and laughed. "I can work with that plan."

Chapter 22
Parker

Pinned beneath a strong, warm arm, my body was sated. I reveled in the way I sank into the mattress, stretching languidly.

I'd been sleeping alone for so long I'd forgotten how good it felt to wake up next to someone.

But as I opened my eyes. The realization hit me hard.

Sucking in a sharp breath, I bolted upright. Except the second my back left the mattress, his arm tightened around me.

"A few more minutes," he grumbled.

In all the time I had spent thinking about Paz, analyzing him and spinning out some fun sexual fantasies, I had never, ever pegged him as a cuddler. But here he was, nuzzling my hair and treating me to the full man bear snuggle experience.

Under normal circumstances, I would be in favor of this. But right now, I was reeling.

We had crossed the line.

The better part of the last eight hours had been spent naked. And damn if Paz hadn't brought his signature intensity into the bedroom.

Not that we'd even made it to the bedroom until the third round. No, he had bent me over the couch first. Then we'd found our way to the floor in front of the fireplace. Finally, he'd carried me up to bed, where he went down on me until he recovered and was ready to do it all again.

No, we hadn't just crossed the line. We'd decimated it. Smashed it to bits, burned what was left, and danced all over the ashes.

He was my client. I was on a job.

Somewhere along the way, the fake part of the relationship had blurred, but it was shimmering back to life now. Because this wasn't supposed to be more than a cover. A means to an end so I could solve a murder.

We weren't supposed to fuck each other senseless and spend the early morning hours cuddling naked.

But the world around us had shifted. My brain was jumbled, my stomach was growling for breakfast, and my lady parts were tingling, begging me to turn this snuggle session into something a little more orgasmic.

Suddenly, I was sweating and panicking. I needed to flee to the safety of my own room.

"Sorry," I said, pushing his arm off me and sitting up. When I realized I was buck naked, I pulled the sheet up quickly. Though I was instantly annoyed with myself for being self-conscious in front of him.

"Don't do that," he said, tugging it back down. "I didn't get my fill of you last night."

Oh, I was in trouble. Because I didn't think I'd ever seen anything as attractive as sleepy Paz. His hair was mussed, and he had a long sleep line across one cheek. Even soft and tender like this, he was still masculine and strong. Like he could cuddle me forever and protect me from all the evil in this world. But I wasn't that woman, and let's face it, he wasn't that man.

"You look panicked. Did I do something wrong?"

"No," I said, my voice way too loud for seven a.m. "I'm trying to figure out where we go from here. I can't believe I was so unprofessional. Please know that I won't let anything distract me from the work I'm doing for your family."

He squinted for a moment, like he was considering my words. "I'm not judging your professionalism right now, Parker. I'm half asleep, and I'm trying to figure out how I can get inside you again." He glanced down at his cock, which was very much awake and making its presence known through the thin sheet.

"This was a mistake," I whispered.

His face fell, but he recovered quickly, donning a mask of indifference I'd become familiar with over the last few weeks.

"Listen." I was ruining this with my crazy, but this was uncharted territory. I had never woken up after having acrobatic, intense sex all night long with a client who disliked me before. "It's not personal."

He laughed. "Of course it's personal."

Shit. "Okay, fine. It is personal. But we can't do this again. Not only because it's grossly unprofessional, but because things are already hard enough. It's not a good idea."

"So what *do* you want?" He rolled over and propped his head on one arm. Damn, the curvature of his bicep could inspire a sonnet, I swear. Paz was strong.

Underneath all those dress shirts was the body of a lumberjack. Not shredded like a bodybuilder, but thick and strong and capable. Muscle meant for real work. And chest hair. Fuck, it looked so sexy on him. Just enough and unbelievably manly.

Shit. I was trying to let him down easily, but I couldn't stop staring at his stupid hot body and face.

"Let's chalk this up to a snowstorm fling and move on with our professional relationship."

"What about our friendship? We are friends, aren't we?" he asked, leaning closer.

"Yes. We are friends. Friends who disagree and fight constantly, but we're in this together."

He scrunched up his face. It was silly and charming and *so* not what I needed at this moment. Where were his rude comments when I needed them? Where was the all-business grump who'd roll out of bed and never speak of this again? Dammit. Why was it that Paz steadfastly refused to ever meet my expectations?

"This was snowstorm boredom," I said slowly, hoping he'd agree. "Never to be repeated."

He jumped up, buck naked and putting that glorious ass on display, and strutted to the window. Pulling the curtain back, he pulled in a deep breath and surveyed the scenery for a moment before climbing back into the warmth of the bed.

"It's still snowing," he said with a wink. A *wink*. This fucker did not know how to stand down. Ninety percent of the time, he scowled at me. And now that I was naked and orgasm drunk and vulnerable, he turned on the charm?

"What are you implying?"

He fell back against his pillow, hands behind his head, making his arms bulge even more. "The snowstorm isn't over, so we don't have to leave this bed *just* yet."

I looked away, searching for the willpower I must have shed with my clothes last night. He was too seductive right now. The damage had already been done. What did a few more hours matter? I looked down at him, feeling the heat of his eyes on me. "Stop staring at me like that," I snapped.

"Like what?" His smile was wide, and his eyes fucking *sparkled* with mischief. I had to be living in an alternate reality.

I sat up straighter, pulling the sheet up over my breasts. "Like you want to eat me for breakf—"

With a hand on either hip, he hauled me against him and pinned me to the mattress.

"I would eat you for every single meal," he whispered as his lips ghosted over my earlobe. "In fact, I think I want some right now."

He pulled the sheet back dramatically, exposing my body. His focus roamed hungrily all over me, making me squirm.

He grasped my thighs with his callused hands, spreading them forcefully, and pierced me with a predatory look. "What's that? You don't want my tongue?"

I bit my lip and stared down at him. At where his lips hovered inches from my clit.

"You are a bastard," I spat.

"Nah," he said, chuckling as he lowered his lips to me. "I'm your good boy."

Chapter 23
Parker

I should have known better. Should have hydrated and stretched. I was working harder and digging deeper than the run-of-the-mill cheating husband or embezzling employee investigation required.

And the living situation wasn't making things easier. I had Mr. Sexy Cranky Lumbersuit all up in my business all the time, and I was walking on eggshells in his precious home, trying to remember not to leave dishes in the sink while also, you know, solving a murder.

Not to mention the big, sexy, orgasmic elephant in the room. We'd had sex. Many times over a thirty-six-hour period. In several locations all over this house, including the massive walk-in shower.

Now, though, we were back to business as usual. Bickering, attempting to stay out of one another's way, and ignoring the awkwardness that came with seeing each other naked. Or attempting to, at least. To Paz's credit, he was making it easy on me. He was back to acting like a surly jackass, effectively erasing the memory of the cuddly, seductive, hilarious body snatcher who'd inhabited his being during the blizzard.

I had been so distracted by the case, by the jaw-dropping, consciousness-altering sex, and the nonstop tension with my stupidly handsome roommate, that I hadn't felt this coming on.

I should have known. I had been constipated and moody. I chalked it up to a combination of irritation with the aforementioned jackass and PMS, not realizing I was in the middle of my cycle, not the end.

By the time it dawned on me, it was too late. It started with a pounding behind my left eye. Then the squiggles appeared. The zigzag pattern I saw in the light. The aura. It was the death knell each and every time. A signal that things were about to get bad.

I stumbled up from my makeshift desk in one of the empty bedrooms, slamming my laptop and shoving it under one arm. Shit. I needed meds, water, and my bed. Because this was not going to be pleasant.

It had been at least a month since my last migraine. And usually, with meds and healthy lifestyle choices, they were manageable.

But I hadn't recognized the signs. And meds could only do so much once the aura hit.

I made it to the bedroom and yanked the curtains closed, then rummaged through my bag for the damn meds. After several passes, I resigned myself to the fact that they weren't where they should be.

Before I could look further, a wave of nausea overtook me. I dropped to the floor and closed my eyes to keep the dizziness at bay.

The pounding behind my eye socket was so intense it felt

like the bones of my skull were throbbing. With a fortifying breath, I hauled myself up, then crawled into bed, feeling every vertebra ache as I lay down. My arms shook as I tried to find a comfortable position, shifting on the mattress as the pain intensified.

Tears stung my eyes as I cursed myself for ignoring the signs. I had experienced my first migraine at nine years old. I knew how to prevent them, or at least minimize their impact. How could I have been so irresponsible?

I cracked one eye open just a little and homed in on my phone on the nightstand. Paz and Henri were expecting me at the office tonight. We planned to review files and work up a list of potential persons of interest. Now that I had done the basics and had learned the ins and outs of the business, it was time to start looking at individuals in the Gagnon Lumber world and create a list of people who could have sabotaged the truck.

It was already three. There was no way I could make it out of this bed, never mind across town in a couple of hours. Migraines like this one could take days to subside. And until my vision cleared up and the pounding dissipated, working and driving would be almost impossible.

I inched toward the nightstand gingerly so I didn't jar my head and neck while I reached for the phone. When I got it, I unlocked it with my thumb print and shot off a quick text to Paz to let him know I couldn't make it.

Then I collapsed into the pillows and breathed through the pain.

Sometime later—it could have been days or hours, I wasn't sure—my bedroom door creaked open, and a shaft of light lit the room dimly.

"Parker, what's going on?"

I kept my eyes shut but turned my head toward him.

The light dimmed as he shuffled over to the bed.

I cracked one eye open when I could feel him hovering over me.

He wore a concerned frown, and he was still wearing his coat. "Are you sick? Your text didn't make sense. Why are you in bed? What can I get you?"

"Migraine," I rasped, pulling a pillow over my face.

"Oh shit. I'm sorry. What can I do?"

I waved him off. There was nothing he could do.

The pain throbbed so forcefully, even my jaw ached. It felt like my back teeth might fall out of my mouth.

"There must be something I can do. What makes it worse?"

"Light," I said, my voice cracking. "And noise."

"Do you need medicine, water?"

"I couldn't find the medicine," I said.

"Okay. I'm going to move you. My room has blackout shades. That way the sunlight won't bother you. And I'll find your medicine."

"No. Can't move."

"I'm going to pick you up and carry you there. Okay? Then I'll get you anything you need. Let me know if this hurts too much."

He slid his thick arms under me and lifted me with ease, then cradled me against his chest with more gentleness than a man his size should be capable of.

I winced and rested my head against his chest as he stood up straight. His heart was beating wildly against my cheek, and warmth radiated from him, seeping through his jacket and calming me instantly.

"Okay," he said softly, "I'm going to carry you down the hall. Ready?"

"Mm-hmm."

With slow, deliberate steps and a warm, firm grip, he carried me down the hallway to the other side of the house. Even in my impaired state, I couldn't help but notice how delicately he held me. How careful he was not to jostle me.

I buried my head against his chest, channeling all my focus into breathing.

The last time I was in his room, we were naked and fucking each other senseless. It had only been a few days since then, but in my current state, it felt like it had been years.

He eased me onto his king-size bed, and I sank into an ocean of pillows and a fluffy duvet.

I peeled one eye open, trying to make sense of my surroundings. "Do you really make your bed every day?"

"Of course. I'm not an animal."

"Figures."

"Are you comfortable? Can I get you clothes?"

"Let me get off these jeans. They're pretty tight." I groaned as I tried to wiggle them over my hips.

"Here," he said. "Let me."

His fingertips grazed my hips as he slid the denim over them. He brushed against the soft skin at my thighs, then continued to gently ease them down my legs. Goose bumps erupted on my exposed skin. Regardless of the excruciating pain I was in, I was fixated on every brush of his fingertips and how good it felt to have his warm, strong body so close to me.

I was having sex flashbacks in the middle of a massive migraine. God. Could orgasms have medicinal properties? Why were we not conducting double-blind placebo-controlled studies on that?

"Do you want a T-shirt?"

I didn't move or respond. Now that my legs were free, all I could do was curl up tighter.

"Here," he said. "It's really soft."

Slowly, I propped myself up on one arm. "Help me?"

"Okay." He guided me to a sitting position and lifted my sweater over my head, leaving me in only a black bra. And then he helped me put on the softest T-shirt I'd ever felt.

With an arm on my shoulder and one behind my back, he eased me back onto the mattress. "I'm going to go find your medicine," he whispered, pulling the fluffy duvet up to my chin. "I'll be right back."

I wasn't sure how long he was gone, but eventually, he returned and softly closed the door behind him.

"Parker," he whispered. "I found this box. It says ergotamine."

"That's it," I said, reaching out. "Pop one out. I dissolve it under my tongue."

He obeyed, and I put it in my mouth, praying for relief.

"I googled migraine treatment. Does a cold compress on your neck help?"

I blinked up at him. His face was marred by a worried frown.

"I'll try it," I said, rolling over onto my stomach. He brushed my hair out of the way and placed the cold cloth on the back of my neck. It stung my skin a bit, but I settled into the softness of the bed and let the cool sensation wash over me.

"I brought water, Gatorade, and crackers. I'll leave them on the nightstand. What else can I get you?"

"Nothing," I said, luxuriating in his pillows. When I got home to Portland, I'd have to invest a portion of the profits from this job in really fancy pillows. I wasn't sure I'd ever recover from my addiction to the luxurious bedding in this house. "Just darkness and silence."

I woke up some time later, still in pain but grateful I had at least been able to sleep, which was rare. As I regained consciousness, I felt his presence nearby.

Through the darkness, I spotted him sitting on the other side of the room, his phone in his hand.

He looked over at me, his face still lined with worry and frustration. This unexpected kindness was jarring but comforting. How tragic that he kept this part of him locked behind several layers of defenses. His feelings were deeper than most, and he was intensely protective of the people he cared about. Did he care about me too? Thinking about it made my heart flutter a tiny bit.

Because having that protective instinct turned on me, if that's what this was, made my chest ache with affection.

I wasn't used to being cared for. Other than Liv, I didn't have a lot of people I could count on.

But this was comforting. To know I wasn't suffering alone.

The room was dark and cool, and he'd loaded me up with plush blankets. Like he'd done his research and discovered the best way to accommodate a person suffering through a migraine.

"I'm here," he said, reaching for a large stainless steel water bottle. "You need to stay hydrated."

I propped myself up and took it from his hand. My throat was dry, and the cool water felt amazing.

"What else can I do?"

"Nothing," I said, sinking back into the pillows once more.

"Okay. I'm going to sleep on the floor. That way I'm here if you need anything."

"Don't sleep on the floor," I protested. "Come up here."

"Okay."

The bed shifted as he settled next to me. Then his body heat radiated from the other side of the bed, and I eased into its comfort. So often, I'd spend days in a dark room alone, trying to get through this.

He said nothing. He sat silently by, but that was more than enough. Just the company of another person when the pain was unbearable. For once, I wasn't on my own. And the realization sent a little bit of my walls crumbling.

When I woke up, I finally felt human again. The sharp, pounding pain had settled into a dull, manageable ache, and I was starving. As I stretched, rolling to my back, I caught sight of Paz propped up against a massive pile of pillows, typing away on his laptop.

"What time is it?" I croaked.

He checked his watch. "Ten thirty."

"A.m.?"

"Yes. It's Wednesday."

"Why aren't you at work?"

The typing stopped, and he examined me, his gaze feeling especially sharp. "Because there was no way I was leaving you. I can work from here." With that, he turned back to his laptop and resumed typing as I rubbed my eyes and processed the last almost twenty-four hours.

"I'm sorry."

"Why?"

"I really put you out. You had to take care of me, give up your bed, and miss work."

"It's no problem. I'd never leave my fake girlfriend to suffer alone." He smirked. With his mussed hair and the plain white T-shirt and sweats he had on, I had never seen him look so casual and relaxed.

"Right. Of course," I croaked. Silly me, imagining there was meaning behind his actions.

"You're not just the PI I hired and my fake girlfriend. As much as I hate to admit it, you're my friend too. I was worried about you."

His dark eyes were soft, and his forehead was furrowed in concern rather than annoyance for once. Shit, that look made my belly do a tiny flip. He was sexy when he was cold and grumpy, but like this? Worried and sweet and helpful? Hot damn. If I wasn't recovering from a vicious migraine and rocking three-days-without-a-shower hair, I'd have a difficult time controlling myself.

"Now," he asked, snapping his laptop shut. "How do we get you back to full strength?"

"Water, caffeine, and lots of food."

He twisted at the waist and snagged a fresh metal water bottle from his nightstand. "Start with this. I'll make breakfast."

I chugged the water, nodding.

"And," he said with a smirk, "if you're willing to relocate, I have a surprise for you."

He tried to carry me, but I insisted on walking. I had a little pride, after all. Even so, he kept one arm protectively around me as we made our way down the hall to my room.

Inside, I scanned the furniture in search of my surprise and grinned when I spotted it.

"You got a TV for me?" I could barely contain my excitement. Because there, on the wall opposite the bed, was a sleek flat-screen TV.

He shrugged and ducked his head like he was embarrassed. "I thought you'd like it."

He looked so bashful and un-Paz-like in that moment. I had to resist the urge to hug him. Normally, that's exactly what I'd do when given a thoughtful gift, but with him, I was afraid of what might happen if I touched him. The last time our bodies had been pressed together, *things* had happened. And I was determined not to let them happen again.

It was imperative that we maintain our boundaries. But with every passing day, it felt less like a dalliance or mistake. Instead, it felt inevitable.

We had been dancing around each other for weeks now. And the mutual dislike was beginning to feel more and more like pretense for something else. Something bigger that I was in no way ready to confront.

So instead of a hug, I clapped my hands and plastered on a smile, doing my best not to wince at the ache in my head as I did so. "I love it. I missed TV. I have so many episodes of *Housewives* to catch up on. Jersey just ended, and Atlanta has already started."

An hour later, we were both full of scrambled eggs, pancakes, and coffee, and I was giving him context for what we were watching.

"This is Teresa," I explained again. "She's an iconic housewife. She once flipped a table at one of her friends because she told her to pay attention. She even went to jail for a bit, but she's back."

He nodded, still sipping his coffee. It was well past noon, and he'd given up on working. Instead, he was reclined on the pillows next to me.

"And the man she's screaming at is her husband?"

"No. That's her brother. She hated him for a while because

he tipped off the feds, and that led to her arrest. But then they made up and opened a restaurant together. But now they hate each other again because he didn't come to her second wedding."

"I'm so confused."

"Shh," I said, patting his arm, secretly enjoying the feel of his bicep beneath my fingers. "It'll ruin the fun if you think about it too hard. Just relax and let your brain cells die."

Chapter 24
Pascal

"Wow. When you said backyard wedding, this was not what I anticipated."

Parker gripped my arm as we walked toward the wedding tent. The church ceremony had been blessedly quick. Now it was time for the reception at Henri's house.

It was chilly, and Parker's cheeks were pink as we trudged along the walkway. She was wearing a down parka over a pretty purple dress. The long sleeves and swishy skirt made her look soft and pretty. Nothing like a gun-toting, ass-kicking PI who investigated murders. I liked this side of her. Actually, I liked all sides of her. And it was beginning to be a problem.

I squeezed her arm. "My brother is madly in love."

Henri had always been a quiet, stoic motherfucker. But then he'd fallen in love with Alice, and shortly after, he'd met Tucker and Goldie, and it was like his frigid heart cracked wide open.

That asshole smiled all the time now. It was terrifying.

And he certainly had spared no expense on his "casual, last-minute" wedding. The tent was the size of a stadium and equipped with state-of-the-art heaters.

A patio area with a fire pit and twinkle lights lay just outside, with Adirondack chairs set up so guests could enjoy the sunset over the mountains.

Alice's family and friends were visiting from Massachusetts and staying in one of Henri's rental properties up the river.

I was truly happy for my big brother. He deserved this. The wife and the kids and the happy family home filled with memories.

When he built this place, I thought it would be his fortress of solitude. Only him and the mountains and the forest.

But the sight of it now? Elaborately decorated, hosting half the county, bursting with laughter and music, with kids running across the lawn? It was obvious this place was meant to be shared.

My empty house seemed even more like a fortress of solitude by comparison.

We stepped into the large tent and were hit with a burst of warm air. "Just goes to show you never know where life is going to take you."

"Fuck if that isn't the truth. I never expected my life would bring me here."

She stiffened and peered up at me, biting that plump bottom lip that made my brain short-circuit. "I'm sorry you're stuck with me."

My stomach dropped. That was not what I meant. If anything, I was thrilled to have her here as my date. Not that I could tell her that, of course, because that would start a whole conversation about the sexy snowstorm, the stakeout, and my general feelings. None of which I wanted to discuss, especially at my brother's wedding reception.

She should feel comfortable and welcome here. I should have been the one making her feel that way. Instead, she felt like I didn't want her here. Shit.

I pulled her a little closer to my side. "If I had to bring a fake date to my brother's wedding, I'm happy it's you. Not only are you gorgeous, but you're far more social than I am." It was an understatement. With Parker on my arm, I stood a little taller and actually smiled as I greeted the various guests. She made me want to be better. Around her, I was constantly upping my game, and it was doing a number on my head.

Because I had never worked hard to impress women. Usually, it was the other way around. Once I'd made money and hung out at hotspots, women were just *around*, approaching me and making things really easy.

Nothing about Parker was easy. And I found myself more intrigued by her every day.

She shrugged. "I'm good at talking to people."

"I noticed."

"Everyone is drunk and celebrating." She rubbed her hands together like a comic book villain. "It's the perfect time to gather intel." She reached into her cleavage, making my eye twitch, and pulled out her phone. "I've been using my Notes app to keep up with bits and pieces."

I was both horrified and deeply impressed. As a workaholic, I admired her dedication and clever electronic storage plans, but part of me wanted her attention tonight.

She took a step away from me, straightening her dress. "I see Ellen and a couple other admins. I'm going to get her to introduce me to Richard."

"I can introduce you."

"I know you can, but working the sweet old lady angle could get me intel I wouldn't get with a Gagnon present."

I gave her a mock salute. "You're the boss."

A slow smile spread across her face. The dark red stain on her lips made her look positively sinful.

Then she turned abruptly and sashayed across the dance floor, her round hips swaying and begging me to chase after her as she closed in on the bar. I wished I could tear my eyes away, play it cool, but it was impossible. Everything inside me was shifting, and she was the cause.

I was admiring the view when a hard shove in my shoulder knocked me forward a step.

"You promised," Adele said, appearing at my side with a glass of wine.

I elbowed her in retaliation. "You look nice," I said, quirking a brow. "Didn't know you owned a dress."

"Very funny, asshole. Joke's on you. I own four dresses. You didn't think I'd show up to the wedding in coveralls, did you?"

I rolled my eyes. Honestly? Yeah, maybe.

"I respect Alice too much for that. Plus, I promised Goldie I'd dress up. Speaking of which"—she craned her neck and scanned the tent—"she told me she wants to dance with you."

I smiled. Goldie wasn't officially my niece yet, but the second I'd met her, I realized blood didn't have a whole lot to do with making up a family. I adored her.

"For some reason, you're her favorite. I'm worried about her taste in men." She shook her head in mock disappointment. "I should talk to Henri about it."

"Stop. It's mutual. I like her much better than I like the rest of you."

We were all anxiously waiting the adoption finalization, even if we didn't say the words out loud for fear of jinxing it. Henri and Alice were their legal guardians indefinitely, but adoption was not a sure thing. They had the best lawyers, who'd dotted every *i* and crossed every *t*, but if anyone knew how easily shit could go sideways, it was the Gagnons.

Once it was official, we could breathe easily.

Across the dance floor, Parker chatted animatedly with Ellen and another woman from the office. The sight of it made my chest tighten, so I did what I did best to distract myself.

"Where's your boyfriend?" I asked. "We were supposed to finally meet him."

Without a word, she yanked the plastic cup out of my hand and chugged the champagne in it.

"I see."

She shrugged.

"Do you want to talk about it?" I knew the answer, but I asked anyway.

She turned toward me, her whole body moving slowly and her face completely blank. "What do you think?" she asked, her voice eerily calm.

"Ah. Good talk," I said, turning back to creeping on Parker. She looked so goddamned beautiful. I didn't want to be the weirdo standing here staring, but I wasn't sure how else to handle the emotions she stirred in me.

I was thinking things and feeling things, and my mind spun with possibilities.

Generally, I was not a fan of weddings. And despite popular belief, it wasn't because I didn't believe in marriage. It was great for some people, like my brothers. But because I found the big, generic party with predetermined rules and antiquated etiquette absurdly boring. These days, I was thankfully past the age where I'd have to attend multiple weddings a year.

But this was unlike any wedding I had ever been to. Figured my brother wouldn't be traditional.

For once, I was enjoying myself at a reception. I was happy for Henri and Alice. And for Tucker and Goldie, who looked positively overjoyed. The way their family had come together and fought for one another was one of the most beautiful things I had ever witnessed.

The devotion my brother showed to his new wife and kids reminded me so much of my dad's.

He was on my mind constantly. Not only because of his death and Parker's investigation, but because the longer I stayed in Lovewell, the harder it was to avoid his legacy and his influence.

My dad loved big. He adored this town and its people. He loved logging. And most of all, he loved my mom.

I would love to say I blamed my commitment issues and general distrust of monogamous relationships on my parents. But they had provided nothing but a rock-solid example of partnership and unconditional love and a home filled with love and constant support.

Near the dessert table, my mom was laughing with friends and sipping champagne from a red plastic cup. Only a couple of years ago, she'd been in such a dark place that there were days she couldn't get out of bed. Days she was debilitated by her grief and could not move forward.

But now she was an administrator at the elementary school and a doting grandmother. She was once again volunteering, throwing parties, and nagging her kids about eating vegetables.

I slapped on a fake smile and worked to look relaxed while the party swirled around me. Guests ate barbecue off paper plates while the band warmed up. The tent was warm, thanks to heaters, and kids ran wild across the grassy hill as the sun began to set.

And I found my mind wandering. This wasn't so bad. The stability and partnership that Henri and Alice had was enviable, though I was loath to admit it. Alice and the kids invigorated my brother. His surly attitude still came out here and there, but he was far from miserable as a husband and father. Could this even be possible for me? For so long, I hadn't thought so, so at the moment, I still couldn't quite conceive of it.

I wasn't a monster. I respected women. But after my one and only serious relationship, things changed. A numbness settled in, and I'd reveled in it.

Going out to bars and clubs had never been my thing, but at some point, I'd found myself tagging along with the guys from work. I typically wasn't one to generalize, but the private equity firm I landed at tended to recruit former jocks and frat boys who lived by the work hard, play hard mentality.

And since I didn't have anything in my life but work, and since the plans I had so meticulously crafted for my future had gone to shit. I started hanging out with them too.

Work till eight or nine, loosen the tie and then head out to restaurants and clubs, where we would be surrounded by women. It wasn't fulfilling, but it was easy.

As a Gagnon, shutting down and ignoring my feelings was really the only coping mechanism I had. That and drinking, of course. Chopping wood too.

But then my brothers went and evolved. Fell in love. Learned to be vulnerable and shit. Then looked to me to do the same.

Didn't they understand? If I stood still, if I thought too much, then it would all fall apart.

All the pain, all the loss, would come crashing down around me.

Better to keep those balls in the air and continue on. Bury the hurt bubbling up inside me. So though that period of my life—working too many hours, casual hookups, avoiding Lovewell—was only meant to be temporary, it had become a defining characteristic. Traits people now associated with me.

Which made this whole Parker situation that much more difficult. Because I was dealing with the judgment that had plagued me since I'd come back to Lovewell as well as the blatant shock, from what seemed like everyone, over the news of my relationship while also trying to show her that I could be more than the shallow guy she had me pegged for if she would give me the chance.

Because although the vision was hazy, I could see it. We had an innate connection, and I desperately wanted to explore it. Not that I was capable of saying that out loud. But every day, it was getting harder to deny my feelings for her.

Before I could compose myself, Parker was approaching with two cups of champagne. Her face was bright and her smile genuine. I stood a little straighter, proud that this dynamic woman was here with me.

"This is quite a wedding," she said, handing me one cup and surveying the crowd.

"Lovewell really turns out for the big events. And Henri runs one of the largest companies in town. Not to mention Alice is the school principal. They do so much for everyone. So I'm not surprised so many people wanted to celebrate them."

She threaded her arm through mine, bringing our bodies flush, and tapped her cup to mine.

"They seem really in love," she said softly, bringing her champagne to her lips.

I stared into my cup, unsure of how to calm my racing heart. Her proximity was doing this to me more and more. Setting my skin on fire and sending my heart soaring.

Sucking in a deep breath, I pushed it all down. "They are. Henri is so much like my dad. The right woman came along, and he was all-in from day one."

She leaned her head against my shoulder. "I have a hard time even conceptualizing that. But I'm happy for them. And for your parents. Mine are divorced."

"Sorry."

"Don't apologize." She shook her head, but she didn't pull it away. "I'm happy about it. As a kid, I used to dream of the day they finally split up. It was an abusive relationship. My mom is doing a lot better now, though I doubt she'll ever fully recover."

My heart sank. How was I supposed to respond to that? She had alluded to her dysfunctional upbringing a couple of times, but this was the first time she had mentioned abuse. It made sense, though. Her fierce independence, the constant physical training, and her desire to help people and do good.

"Jesus. I'm so sorry you had to live through that."

"It's okay. But that's why I don't have very high opinions of love and marriage."

I shrugged. "I'm anti-marriage too, and I don't have a good excuse."

She turned and shot me an annoyed glare. "Oh please. You're a family guy. And you bought that giant farmhouse. You've got to fill it with a doting wife, a few wild kids, and at least one dog. I can see you tripping over Legos on the stairs and building a tree house out back."

I frowned. "Then you should definitely rethink your line of work. I'm not interested in staying in Lovewell, and I'm certainly not interested in living in that house and filling it with kids and dogs."

She elbowed me in the ribs. "More of a cat person?"

"You're ridiculous."

"Yup. Standoffish, grouchy, and makes you earn his affection. Definitely a cat person."

Chapter 25
Parker

Weddings were weird. On the one hand, eternal love, the joining of two families, the booze and the food were all great. On the other hand, they gave me a stomachache every damn time. Like I was missing some components necessary to function correctly in society, but I couldn't for the life of me figure out which ones.

Tonight, the guests were living it up. The bride and groom, as well as their adorable kids, were delirious with happiness too.

The sight of it filled me with joy, but at the same time, my brain was whirring along on overdrive, assessing every guest, planning out who I needed to talk to, and sneaking quick looks at my date.

Paz was handsome. That had never been up for dispute. And he wore a suit so damn well. That I knew for certain. It was his default setting.

But standing up with his brothers while wearing a flannel shirt and suspenders? H.A.W.T. The theme of this wedding was upscale lumberjack, and I was drinking up every detail.

His beard was growing in. He scratched at it endlessly, but it looked damn good. Especially with the few grays sprinkled throughout. He kept it closely trimmed to keep with his biz aesthetic, but deep down? Yeah, Paz had a wild side. I'd seen it. I'd *benefited* from it. And now it was difficult to look at him and see the stuffy suit he pretended to be.

He was layered and complex, and he didn't let many people in. But I had been elbowing my way past his defenses for weeks. I wanted all the information all the time. It was a side effect of the job. But the end result of all my digging was a jumble of frustration and admiration wound together with a healthy dose of lust.

But I was here to work. A fact I had to continually remind myself of.

This was likely the only time the entire Gagnon Lumber team would be in one place. Guys who worked seasonally and guys who lived in other parts of the state were all here to support their boss. And I'd never have another crack at them.

So I casually worked my way through this wedding, utilizing Ellen and a few others I'd befriended over the last few weeks to make introductions. I matched faces to names and read body language while holding innocent conversation. The only thing that would make this night better was access to my laptop so I could update my notes and spreadsheets, but that would be beyond strange at a backyard wedding. So instead, I was filing everything away and discreetly typing notes into my phone.

I approached a group of old-timers who were nursing beers and trading stories by the fire. I had been dancing around Richard Bernard all night. From what I'd gleaned from his interactions, he seemed to keep to himself.

"Richard, right?" I asked, like I didn't know that he was the operations director who had also been Frank Gagnon's best friend and had been employed by Gagnon Lumber longer than any other living employee.

He was a tall, thin man with military-short silver hair and a permanent scowl.

I held out my hand.

"Yes," he said, scrutinizing me behind a pair of round glasses and giving me a wary smile. "That's me."

"I've only been here for a few weeks. I'm still trying to learn names."

Little did he know I was privy to his social security number, his mother's maiden name, and how much he still owed on the blue Tacoma parked down the hill. "I'm Parker. Pascal's girlfriend."

The rest of the men around the fire introduced themselves, and I made small talk, asking dumb questions about their jobs and pretending to be fascinated.

"Cutting down trees for a living must seem boring to someone like you," Richard said, his smile not reaching his eyes. "Word around town is that you're a famous author."

I shrugged. "Hardly famous."

"But still. Murder mysteries? How does a pretty little thing like you come up with this stuff?"

I blinked back the desire to tell him to take his condescension and shove it up his ancient asshole. I tapped my temple. "Got a lot of ideas up here." I flashed him a megawatt smile. "And looks can be deceiving."

He nodded at me, sipping his beer.

The other guys were easy to chat with. Nate, who was a recovering alcoholic with a baby on the way, had been hired by

Frank when no one else would give him a chance. He was loyal and, according to Paz, extremely hardworking. He likely wasn't bright enough to evade the authorities, and he didn't have any debts, shady relatives, or other possible motive. Plus, he'd been living in New Hampshire at the time of the accident.

Al was nearing retirement, and he was a deacon at the church in town. Although religious types usually raised my suspicions, he was clean as a whistle. His wife could get a bit rowdy at bingo, but that was really it. After years in the woods, he'd moved to a desk job at headquarters a few years back.

And that left Richard.

Longtime employee, trusted adviser, godfather to Pascal.

Had no wife, no kids, no life beyond the business.

Owned a modest cottage in town, spent his downtime during the warmer months kayaking, and spent the majority of every winter up at logging camp, where he ran the show, nurtured the next generation of loggers, and oversaw operations.

"Timber companies seem like they're usually family owned, huh?"

"Oh yes," Al said. "My father was a logger. Learned everything from him. My brother and I started after high school. My son is going to college but plans to work in the industry someday."

I beamed at him. "That's so great. What about you, Richard?" I asked casually. "Any family in the business?"

He shook his head.

"What about your nephew?" Nate asked with a tilt of his beer bottle. "Didn't I train him a few years ago?"

Richard's face shifted from neutral to furious in seconds. "He moved away," he gritted out.

Okay. That right there told me I should dig deeper into

Norman Bernard. There was definitely a story behind that reaction.

"I'd love to take you to lunch sometime," I said in the sweetest voice I could muster. "I'm writing a series of books set up here. They'll all revolve around the timber industry. From what Paz has told me, you're the expert."

His eyes never left the fire. "I doubt I've got anything interesting to tell you."

I bit the inside of my cheek and forced a smile. "Online research can only get me so far. Talking to someone who's been doing this for as long as you have would really help me out."

He nodded and gave me a sidelong glance but didn't respond.

Shit. I was coming on too strong. I shouldn't have come out with the ask so quickly.

Richard was skittish. Everything I'd dug up indicated that he kept to himself. Our interaction tonight confirmed it, and I couldn't afford to burn this bridge. Henri trusted him, and he was a mentor to Pascal. He would be my best chance at figuring out what happened.

And my gut told me there was so much more here. He had an alibi for the day of Frank's accident, but I had no doubt he was hiding something.

While Nate and Al were happy to talk shop and ramble on about all the boring details, Richard was more reserved. He'd turn my questions around on me skillfully. And while he was always polite, he was distant, closed off. And it only made me want to know more.

The sun had gone down, and the reception was in full swing. The guests were all full of barbeque, and spirits were high.

The local band played a mix of oldies, country and pop hits, and the dance floor had been full all night. The general ease of the evening had my guard slipping a little, and I didn't mind it one bit. The happiness was contagious.

"Dance?" my date asked, offering his hand.

The last thing on earth I wanted to do was dance with him. Because no good could come of this. My poor lady parts were already so confused around him, and my brain was too.

But instead of feigning an injury or coming up with a clever excuse, I took his hand and followed him onto the dance floor.

The heat of him soaked into me as he wrapped an arm around my waist. Subconsciously, I wanted to snuggle in closer, nuzzle into the crook of his neck, but the sliver of my brain still on guard reminded me that distance was necessary and healthy.

"Having a good time?"

I nodded silently. Talking right now would lead to one of two things: fighting or more vulnerable revelations. I wasn't interested in getting involved in either.

This was the closest we'd been since we slept together. We'd been staying out of each other's way, and that had helped cool things off a little. But now, dancing with him, wrapped up in his warmth and his scent, I had to fight the surge of lust only his proximity was capable of creating. And damn if it didn't make it hard to stay professional.

But I persevered, remaining quiet, pushing thoughts of the case out of my mind. For once, I took the time to let myself be. I was dancing with a strong, handsome man I happened to have a massive crush on. Life didn't get much better.

"Parker," he rasped, his tone loaded with more vulnerability than I'd ever witnessed from him.

When I pulled back to respond, he was watching me, his brown eyes molten.

His grip tightened on my hip, and I arched toward him, needing him closer. He said my name again, this time just a whisper, as he tilted his face closer.

"Everyone is watching us." I said lamely.

"Good. Then we'll give them a show." He leaned forward and every cell in my body anticipated his kiss. I needed it. I needed him in this moment.

His lips were centimeters from mine when a shrill scream rang out.

I jerked back, scanning the tent for danger, wishing I had a weapon or at least a can of pepper spray.

Not, even for an instant, would I have fathomed what had the guests around us in a panic. It was a moose—enormous, with a full rack of antlers—and it was standing in front of the ornate cake table at the end of the tent.

He was devouring the exquisite wedding cake we had admired earlier. The creation was massive and decorated to look like tree bark with Henri and Alice's initials carved into it.

And now a moose the size of a shipping container was going to town on it, working his way through the intricate leaves and acorns while guests backed away in horror.

The tent was large, but being trapped inside it with an angry moose was likely incredibly dangerous. Thankfully, the people nearest to the creature were already cautiously putting distance between themselves and it.

But a shrill scream rang out behind us. "*Cliiive*!"

A whir of blond curls and a sparkly purple dress whizzed by me as Goldie charged at him. Clive, to his credit, was unbothered as he used his massive tongue to swipe at the frosting on his snout.

Dropping my arm, Paz snagged Goldie by the waist and scooped her up.

"Goldie," Paz murmured, holding her tight as she wiggled and thrashed against him, "get in the house."

"But I wanted cake," she cried, tears running down her cheeks and mixing with a layer of grime. Her fluffy dress was already streaked with dirt.

Suddenly, Henri appeared in front of us, holding up both arms. "Please exit the tent on the opposite side and head toward our house. Your safety is the most important thing right now."

Goldie let out a sob as we shuffled off the dance floor.

"We don't want to scare him or make him feel threatened," Paz explained to her as she wiped her nose on his shoulder.

The band had stopped playing, and half the guests were still frozen, watching as a moose slowly ate what had been a very beautiful and probably very expensive cake.

After Clive had decimated about half of it, he moseyed away, seemingly unconcerned by the commotion he had caused. At this point, a good chunk of guests had left, and others had sought the warmth and safety of Henri and Alice's house.

We stood on the porch, watching the carnage. Beside us, Alice was laughing hysterically. "It's payback," she said between giggles. "For the time I threw tampons at him."

My head snapped around. "What?"

Henri had his arm around her and was chuckling as well. "Asshole moose," he said, shaking his head.

"One time he stole our clothes when we were skinny dipping," Remy said as Hazel's face reddened.

How was this possible?

I turned to Paz for an explanation. Why was his family acting like a moose crashing a wedding was a regular occurrence? And how could they be so casual about the sentient and clearly vindictive wildlife?

"Clive is not your average moose."

Chapter 26
Pascal

In the parking lot of the Ape Hanger, I killed the engine and looked over at her. "Are you sure you wanna do this?"

She pulled down the visor and fluffed her hair. It was not in its usual ponytail today. Instead, it was cascading down her back in all its dark and shiny glory. Basically begging me to run my fingers through it and give a gentle tug.

We were in Heartsborough, which was across the river from Lovewell. Our town rival for generations, it was home to a small downtown, a few doctors' offices, and the headquarters of LeBlanc timber.

It was also the home of the Maine Marauders, a local biker gang. We'd always steered clear. Dad had distrusted the bikers, and they rarely worked on our crews, but they'd been around my whole life. Everyone knew the bikers sometimes got mixed up in shit, so I was concerned about walking into their headquarters.

And after learning about the threatening note and our stakeout gone wrong, the stakes were feeling even higher.

Parker was no longer a cop, but that didn't matter to these types. I didn't want her going in there at all, but I had to settle for going with her.

She slipped a small canister of pepper spray and what I suspected was a taser into her girlie purse, then reapplied her red lipstick.

"You're a hell of a woman." Censoring myself around her was damn near impossible anymore.

She turned and winked. "Don't get in my way in there. I've got criminals to uncover."

"You know most bikers are not criminals, right?"

She squinted at me, annoyed. "Yes, but according to the federal tracking database, some of these bikers are. And they have ties to oxycodone trafficking. I have a feeling we can get some leads here."

Since our run-in with her FBI agent ex, Parker had been more focused than ever. I had no doubt that finding my dad's killer was still her top priority, but it didn't hurt that she was motivated to show that asshole what she was capable of.

"Let's go."

The Ape Hanger made the Moose look like the Ritz. The only word I could use to describe this place was scuzzy. I wasn't usually weird about germs. How could I be? I had spent my childhood in the woods. But hot damn, I already wanted to shower in a full vat of Purell.

The parking lot was unpaved, and rows of motorcycles were lined up, despite the fact that it was three p.m. on a Wednesday and the middle of winter.

The building was wide and squat, with small windows high on either side of the entrance. An old neon sign that probably hadn't worked in years hung above a scratched door that was hanging off its hinges and rotted in some spots.

The lights inside were dim. One wall was covered in dartboards, while pool tables took up the open space in the center of the establishment. There was an old-school jukebox in the corner playing a hard rock song I didn't recognize, and the linoleum floors were covered in at least an inch of grime.

But Parker was oblivious to it all. She was in the zone, watching every patron and employee, soaking in every detail as she traipsed through the bar with a disarming smile.

Heads turned. Every damn one of them. Making the hairs on my arms stand up.

This place was packed for a Wednesday afternoon. I guess bikers did not keep business hours.

Parker was wearing skintight jeans with combat boots and a soft black sweater that kept falling off one shoulder, revealing her bra strap. Her hair was down, and she'd put on dark eyeliner and deep red lipstick. She looked a little hard edged and sinfully sexy.

She walked up to the bartender, a grizzled man who was somewhere between his midforties and his sixties. It was hard to tell. His face was weathered and tan under a long white beard that hung halfway down his chest, and he wore a leather vest over a black T-shirt.

Tattoos peeked out of the collar of his shirt and snaked down both arms.

"Hello," Parker singsonged in that girly voice that made people underestimate her, just like she wanted them to.

"You lost, sweetheart?" the old guy asked, his arms still crossed.

She plopped onto a stool, putting her purse on the scratched bar top. "Oh no. I only came for a drink. Whatcha have on tap?"

"We don't got any girlie shit."

She leaned forward with a grin. "Good. Because I'm in the mood for whiskey. How about a shot of Jameson and a beer to chase?"

Behind her, I hovered closer. The back of my neck was already dotted with sweat. "You with her?" he grunted.

I nodded. "I'll have the same."

"And pour yourself one," she said, her smile never wavering. "What did you say your name was?"

"Didn't."

"It's Otter," someone hollered from the pool table.

"It's a pleasure to meet you, Otter," Parker said with a prim nod.

He placed two beers in front of her and scowled. "Really. What are you doing here?"

She tossed her hair, and her smile turned even sweeter. "Day drinking. My friend Pascal over here needs to loosen up." She threw a thumb over her shoulder, and every eye followed, glaring.

"He's got a big ole stick up his ass. So I saw this place and figured you probably pour a strong drink."

Otter's lip quirked. It was probably the closest he came to smiling. Then he busied himself pouring our whiskeys.

Damn. That was all it took for her to disarm them. The interest died down and people mostly went back to their conversations.

With the waning scrutiny, I let my shoulders sag and took in my surroundings.

There were probably two dozen men here, all of whom looked like bikers. But only about half wore the Marauders vest. While there were hundreds of tattoos on display, no one was carrying a weapon, that I could see at least, and they were all either immersed in easy conversation or playing darts.

Parker handed me a shot of whiskey and clinked my glass. With a quirked brow, she held hers up, silently signaling me to do the same. I obeyed and tossed it back, soaking in the way it burned on the way down.

Parker looked completely unfazed by her shot. Her expression was still overly bright. And suddenly, she spun on her stool and waved at a group of older men playing darts. "Can I play winner?"

They all wore leather vests and scowls, but they grumbled when she smiled at them.

Beer in hand, she wandered over and introduced herself, being sure she caught their names too.

Fascinated, I watched her work the small crowd like she had with the people of Lovewell, leading the conversation where she wanted it to go.

"I'm a writer, actually," she said, flipping her hair over her shoulder. "Murder Mysteries. I can already tell this one is gonna be my best. It's set in a fictional town like this one. Logging industry and all. I'm up here visiting to get inspiration."

"We've got stories, cutie," one man said, patting his lap. "Come sit, and I'll tell you some scary shit that happens out in those woods."

She wrinkled her nose. "Thanks for the offer, but my boyfriend over there wouldn't like it. How about I kick your ass at darts and then I'll listen to your stories?"

Without waiting for a response, she sauntered toward the dartboard, her tight jeans cupping her perfect ass. She had completely charmed a bunch of old bikers and was about to destroy them at darts.

How had I ever doubted her? Because there was literally nothing this woman couldn't do—aside from pick up after herself.

Turned out that Blaze, Rubble, and Popeye were retired loggers who'd worked for a few outfits over the years. Parker bought them a round after handily defeating each of them at darts.

Although they probably all carried AARP cards, they had their fingers on the pulse of things around here.

"It's those damn drugs," Popeye said, rubbing the back of his neck where he had a tattoo of a skull on fire. "It's so sad."

No community up here was immune to the toll the opioid epidemic. My sister-in-law Hazel was working on a doctorate in public health and had devoted years of her life to studying the impact of opioids on rural communities. And everyone here seemed to feel the toll it had taken as well.

"I guess it's easy to run drugs up here," Parker mused, playing especially dumb. "All these unpopulated areas, lonely roads."

"Exactly," Blaze said. "It's too easy. The logging roads head right to Canada, and they're private, see. So it's not like law enforcement is patrolling them."

"Private? So who owns them?" she asked.

"The logging companies. Up in these parts, it's split between four families. Hundreds of employees between 'em. Hauling logs every day down those roads," Rubble explained. "Drove for the Clarks for twenty-one years, but my back's shit now."

"And no one's caught on to it?"

The men laughed.

"People work very hard not to catch on, if you know what I mean."

"Some stay out of it and fire anyone who touches the stuff." This from Blaze. "Work with the cops. That kind of shit. But others turn a blind eye."

"And some participate," Rubble added, one brow cocked. "Pills pay much better than trees these days."

It took everything in me to keep from jumping out of my chair, pinning him to the wall, and demanding he tell me what he knew. But I was background noise here. I had to let Parker work.

No one recognized me. Granted, I had a beard, and I was wearing a black baseball cap and a plaid shirt with a puffy vest. It was my Henri costume. But it was working. Information was flowing far more easily than I could have anticipated.

I mentally kicked myself for ever doubting Parker. Since the day she showed up in Lovewell, she had been impressing me with her skills, ingenuity, and intelligence.

It was hard not to slip into overprotective mode. Because the urge to protect her, to provide for her, and keep her happy, was shaking me to my core. I'd never been the guy who got attached, but I was long past attached to her.

Parker leaned in and lowered her voice. "Are you saying some of the loggers are involved?"

Blaze nodded. "It's an ugly business, but some guys from the club have been involved off and on. Mostly in the northwest."

I kept my head down, sipping my beer slowly. The northwest? The Golden Road was an unofficial dividing line for several of the timber holdings. It helped orient what was our land from that of the other families. Looking at a map, Gagnon land took up most of the northeast section. Heberts owned much of the land to the west of the main road.

But no-man's-land, where Remy and Hazel had found the

stash hidden in a container outside an old cabin, was an undeveloped parcel that was technically property of the state. It had been part of some claims long ago, but the lines on the map had shifted over the decades. And no-man's-land? It sat directly in the northwest corner of logging territory.

"I shouldn't have said anything," he gritted out as the others glared at him. They were old-timers, sure, but the club had a code, and he was definitely speaking out of turn.

"I understand. But you've been *so* helpful." She gave them all a flirty smile. "I've been behind on my book research. This is so great." She tapped her chin. "I wonder who else I can talk to about this. Maybe some of your friends?"

They shook their heads in unison. "Don't," Rubble said. "Pretty thing like you can't be goin' around asking too many questions. Especially at a place like this. Stick with researching on the internet. Don't get mixed up with people here." He looked around the bar. "During the day, this place is usually filled with old-timers. But the young ones? They're trouble. Stay away on Friday nights. And don't go talking to anyone named Stinger."

Her eyes flashed for a fraction of a second, but her face betrayed nothing.

"Stinger?"

"Yes. Bad dude. Piece of shit and a drug pusher, to boot."

"I'm shocked that dumbass hasn't gotten arrested yet. Always gallivanting around, selling drugs, and flashing money."

Parker nodded, her face a mask of innocent concern.

"He's dumb, but he's well connected. In with some pretty powerful folks."

"Must be, because he hasn't gotten caught or killed yet. He's always drunk and bragging about his big scores and acting tough. Saying he killed someone."

I gasped. Not loud, but loud enough for Parker to pin me with a glare.

"And his bike? Who the hell drives a Ducati up in these parts?"

"What a fucking waste on our shitty Maine roads."

Parker pressed her lips together. Hiding a smile, no doubt. I already had my phone in my hands, searching local foreign motorcycle dealers. A rare European bike would be easy to track down up here.

We were closer than ever, and I had Parker to thank. Despite sitting incognito in a shady biker bar, I felt a rush of pride and admiration bloom in my chest. Parker was so much more than I had bargained for. And as I looked over at her, chatting with her new biker friends over a beer, I knew it was too late for me. Because I was head over heels for this woman. And there was no going back.

Chapter 27
Parker

Back at the house, my fingers were flying over the keyboard. Stinger, whoever the fuck he was, would be caught like a rat in a trap soon, if I had anything to say about it.

My friends at the Ape Hanger had given far more information than I could have anticipated. In my wildest dreams, I never thought I'd be leaving there with confirmation of the connection between the logging roads, the local timber companies, and the Canadian drug traffickers, let alone the name of the local dealer who seemed to be both stupid and indiscreet.

This was the stuff investigator dreams were made of.

I was so deeply in the zone I didn't even notice Paz, who'd set himself up at the bar. For the first time since I'd met him, he actually sat back and let me work. Our mutual respect continued to grow, and if I wasn't mistaken, he was beginning to trust me.

Before our little mission, he had been twitchy and frustrated. Angry that I was even going to the Ape Hanger and then annoyed about being with me, even though he'd insisted.

I was more than capable of handling myself, and I think he may have finally realized it.

Several times, he gave me meaningful looks, like he was acknowledging significant moments. But he didn't interfere, and he only participated enough to keep our cover.

He'd trusted me to do my job and gather intel. To say I was shocked would be an understatement, since we'd done nothing but bicker and disagree since he approached me about the case.

Since coming back to the house, Paz had been careful to give me space to work. He had thoughtfully cooked dinner and done the dishes while I pored over online vehicle registration databases.

I was going to find this motorcycle. Sadly, as a PI, my access was far more restricted than it had been back in my cop days, but I still had plenty of tricks up my sleeve.

Without the model or even the color of the bike in question, it would take some time to track down. Luckily, there were only eleven Ducatis registered in all of Penobscot County. That was one of the benefits of being in the sticks, I guessed.

I stretched my neck, tilting my head one way and then the other to alleviate some of the tension, and rolled my shoulders. Blowing out a breath, I tugged my hair tie free and scratched my scalp before twisting my hair back up into a messy bun.

I shook out my hands, ready to get back to it, and caught sight of Paz. He was at the kitchen island, staring at me. And not in his usual superior, judgmental way. But with heat and longing. My eyes snapped back to my computer screen as my heart pounded against my ribcage. Damn Paz and his killer good looks. Couldn't he see that I was chasing a hot lead?

My fingers twitched as I waited for the results of my motor vehicle search to populate. Was it just me, or was the Wi-Fi lagging? His eyes were boring into me, sending tremors coursing through me. God dammit. It made me want to run up to my room and lock the door.

This day had been intense already. I didn't have the bandwidth to think about the way his attention ignited a fire in my core or how ridiculously hot he looked in that shirt. And I couldn't rehash the things I had said to him. That sleeping with him had been a mistake. That I didn't want things to go further. At the time, keeping my distance had felt necessary.

Because right now? That all felt like a total crock of shit.

We were in this together. He'd driven my car at a giant moose to make sure I was safe. He escorted me everywhere like an impeccably dressed bodyguard. And he let me be me. With my mess and my chaos and my habit of falling down the research rabbit hole. The man was making me dinner because he knew there was no way I'd remember to eat tonight with all this fresh information in my brain.

Focus, Parker. I scrolled through the registrations. Despite the small population, the county was geographically massive, so I didn't even recognize most of the towns.

I was about to start running checks on each name when my attention snagged on two words.

"What the fuck?" I gasped, dislodging my laptop. Thankfully, though my brain was a jumbled mess, my reflexes were in tip-top shape, and I grasped it before it could slide off my lap.

I blinked several times, and finally, my tired eyes cooperated and homed in on the details.

"You okay?" Paz was looming over me, looking particularly protective and masculine.

"Sit down."

He joined me on the couch, our bodies flush against one

another. And I couldn't help it. I sank into his warmth, a little too physically comfortable with my fake boyfriend and client.

I pointed at the screen. "Look familiar?"

He leaned forward, examining the database until his focus landed on the state registration number for a 2021 black Ducati Streetfighter V4.

"Are you fucking kidding me?"

"Nope." I tracked the line on the spreadsheet with my finger. "The owner of this very fancy imported Italian motorcycle is a company called Pattes Holdings. Which is headquartered at Mountain Meadows trailer park. And the registered owner of this company happens to be one Mitch motherfucking Hebert."

Paz stood, tugging at his hair and pacing around the living room. "How is this possible? The local drug dealer drives a flashy bike registered to a shell corporation owned by Mitch Hebert? The CEO of the largest timber operation in the state? Who happens to control hundreds of miles of remote roads leading to Canada?"

I bit my lip, a smile spreading across my face. "You were the one who told me he was dirty. And now we know he's deep in this shit."

Pulling up the photos from our stakeout, I patted the cushion next to me. Once he sat down again, we scoured each image for even a glimpse of the motorcycle. The photos were dark and blurry, but in one photo, part of the license plate was visible behind the two street bikes. And what we could see matched the registration database.

"Zoom in on their faces," he said, scooting closer and putting an arm across the back of the couch.

My face flushed at his proximity. I hadn't had this type of hormonal reaction to a boy since the sophomore homecoming dance. It was embarrassing and unprofessional. Could I blame my body? This man had doled out orgasms during a blizzard, and since then, sexy times had been nonexistent. Of course my nipples were begging for his attention while my clit complained from inside my sensible cotton panties.

In several of the photos, Mitch and his brother Paul were easily recognizable, but images of the others were less clear.

"One of these guys has got to be Stinger," I said.

Beside me, Paz was still examining the photos. "The one with the sunglasses looks younger than the others. And sort of familiar."

I took in the mystery man. In comparison to the others, he looked to be below average height, with a lanky build. His hair was long, obscuring part of his face. The large sunglasses did the rest.

The edges of a couple of tattoos were visible near the collar of his leather jacket, but not much else.

"What's that on his face?" Paz asked.

"I think," I scooted closer and squinted, "it's a tattoo. Or a really bad scar."

The damn sunglasses hid the mark, but the thin lines looked to be part of a small tattoo.

"I don't get it," Paz said, his frustration mounting, "how is a drug dealer with a fancy motorcycle and a fucking face tattoo gallivanting around town, and no one has noticed?"

"He must be better at this than we give him credit for."

"Or maybe he's well protected." He balled his fists and hauled himself up. Muscles taut with tension, he paced across the room and stopped at the fireplace. "What if he had something to do with my dad's accident?" he asked, his back to me. "I feel it, Parker. It's all connected."

I stood and put my laptop aside. "I'll find out," I said, shuffling over to him. "Maybe Mrs. Revelle has seen him and can give us more info. I'll bring him down. I promise. And Mitch Hebert too. That fucker's laundering money through a bogus dog walking business and buying flashy gifts for the local drug dealer. You can bet your muscular lumberjack ass that he'll pay for it."

Paz turned to face me. For one moment, we were frozen, staring at one another, sharing the weight of this discovery.

But then we were kissing. Maybe I kissed him first, or maybe he took the lead. I didn't know. All I knew was that once we started, my body took over, launching itself at him and pressing even closer.

I was desperate for an outlet. A way to expend some of the pent-up feelings raging inside me. I was desperate for him. The feel of his warm, rough hands on my skin, the taste of his lips.

He was gentle, even a bit tentative. Exploring in the most unhurried way. I had always assumed Paz would be a master at efficiency, but this kiss was a journey, not the destination.

The pressure increased as his hands found my hair, one stroking the back of my neck. My hands were on his chest, gripping his shirt and soaking in the heat emanating from the thick wall of muscle beneath it. Unable to control myself anymore, I gasped before diving in deeper, pulling him close, and making it clear just how much I wanted this.

But a moment later, he pulled away. "I'm sorry." With one long step back, he took all his warmth with him.

My lips tingled and my chest heaved as my brain tried to catch up and form words. I still didn't know who'd initiated the collision. Because that's what it was. Our bodies colliding in a rush of heat and passion. I had been just as willing as he was. We both knew it was a bad idea, but I was having trouble remembering why.

"Actually," he said, "I'm not sorry. I've been wanting to do that for a while. Fuck. I respect you, Parker. And I respect the boundaries you drew after the snowstorm. But it's killing me to stick to them."

I nodded, touching my swollen lips. Why had I established those boundaries in the first place? Because this felt incredible. How could I delude myself into thinking it was even possible to stay away from this man?

He wrung his hands and searched my face. His shoulders were slumped, and his expression was more open and vulnerable than I'd ever seen it. I wanted nothing more than to jump into his arms and kiss all that self-doubt away.

"I spend every single minute of my day thinking about you. How gorgeous you are. How smart and fearless. How badly I want you. Your body and your mind."

His words hit me like an arrow to the heart. He was so sincere, so impassioned. I stood, blinking at him while my brain processed this new information.

"You don't have to say anything," he said, taking a step back. "I've never met a woman I felt was made for me. Someone who could push my buttons and go ten rounds with me intellectually, then wake up ready to do it all again the next day. You see through my bullshit and all my masks. And I hate it. But fuck if it doesn't make me respect you that much more. You're fucking spectacular."

Without my permission, my body moved toward him. I was desperate to feel his skin beneath my fingers, the weight of his body against mine. It was wrong, to let myself fall back into bed with him, but I couldn't stop the feeling that this was a foregone conclusion.

I gripped his shirt with both hands. "You want me?" I asked, biting my lip hard to keep from throwing myself at him.

He didn't kiss me. He didn't throw me over his shoulder. He didn't even touch me.

"I don't want to fuck you, Parker," he said, tipping my chin up with his finger so I was forced to meet his dark glare. "I want to possess you. I want to own you."

I gasped. What the hell was he talking about? We were flirting. Hopefully headed toward some fun naked time. Weren't we? But his tone and face were dead serious.

"You challenge me. And you fascinate me. And it's not superficial. You have dug so deep into my brain that you make me want things I've never allowed myself to want before."

I dropped my chin and focused on his shirt, needing a break from the intensity of his gaze. But all I saw was the way his chest heaved. Like he couldn't slow his breath. Like his heart was racing as quickly as mine was.

Trying to lighten the mood, I took a step back. "Stop." I swatted at his chest. Because damn if I wasn't feeling uneasy right then. It was one thing to acknowledge the mutual attraction between us, or even act on it—with clear boundaries in place.

But what he was saying? This wasn't my "let's bang to get it out of our systems" philosophy. This was so much deeper. And I was way too chickenshit to let this unnerving conversation go any further.

"We can't do this," I whispered.

He grabbed my shoulders, startling me. "Why not? Tell me you're not attracted to me. Tell me you don't feel the connection between us. Tell me that we don't fit together perfectly. That we don't smooth out each other's sharp edges."

My rebuttal died on my lips. The words vanished from my vocabulary. He was asking for so much more than I could give.

And he'd bared himself. Those words, speaking them like that, had to have been one of the most frightening things he'd ever done. He'd opened himself up to me completely. And in that moment, I believed him.

So, for once, I stopped. "Kiss me."

Chapter 28
Parker

But he didn't kiss me. Instead, he picked me up, threw me over his shoulder, and promptly ran up the stairs.

"We're doing this right," he growled, giving me a hard spank.

My body shook with anticipation. Or perhaps it was all the blood rushing to my head. Either way, being manhandled by Pascal Gagnon, the grouchy Lumbersuit, was intoxicating.

He took me directly into his bedroom and flipped me over so I stood in front of the massive bed.

"That's better." He ran his fingers down the sides of my torso and grabbed my waist, pulling me in. "Now I'll kiss you."

And kiss me he did. Soft but firm. Hungry yet controlled. Teasing me and testing my resolve.

How on earth did I think it was possible to stay away from this? From the electric current that flowed between us? Because it grew stronger with every touch, every look, every kiss.

"Did you mean what you said earlier?" I asked, studying his face.

His words and his actions, they all had meaning. But I wasn't sure I was prepared to face the implications.

"Yes. I meant it all." He ran his hands through his hair, his eyes locked on me. "Trust me. I wish I could control these feelings, but I can't."

"Thank you for being honest," I said, placing my hand on his chest. "Vulnerability is hot. We're all flawed humans."

He laughed. "Glad you think so, 'cause I've got more flaws than most."

I slid my hand down until I was palming his erection. It strained behind his jeans, hot and hard and thick. "Except this," I whispered. "No flaws detected here."

He growled and picked me up, then dropped me on the bed and covered me with his body.

"Stop being so fucking sexy. I'm trying to take my time here."

I wiggled underneath him, desperate for friction. "There's plenty of time later. Get those pants off. You want to possess me? Show me."

Before I could even blink, he had torn off his shirt and stepped out of his jeans. Clad in only his boxers, he retrieved a condom from the nightstand and dropped it on the bed.

And then he was on top of me, kissing me senseless while my body trembled in anticipation.

I couldn't get the phrases out of my head. Every kiss, every stroke of his hand. All I could hear was *I want to possess you* and *I want to own you* on repeat. What should have scared me, what should have been a bright red flag, felt like a starting line.

Because the need I felt for him was greater than anything I'd ever experienced before.

"Please," I whispered as he pulled down my leggings. I lifted my hips, desperate to feel his skin against mine.

He took me in as I lay naked under him and shook his head. "Do know what it's been like watching you walk around and knowing you had no panties on?" He threw my leggings onto the floor. "I used to obsess about your braless tits in my house. Then I had the unique torture of knowing your bare pussy was just a scrap of fabric away."

"Sorry," I said, not even remotely sorry. "But you haven't exactly made it easy for me either. Not only does your ass look delicious in those sweats you're always wearing, but I can see the outline of your thick cock too. And then I daydream about how good it felt when you were fucking me."

"I guess we've both had a lot on our minds, then." He traced his fingers across my jaw.

I dipped down, taking one into my mouth.

"*Fuck*. I need to be inside you."

"Hurry," I said, more than ready for him.

He sat back on his knees, putting his big, strong body on display as he rolled the condom onto his thick cock. Every physical attribute was powerful and serious, but there was so much more beneath the surface. And it only made him hotter.

"I want you on your back," he commanded. "Your ass is spectacular. And while I thoroughly enjoy fucking you from behind, there is absolutely nothing better than watching your face as you come on my cock. It's so beautiful. The look of pure bliss in your eyes. The way you cry out. The feel of you."

He lined himself up slowly, making me shake in anticipation.

"I need to see that. Need to see your gorgeous face. The way your eyes widen when I push inside you. The way you relax once you adjust to my size." He spread my legs wide. "That's a good girl," he murmured, pushing into me one inch at a time. "Yes. Feel that? How perfectly we fit? This pussy was made for me, Parker."

He began to move, slowly at first. But I needed more. I was already on the brink. So I bucked my hips against him as I cried out. "You're so thick."

His lips ghosted over my earlobe as he chuckled with pride. "Patience. I'm only getting started."

Fuck. I dug deep for restraint and let him lead. Because if I had my way, I'd stay like this all night. Together, naked, joined, and fulfilled in every way.

He tilted his hips, changing the angle, and thrust deep, moving slowly while circling my clit with his thumb. The steady rhythm and the way his attention on me lit me up inside had my body flushed and ready in minutes. Primed for what I could only imagine would break me.

"Look at me," he commanded.

Obediently, I took in his scruff, his dark eyes, and those broad lumberjack shoulders. I grabbed his perfect ass, delighting in the feel of his muscles clenching as he pistoned in and out of me.

My orgasm was gaining steam as he lavished attention on both my greedy nipples. The tension mounted as he pushed me higher.

"I dream about this." He grunted. "Every single night. And I wake up every morning alone and hard and desperate for you."

His confession was jarring, but it further fanned the flames in my core. "What do you do about it?"

"Fist my cock and think about fucking you. Fantasize about sliding in and out of you from behind. What you taste like when I eat your sweet pussy. I've been tortured, Parker. And it stops now. You're mine. This pussy belongs to me. And that mouth. Oh fuck, that mouth."

Every nerve ending in my body lit up as he spoke, and the combination of his thumb on my clit, his thick cock buried inside me, and the word *mine* echoing between us sent me crashing over the edge.

I came hard and fast and loud, enjoying how his thrusts became jerky and uneven as I spiraled into bliss. He collapsed on top of me, still twitching inside me.

I wrapped my arms around him and squeezed, feeling the weight of what had passed between us. And then he kissed me softly before getting up to deal with the condom.

And as I watched him walk away, admiring the round globes of his ass, all I could think about was that word. *Mine.*

Chapter 29
Pascal

"Coffee?" Parker had one hand on her hip and was tapping her foot. With a growl, I sidled up behind her and slapped her ass as she turned on the machine.

She danced around the kitchen, putting slices of bread into the toaster and leaving a pile of crumbs on the counter. For the first time, I was grateful for her hatred of bras. She looked really fucking good in my T-shirt and nothing else. So good I couldn't remember why we had even ventured into the kitchen. Grabbing the hem of the shirt, I pulled her toward me and planted a sloppy kiss on her lips. For the first time since her arrival, I let myself acknowledge how much I liked having her here. How I looked forward to coming home, knowing she would be here with her girlie music and chaos.

I turned the coffee maker on, and she put a few slices of bread in the toaster. It was all very domestic and calming. Fuck. Who knew something so simple could make me so deliriously happy? Not that I would ever admit it out loud. Was this what had my brothers smiling all the time? Morning snuggles and making coffee in their underwear? Because it was kind of wonderful.

"Out of paper towels," Parker said, removing the roll from the holder. "Are the extras in the basement?" She headed toward the door that led downstairs before I could stop her.

I froze, fear twisting my gut. Oh shit. She was going to run away screaming when she saw it.

She flipped the light on and plodded down the steps without looking back. Cringing, I shut off the sink and followed her, already sweating.

Her footsteps stopped at the bottom of the stairs, and she inhaled sharply. "What the fuck?"

I winced and hurried down, racking my brain for a way to explain without looking completely insane.

"Paz?" She was standing in front of a large steel rack—one of several, actually—that was carefully organized and labeled with supplies.

"You have a lot of stuff here." She raised one eyebrow and crossed her arms. "It's like a fucking Costco."

"I like to be prepared," I said lamely, studying my feet.

She walked along the racks, reading each label. "You don't have a coffee table or a dining room table, but you have freeze-dried food? Iodine tablets? What are these even for?"

Despite my better judgment, I opened my big, dumb mouth. "I have enough here for a handful of friends and my family for at least thirty days, which, in the event of radiation exposure, is essential."

"Radiation exposure?"

I nodded. Being prepared for an industrial accident wasn't irrational.

She turned on her heel and went back to her perusal.

"Water, water purification tablets, water jugs, water purifiers." She ran her hand along the shelves.

"I like to be prepared." I shrugged. "We experience extreme weather up here."

She shuffled over and draped her arms around my shoulders, calming my racing heart immediately. "I'm not judging you. I just want to understand."

I nodded.

"Because," she said, "that's a lot of batteries. Like an excessive amount. There have to be hundreds here, all labeled and in bins. And the flashlights."

"They come in handy."

"Of course. But you only have two hands. There are like fifty."

She pulled back and snagged a roll of paper towels from the shelf. "Let's go upstairs and talk."

Feeling more than a little exposed, I followed her. I wasn't ashamed. On the contrary, actually. Preparation was important to me, and I took pride in my ability to provide for myself and my family. But this thing between us was so new, and Parker wasn't like me in this respect. She was wild and free and spontaneous. And now that she'd seen what was hidden behind the curtain, I couldn't imagine she'd want anything to do with me.

She led me up to the couch and returned with two steaming mugs of coffee.

"Help me understand," she said, her eyes soft and her head tilted a little.

Fuck. I was an anxious mess. Why couldn't I be the kind of guy who could go with the flow and have a good time?

"I've always been like this," I explained. "Even when I was a kid, my brain couldn't slow down. I couldn't let go of my concerns and just have fun. Instead, I'd picture catastrophe after catastrophe. Like a movie playing in slow motion." I was always preparing, always planning. It was the only way I knew how to protect myself and my family.

With a sympathetic smile, she placed both our mugs on the coffee table, then snuggled up next to me silently, giving me the space to continue. Giving me the physical support to encourage me. The warmth of her body against mine made me feel less alone.

"I'm not even sure how it started. I knew, even when I was probably too young to understand, that my dad had a dangerous job. It wasn't uncommon to hear about people we knew being seriously hurt or killed on the job. And then the roads. Every winter, there were horrible accidents."

She nodded, almost like she understood.

"Things are extreme up here. It's important to know how to handle yourself and the equipment. From an early age, I needed to make sure everyone was safe."

I squeezed my eyes shut. My chest felt tight, and my hands shook, but I had to get it all out if I really wanted more with Parker, something lasting. I had to be honest with her. And to be honest, first, I had to be brave.

"It started as small stuff. I used to keep Band-Aids in my backpack, because Remy was always climbing trees and getting cuts and scrapes. And then it was a big water bottle and extra snacks, in case my siblings got hungry or thirsty while exploring the woods."

"It's how you love," she murmured. "And I think it's beautiful."

My heart clenched. "It was my role. I was the organized one. And I relished it. I guess the scary things seemed a little more manageable when I felt like I had some control."

"And your dad's accident?"

I pulled her close and took a deep breath, letting the smell and feel of her strengthen me. "My brain shut down. And it's never been the same. The fear, the constant panic. The need to be vigilant. It never goes away. I'm always waiting for the next terrible thing."

She peered up at me. "Thank you for telling me this."

"You probably think I'm crazy." My shoulders slumped, and I dropped my chin. Fuck.

"Not at all. I think you're human."

"Some days it feels like the fear is all that's left of me." I pressed my lips together and closed my eyes. "That I have nothing else to give."

She pushed up, putting her hand on my chest. "That's not true. You are so many things. You contain multitudes. You do not exist only to worry and stockpile supplies."

"But I do. Getting the company back on track, providing for everyone—that's what I'm here for. They have each other. And this? It's all I can do."

"That is straight-up bullshit." Her face flushed, and she went rigid. "I've been here a month," she gritted out, anger radiating off her. "And you know what I've seen? A family that constantly reaches out to you to include you and consult with you. Siblings who value your intellect and perspective. A mom who'd kill to spend more time with you. Who drops off fresh banana bread, even if you eat it without chocolate chips."

She stood and paced to the windows. Damn, she was adorable when she was mad.

"Do not talk about my boyfriend that way."

I froze. Real boyfriend or fake boyfriend? I opened my mouth to ask, to clarify the label, but she was on a roll.

"Stop reducing yourself." She fisted her hands at her sides.

"Start trusting that there is a well of good inside you just bursting to be let out."

"How do I let it out?"

"By being fucking vulnerable. Saying what you feel for once. Stop hiding behind the grumpy exterior. You're basically Oscar the Grouch in Brooks Brothers."

I laughed. She wasn't far off. I hauled myself off the couch and pulled her against me. My affection for her swelled in my chest.

With one finger, I tipped her chin up and stared into her gorgeous eyes. "Thank you." I leaned down to place a kiss on her lips.

"Fear and anxiety are healthy and normal. Don't forget that. But I'm always here to listen. And I'm on your team, if you want me."

"I want you so fucking much," I said, kissing her again.

Chapter 30
Pascal

I missed her. There. I said it. Henri had taken Parker up to camp the day before so she could inspect the buildings and see the machine shop. I wanted to be the one to take her, but it was almost Thanksgiving, which meant endless year-end spreadsheets and meetings with the finance team.

We should have done it weeks ago, before winter really kicked up, but there hadn't been time between stakeouts and fucking her on every available surface in my house. I was the luckiest guy in the world, and I wouldn't take any of this for granted. I'd already learned that lesson. For once, work hadn't been my first priority.

And it wasn't just sex. Parker saw right through my defense mechanisms and bullshit. She'd seen my damn basement, and instead of judging me or running away, she embraced that side of me. Every single day, she was inspiring me to push myself and to grow.

I was a planner, a prepper. Always imagining every scenario. And right now, all I could see was a future with Parker. I wanted it more than I had ever wanted anything.

But right now, she was over a hundred miles away in the damn woods with no cell reception. With my brother. So instead, I was stuck here, in my office, thinking about her and how cute she looked when she wore my T-shirts.

How strangely things had turned out. When Dad died, my life stopped.

The anchor of our family. The man I had spent my life trying to impress.

Gone in an instant.

A freak accident.

And I was hundreds of miles away, in the city, trying to make rich people richer.

It was only when the shock and grief were so bad that I made a mistake. One email, attaching the wrong document. And suddenly, my career was gone, and Parker's case was blown.

Henri, Adele, and Remy had already worked for Dad. Henri had been his right hand since we were teenagers and was heir apparent to the Gagnon Lumber business.

Not that I minded. I had wanted nothing to do with it. I'd gotten out of Lovewell, my stiflingly small hometown, as I'd always dreamed of doing, and I'd made a life for myself far away from the woods.

But everything ended. All the things I cared about. Lost in an instant.

So then I'd been pulled back in.

The business was failing, and we could barely make payroll. Things were a fucking mess.

Henri begged me to come on as CFO and iron things out. For years, Dad had been in charge of the financials, and he'd left me with an endless number of messes to clean up.

Frank Gagnon had been a beloved pillar of the community.

He was kind and helpful, and in a place like Lovewell, neighbors helped each other.

He gave people jobs and fought hard so every employee could keep those jobs. He donated his time and energy and always had kind words for everyone.

He was my exact opposite. So when Henri called looking for my help, I offered him money. A large enough sum to keep the business afloat while he picked up the pieces. That had been my goal, after all. Make a lot of money so I could provide for my family while keeping a healthy distance.

But the bastard refused. Even acted insulted. Strong-armed me into hauling my ass back here. So I did. And we got to work. And now, two years later, I got it. What I couldn't understand at the time. Wealth and status and success mean so little. It was about what I was willing to do to get there. And somehow, coming back here, reconnecting with my family, and putting in the work had changed me.

So now, instead of taking work home or drinking alone while I played the piano, I was heading out to meet my little brother. I wasn't sure what the new Paz would look like, but I was beginning to think he would be an improvement.

My baby brother was infuriating. He was good at everything, especially pool. He had just beaten me for the second time, and now I had to buy dinner. He had invited me to hang out with him at the Moose while Hazel bartended.

The pathetic sap couldn't go even a few hours without his wife, so he insisted on parking himself at the bar and making eyes at her while she worked. It was disgusting.

But he was healthy, sober, and in love. And I had let my

own bullshit get in the way for too long. Parker was right. It was time to man up and own my shit.

I took a deep breath and closed my eyes. I had to do this. Parker said growth was painful and difficult. But I needed to clear the air.

"I owe you an apology."

Remy quirked his head. "Really?"

"Yes." I thrust my hands in the pockets of my jeans because I didn't know what else to do with them. "I owe apologies to the whole family, actually. But specifically to you. And Hazel."

He narrowed his eyes. Remy was generally the happy-go-lucky, not a big deal type, but I knew I'd hurt him.

"I've been carrying around so much anger. Most of it directed at myself. And instead of dealing with it like a fucking adult, I lashed out. At everyone, but mainly at you."

I rubbed at my chest. Fuck, that was hard. But once I opened my mouth, the right words did fall out. I had to accept the consequences of my actions and push forward in the right direction.

"Honestly, Remy, you scared the shit out of me when you fell apart. Losing Dad rocked my world, and I hated myself for not being closer to him, for not being here like you guys were. And then Henri's accident and your issues. It was too much. I shut down and let my inner asshole take over."

There. That was a start. If I had any hope of maintaining my relationships and keeping Gagnon Lumber going for future generations, then I had to start living up to my dad's example, and owning up to my mistakes was priority number one.

"So what I'm trying to say is that I'm sorry. According to Parker, I'm an emotionally stunted man child who lashes out as a defense mechanism."

A slow smile spread across Remy's face. "Shit, she's smart."

"Yes, she is. It's annoying as fuck, actually." I shook my head.

The way she could read me was terrifying. But in this moment, I understood how valuable her insight was. "When you had your breakdown, then Henri got hurt, I snapped. The fear became all-consuming, and I couldn't shake it, no matter how hard I tried. I was so mad at you for putting yourself in danger. Because the thought of losing either of you paralyzed me."

And then I went numb. Too much loss, too much fear. Because suddenly everything felt out of my control. I fixated on fixing the business and keeping everyone safe. I'd spent my entire life thinking that if I just worked hard enough, I could wrap everyone up in a protective bubble, and my money would insulate us. But that wasn't real life.

Remy stepped toward me and opened his arms. "I accept your apology," he said, pulling me into a tight hug.

"You don't have to. You can hate me."

He punched my shoulder. "I could never hate you. I've been a shithead too."

"I've been spiraling for years and only recently realized it. Not sure I can correct all my issues, but I want to make things right with the family."

He shrugged and dropped the rack onto the felt. "Who cares? You can fix it. So do it."

"You're a really good person, you motherfucker," I said, laughing.

"Lord knows I didn't learn it from you."

I chalked my cue, preparing to break. "I'm happy for you," I told him. "And I'm proud of the man you are. A year ago, you were a drunken disaster, and now you're a pro athlete, sober, and married to the love of your life."

"Exactly. See? If I can grow and mature and shit, so can you."

I shook my head. "Nah. I think I might be too far gone."

Remy had always been an optimist, a believer. He'd hit some rough spots, but deep down, he was always going to find his way.

"No, you're not. Maybe don't fake marry someone like I did." He gazed over at Hazel, who was filing pints. "But ease up on trying to control everything all the time."

"When did you get so wise?"

"It's my wife. I married a genius, so I had to up my game."

"I can tell." I broke and lined up my follow-up shot while his words rattled around in my brain. I had changed. I felt it. And maybe I could keep this up. Push myself a little harder to evolve the way Henri and Remy had.

After playing quietly for a few minutes, Remy spoke up. "You gonna tell me what's happening with Parker?"

I looked up. "The investigation?"

"No. Between you two."

I opened my mouth to deny it, but nothing came out.

"Tell me the truth, Paz. We've already gone deep tonight."

He was right. No sense in taking a step back after all that.

"I fell for her," I said softly. "And I don't know what to do about it."

Remy pumped his fist. "I knew it! But I won't tell anyone. I know what it's like to develop feelings for someone who is off limits."

He certainly did, though that didn't make me feel a lot better. "She's gonna solve the case and leave. And while I understand that, it's like my brain can't accept it."

"Have you talked to her?"

"About my feelings? Sort of."

"Okay, so that's a no. Maybe have a conversation, lay it out there. Is this a hookup situation or something more?"

The mere the suggestion that this was only a hookup made me angry. I frowned at him. "No. It's real." And now that I'd said it out loud, I knew with certainty. I was in love with her. Because the thought of casual, the thought of not having her forever, made me see red. Parker was mine. And I had to find a way to make it permanent.

Remy and I played pool for hours, talking about his upcoming competitions and how Hazel's research was coming along. And for the first time in a long time, I felt like myself in the presence of one of my siblings.

Hazel was stacking glasses behind the bar, and Jim, the ancient and cranky owner of the Moose, was wiping down the countertops.

"Hey, Paz," he said, "can you do me a favor? Richard left his credit card here last week. Could you take it to him?"

I opened my mouth to tell him it wouldn't be a problem, but snapped it shut again. Richard? Here? Not possible. He kept to himself when he wasn't at camp. Almost to the point of being reclusive. He was all about clean living. He never came to the Moose, and when we were kids, my mother had to drag him over for Sunday dinners with our family.

Jim slid the card over to me, and sure enough, it said *Richard Bernard*.

"Mind giving it to him? You'll see him before I do."

"Sure." I slipped it into my wallet, confused. "He was here?" I'd never seen the guy take a sip of alcohol, and between the socializing and the fried food, I couldn't imagine this place holding any appeal for him.

He nodded. "Hadn't seen him in a few years, actually. Not since that night I threw him out."

My eyes widened. I had known Richard since the day I was born. He was the epitome of self-control and respect. Not exactly the type to get thrown out of a bar.

I planted my elbows on the bar and squinted at Jim. "What the hell are you talking about?"

He didn't look up from where he was wiping down the already clean countertop. For a wannabe dive bar, the Moose was spotless. "You didn't know? Couple years ago, he came here and made a big scene. He and your dad went out back and had words."

What?

"So strange, now that I think about it. Your dad, may he rest in peace, never had any trouble with anyone."

"Especially not his best friend and best man."

"I don't know what it was about. My dishwasher heard them fighting, so I went out back. They were yelling. Things got ugly. There were some other men there too. Young ones. Maybe employees?" He looked up and tilted his head for a moment, then went back to cleaning. "I dunno. Anyway. I kicked Richard out. Told him to get outta here before I called the chief."

"And my dad?"

"Came back in, closed out his tab, and left a hefty tip. Said polite goodbyes to everyone and then left."

I was dumbfounded. My father never let himself get caught up in arguments like that. He was a sit down, have a beer and hash it out type. And with Richard? In public? It strained credulity.

"Do you remember when this was?"

He shrugged. "Couple of years ago. Not long before your dad passed. It was fall. I remember how cold it was when I went out back that night. And the Patriots had just lost to the Jets, which meant I owed Bernice and Louie free dinner when they came in for their next date night."

My mind was spinning. I pulled out my phone and found the Patriots schedule from two years ago. The Patriots had played the Jets on November twelfth.

Three weeks before my dad died.

Maybe it was unrelated. They had been friends for decades, and the business had been experiencing troubles for some time, after all. But the timing was a little too convenient.

Richard had taken leave shortly after the argument. He'd been in Florida with his sister when the accident happened. That was why Dad was driving a truck in the first place, because it was the busy season, and he was covering for Richard. Deliveries were delayed, early snow had impacted quotas, and everyone was scrambling.

It had to be connected. But how?

Richard couldn't have sabotaged the truck. He was my dad's best friend. He loved him, and I couldn't believe he'd ever hurt him. Not to mention he had been gone for two weeks when it happened.

So why were all the hairs on the back of my neck standing up?

Chapter 31
Parker

The ride up to Gagnon Camp was bumpy and long. Thankfully, Henri had all kinds of stories to share about his kids. The surly man seriously glowed when Alice, Tucker, or Goldie were mentioned. Even talking about the mundane aspects of parenthood made him smile.

He was so much more than the grumpy recluse Paz had described. Maybe marriage had changed him. Or maybe it was parenthood. Two things that had never really been on my radar until recently.

Now my brain was awash with all kinds of things I'd never given much thought to. My independence had always been so important to me. But now, it felt less like a badge of honor and more like a millstone around my neck. Maybe it was okay to depend on other people. Could I start with just one person? And could he trust me in return?

We rode companionably while Henri answered every single one of my dumb questions about logging and machines and roads. After more than two hours of weaving through the dense forest, we reached what I could only assume was the camp. The road widened into a flat, open area that housed several buildings and dozens of vehicles. A creek ran along one side, lending some natural flair to this desolate corner of the wilderness.

The buildings were wide and stout, each with a metal roof and minimal windows. The architectural vibe was definitely Soviet-era prison, but it was teeming with activity. An American flag flew proudly on a pole, men rushed around in brightly colored workwear, and country music was filtering through the air.

Every single person stopped and greeted Henri. Some with waves, but most with handshakes and hugs.

"Did you bring banana bread?" one man asked, removing his protective headphones.

Henri rolled his eyes. "I was wondering why you all were pretending to be happy to see me. Yes. Mama Gagnon made enough for all of you." He reached into the back seat and pulled out two cloth shopping totes filled with loaves wrapped neatly in aluminum foil.

"But," he said, holding up the bags as other workers walked over in search of baked goods, "there is a price. This"—he gestured to me—"is Parker. She's Paz's girlfriend."

Several eyebrows shot up at the use of that word, but Henri ignored the reactions.

"She's doing research for a book she's writing, and I expect you all to welcome her, answer any and all questions she has, and make sure her stay here is as comfortable as possible."

The assembled men nodded, some giving me friendly smiles.

After he'd handed off the baked goods, Henri took my bag and lumbered toward the main building. "This ugly-ass building is the dorm. We've also got a few small cabins, an office, and a small shop for repairs. Out back are a couple of pole barns and other structures for storing materials and fuel."

I nodded, taking it all in. This was certainly not what I had expected. Granted, my internet research showed lots of photos of men in old-timey suits cutting trees with long saws and floating logs down rivers. Not exactly twenty-first century methods. I supposed this scenery shouldn't have come as a surprise.

"This cabin is yours," he said over his shoulder. "It's not fancy, but my dad built it for my mom after they got married. She used to come up here and stay with him."

He unlocked the door and led me into a small home. A wood stove that was already putting off heat stood in one corner, and a large bed took up the other. It was covered with a lovely handmade quilt. A small table and loveseat were on the other side, where one small door led to what I assumed was a bathroom and another to a sizable closet.

"Does this get used?" A framed photo on the wall drew my attention. It was Frank and Loraine on their wedding day. He was wearing a suit, and she was wearing a simple white dress. Her hair was feathered and enormous in the way women wore it during the early '80s.

"Not really. But we clean it and keep it warm in case my mom wants to visit. She hasn't since Dad died. But they spent a lot of time here together. I hope that she'll want to return someday."

"The man built her a cabin for her occasional visits? Seems extreme."

Henri laughed. "You didn't know my dad. Gagnon men? We love with everything we have. And my dad was devoted to my mother. Lived every day of his life working to make her happy. And he wouldn't have had it any other way."

I smiled, trying to wrap my head around that kind of devotion. That entire experience was so far removed from my childhood it was hard to comprehend.

"But you should know that, dating a Gagnon and all." He winked.

A jolt of panic ran through me.

Did he know? That our fake relationship wasn't actually fake? That I had been waking up next to his brother every morning and was already concerned that I wouldn't be able to sleep without being wrapped in his strong arms?

Or was he joking about our fake relationship cover story? Shit. My paranoia was at an all-time high.

"I've got to head a few miles north to a felling site for a bit. Follow me to the office, and I'll get you a radio so we can keep in touch. The dormitory building has a large kitchen, and we've got coffee brewing twenty-four hours a day. You can work wherever you'd like, and feel free to poke around the office. I'll leave you my keys."

An hour later, I was settled in the kitchen, drinking hot coffee and poring through the most recent batch of personnel files Ellen had helpfully found for me.

I caught myself skimming over details because I was preoccupied with missing Paz. It had only been a few hours, but I wanted him near me. Being out here in the middle of nowhere without him was overwhelming, not to mention I'd gotten used to bouncing ideas off him as I researched, so going through these files alone felt more tedious than it should have.

In addition to being hot, great in bed, and a decent cook, he had become a trusted thought partner. That wasn't something I had ever wanted before, but now I couldn't live without it.

My eyes were starting to blur and words were running together on the page when a stocky man with patchy stubble and a backward hat poured himself a cup of coffee, then dropped to the seat across from me.

"Want a piece of my Mama Gagnon banana bread? I'm happy to share."

"That depends," I said. "Does it have chocolate chips?"

He reared back in mock offense. "This is America," he groused, though his friendly eyes sparkled, and his ruddy cheeks gave away his good humor. "Of course it does."

"Okay, good."

He held a hand out over the table. "I'm Ace."

"Parker," I said, taking it.

Ace turned out to be the chatty sort. He was in his late twenties and had been working out here for seven years. He'd recently been promoted to crane operator, he'd boasted with a genuine grin, which was a designation that took some training and licensing to accomplish.

Together, we put a dent in the banana bread. "This company is my home. I was such a shithead when I was younger. Bouncing around from job to job, partying too much, getting into all kinds of bad shit. But my friend's uncle worked here and hooked us up."

"That's great."

"Yeah. Still can't thank Richard enough for setting us up."

I perked up at the mention of Richard Bernard. He was still an enigma I was trying to figure out.

"I was such a fuck-up. I wasn't used to such hard work. But I liked it. Being out here, breathing fresh air and actually accomplishing something beats the hell out of serving fast food, you know? And Richard has been a mentor to me. He's the one who promoted me and pushed me to go for my operator's license."

"And your friend?"

"Worked here on and off, but it never stuck. Richard's upset about it. Always wanted Norman to have a good life."

I smiled. Ace was a good kid, and while I had very little interest in operating a crane, I did want to know more about his friend Norman.

Turning back to my computer, I pulled up timesheets from a few years ago. "Is this him?" I asked. "Norman Bernard. Birthday April thirteenth, 1995?"

He nodded, his mouth full.

"It says here he last worked for Gagnon four years ago."

Ace shook his head and took a sip of his coffee. "No, ma'am. I've seen him around camp off and on the last couple of years. Pretty sure he was here within the last year or two."

My eye twitched as I typed, capturing every word out of Ace's mouth.

"Yeah. Richard sometimes has him up here doin' odd jobs and helping out during the busy season."

"Recently? Are you sure?"

He pursed his lips and squinted like he was digging through memories. "Yes. I keep my distance. I've got a great job and a fiancé now. I'm not looking for trouble. He's gotten pretty hard over the years. Mixed up with bikers. Lots of ink."

Schooling my features and twining my hands in my lap, I suppressed the urge to hug Ace. He didn't know it, but he was giving me absolute gold right now.

I scratched my head, playing dumb. "Huh. That's so weird. He's not in any records from the last couple of years. And it says he was terminated four years ago. The file says erratic behavior, being late, mishandling equipment."

"Sounds like him." He nodded with a frown. "We were both full-time employees, getting benefits and the whole thing. I kept moving up, and he got fired. But sometimes people come back for seasonal work."

"But there are no records."

Ace smiled. "That's normal. Some guys, usually the more, shall we say, unstable ones, like to be paid in cash. Every winter, a handful will show up looking for work, and depending on how far behind we are, Richard might hire them."

"But doesn't the company have to train them?"

"Most people around here practically grew up doing this. They know the ropes. Plus, they're not the guys driving trucks or operating machinery. They put the straps on the trees after they're felled, run wood chippers to get rid of brush, drive the trash to town so we don't attract bears, that kind of stuff."

"Ah." I nodded, still typing.

"The last several times Norman was hanging around here, another guy was with him. Big dude. Older, with a gray beard. He's a biker. Don't know his real name. Everybody called him by his nickname." He closed his eyes and rubbed his temples. "I wanna say it's Grinder."

I was furiously typing when Ace's eyes narrowed. "You puttin' this all in your book?"

I paused and gave him my best disarming smile. "It's going to be a series of books, actually. And I like to do really thorough research so I can make things as realistic as possible."

He nodded. "Okay, good. 'Cause I don't want Norman or Grinder to know I was talking about them. They have connections to some scary people."

"I understand. This is all background so I can start getting the stories going in my head. Sorry. I should have made that clear."

He checked his watch. "Break's over. I gotta head back out. Good luck with your books."

I waved him off and immediately cursed these woods for the lack of Wi-Fi and cell signal. Because I needed to run Grinder through every possible database on earth.

And more importantly, I needed to tell Paz. Norman had been up here, and Richard had allowed it. I had a very bad feeling about all of this.

Chapter 32
Parker

As soon as Henri's truck stopped in the driveway, I was jumping out and running into the farmhouse. It had only been two days, but I missed him. The feeling was so foreign to me. For most of my life, I'd prided myself on being fiercely independent, but it was hard to deny how downright painful it was to wake up without him next to me.

And I had so much to tell him. Not only about the investigation. I'd learned so much about his business and family and background. Being out there in the woods opened my eyes to where he'd come from and how he saw the world.

I could hear the piano from the driveway. He was playing, clearly working something out, and it made me even more desperate to see him.

"You're home." He met me in the kitchen.

I dropped my bag and jumped into his arms.

"Fuck, I missed you," he growled between kisses.

"It was only two days."

"Don't care." He carried me toward the stairs. "I didn't trip over any shoes. It was so sad."

I gave him a light smack. "Always talking shit."

He kissed my neck. "Let's get naked."

"I have so much to tell you."

"Great. Naked first, talk later." His rational brain had clearly left the building, and I was dealing with caveman Paz, which was usually good news for my lady parts.

But as he carried me from the kitchen, an Amazon package on the counter caught my attention.

"Wait. Put me down."

With a huff of annoyance, he lowered me to the ground.

"It came!" I cried as I tore open the shipping bag. "Yes!"

He stalked toward me, and I ran, hiding the delivery behind my back.

"I will catch you," he said, prowling my way.

I giggled, pressing myself up against the living room wall with my hands still behind my back. "First I have to give you your present."

He walked toward me, taking his shirt off and throwing it onto the floor. Fuck. The way he was looking at me, like he was going to devour me, made my thighs shake.

"It's a very romantic gift," I said.

He slapped his palms against the wall, caging me in, and planted his lips on mine.

I placed the hat on his head and kissed him back fiercely.

With one more nip at my bottom lip, he stepped back and took off the hat. "Stud Muffin?" He inspected the trucker-style hat like it was on fire.

"Yup." I smacked his ass. "You're my stud muffin. Now let's get those pants off."

I unhooked his belt and jeans and pushed them down, along with his boxers. I was a woman on a mission, and more than anything, I wanted to tell him with my body what I couldn't with words—that this was real and scary and exhilarating.

Slowly, I dropped to my knees, admiring the thick erection standing before me. "And now I'm going to show you how much I missed you."

"Parker," he said, "you don't have to."

"Put the hat on. I want to."

He put it back on his head and looked down at me with hooded eyes. This was right where I wanted him. I ran my fingers along his cock, taking in every ridge and vein. It was even more spectacular than I remembered.

I gripped it firmly and lowered my mouth.

"*Fuck.*" He groaned, throwing his head back until it hit the wall. As I swirled my tongue along the ridge, licking the bead of wetness off the tip, his hand slid down to my head and held me gently.

I breathed through my nose as I work my mouth over him, taking him far back and swallowing. The incomprehensible mutters and noises he made confirmed that he was loving the attention.

With one hand, I tugged on his balls while I picked up the pace, lips and tongue swirling and working his shaft.

His grip tightened, caging my ears, while he jerked his hips. I reveled in the power I possessed. In my ability to make him wild like this. Stoic, buttoned-up Paz shaking with lust thrilled me to my core.

And speaking of core, I was drenched. Figured that the one time I actually wore panties, I soaked them right through.

Above me, his face twisted as I picked up the pace, anticipating his release. But before I could finish the job, he pulled me up and hauled me toward the kitchen.

He set me on my feet and stripped off my jeans and panties, then lifted me up, carrying me silently and with total focus before placing me gently on the closed lid of the piano.

Before I knew what was happening, he had two fingers inside me. At the initial breach, I cried out, already so damn close.

"Yes," he growled, pulling me forward until my ass teetered on the edge. "Seeing you laid out on my piano? Fuck. I've fantasized about this so many times." He didn't slow. "You're ready for me, aren't you? I was so close, but I'm not coming without you."

All my nerve endings were on fire as he notched himself at my entrance.

"Shit." He took a step back and brought his attention back to my face. "I gotta run upstairs."

"I have an IUD," I said, angry at being denied what I needed. "And I've been tested."

"Me too. And it's, uh, been a while."

Mouth agape, I stared in surprise, but I slammed it shut again and nodded. "I've never."

"Neither have I."

"But I want you to be my first," I said, taking off my T-shirt and making quick work of my bra.

He bent down to take one needy nipple into his mouth. "Tell me you want nothing between us. Use the words, Parker."

"I want it." I gasped. "I want you bare."

Before I could say another word, he grabbed my hips and pushed into me. It was just forceful enough to make me grab his shoulders for balance. He must have hit the keys as he surged inside, the clanging noises reverberating through the empty room.

"I'm not gonna last long," he said through gritted teeth. "I'll make it up to you later."

"I don't care." I moaned, feeling him hit entirely new spots with this angle. "I want you wild and unleashed."

"Don't hold back, Parker. Tell me exactly what you need."

With my arms extended behind me and my palms flat against the fine lacquered wood of the piano, I propped myself up. I arched my back, letting my head drop as I climbed higher with every one of his thrusts. Fuck. I could feel every single inch of him.

"I need you," I rasped as my muscles contracted around him.

"Mine," he growled. "Only mine. Tell me I'm the only one who gets you like this."

"Only you, Paz."

His hands slid down to my thighs, spreading them as wide as they could go and thrusting deeper. "That's it." He groaned, his movements becoming erratic. "Take it all. Take everything. Look at me while you take every inch of my cock."

And I was lost. The wave that hit me crashed hard and fast, sending me into a spiral of shudders and cries that seemed to go on forever. I clung to his shoulders as my body trembled.

As I spiraled, he twitched inside me. The slightest movements were incredible with nothing between us. And it was in that moment that I knew what it was to be possessed.

When I finally came back to consciousness, I opened my eyes, and there, in front of me, Paz was sweaty and smiling.

He dropped his head to my shoulder. "Tell me," he said, catching his breath. "Tell me what I need to do to make you mine. I'll do anything to have you forever."

This was too good. Too right. The way he made me feel. I was such a goner. And it was time to stop fighting it. Because I wasn't *falling* for him. I had already fallen.

Chapter 33
Pascal

"God, I missed you," I said into her hair, rolling her over so I could see her face. "It felt like you were gone for a week."

She nuzzled against my shoulder. "Same here. I have so much to tell you. And so much work to do."

She sat up and scanned the room for her clothes.

I pulled her back down. "I've got a lot to tell you too. But getting you naked was my top priority." I kissed her deeply, relishing the feel of her body relaxing as my hands roamed over her smooth skin. "And now I have to get the piano tuned. Not that I mind."

"Was that really your fantasy?" She tucked a strand of dark hair behind her ear.

I nuzzled her neck. "Yes. I thought about it so many times. Next time, I'll eat your pussy up there first."

She groaned and pulled me closer. This was so perfect. I didn't want to ever move.

The past day had been torture. Roaming around my empty

house had reminded me of how gray and awful my life had been before Parker showed up and turned things upside down.

I rolled, pinning her beneath my hips, and sucked gently on her pulse point.

"Seriously," she said, squirming beneath me. "We've got so much to talk about."

"Hmm." I kissed across her collarbone, loving the way her chest heaved as I did. "Let's talk about how I'm totally crazy about you. It's literally testing the bounds of my sanity."

"Really?" She dragged her nails down my back and gave my ass a hard squeeze.

"Yes. I want you here with me all the time. When you're here, annoying me with your chatter and your bras and your ponytail, I feel like things are the way they're supposed to be. Like I'm normal and healthy and sane, and life could be amazing." I kissed her jawline and pulled back. "I'm not the angry, repressed son of a bitch I usually am when you're here."

She blinked up at me. "That was oddly beautiful. But I need caffeine before I'll go another round."

"Fine," I grumbled, heaving myself up but dipping down quickly to bite her nipple for good measure. "I'll start the coffee maker."

Half-dressed, we stumbled our way to the kitchen, where my laptop and papers were spread out everywhere. Apparently, Parker was rubbing off on me in more ways than one.

"We should talk," she said between kisses.

With my hand halfway up her thigh, I froze. Those were literally the worst words in the English language.

I dropped my hand and took a step back. "About what?"

Her eyes were on the floor, and her usual brisk confidence was missing. "I guess... oh, shit, this is so hard." She toyed with the hem of her T-shirt and shifted from foot to foot. "I've gotten pretty attached to you over the past month..."

I bit the inside of my cheeks to keep from smiling too broadly as she peeked up at me. She was adorable when she was nervous.

"And, well, you know all about me and my career change and my family and shitty childhood. My baggage is all out there."

I nodded.

"So before I'm in too deep. I wanna know. What's your deal? Who hurt you?"

While her question certainly threw me, it was the earnest delivery that really knocked me on my ass. Because I could see it in her eyes. She didn't want to get hurt.

She *had* always been honest with me. About her shitty ex and her dad and how hard it had been to climb the ladder at the state police. I wanted to reassure her, wanted to give in to her every request, crack myself open and reveal every shitty part of me and beg for her affection anyway.

But how? I didn't even know where to begin.

"Because this." She waved a hand at me. "This whole stoic, closed off, feelings are for the weak facade." She licked her lips and searched my face. "It reeks of coping mechanism to me. So if we're sleeping together and in a fake relationship—"

"Stop right there. I think we both know this has grown beyond sleeping together."

"Okay, if we're in a relationship of indeterminate reality..."

"Better."

"Then let me in." She tapped my chest and looked up at me expectantly.

I chuckled. God, I was totally smitten with how her mind worked. "I thought you were a skilled interrogator?"

She raised one eyebrow in response. The look made me want to take her over my knee and spank her.

"I am. And I have extensive training in psychology. In my expert opinion, it seems that you're used to being the smartest guy in the room. And you wear your self-control and stoicism like badges of honor instead of the clear trauma responses they are."

There it was—the smart mouth and sassy attitude that had me hard as a rock every fucking time. Sadly, I had the distinct feeling I wouldn't be inside her until I had sufficiently bared my soul.

"I hate to disappoint you, but there's no story here." I attempted to turn up the charm to divert this line of inquiry. Fucking would be so much more interesting.

Instead of answering me, she turned around and pulled a coffee mug from the cabinet, letting my T-shirt ride up, exposing that delicious ass. She poured a cup, blew on it, and took her time taking a sip, all the while ignoring me. It was infuriating how she could control the pace of a conversation like this.

She placed the mug on the counter and took a hair elastic off her wrist. Just as placidly, she took her time gathering up her hair on top of her head into a messy knot.

The shirt rode up again, this time giving me a tiny glimpse of her delicious pussy. I clenched my fists and shifted on my feet, knowing this was a losing battle.

"Sweet, sweet Pascal. I know your family, your hometown, your job. I've seen where you came from. So while I know how badly you want to bend me over this lovely quartz countertop right now, I have to insist we do a little talking first."

Fuck, now I was sweating. She was clearly a witch sent to

tempt me. But instead of walking away, attempting to save my sanity, I opened my mouth.

"It's not an interesting story," I said, grabbing my own mug. If we were gonna talk, I'd need to caffeinate. "For as long as I remember, I wanted to do big things. Get far away from the predictable small-town life path."

She nodded.

"And so I avoided commitments and attachments and focused on money and prestige. Getting my degrees, getting the right job, moving up, and making more and more. I never wanted to be the guy with a nine-to-five and a wife and kids. I thought I was better than that."

Back then, climbing the ladder felt like the only path forward. Pulling all-nighters and ping-ponging around the globe closing deals was natural. Everyone I knew then lived like this.

"I lived a big life in the city. Deals and travel and cars and girls. But then my dad died, and everything fell apart. And I realized that I had done the exact thing I had tried to avoid. I was nobody doing nothing. My existence was empty and superficial, and it was too late to fix."

She placed her mug down and grabbed my hand. "It's not too late."

"But it is. My dad is gone. I lost out on so many years with him. And so much advice I wish I'd been around for him to impart to me. All I wanted was to avoid turning into him. And I succeeded. But it's all empty. My siblings are growing and leading a productive life. Even my mom is finding her purpose. But I'm stuck."

I pulled her close, tucking her into my chest. This was the opposite of empty. With Parker, even the most mundane things felt so significant. "Honestly, I've spent most of my life alone. I always assumed it would stay that way. I had casual relationships because it was convenient and fun. At least for a while. And now I'm back in Lovewell, older, maybe a little wiser. Realizing that it's okay that there isn't one perfect person out there for me."

She pulled away from me. She didn't say anything. Just picked up her mug and took a quiet sip of coffee. Then she carefully placed the mug on the counter, wound up, and punched me in the shoulder.

"Ow," I said, jumping back and rubbing the spot. Shit, she was strong.

"You expect me to believe that shit? There is no right person for you? That you're empty and stuck and there's no hope? Talk about self-pity bullshit."

Jesus, she was feisty. "You don't have to believe me. I know it in my bones. I'm an asshole. I'm selfish, inflexible, and obsessed with work. Not exactly a dream date."

She turned around and leaned on the counter, putting her head in her hands. "You're gonna make me say it, aren't you?" she asked between her fingers.

I cocked my head to the side. Because I had no idea what "it" was.

She stood tall and rounded on me. "You are making excuses. I've been your roommate and fake girlfriend for what, a month now? And I don't see any of those things. Want to know what I see? I see someone intensely devoted to his family, at the expense of his own dreams and feelings. Someone who gives of himself every day for the betterment of his community. Who goes to extremes to protect the people he cares about."

I stood, frozen, my heart in my throat. She didn't see me as some closed-off prick who used women and alienated people?

She poked me in the chest. At this rate, I'd be covered in

bruises from this woman. "And selfish? You visit your mother constantly. You bankroll every need this town can come up with, and they don't even know it."

I shrugged. "I'm a Gagnon. It's what we do."

She poked me again, even harder this time. We were standing chest to chest, and she was fuming. God dammit, the image made me wonder whether I should make a run for it or drop to one knee and propose. Parker saw me. Really saw me. And it terrified the living shit out of me.

"Nope. Not buying it. You don't have to stay here if you hate it."

"I don't hate it."

"Then why all the resentment? Why do you lash out and push away the people you care about?"

Pain and shame and sadness bubbled up inside me, right along with hope and fear. And as much as I wanted to push them all back down like I'd done for the last thirty-five years, I couldn't do it. Parker, standing in front of me looking beautiful and raw and like she really, deeply cared about me, made me want to be that guy. The guy who could be good enough for her.

"Because I'm angry at myself," I said finally. "I hated this place, and I got out of here as fast as I could after high school. I was ashamed of this tiny town. Ashamed of how generations of my family had made their living. I wanted a white-collar job and a fancy imported car, and I didn't want to be out in the woods every day."

She brushed a finger across my cheek. Shit. I was tearing up.

"There is nothing wrong with wanting to pave your own way."

I shook my head. She didn't get it. "But I pushed all this

away. I detached. Wasn't there for my parents or my siblings. And then my dad died. I'll never get to be close to him. We'll never have the relationship I always wanted. I will forever be the child he didn't have a connection with."

The tears fell freely now. I wasn't a crier. Hadn't cried since Dad's funeral, and that was in the privacy of my own car. Fuck. I should stop. I should be ashamed to cry in front of Parker.

But this was necessary. I had to tell her my secrets and break down in front of her in order to do this right. To build something solid with her.

Because I desperately wanted that. The very thing I had never allowed myself to want. And if I didn't get past all this other shit, I'd never have it.

"I never met your dad, but it's obvious he loved you as much as he loved your siblings. Your mom loves you so much, she puts up with your overprotectiveness. And your brothers and Adele? They respect you, despite the shit that comes out of your mouth." She wrapped her arms around my neck, pressing her head to my chest.

Closing my eyes, I tucked my chin and breathed her in, let her scent wash over me.

"If you were my brother, I'd kick your teeth in for the way you speak to Remy. But he idolizes you. You just can't see it."

She held me close, never wavering as I cried in my kitchen. I kissed the top of her head as my tears fell into her hair. Everything hurt but somehow felt lighter at the same time. Parker was slowly undoing all the knots I'd been tying myself into for all these years.

"You can always apologize, you know." She looked up at me with a small smile.

If it meant she'd look at me like this again, I'd do anything she asked me to.

"And above everything, it's time to figure out how to forgive yourself. You're allowed to change your mind and shift priorities. Just because you hated it here when you were a kid doesn't mean you can't love it now. Maybe you do want to be here, but you don't *want* to want that."

Most days, my only priority was the family business. Keeping the trees falling and the trucks running would provide for my family and keep them safe. But she was right. I had been shifting and changing over the past two years. I'd been stuck.

"The lumber CFO who is close with his family and dotes on his niece and nephew? You know him? The guy who lives in a big farmhouse and loves to hike? That guy doesn't fit with the vision of your life you've had in your head for all these years. And now you're scared. Scared that you wasted all this time on something stupid and unfulfilling."

I dipped low and kissed her. I needed her lips on my lips and her hands on my skin. To ground me and reassure me that all the things I was feeling were real.

She was right. My situation had changed. My life had been turned upside down. And it turned out that all the things I thought I wanted were making me miserable.

And as I kissed her, I vowed to be better. To give more of myself to my family. Because maybe, just maybe, I could turn all of this into something special.

Chapter 34
Parker

"Okay. We've got Grinder, a.k.a. Frank Demers, dual US and Canadian citizen."

I was lying on the couch with my laptop while Paz stood at the stove. Whatever he was making smelled delicious. We had been up almost all night talking, making love, and strategizing.

"How does he fit in?"

"He has a record. Did some time in Montreal for drugs about ten years back. Known affiliates include some notable criminals across the border."

"So he's our link."

"Possibly. If Stinger is indeed Norman, then we've got some really good connections. Because he's not a kingpin."

"Definitely not. He's a henchman at best."

"This Grinder guy's a biker who's done lumber work and also has connections across the border. This all tracks with our theory. Now we need to determine how your dad fit in. What did he know? And who knew that he knew?"

Paz sat next to me, placing a mug of coffee on the table. "It's hard to believe Richard could be involved." He shook his head.

"I don't have evidence that he was." My heart broke for Paz and his family. Reliving this, wondering and worrying, it was clearly taking a toll. "I'm just saying that he could be how these guys gained access. Think about it. Richard goes to Florida to help his sister. He runs camp and is loyal to the Gagnons and the business. But his nephew is not. He's a wash out who got into drugs. But he knows his way around up there, and he's got access. He's always welcome to take on work because of who his uncle is."

Paz nodded. "So Norman is working for traffickers, and he takes advantage and uses this access when his uncle is gone."

"Yes. And the traffickers likely include Mitch Hebert and his rival lumber company."

He balled his hands into fists. "Fucking Heberts. As much as I would love to see the fucker rot in jail forever, if he had anything to do with my dad or Henri, then he's not going to make it that far."

"There's a bigger question." I bit my lip. This was the hard part. "We're very close to proving that Norman Bernard and Mitch Hebert are engaged in a criminal conspiracy to traffic opioids across the US/Canadian border."

He nodded. "Should we go to the police?"

I hedged. "Yes and no. On the one hand, this info could be helpful. But on the other, it's not confirmed."

"Okay..."

"But here's the bigger issue. If we show our hand to law enforcement now, they'll act. If they come down on Hebert and Norman and the others, it will compromise our ability to find out what happened to your dad. They'll likely be interrogated or arrested, and everyone else will go underground."

His eyes widened. "Public safety is more important. As close as we are, I need to keep my family and this community safe. If anything else happened, I could never live with myself."

My heart clenched. He was such a good man.

"What do we do? Who do we contact?"

I tugged on my ponytail. "We could go local, but they have limited resources."

"Plus the chief is in the Heberts' pocket."

I shrugged. All I'd been able to pin on Chief Souza was laziness. It was entirely possible that this had been going on under his nose for a long time, but the alternative was downright scary. "If so, he could tip them off and cause more problems."

"And there could be other officers working with them. Other guys who could tip them off, even if Souza isn't involved. There's a reason they've been getting away with this for so long."

I sighed. "Our best option is for me to go to Bryce and the FBI and share everything."

"Will he take it seriously?"

"Not sure. Without evidence confirming Norman is Stinger and Mitch is actively participating in the trafficking, he might not follow up on it."

"So let's get it. The evidence. And then turn everything over. "Let's see what we can dig up over the next couple of days. If we're gonna do this, we need to know the FBI is going to crack down and keep everyone safe."

He paled and focused on something over her shoulder, probably turning over the realization that his family could be in danger again. And that he would be powerless to prevent it.

Because no number of batteries and no amount of bottled water could protect against this. We needed to finish it. We had to ensure that those responsible went to jail for a really long time.

He was deep in his head now, if his slumped shoulders were any indication.

"Stop," I said, placing my hand on his chest, feeling his heart pound beneath my fingers. "We're close and making progress every day. As hard as this is, we've got to stay objective."

He placed his hand over mine, and we stood like that for a minute.

"I'm so glad you're here," he said softly.

I put my laptop down and crawled into his lap.

"And I'm not going anywhere." I wished I could make this better. But I couldn't. His father was gone, and the best I could do was help him achieve the closure he desperately needed.

He wrapped his arms around me and sniffled, so I held him tighter. Paz always presented as the cool, unemotional type. But now that we had peeled back the grouchy exterior, there was so much more there.

And he shared it with me. That realization made my heart flutter.

"You do not need to clean," I said, scooping up my files to save them from his manic scrubbing.

"Of course I do. We've got a guest arriving in"—he flicked his wrist and checked his watch, and damn, was it sexy. Since when was checking the time so hot?—"two hours."

"It's only Liv." The timing was not ideal. But when she called an hour ago, she was already on her way. Granted, I had begged her to visit several times since I'd been here, but I assumed we'd agree on a date before she hopped in the car and made the drive.

Paz and I were balancing on a precipice. With one another, as well as with the investigation. And the next few days were key. We couldn't sit on this information forever, and we were so close to putting the pieces together.

So the arrival of my best friend would throw a bit of a wrench into the plan. But knowing Liv, she'd get a burst of inspiration and spend the entire time writing furiously. Or she'd immediately pick up on what was happening between Paz and me, and I'd have to face the music. Because it was official: I was absolutely falling for him.

But at this moment, when he was in full on grouch mode, it was a bit easier to be objective.

"Have you seen my AirPods?" I asked, searching through my bag.

"I thought you found them yesterday."

"Yes," I said, dumping the contents onto the counter. "I found them in the linen closet. But then I lost them again."

"This house is four thousand square feet," he said, gathering up what looked like a sweater, a pair of sunglasses, and several empty sparkling water cans. "How do you generate this much mess?"

I took the stuff out of his hands. "Deep breath."

But he was in full-on rant mode. "Dishes in the sink. Bras hanging from every doorknob. Papers everywhere. And that doesn't include all your girl shit. The makeup and scrubs and lotions."

I put my arms around him and gave his ass a firm squeeze. "Liv is going to love you, and everything is going to be fine."

He frowned down at me. But it was a sexy frown, if such a thing existed. "I'm gonna have to start punishing you. Every time you're naughty and make a mess," he growled, fire flashing in his dark eyes.

I gave his ass another squeeze. Because I knew exactly how to improve his mood. "Then I'm going to be a lot less motivated to clean up."

He tipped my chin up. Eyes ablaze. "Not sure if I should spank you or make you suck my cock."

I licked my lips. "Neither is much of a punishment. You know I love giving head. And I'd much rather blow you than vacuum."

His eyes bulged, and that cool confidence wavered. "Then I suppose we can come to some kind of arrangement."

I trailed my fingers down his chest before sinking to my knees. "Hmm. Then I should probably give you a preview of my skills."

He threw his head back and groaned. "You can make a mess anytime."

Chapter 35
Parker

Of all the people to arrive in Lovewell and make herself right at home, the last person I expected was Liv. But here she was, charming patrons in the diner, tossing her red hair around, and soaking up all the charming small-town details.

She had taken one look at me and one look at Paz and demanded to know what was going on. So I shoved her into my car and headed to the diner, hoping the greasy food would subdue her curiosity.

"Holy sexual tension, Batman!" she said, sliding into the vinyl booth. "Don't lie to me. I know you're hitting that. The fucking steam between you! I could have written on the windows with my finger." She fanned herself with the menu. "I need my laptop. I should be writing a romance right now."

"You're ridiculous."

"Yeah, you're right. If I were to switch genres, I wouldn't go for a sappy small-town love story. It'd definitely be a why choose. A handful of bear shifter lumbersnacks for sure." She tapped her chin. "Ooh, maybe moose shifters. Not sure that's been done."

"Gross."

"Do not yuck my yum, lady. I've got all kinds of recs for you when you decide to broaden your literary horizons." She scooted forward in the booth and dropped her elbows to the table. "Tell me all about it. I imagine this"—she waved an arm, indicating the diner—"is the best we've got in this one-horse town, so let's get a milkshake, then give me all the dirty details about the lumbersuit."

"They have a bar."

"Ooh, a seedy dive?"

"Sort of. It's not what you're picturing, I'm sure. Not fisherman and dockworkers."

"A lumbersnack dive? I'm down for checking that out tonight. But if you do not start talking right now, I'm gonna ask all these nice, nosey people about your sex life instead."

I glared at her. There were only two people who truly had my back in this life: My mother, who I would do anything for. And Liv. She had taken one look at me at the start of our freshman year of college and decided we'd be best friends. And we had been for sixteen years. In all that time, I had never once doubted her loyalty or her love for me.

We didn't compete with one another, and we didn't get jealous. Ours was a friendship born out of mutual weirdness and a desire to be understood.

She was the creative free spirit with a goth edge, and I was the goody-two-shoes who was afraid of her own shadow. We were both only children with divorced parents who'd bonded over our mutual love of Britney Spears and Jane Austen.

Before I could sate her curiosity, Bernice wandered over, eyebrows almost touching her beehive while she took Liv in.

Waist-length red hair, flowy black dress, multiple earrings in each ear, and a massive evil eye pendant around her neck. Not to mention the black eyeliner thick enough to line a parking lot.

We placed our orders while Bernice gawked. Liv was gorgeous, and in a town like this, her style was light-years past unique. While I had spent a lot of my life blending in, Liv had an innate understanding that standing out was her only option. And she embraced it wholeheartedly.

She leaned forward. "It dawned on me that the people here think you're me." She grinned, giddy at the prospect. There was nothing a dramatic soul like Liv's loved more than role playing and general shenanigans.

I shook my head. "They think I'm L.T. Shipman. They think I'm up here researching a series of books set in a small logging town."

"Ooh. I knew that was a great idea. The woods, chainsaws? Creepy as fuck. I could definitely work in a psycho sexual angle." She tapped the table rhythmically with her hands, signaling that she was coming up with a book idea.

"Okay, okay, okay. But up here, I'm the writer, got it?"

She smiled broadly. "And what do I do?"

"I dunno. What do you want to do?" I regretted the question the second the words left my mouth.

She fluffed her hair. "Obviously, my character needs a backstory. I need to commit fully in order to convince the townsfolk of Lovewell, Maine, of my identity." She tapped her chin, a maniacal look in her eyes. "Hmm. I'm a disgraced socialite. Cast away by my blue blood family because I fell in love with the help. A chauffeur?"

"Isn't that from *Downton Abbey*?"

"Oh shit, yeah. I'll work on it."

"I really missed your dramatic ass," I said, squeezing her hand on top of the table.

She blew me a kiss, but before she could respond, her eyes widened, and her mouth dropped open. Leaning halfway across the table, she whisper-yelled, "Lumberhottie alert!"

"Liv," I hissed. "Keep it down. The population here is smaller than that of your Pilates studio."

Casually, I spun so I could get a look at who she was drooling over. Two men were entering the diner, one of which was Remy Gagnon.

I gave him a small wave. "That lumberjack is married, and he's Paz's younger brother."

"No. Not the skinny one. The thick plank of hardwood."

"That's Remy's brother-in-law, Dylan," I said. "I don't know him, but he's a teacher."

She waved a French fry wildly. "Oh shit. I am hot for that teacher."

I stepped on her foot under the table. "Tone it down. I think he has a girlfriend."

"Hope it's not serious. Should I go say hello?" She was tilting her head so she didn't lose sight of him.

"No. Eat your grilled cheese."

"I'm just saying. I drove all the way up here to see you, but you're distracted by the lumbersuit. Maybe I need a distraction too." She craned her neck, and I swear she licked her lips.

I threw a fry at her. "I'm not distracted."

"Your pupils dilate every time I mention him. He's clearly dickmatized you. No doubt it's an excellent dick. A big, strong axe."

"Please stop."

"I'm only getting started. The muscles, the beard, the weirdly sterile house. I sense a freak with control issues. Probably dominant but likes to be submissive sometimes too. I bet he goes down on you all the time."

My face heated. Jesus. Liv could crack me open and read me like a damn book.

She raised one eyebrow and huffed out a smug laugh. "He fuck you outside yet?"

"No," I said, inspecting my sandwich.

"Liar."

"Does in a barn count?" I grumbled.

"*Bingo.* Knew it." She pounded her fists on the table, garnering annoyed looks from everyone in the diner.

She took a big bite of grilled cheese and blinked at me, waiting for me to spill.

But where did I even begin? I was here to work, and the stakes were impossibly high already. And it wasn't only sex. If it was, I could compartmentalize.

Our connection was more complex than that. I wanted a future with him. Or at the very least, a shot at a future with him.

But I lived in Portland, and there was this whole pesky murder investigation. Our chemistry was so hot and so intense, but was this even sustainable? And could I survive if we couldn't make it work?

"I'm conflicted," I said, finally breaking the silence.

Liv frowned. "Babe, I'm here to help. Anything you need. Is the sex bad? Better come home with me tomorrow, then. No use sticking around for bad dick."

"No, it's not bad at all."

"You seem pretty upset for someone getting good dick on the regular."

I squeezed my eyes shut, already regretting what I was about to tell her. "Book sex," I said softly.

"Book sex? For real?"

I nodded. Yes. That was the best way to describe it. Sex with Paz? It was the desperate, sweaty, can't get enough, have to have you kind of sex. And our connection? It was like I needed him as badly as I needed my next breath. Where being separated was painful, and the sound of his voice alone instantly made my day better.

"Oh shit. They serve booze in this place? Mama needs a cocktail." She scanned the diner, probably searching for Bernice, who, in typical fashion, had dropped our plates of food and disappeared.

"You found yourself a real-life unicorn? A guy who fucks you like a book boyfriend. Like you're the most desirable woman on Planet Earth, and he will drop dead if he's not inside you, giving you orgasm after orgasm?"

I nodded and smiled weakly. "Pretty much."

"Okay. This is what you need to do." She sat up straight and locked her gaze on me. "You have to marry him. Does this Podunk town have a jewelry store? Let's go buy a ring so you can *lock it down* immediately."

"Stop it. You know I don't want to get married. And I don't know if these feelings are real or only the result of being orgasm drunk for the last two weeks."

"You're clearly in love with him. You just don't want to admit it because then you'd have to deal with all your baggage and trust issues."

I glared at her. Once again, Liv saw right through my shit. It was a quality I usually loved, but was it too much to ask for her to go along with my delusions and let me pretend I hadn't fallen in love with Paz?

"You know," she said, looking out the front window of the diner. "I've changed my mind. I love it here. You should move here. Ride that good lumberdick and live happily ever after." With a sad smile, she cupped my cheek. "I'll miss you, but I'll never stand in the way of true love and earth-shattering orgasms."

Liv was right, as always. If this was it, if this was the real deal, then I'd have to consider moving here. This town, the business, they were part of Paz's DNA, no matter how much he tried to deny it. And I would never take that away from him. Relationships may have been strained, but his family was here, and they loved him. This town supported him more than he realized. Not being lucky enough to have had that myself, I could see how rare and precious it was.

Clearing my throat, I braced myself, ready to be the most honest I'd ever been. I'd put it out there, tell Liv that I wanted to try for real.

But before I could, the bells above the door chimed, and in walked Mitch Hebert. The motherfucker in the flesh.

"You okay?" Liv asked, her eyes swimming with concern.

I nodded woodenly as ideas churned in my head. This was the opening I had been waiting for. While not strictly legal, and certainly not admissible, a plan had been brewing in my mind for some time. And the Apple AirTag I had purchased a couple of weeks ago was beckoning from the depths of my purse.

I eyed Liv. "Can you create a diversion?"

She nodded and grinned. "Always."

"Good." I grabbed my purse and headed toward the ladies' room, hoping to slip out the kitchen door. I was halfway across the dining room when a crash echoed around the space. Liv could always be counted on to amp up the drama.

I waited until Bernice and her husband, Louie, rushed out of the kitchen to check on the commotion, then slipped out the back and crept along the side of the building. It was hard to be stealth in broad daylight, but I worked with what I was given. Naturally, Mitch had parked right in front of the diner in a handicap spot. That alone warranted a one-way ticket to hell. Never mind the rest of his shit.

It only made it more fun to turn on the AirTag, sync it to my phone, and place it on the rear bumper of his giant white Mercedes. With any luck, this baby would help me collect enough evidence to put him away for a long stretch.

Once it was secured, I scurried along the back wall of the building and slipped back inside, then casually strode through to the dining room.

As promised, Liv had captivated the entire diner. She was sitting in a booth, surrounded by a crowd of people, with a damp towel over her brow and a glass of water in her hand. Dylan Markey was front and center, clearly digging the damsel in distress act. I could have sworn he had a girlfriend, but I'd be shocked if Liv didn't walk away from this ordeal with his number.

I gave her a wink, which prompted her rapid recovery, and thanked everyone for their kindness as I ushered her back to our booth.

"You are frighteningly good at that," I said.

"We all have our strengths, bestie."

Chapter 36
Pascal

"So he's using the dog walking business to launder money?" Liv sat on the couch while Parker walked her through the evidence on the whiteboard she had made me roll into the living room. We were brainstorming and revisiting everything we'd learned in the last few days.

Liv, while loud and pushy, was a helpful addition. Her imagination was wild, and no theory escaped her analysis. Plus, Parker lit up around her.

I'd been instructed to meet my brothers at the Moose tonight so they could have a girls' night. Apparently, that involved wine and Korean face masks. I wanted nothing more than to spend every waking moment with Parker, but it was obvious by the way she'd been clinging to Liv that she'd been lonely up here. She'd laughed and smiled more in the last few hours than she had in weeks. Damn, I'd happily build a guest house on the property so Liv could visit whenever she wanted.

Jesus. I was in deep. It was the Gagnon curse. Once we fell, we fell hard.

"Yes," Parker replied. "There's no evidence that dogs are

actually being walked, but they file taxes every year and have a website. They've gone to great lengths to make it look legit."

I sat down and admired how hot Parker looked sketching things out. Could we make this work long term? For the first time in years, I was willing to try. If it meant going back to Portland, I'd do it. At this point, I'd follow her anywhere.

Granted, I hadn't told her that yet. But I would. And I'd tell my brothers tonight. Give them the full truth and take all the teasing. Hopefully, I'd also walk away with tips for how to make her stick around.

"And Stinger?" Liv asked. "He's the drug kingpin?"

"No. We believe he works for the trafficking organization. Maybe Canadians, and likely involving the Heberts. His real name is Norman Bernard and he worked for the Gagnons for a while."

"Do you think he did it?" Liv asked softly, looking between Parker and me.

"Not sure," I replied. "But we have a strong suspicion. Especially since we know now that he's been up at our camp a few times over the last few years. Henri and I spend most of our time at our headquarters in town, and Richard runs operations up there. We don't have a lot of insight into how and when he was around, but we're not ruling anything out."

I kept my concerns about Richard to myself for now. Was he involved? And how the fuck was his nephew working for us under the table without my knowledge? Was that what he and my dad had been fighting about?

All of it made me sick. Because someone somewhere had wanted to harm my family. And what if they tried again?

I looked at Parker. She was my family now. And I'd do anything to protect her.

I had worked out some of my pent-up anxiety over the case and showered before dressing to head out to meet Remy and Henri. I came downstairs to find Liv typing at the kitchen island with a glass of wine.

"Parker ran out to get more wine and snacks," she said without looking up. "I had a great chapter idea, so I stayed here to write."

I nodded, pulling a glass from the cabinet. "She's pretty amazing," I said, because I could no longer keep all my feelings from spilling out of my mouth. God, I was as bad as Henri. But there was no use hiding it from her best friend.

"I'm glad we have a minute, actually," Liv said, slowly closing her laptop and scrutinizing me from across the room. "'Cause you and me? We need to talk."

My stomach sank. Shit. I brought my water glass to my lips, mostly so I could hide my panic behind it.

She steepled her fingers and narrowed her eyes. Liv's whole vibe was very Stevie Nicks with a sordid past. And despite her small stature, she didn't seem like someone I'd want to mess with.

"Parker is an absolute badass, but deep down, she's scared and hurt and has a hard time trusting."

All I could do was nod in response. She wasn't wrong, but what was with the warning? Was she teeing me up for a brutal takedown?

"She likes you. And while I'm not convinced any non-fictional man is good enough for her, I'm willing to give you the benefit of the doubt."

"Um..." I hedged, sticking my hands in my pockets. "Thank you?"

"Listen, I may not have a law enforcement background or be able to shoot a gun to save my life, and I definitely don't have her ninja skills. But I'm even more dangerous. Because the thoughts in my head are so depraved and violent and terrifying, I get paid to write stories about them."

"*Okay.*" Maybe I wouldn't build a guest house so she could visit any time she wanted.

"I've committed more murders in my head than even the most prolific serial killers. So step out of line, and I'll take it from fantasy to reality in a heartbeat. Because no one hurts my best friend."

Shit, this woman was what nightmares were made of. But I also respected the hell out of her. That kind of loyalty was exactly what Parker deserved. "You're scary," I said.

She crossed her arms. "Correct. And Parker is my best friend. And for some crazy reason, she's into you. So. Do. Not. Fuck. This. Up."

I had no intention of fucking it up. On the contrary. I was trying to figure out how to keep her forever. Historically, I didn't get attached easily. And that alone was how I knew Parker was the real thing. Because the trust and respect and desire that had grown between us so quickly was worth keeping and fighting for.

"Also"—she pointed a finger at my face—"never, ever, stop going down on her. I've heard your skills are excellent, but don't slack off once you lock her down."

Shit. My cheeks went hot immediately. Should I be flattered that Parker had bragged about my skills? Or embarrassed? Probably both, but I'd focus on the former.

"I can't believe I'm having this conversation with you." Every cell in my body was telling me to run far away from this.

"Believe it. You may be a rich, handsome lumbersuit, but no one fucks with my best friend. Hurt her and die."

I was saved from further discussion by my ringing phone. "Gotta take this," I said, pulling it from my pocket. Parker had no idea how perfect her timing was. She'd unwittingly rescued me from the clutches of her tiny and terrifying friend.

"Paz, it's happening," she shouted on the other end of the phone. "Mrs. Revelle just called me."

My heart lurched, and my pulse took off at a sprint. "Okay. Slow down and explain."

"He's there. Stinger is at the trailer. I'm headed straight over."

"No. Do not go alone."

"My camera bag is in the car. I'm gonna get some long-range photos. Confirm it's Norman, confirm the motorcycle, and see if I can ID any of his associates. If we're really lucky, our boy Grinder will show up too."

On the other end of the phone, her voice was high-pitched with excitement. She was so confident that this would give us what we needed to close the loop.

But I felt sick to my stomach. "Parker, it's not safe. I'll meet you there."

"No." Her voice was firm. "This is what I do, Paz. I can slip in and out. Tonight, we compile everything and hand it over to the feds."

Every one of my instincts was screaming to go to her, to protect her. To tell her to stop for a minute and work out a plan. But I held back. I had to trust her. And I had to trust myself. We were a team, and she was trained and smart and ready.

"I'll be waiting here. Text me in an hour. If I don't hear from you, I'm showing up with the police."

Her sigh crackled down the line. "Fine. I'll text you when I get the photos, and then we can plan the next steps."

I paused, my heart in my throat. My gut was telling me that things were off. I so badly wanted to tell her to be safe, that I loved her, and that I didn't even care about the investigation anymore if it meant she was safe in my arms. But I couldn't say that. Not yet.

I couldn't get in her way. This was her job. And she was great at it. Her words rang in my head. I needed to trust her. It was only a few photos. What could go wrong?

Chapter 37
Parker

I knew it. I fucking knew it. Dumb is gonna dumb. It was only a matter of time before Stinger—or should I say Norman Bernard?—surfaced. I had to see him and confirm the face tattoo, then I could turn everything over to Bryce and the feds.

Did the idea of handing all my carefully collected evidence over gut me? Yes. But it also thrilled me. Because Bryce would know it came from me. And that would have to be enough.

After six weeks of digging and hunting and boring stakeouts. It was time to strike. And though I had a great deal of confidence in my investigative skills, I wasn't equipped to bring down an international drug cartel on my own.

Nor did I want to. Those kinds of desires belonged to Parker of the past. I was in the business of helping people now. And I was ready to end my professional entanglement with Paz so I could officially start my personal entanglement with him.

As terrifying as that sounded, it felt right. We had a lot of details to hash out, but I had fallen for my grouchy lumberjack, and I wasn't giving up on him.

As promised, Mrs. Revelle had called me when two motorcycles pulled up to the trailer. It was only two p.m., but it was cloudy, and snow had begun to fall. The perfect type of weather to help me stay concealed while I took photos and got close enough to get a shot of his face.

My plan was to slow roll through the trailer park and find a spot to drop my car so I could sneak up on foot. There were enough tall trees and structures to let me get close without being seen. And if I did end up being spotted, the snow would make it harder to ID me.

After confirming the Ducati was in front of the trailer, along with one other motorcycle, I circled around and left my car near the entrance on a dead-end street. I put my camera under the gray down jacket I had borrowed from Paz, then slowly walked along the edge of the forest, keeping an eye out for both bikers and that fucking moose.

The place wasn't totally deserted. Cars came in and out of the park, and kids were out, throwing snowballs at one another on the opposite side of the street, so I pulled my knit cap lower and walked casually as I made my way toward the trailer.

Sure enough, there were two motorcycles parked out front, including a black Ducati Streetfighter V4. There was a weathered woodshed about twenty yards from me, so with a subtle scan of my surroundings, I headed toward it and ducked behind it for cover before pulling my camera out.

From this angle, the bikes and their license plates were visible, so I snapped a dozen or so photos to be sure I captured every detail. The large window on one end of the trailer was partially covered by curtains, but the light inside was on, and I could make out shadows.

I crouched down, waiting and watching. After several long moments, a large and imposing figure with a beer gut passed by the window. Not a match for my profile of Norman at all. So I waited, my teeth chattering in the cold, wishing for just one good look at his face.

Eventually, after my fingers went numb and my back was aching, I got it.

The door opened, and the larger man walked out, but a second man stepped onto the porch.

I was ready, pointing my lens and praying that I could get what I needed.

Because that man was tall and gangly, with strawberry blond hair tied back in a ponytail, and he had a tattoo on his right cheek.

I zoomed in, and there it was. A dragonfly. Small but unmistakable. I clicked the shutter, getting as many shots as I could.

He wore a vest over a black T-shirt, leaving his arms exposed, despite the cold, and I captured a dozen photos of the full sleeve on his left arm.

The other man wore a heavy coat and knit hat, but his face was partially visible, so I clicked away.

I promised Paz I'd get my shots and go home, but I was on a roll. And as the snow picked up, I became more and more eager to scope out the inside of the trailer. Because while I had connected the dots on the drug operation, we still hadn't officially confirmed that the Heberts were responsible for Frank's murder. And I was too close to give up now.

Carefully zipping up my camera again, I resolved to head back to my car, warm myself up, and wait for Stinger to leave. It was getting dark, and once I could use that to my advantage, I'd take a closer look.

So I slipped out from behind the wood pile and headed back to the other side of the park. It was eerily quiet now. Most people were indoors since the storm was picking up. It was nothing like the blizzard from a few weeks ago, but it was heavy enough to make driving difficult.

My phone, which had been on silent, was likely full of texts from Paz, warning me about weather and slippery roads, but I could not wait to show him these photos. Finally, I had concrete evidence. And with this addition to the evidence we'd already collected, I had hope that law enforcement could do the rest.

Sliding into my car, I carefully removed my camera from my coat, gently wiped it down, and put it back in its case. With the heat cranking, it didn't take long to thaw out. Once feeling returned to my fingers, I opened the glove box in search of my lip balm. I couldn't help but smile at the supplies Paz had packed for me. This man's love language was definitely preparation. He needed to make sure everyone he cared about was protected and taken care of.

Funny enough, this stuff had been here for weeks. He'd done it all before we even kissed. Was he feeling something even back then?

I slid the seat belt cutter into my hand, admiring the smooth steel.

Without warning, the car lurched, and my shoulder was yanked back so hard it slammed against the seat before I was thrown forward so my head hit the steering wheel. I reacted, throwing up an elbow and trying to wiggle loose of the grip on my neck.

"Get the fuck out," an angry male voice said, pulling on my hair.

I used my legs to brace myself and slammed one fist up, making contact with a satisfying crack.

Before I could pull free, though, I was being dragged out of the car. I squeezed the seat belt cutter in my palm and scanned the interior for my phone. Shit. It had been knocked to the floor on the passenger side.

I lunged for it but was pulled back again, my shoulder hitting the door frame.

It was only then that I could see them. Two men hovering over me, laughing, while another pinned my arms behind my back.

"Stop fighting," the older one said. "Don't make this harder. It's fucking freezing out here."

I froze. It was the man from the trailer. Dark gray beard and a beer gut. Still wearing a wool hat.

And the man next to him?

Stinger. Norman Bernard.

I let out a blood-curdling scream and thrashed against the man holding me, taking out one of his knees in the process.

When his grip on me loosened, I ran for it, screaming for help while I did so. But I didn't make it more than five feet before a large body tackled me, and I hit the ground. The impact knocked the wind from my lungs, and before I could suck in a breath and scream again, a rough hand covered my mouth.

Another set of arms hauled me up, and the two of them dragged me toward the trailer while I continued to kick and thrash.

I bit the hand covering my mouth as hard as I could, making the man yelp and pull it away, but before I could get free, he hit me square in the jaw.

"You stupid bitch," that same voice said.

My head snapped back as they pushed me into the back of a dark van. One man kneeled on my back while another tied my hands together.

I lay there, panting and racking my brain for a way to escape.

"Got her, boss," Stinger said into a cell phone.

"Yeah. Hold on." He came back a moment later with my phone and held it up to my face to unlock it. "Yup. I'm in. Okay, what should I text?"

"Help!" I yelled as loud as I could. "I'm being kidnapped by drug dealers."

I heard the crack before the pain registered. As my cheek throbbed, I was pushed back and held down, then my mouth was covered with a strip of duct tape.

Stinger grinned at me from where he was typing on my phone. "This is gonna be fun."

Within minutes, we were headed away from the trailer park, tires squealing.

With a defeated breath, I closed my eyes and went through everything I'd ever learned about abductions. Fuck. I needed a plan to get myself out of this.

I had no phone, and I didn't know where I was headed. All I had was the seat belt cutter. It'd get me out of these ropes, but it wasn't an ideal weapon, and I didn't know how many people were waiting at our destination.

First, I needed to calm down. I closed my eyes and focused on my breathing until my heart rate slowed. I concentrated on squeezing the seat belt cutter, feeling the cool steel in my hand. I was getting out of here and back to Paz. But first, I had bad guys to take down.

So far, all the evidence pointed to them being amateur morons. I'd almost fought three of them off on my own. That was clue number one. And rope? Did they not have zip ties this far north? What kind of old-timey retro heist was this?

I chuckled to myself, letting my thinking brain take over.

The more relaxed and focused I was, the greater the likelihood that I would get out of this alive.

The paracord wrapped around my wrists came off easily. Whoever these junior varsity kidnappers were, their knot tying skills left a lot to be desired.

As promised, the cutter slipped through the first layer, and then I untied the rest. Paz was right. This thing was pretty handy. After tearing the tape off my face—fuck, that hurt—I tucked the seat belt cutter into my bra.

The van turned sharply, and we bumped down what was likely a dirt road. If that was the case, there was a good chance we were headed out of town. Getting out of the van wouldn't be an issue, but surviving the night in the woods in the winter was another story. I was wearing a coat and boots, but they weren't heavy duty enough to hold up if I had to walk thirty miles back to town.

Suddenly, the music died, and murmurs were audible.

"You found him where?"

"That dumbass." A scoff. "All that fancy education, and he fell right into our trap."

"It wasn't exactly our trap. It was the boss's idea."

They fell silent for a few moments. The only sounds were tires on bumpy gravel. I inched up closer to the cab, where the stench of cigarette smoke got stronger, hoping to catch more of their conversation. The back of the van was dark and empty, but I could use that to my advantage.

"It's so funny," one voice said as the van slowed a bit, "Paz Gagnon, that corporate motherfucker. Do you think the boss will let me shoot him in the head?"

"That prick thinks he's better than everyone. Boss will probably shoot 'em himself. Besides, you took out the dad."

"Yeah, but I didn't get the satisfaction of watching it happen."

"Doesn't stop you from getting drunk and bragging about it."

"Oh, fuck off."

I stiffened and held my breath. Did they have Paz too? Where were they taking him, and who was the boss? This was a lot more serious than I had anticipated.

I moved around quietly, feeling for anything that could help me. But other than the ropes I'd shed, the cargo area was empty. Shit. I was going to have to get out of this using my brains and my fists. And while I certainly had training and IQ on my side, they had strength in numbers.

What had to be an hour into the trip, we were still bumping along, and I was still strategizing. The van was windowless, and the door was locked. There was a good chance I could get it unlocked, but that still left me with the issue of being stranded in the middle of nowhere in the cold. And a tumble from a moving vehicle would only make that worse. So I stuck around. Especially because I needed more information about where they had taken Paz.

Professional criminals would never bring two hostages to the same place, but based on what I'd seen, these jokers were wannabes who had gotten lucky so far. So the odds were in my favor.

I spent the rest of the ride stretching and warming up. I'd need to be ready to fight and run like hell.

After another turn, the van came to a stop, and both front doors opened.

It was go time. The guys were outside the van, and it sounded like one was hollering to another person nearby. So I used the opportunity to crawl to the back corner of the cargo area and crouch on my left side.

The doors opened, shedding dim light on the space.

"What the fuck?" came a raspy voice. "Where is she?"

I stayed perfectly still. The light wasn't bright enough to give my position away.

So I waited. And sure enough, he opened the doors wider, leaning in to search for me.

Once the man nearest was within range, I kicked him square in the head. Grinder went down hard, just as I knew he would. My side kick was brutal, and all the squats with Adele had only made me stronger.

I only had a moment, so I leapfrogged over his bloated body toward the door, only to be faced with Stinger.

"You fucking bitch," he growled, lunging for me.

But I had another trick up my sleeve. A punch straight to his balls. While he doubled over screaming, I landed an uppercut to his jaw. He shifted and pawed at me, giving me just enough room to jump out the door and make a run for it.

There were about half a dozen men hovering in a large parking area. Big flood lights illuminated the space that looked like a camp or a work site.

I didn't have time to take stock. I headed straight for the tree line, running right into the woods where I could be concealed.

"Get her," Stinger yelled, his voice strained.

I would have loved to stop and admire my work, but I had shit to get done. So I kept running, dropping low and looking for potential cover as I moved deeper into the woods.

The foliage was so dense and the starless sky so dark that I kept tripping over tree roots and stones. So I dropped to my hands and knees and crawled. Yes, the snow was wet and freezing, but it was better than getting shot.

The shouting continued, and beams of light penetrated the forest as the men moved into the woods with flashlights. Their attempts were halfhearted at best. It was cold, and these woods were dense and dark. I waited and watched. They couldn't see me, but that didn't mean I couldn't see them.

The open area was decently lit with industrial lights, showcasing logging equipment parked on the far side. There was a big, newish-looking pole barn and a smaller, older structure next to it. We were out in the woods, that was for sure, but the Hebert Timber logo on the side of my kidnap van brought a smile to my face. The idiots were doing my job for me.

From my vantage point, I could only make out one road leading to the clearing.

So I huddled up, grateful I was wearing Paz's big jacket, and waited. I could run or attempt to steal one of the trucks, but Paz was in danger, and I wasn't leaving without him. I didn't care if I lost toes. We were in this together.

Thankfully, I didn't have to wait long. About thirty minutes after the henchmen had given up their search for me, a white Mercedes G-Wagon pulled up. Mitch Hebert got out, wearing one of those thousand-dollar Canada Goose jackets. His brother followed and opened the back door.

My heart seized. I had no weapons, no phone, and no backup. I almost screamed, but I controlled myself.

Because there was Paz. Being pulled out by his jacket. His face was battered, and his hands were tied behind his back. His mouth was taped, but even from here, I could see his dark eyes flash with anger as he was dragged into the large building.

The rest of the men followed, all but forgetting about me.

Bile rose in the back of my throat. Stinger had said they were going to shoot him. Fuck. I could not let that happen.

I closed my eyes, took a cleansing breath, and then took off through the forest around the back of the building.

Because no one would hurt a single hair on my lumberjack's head. Not if I had anything to do with it.

Chapter 38
Pascal

My head ached and nausea rolled in my gut. The small, dirty room I'd been thrown into was empty, save for the folding chair that I was currently tied to.

Where was Parker? Had they hurt her? The thought made me even sicker. I never should have let her go to the trailer park alone.

I hadn't even told her that I loved her. And she could be hurt. Or worse. The panic rose up within me, sending me spiraling again. My throat felt like it was closing up as fear gripped my heart. But I had to keep my wits about me.

Fucking Heberts. I'd always suspected they were criminals, but to go this far? It was almost unfathomable. But now I knew the truth. Mitch and Paul Hebert were running a large-scale drug operation through their logging business and laundering the proceeds in a variety of shell companies all over the state.

But of course, the idiots had failed to properly cover their tracks. Law enforcement would catch on eventually. But right now, my only concern was Parker.

She had to be here too. We were in the woods. The hard left they'd taken off the Golden Road meant we were likely in the south quadrant, near the border of the Heberts' land.

We weren't at their camp. This was an outpost at best, and the ride hadn't been long enough. So, on the plus side, we weren't terribly far from civilization and potential rescue. If I could get out of this room and get a look around, I could make a plan.

My next panic attack was knocking at the door of my mind, ready to take over, but a shifting sound at the sole window in the room drew my attention.

A light shined through the small pane of glass, temporarily blinding me. I blinked rapidly, and the light was diverted. And there, at the window, wearing my jacket and shining a flashlight, was Parker.

My heart soared. She was alive. But what was she doing here? Outside the building?

My hands were tied, so I couldn't unlock the window. She waved an arm, signaling me to move back. Following her wordless instruction, I shifted my chair so that I was blocking the door. That way, if someone in the building heard us, I could block them from getting to Parker so she'd have a chance to escape.

She gave me a thumbs-up and struck the window with a small object. The crack of the window was relatively quiet, and from the impact point, fissures spread like a spider web. Then she used her boot to push the glass out of the way.

The sound of the glass clattering to the ground was louder than the initial break, but the building was large, and a massive generator was running outside, providing plenty of background noise. With any luck, she hadn't garnered any attention.

She wrapped her hand in what looked like a sweatshirt and

gently swept the glass away from the sill. Then she draped the shirt over the frame and swung her legs through before dropping to the floor like a spy in an action movie.

She was wearing winter boots, leggings, and my down jacket, and her face was pale.

"Hey, stud muffin," she said, walking towards me. "What the fuck did they do to you?" In a heartbeat, she was in front of me and cupping my face.

She gently ripped the tape off my lips, then tipped forward and kissed them.

"What are you doing here?" I hissed.

"Saving your dumb ass," she replied. "Did they hurt you?"

"Let's get into details later. We've got to get you out of here. I overheard Mitch saying he was going to 'personally shoot that cop bitch in the head.'"

She shrugged, brandishing the seat belt cutter I'd stowed in her glove box. "Did you break the window with that?" I asked, impressed.

She nodded. "And I cut through my wrist ties," she said as she sliced through mine.

I rubbed my wrists and pulled her into my lap.

"That is fucking hot," I said, reaching into my pocket and pulling out my multi-tool.

"Of course you keep a Swiss Army knife in your jeans."

"Damn right I do. Dumbasses didn't think to take it off me. They also didn't take my phone, so I've been voice recording them for the past few hours." I removed it from my pocket, where, sure enough, it was still recording.

"Any signal?"

"Nope, but we're not that far out. Once we get closer to town, we can call the police."

She buried her head in my chest. "I was so worried about you."

I held her close, only for a moment, and pulled in a deep breath, thankful she was okay. "After I got that text, I panicked. I knew I had to get you back."

She pushed me away. "What are you talking about?"

"About the time you were supposed to check in, I got a text from your phone. It said you were going to meet me at the Ape Hanger. Except whoever wrote it used the wrong *there*, so I knew it wasn't you."

"And you went anyway?"

"Fuck yes, I did. No way was I going to let anyone hurt you."

"And you didn't call the police?"

"Couldn't risk it. What if they found out and hurt you?"

She crossed her arms and glared at me. "You're telling me you willingly let yourself get kidnapped?"

"Yes." I couldn't fight my grin. "But don't worry. Liv and I have a plan."

"You dragged Liv into this?"

"Like I could keep her out. She agreed that it was probably a trap. So we decided that if I didn't text her within an hour, she'd call the police. She's got your laptop with everything on it ready for the feds."

Parker didn't let up on the glaring. She only sat a little straighter. "What's your code phrase? No way Liv didn't give you a code phrase."

I looked at my feet. "Keep the change, ya filthy animal."

Parker laughed. "That tracks. I'm fucking furious with you, by the way. You can't put yourself in danger like that."

"I didn't think. I had to make sure you were safe. And Liv

agreed. You don't have to do it all by yourself anymore. We're in this together."

"Fine." She hauled herself off my lap. "Climb out that window, steal one of the cars, and call the police as soon as you can." Yanking me by the arms, she pulled me to a stand, then she pushed me toward the broken window.

"No fucking way." I spun on her. "You're coming with me."

She shook her head. "I am so close to getting enough evidence to put everyone here away for at least a few decades. I gotta stay."

"No. I'm not leaving without you."

"Yes, you are. You're going to take that phone and my laptop to the FBI and nail these fuckers. I'll stay here, keep them busy while you escape. Hopefully, I can confirm that Mitch Hebert killed your dad. No one knows where we are. You'll need to bring the police here to recover the evidence."

"No."

I'd spent almost two years desperate to know what had happened to him, but I wasn't willing to sacrifice Parker for those answers. She was too important to me. And if anyone would understand that, it was my dad.

"I'm not leaving without you. All I want is to get you out of here. Nothing else matters."

She regarded me, naked fear swimming in her irises. All that self-confidence, all the police training, melted away, leaving behind only the woman I had fallen in love with. I would not let harm come to her.

"I fucking love you," she said through gritted teeth.

I pulled her close and kissed the top of her head. "Not as much as I fucking love you."

"We're so gonna fight about this later."

"Yes. I promise to let you yell at me as much as you want, but first, we need a plan."

I rolled my shoulders and shook out my arms. My blood was circulating now that I wasn't tied up, but the cold wind whipped in through the broken window.

"They brought me here with no blindfold, so I got a good look at the entrance and part of the building. And I'm pretty familiar with these layouts. The giant garage bays on the other side? That's where they keep whatever they're hiding and distributing. I heard music coming from over there. Typically, several of these small rooms are clustered along the front wall. So if we unlock that door and head right, there should be another room or two before things open up. We could potentially hide in one of them if necessary."

She took my phone and wedged it in her bra. "I'll see what I can record. Grab the folding chair." She nodded to where I'd been tied up. "It's a good weapon."

Fuck, she was good. I folded it up and waited while she tested the lock. "When they threw me in here, I overheard an order about pulling out the snowmobiles. I think they were sending people out to look for you."

"Even better. Fewer henchmen out there. Give me that multi-tool."

I handed it to her, and she took a moment to assess the different functions. But I didn't have the pleasure of witnessing Parker's lock picking skills because voices echoed from the hall on the other side.

She flipped up the tiny knife on the multi-tool and plastered herself to the wall next to the door. I picked up the folded chair and did the same.

I stood, my heart pounding in my ears, for several moments that felt like hours.

Parker was totally focused, totally calm, watching the door, ready to pounce. She turned to me and mouthed, "I love you."

My heart squeezed at the same time the nausea still roiling in my gut threatened to take over. How the fuck had I ended up here?

The door opened slowly, and when Parker nodded, I stepped forward, smacking the man who had walked in square in the face with the chair. Couldn't tell who it was, but I hit him hard, and he fell to the floor. Only, he grasped the chair and dragged me down with him. Parker darted out of the room as I struggled to get back on my feet.

I didn't recognize the man I'd hit, but he was barely conscious. So I pulled myself up off the floor and took off after her, locking the door behind me as I went. The hallway was well lit and, as I suspected, lined with small offices leading to a larger, open space. I hugged the wall, crouching low and searching for Parker.

The space was bare bones, with spotty fluorescent lighting and small, drafty windows. At the end of the hall was an open warehouse-style space that I could just make out from my vantage point. I stepped away from the doorway, trying to get a better look, and spotted Parker. She was fifteen feet ahead of me, clutching my multi-tool and peering into the warehouse.

A loud shout echoed through the open space. I plastered my back to the doorframe as a large older man came down the opposite end of the hallway. Before I could react, he grabbed her by the hair and was dragging her toward the warehouse.

I sprang into action, ready to fight him, but she locked eyes with me and shook her head. Her eyes were wide in a silent warning to stay hidden. No matter how hard it was to watch someone put their hands on her, we had the best chance of walking out of here if I wasn't discovered.

"I found the cop," a booming voice shouted.

The response came from a voice I recognized. "About fucking time."

Mitch Hebert.

Chapter 39
Parker

I appreciated when a person made it clear who they were. No artifice, no pretense, nothing but total honesty. Mitch Hebert was an asshole and a criminal and didn't even attempt to hide it. He flashed his money, treated people like dirt, and made a habit of casual cruelty. So his presence was no surprise. He was seated in a warehouse filled with weapons, criminal henchmen, and several thousand silver bricks of what I assumed was heroin or fentanyl.

He had been telling us all along. But it was still satisfying to see the evidence laid out in front of me. The space wasn't huge. It was probably a couple thousand square feet, but it was a police officer's dream. Clear plastic totes filled with pills, half a dozen pill presses, stacks of carefully organized cash, and a fuck ton of weapons.

Grinder, that piece of shit, was dragging me into the center of the room, first by my hair and then by my shoulders after I landed a solid kick to his elbow.

He deposited me in front of Hebert, who was standing

behind a folding table. My buddy Stinger stood next to him with a .45 pointed directly at me.

This had not gone according to plan. But at least I had Paz's phone stuffed into my bra. Every word of this conversation would be recorded.

"Oh look. It's the trashy ex-cop," Mitch said. He didn't have a mustache, but the twirl was theoretical. "You have been such a pain in my ass. Sniffing around my business, asking questions everywhere. Running background checks on my employees."

How the hell did he know that? Shit. I couldn't worry about that yet. Instead of getting worked up over the possibilities, I kept my face cool and impassive.

"I know you're working for the Gagnons, and I'll tell you what I told their old man. You can't stop me. I won't let you or them get in the way of my business."

At his side, Stinger studied the gun in his hand like he'd never seen one before.

"But you have, Mitch. You let your arrogance make you overconfident. We both know you've been sloppy. You're clearly scraping the bottom of the barrel with these two numbskulls." I nodded at Stinger, then tilted my head toward Grinder, who was still hovering. "And a dog walking business as a money laundering front? Doesn't get more obvious than that."

Mitch's face reddened, and he clenched his fists on top of the table. "Shut the fuck up."

"Can I shoot this bitch now?" Stinger asked, sounding bored.

I turned to him, narrowing my eyes. "Ooh, Stinger. Such a tough name for a sloppy wannabe gangster with terrible taste in motorcycles."

"It's because of my ink, ya dumb bitch." He pointed to his cheek. "Dragonfly. Stinger. Get it?"

I shook my head. At times like this, I missed the state police. Because I had no doubt I would have won several free rounds of drinks in the "dumbest criminal" competition if I'd submitted this contestant.

"Dragonflies don't have stingers," I deadpanned.

He pointed to his face. "Yes, they do."

"No, that's a thorax, you ignoramus. Dragonflies can't sting anything."

"Fuck you, fuzz," he spat at me while Grinder laughed behind me.

"I'm not a cop. Which is a problem for you. Because I'm not bound by the fourth amendment."

"What does that even mean?"

"I don't need probable cause to shoot your ass."

"Joke's on you. We got the guns."

"For now," I said. "Why didn't you just shoot Frank Gagnon? Would have been faster."

Mitch leaned forward, pressing his palms flat against the table. "I'm not a violent man."

I rolled my eyes. I loved it when these basic bitches lacked even fundamental self-awareness. "The gun pointing at me contradicts that statement."

He ignored me, puffing himself up even more. "I would have shot him myself if I'd had the chance. I hated that do-gooder my whole life. I had a glass of my best whiskey the day of his funeral. He was always trying to do the right thing. You know what the right thing is? Making fucking money."

Grinder laughed.

I glared at the idiot biker, then turned back to Mitch. "But tampering with brakes? That's complicated. You really trusted these dufuses to pull it off?"

"That was a management call," Mitch said curtly. Great. He confirmed he's working for someone else. A few more minutes, and I'd be getting their socials and favorite colors. "I had my doubts." He shrugged.

"I did it, didn't I?" Stinger bragged.

"Yes, Norman. I guess you did. Did you enlist your uncle to commit this murder, or did you do it all by yourself like a big boy?"

He flinched almost imperceptibly, but I clocked it all the same. So Richard had been involved, or at least aware. It wasn't confirmation. But I'd get that eventually.

"We have a lot of product to move before sunrise," Mitch said. "Grinder, radio the other guys. Tell them to circle back."

He turned to Stinger. "Management says shoot her. But don't make a big mess. I've got work to do."

Stinger laughed. "Sweet."

He sauntered around the table, sliding the safety off as he did. *Shit.* Time to act. Run, jump, tackle him. Anything. Otherwise it was lights out.

He cocked the hammer and wrapped his left hand around the grip.

And then a deep scream echoed off the concrete walls. A war cry, really.

It was Paz. Running at me at full speed, yelling.

He hit me like a ton of bricks, sending us both flying as the gun went off. My head hit the cement floor, and his big body pressed into mine, shielding me.

"Paz," I said desperately, trembling. "Are you okay?" Was he hit?

He looked at me and gave me a smile sweeter than a cranky lumbersuit like him should be capable of. "I love you."

It was then that I saw it. Blood on the floor. Pooling next to him.

"Fuck. You're hit."

But Mitch was prowling toward us slowly, pulling a revolver out of his gaudy belt. And now we were both on the ground, vulnerable and defenseless. Paz held me tighter as I froze in terror. This was it. But at least we would spend our last moment together.

"I always thought Henri would be the one I had to take out. Or your loud bitch of a sister. Never you, Pascal. I always saw a little of myself in you. Cool and calm and focused on what really matters. Success and money."

He took another step, and my entire body shook.

"My own sons have been nothing but disappointments. They don't have it in them. The ability to do what it takes to get what they want. I thought you were better than them. But you and your cop girlfriend have got to go. My Canadian friends are angry with me, and my guys are making sloppy mistakes because of you and your amateur investigation." He jutted his chin. "That one over there couldn't even shoot her at close range. So apparently, I've got to end this myself."

He aimed at Paz's head, and I let out a blood-curdling scream.

But my scream was drowned out by a crashing sound. A battering ram held by two officers in tactical gear smashed through the door.

"Drop your weapons," a deep voice commanded. And before I could blink, the warehouse was swarming with FBI agents armed with rifles.

Chapter 40
Pascal

From the back of the ambulance, I watched the flurry of activity. Several tactical teams had descended on the Hebert compound, and the entirety of the alphabet was here. FBI, DEA, DHS, ATF. Every department was here for a piece of the criminal pie.

But I had far bigger problems. Mainly the bullet in my ass. Well, it wasn't there anymore. According to the EMT, it had passed through very briefly, but I'd be on my way to the hospital shortly for stitches, X- rays, and a shit ton of antibiotics.

At the time, I hadn't even felt it. I was totally focused on Parker and keeping her safe. But now the adrenaline was wearing off and the pain was catching up to me.

I lay in the ambulance while Parker sat on the back bumper, giving yet another statement to law enforcement. The questions were endless and repetitive, but she knew better than anyone how important it was to go over every detail carefully. She was only a few feet away, but it was too far. I would never let her out of my sight again. No matter how logistically impossible that may be.

I had almost lost her tonight. After spending my life preparing to keep everyone I loved safe, the reality of what had occurred was crippling. Yes, we were alive. But things could have gone so differently.

"Let me through," came a familiar, angry voice. "We're family."

As I sat up to get a look at the new arrival, my sister hopped into the back of the ambulance, flanked by my brothers. Before I could react, she was crushing me in a hug.

"Ease up, Adele. I got shot."

"Fuck you," she said, hugging me tighter. "I can't believe you got yourself fucking shot."

"Adele, let him go. You can yell at him after he's been to the hospital."

"Okay." She sniffed, taking a step back. The ambulance was bursting at the seams now that all three of my siblings had wedged their way inside. Parker was still sitting on the bumper, her eyes gleaming like she was enjoying watching them bombard me.

"How are you even here?" I asked.

"I called them," a high-pitched voice piped up. Liv appeared at the open doors and looped her arms around Parker. "When you didn't text, I called the police and the FBI, and then we used the AirTag Parker put on Mitch's car to follow you into the woods."

"You were tracking Mitch's car?" I asked.

"Shh," Parker said. "It's not strictly legal, but I needed to know where he was going."

"And it saved your ass," Liv said, defending her friend. "We lost the signal part of the way here, but we followed the roads, and the FBI contacted one of the Heberts, who helped us find the place."

"A Hebert helped?" Henri said, his voice surprised.

Liv nodded. "I rode up here with a few of the plainclothes guys, and they reached out. I didn't catch his name. He's a logger, though."

"Probably Gus," Remy murmured.

Damn. This was all mind-boggling. If things had gone even a little differently—if Liv had hesitated to call the cops, or if the FBI hadn't taken her seriously, or even if the Heberts hadn't been cooperative—we would be dead.

And that realization sat like a stone in my gut.

"Thank fuck you're okay," Remy said. "Did Parker really take out ten guys to save you when you got kidnapped? That's the word on the street."

Parker smiled at me, mischief alight in her eyes.

"Something like that," I said, giving her a wink.

"She's a keeper," he said, raising his eyebrows.

"What did I miss?" Henri asked, looking between Parker and me. "Are you guys together?"

We nodded, not taking our eyes off one another.

"I thought you were fake dating for a cover story." My sister crossed her arms over her chest and gave me that look that had always terrified me.

"They were. But it's real now," Remy said.

"How did Remy know?" Adele asked. "And dammit, Pascal. What did I tell you? I knew this would happen."

"You're dating?" Henri removed his hat and ran his hands through his hair. "Is it serious?"

"He took a bullet for her, dumbass. I'd say it's serous," Liv quipped.

"I'm kind of in love with her," I said softly.

"And I'm kind of in love with him," Parker replied, wearing a soft smile.

"Welcome to the family, Parker," Henri said, giving her a hint of a smile and standing as tall as he could in the cramped space.

"This is so adorable," Liv shouted, jostling Parker. "And romantic! I need my phone. I have so many book ideas."

My siblings bickered like they always did, and Parker got sucked into Liv's newest idea while my body was hit with overwhelming fatigue. The sense of what I could have lost tonight overwhelmed me, and my eyes welled with tears.

But before I could tell them all how thankful I was for the way things turned out, the EMT was shooing them out and updating our arrival information with the hospital in Bangor. It would be a bit of a ride, but I was stable. The FBI agents would drop by tomorrow for more rounds of questions, and although I wanted to help, I was more than ready to put this all behind me.

Because I had other things to look forward to. Including the gorgeous woman sitting next to me. She needed to be checked out as well. The EMT had put her arm in a sling, suspecting she had dislocated her shoulder, but she didn't complain once. She just clutched my hand as the ambulance bounced all over the dirt road.

"You saved my life," she said, gazing down at me.

"You saved mine first," I replied.

Even before her heroics tonight, she had saved me. She'd pulled me out of the downward spiral I'd been stuck in for years, and she'd made me see what was right in front of me. A fulfilling career, a loving family, and a community that was rooting for me.

And her, hopefully, if she'd have me.

"I think I should stay for a while," she said, squeezing my hand. "Supervise your recovery."

I grinned. "Is that right?"

"Yes. Get ready for more mess, Gagnon, because I think you're going to be stuck with me."

In my periphery, the EMT gave me a nod before turning his attention to the equipment to give us some privacy.

"I think I'd like that. The *Housewives* are really growing on me. And I can live with your bras as long as they're never on your body."

She put her hand on my head, as if checking for a fever. "Are you serious? You're strapped to a gurney and hooked up to a morphine drip."

"Don't care. We almost died tonight. I'm done wasting time. I'm in love with you, and I want you and your mess and your smiles and your bad taste in TV forever."

Her eyes softened and welled with tears. "I don't know what to say to you right now."

"Kiss me. We'll work it all out later." And I meant it. After escaping murderous drug dealers and getting shot in the ass, the details didn't seem particularly significant.

"There's a lot to work out. You have a hole in your ass, for God's sake."

"It's fixable. These wonderful EMTs told me it just grazed me. They bandaged me up, and the hospital will do the rest. A gunshot didn't take me out, but having to live a single day without you might."

"As much as I want to argue with you right now, I feel the same way."

Epilogue

Parker

2 Months Later…

"Do you want another drink?" Paz asked, sitting up on this teak lounge chair.

I lowered my sunglasses to ogle him a little. *Fuck, he's hot.* He didn't spend nearly enough time shirtless in Maine. I'd have to institute some requirements when we got home.

"We should move here," I said, leaning back again and scanning the white sand and turquoise water. "Then you wouldn't ever have to wear a shirt again."

He hopped up and stretched before heading to the back of our private cabana, where a full bar was set up, as well as a phone we could use for special requests.

His ass, recovered from the bullet, looked especially round and delectable in his green swim trunks.

"You should be topless too," he said, biting his lip. "It's only fair."

I rolled my eyes. But how could I possibly deny him? I reached back and unhooked my bikini top and let it fall to the ground.

"Much better."

He poured another glass of champagne for me and then sat at the end of my chair. A light breeze blew through our cabana, ruffling his hair and making this moment even more perfect.

"You're spoiling me," I said, holding out an arm and using it to pan our private stretch of beach behind the luxury villa. I had never been to the Bahamas before, but Paz insisted on a vacation. So I had happily let him plan it. But never in my wildest dreams did I think I'd be at the Four Seasons with my own private beach.

Here, in our little slice of paradise, we could get away from the snow and the wilderness and all the drama.

Since the raid of the Heberts' facility, it had been nonstop. Interviews with police and prosecutors almost daily. I had turned over the records from the investigation as well as my phone, but every day, I received calls asking for confirmation of certain details.

There had been over a dozen arrests, and thousands of pounds of drugs were seized. Thankfully, a few of the henchmen were talking. With any luck, the feds were closing in on more arrests soon. If I knew one thing about narcotics trafficking, it was that there was always a bigger fish, always another player in the mix.

And all my cop instincts were telling me there was more to this story. Mitch Hebert, while an evil motherfucker, wasn't smart enough to put together a sophisticated international drug trafficking ring. He had even mentioned "management" several times. Hopefully, he'd squeal and the feds would be able to move on who was really in charge. But I had seen this go sideways so many times.

Deep down, I knew better than to assume the problems had all been solved. Richard had been questioned and released.

They'd determined, apparently, that he hadn't been involved in any of this. But my doubts persisted. There was something happening with him, and I wasn't convinced he was clean. Especially after seeing Norman's reaction when I mentioned his name.

And then there was the matter of Henri's accident. It was nagging at me, burrowing deep in my brain. If Stinger hadn't been there, then who tampered with his brakes? Thank God the accident hadn't been fatal, but it so easily could have been.

Paz tipped my chin up, bringing my attention back to his handsome face and this surreal experience. "I'm selfish," he said. "I booked this place because we have total privacy. You can be naked all the time."

"Maybe I want to be naked all the time."

He took the flute out of my hand and set it on the table. Then he was kissing me again, pushing me back against the chair. "I'm glad we finally agree."

Later, after an amazing candlelit dinner on the beach, we strolled along the surf, holding hands and kissing under the moonlight. My feet were bare, and I swore I could feel every one of my worries floating away. We'd only been in paradise for forty-eight hours, but already, I felt like a different person.

All the orgasms had something to do with that, no doubt.

"I know I promised I wouldn't talk about this," he said, lifting my arm to kiss the back of my hand. "This vacation is supposed to be about living in the moment and unwinding."

I stopped, forcing him to as well as I held his hand firmly. "But...?" I led.

"But I'm a planner. And the thought of not having you

every single day for the rest of my life is literally driving me crazy."

I took a deep breath. Life had been so busy and overwhelming that we had been taking things day by day. His recovery and my nonstop work with law enforcement had taken almost all our time and energy. Even so, things were so right between us, and I was totally committed to him. But I knew he wanted more. He craved permanence.

"Stay in Lovewell," he said, his eyes boring into me. "Or I'll move to Portland. I don't care. I want you forever."

With a grin, I threw my arms around his neck. "I want you forever too. But we don't have to rush to get there. I've got a lot of things to figure out first. What will I do long term? I've been managing things remotely, but I'm not sure how well my business would do in a small town like Lovewell."

He swallowed, the muscles in his throat working. I had bitten them and licked them many times. And the alcohol, exotic beach, and the nudity were making my hormones go wild again. "You can travel when you need to. Take clients up north. We can figure it out."

His response was nonchalant, but this was my life and my livelihood. Granted, I had thought a lot about staying. I was head-over-heels in love with my lumberjack. After what we'd been through, nothing else seemed relevant.

This felt like forever. And I no longer worried about proving myself to my father. His opinion meant nothing to me anymore. It was time to consider my own happiness and live a productive life of my choosing. And right now, I wanted to choose Paz and Lovewell.

He licked his lips, abruptly ending my thought spiral. "Or you could let me take care of you. All I ask is that you never wear bras and you let me eat your pussy every day."

I stood up on my tiptoes and kissed him hungrily. "Wow, you drive a hard bargain."

With a smirk and a shrug, he said, "My negotiation skills are legendary." He cupped my cheek gently. "I mean it. I want you at the farmhouse with me. We can get furniture and hang photos. Maybe rescue a cat. Make it our home. I know there are a lot of details to work out, but we can do anything together. We took down a drug cartel, for fuck's sake."

"They haven't been convicted yet. Don't get ahead of yourself," I said, my cop superstitions rearing up.

"They already have a handful of confessions *and* the recording. I don't think there's a lot to worry about."

He was so handsome and so goddamned persuasive. Especially when his fingers were toying with the hem of my dress, slowly inching it up my thighs. Right now, in this moment, life was perfect. This man, this overprotective, anxious, stubborn man, had completely upended my life. And I couldn't wait to see what would happen next.

"I'll stay."

He picked me up and spun me around, then collapsed in the sand. "Good," he said, already kissing my neck. "Kids?"

"Eventually." I tilted my head to give him more access.

"Let's start trying now. Goldie and Tucker need cousins."

Before I could respond, he had me flat on my back in the warm sand as he pulled my dress up higher.

"Let's start with cohabitation first," I said, gasping as his fingers found just the right spot. "And then we can talk about everything else."

At this moment, everything seemed possible. Because I had fallen for this wonderful, serious, sometimes infuriating man. Someone who challenged me and supported me every single day. I knew I wasn't going back to Portland, because Paz belonged in Lovewell. And there was no place I'd rather be.

Bonus Epilogue

Want more Paz & Parker?

Scan HERE to read the bonus epilogue

Warning: it will make you laugh, cry and swoon!

SCAN ME

Need More Lumberjacks?

You can find the entire Lovewell Lumberjacks Series on Amazon. Free to read in Kindle Unlimited

Book 1: **Wood You Be Mine?**
Book 2: **Wood You Marry Me?**
Book 3: **Wood You Rather?**
Book 4: **Wood Riddance!**

Keep reading for the first chapter of **Wood Riddance** an enemies to lovers, accidental pregnancy romance.

Prologue

Adele

2 years ago

This could not be happening.

I sat up straight and tried to control my breathing. It was a technique I'd learned in therapy after my dad died. There weren't many things I could control in life, so I focused on box breathing. In for four, out for four.

Because the rage that was usually set to a low simmer inside me was threatening to boil up again.

"I think there's a mismatch here," he said, sitting back in his seat with the kind of unearned confidence that made me homicidal.

I clenched my fists. How was this happening *again*? I'd date someone for six months or so, and then they'd dump me. For any number of lame and questionable reasons.

I just wasn't worth hanging on to.

As he explained, ad nauseam, why his work was so important and why he was so special, I zoned out, studying his face for clues as to how things had gone so wrong.

Prologue

Weak chin, patchy stubble, and beady eyes. Long ago, I had learned to never go for the hot ones. They were always full of themselves and thought they could do better. I had liked Blake. He was quirky, and I enjoyed his dry sense of humor.

"I think we have different values, goals," he said expectantly.

Licking my lips, I racked my brain for an appropriate response and came up empty. "Sorry?"

"I'm ambitious, and academia isn't for the faint of heart," he said slowly, like I was a child.

I snorted. I wasn't sure what academia was for most of the time.

"And I'm in my thirties now. I need a partner who will be an asset when it comes to my career."

God, I was such an idiot. I'd left work early and curled my hair, excited for a night out. We had made plans for him to spend the weekend, so I had deep cleaned my house and stocked the fridge in preparation.

In all these months, we hadn't gone out much. Only to the annoying pub near campus where he and the other junior professors would drink cheap beer and one-up each other, each trying to establish themselves as the smartest of the bunch.

We had been dating for six months. Sure, we'd kept it casual. I met him a few months after losing my dad in a truck accident, so I wasn't in a place for serious. But we'd been exclusive and having fun. I'd also spent those six months driving to Orono to see him because, apparently, coming to Lovewell was "inconvenient."

I owned my own gorgeous home, while he lived in a dingy apartment with the other junior faculty. But according to him, staying close to home was important because he needed to ensure he was rested and focused. You know, because his job was so important. Talking to bored, hungover freshman about the fucking Crusades.

And I was "just a mechanic." Novel, sure, but ultimately unimportant to fancy fuckers with PhDs like him. I was less important, despite my higher income, my position leading a large team, or the level the responsibility I was tasked with. The entire point of my professional life was to ensure the safety of dozens of employees at Gagnon Lumber.

I could sense it, the anger and rage bubbling up inside me. It had taken thirty-plus years to learn to control. But right now, I wasn't sure I could stop it, and I wanted to preserve my dignity.

"Just so I understand," I said, sarcasm dripping from my voice. "You're dumping me?"

He nodded, looking way too calm for someone who might be swallowing his teeth in the next few minutes.

"Then why are we here?" I hissed. "Why did you drive to my house and pick me up and take me to one of the nicest restaurants in the state?"

He shrank back. "I planned to do it when I arrived, but you looked pretty, you know, like you made an effort. I felt bad, so I figured we could have a nice meal."

My eye twitched and bile rose in my throat. "Are you kidding me?"

"I don't want to make this messy, Adele. It's one of the things I really liked about you. How no-nonsense you are. Not like other women. I assumed you'd understand."

And now I was ready to explode. It was how I operated. Once wronged, I'd hate you forever. So despite how excited I'd been to spend the weekend with him, the switch had flipped. I now despised him and wanted to throw him into the ocean.

"Understand what? That you think I'm not good enough for you?" I snarled.

He paled, leaning forward. "Keep your voice down."

I smiled, enjoying how nervous he looked. "Get. The. Fuck. Out," I said slowly, swirling the wine in my glass.

"Don't be hostile."

"This is me playing nice. Leave. Now."

I looked at him coolly, determined to retain my composure. Castrating him with a butter knife was oh so tempting, but I wouldn't make a scene. He wasn't worth it. There was no salvaging this. He didn't see me as worthy, and I had learned a long time ago not to beg people to accept me or love me.

Sipping my wine and staring out the window, I ignored him as he walked out. I refused to give him any indication that I cared about his flat, pompous ass.

The waitress appeared, looking nervous. "You can take his beer," I said, picking up my menu and giving her a quick smile. "I'll be ready to order in a minute."

She nodded and scampered off.

Another day, another insecure, unworthy man. Story of my goddam life.

It wasn't like I hadn't put myself out there. I'd joined the apps, and I went out of my way to leave my small town and head to where there were more options. I wore makeup and made small talk and attempted to be less scary.

But at five-eleven and with a traditionally masculine job, as well as a complete inability to suffer fools, most of the male population was scared off on sight.

I was beginning to lose faith. My mom and dad had adored each other, and they'd loved each other fiercely for almost forty years. I'd grown up witnessing the love they had for one another every day of my life.

So I knew it was possible. Companionship, love. Granted, my two older brothers were also chronically single, and my youngest brother, Remy, had an awful fiancée we barely tolerated. So maybe the soulmate kind of love was skipping this generation.

I wanted to hold on to my hope that someone would see the real me. But so far, every guy I'd met had decided I wasn't worth it.

As soon as I was certain he had left the parking lot, I took a look around. I'd order dinner and then cross my fingers I could get a ride share to take me all the way back to Lovewell. If not, I'd swallow my pride and call one of my brothers.

The bar area was bustling with people chatting and drinking as the sun began to set outside. It was one of those industrial style places, with exposed duct work and water served in mason jars. Not really my style, but I was hungry, and I'd be damned if I let shithead Blake ruin my evening.

And then I looked up and met a familiar set of dark brown eyes.

Fuck me sideways.

Finn Hebert. At the bar. Staring at me. I reflexively reached for the butter knife on the table. Of all the cocky asshole shitheads to witness me getting dumped. Why did it have to be him? Was Mr. Canton, my sadistic eighth grade math teacher, unavailable? Did Ritchie LaVoie, who'd taken my virginity and then joked about it with the whole school after, have a previous engagement?

Because while tonight had been humiliating as it was, knowing a Hebert, and *that* Hebert, of all people, had witnessed it, only made it worse.

All while looking especially handsome. His long hair was pulled back into a man bun. He was wearing a plaid shirt with the sleeves rolled up to expose the tats on his forearms, and his dark jeans were molded to his legs. The man wore clothes really well. *Bastard.*

Finding clothes that fit my tall frame was always a challenge. But this asshole was NBA-player tall and looked like he'd stepped out of a hot Viking lumberjack magazine.

He picked up his beer and sauntered over far too gracefully for someone who was the size of a baby giraffe.

"Everything okay?" he asked, looking down at me.

"Yes." I glared at him. "My date had an emergency. I'm trying to enjoy my glass of wine."

"Great. I'll join you."

Before I could protest, he had taken Blake's chair and was leaning over to clink my glass with the lip of his bottle. I held my middle finger up against my wineglass.

He ignored my rude gesture, instead looking around the space. "I've never been here," he said, bringing his beer to his lips.

I watched the muscles of his throat contract and raised one eyebrow. Why was he being so nice? Had he used all his dad's money to buy a better personality? I was in no mood for chitchat, especially with this overgrown frat boy.

Briefly, I fantasized about whipping off one of my heels and throwing it across the table so it lodged in the middle of his smooth, tan forehead. My aim was impeccable. There was a reason I had won so many axe-throwing tournaments. And I knew I could do serious damage.

But then I dipped my chin, taking in my flats. Blake was self-conscious about his height, so I'd stopped wearing heels—though I had quite a collection—in order to appease him.

I smiled to myself. He was such a dickweasel. I wanted to go back to my shop, invent a time machine, and travel back six months so I could decline his offer to buy me that first drink. Because what had I been thinking?

Looked like I had hit the desperation stage. Perhaps I should call it a day and adopt some cats.

"Are you laughing *at* me or *with* me?" Finn said, interrupting my thoughts.

I pinned him with a sharp glare. "Obviously *at* you. I was planning my upcoming cat adoption. I'm prepared to fully embrace my spinster identity."

"Seems a bit premature." He dropped his forearms to the table so his hands rested not far from mine. "I'm single, in case you were wondering." With that admission, he gave me a wink. His posture was relaxed, and despite my better judgment, I was curious. What had led this big, intimidating guy with all the tattoos, a young daughter, and a cocky smirk back to Lovewell?

"I'm not," I snapped a little too eagerly, "interested."

He shook his head and leaned in. "You single? I suspect you may be after that Poindexter stormed out of here."

I shrugged, not willing to give him the satisfaction of being right.

"Good. He's not good enough for you."

I snorted. "He thinks otherwise."

He took another sip of his beer. "Guys like him always do. Not a great loss. Someone better will come along."

I tipped my wineglass back, desperate for a refill. "Not likely," I said, catching the server's eye.

"You're a strong, blond goddess. On what planet are you not good enough for him? You're basically a superhero." He scratched his chin. "I get a strong She-Ra vibe from you."

I laughed, secretly flattered. Most of the time, I felt tall and unwieldy. I was far from one of those tiny, delicate women.

Nope, I was more like the large monster lurching through the city as bodies fell in my wake.

"Definitely. Can you keep a secret? I'm a bit of a comic book nerd. And trust me, you are definitely She-Ra."

Shit, he was good-looking. And he had the good sense to compare me to a beautiful, powerful, feminist superhero. I had to be careful, though. Because beneath the serious Viking facade, Finn Hebert was a charmer.

And in my just-dumped, vulnerable state, I could not afford to be charmed.

"Let me drive you. I'm heading there anyway."

I shook my head, signing the credit card receipt. He had fought me on paying for dinner, but I'd insisted we split it. The last thing I needed was to be indebted to a Hebert. It was bad enough that I'd eaten dinner with him. I'd pay for my own rainbow trout.

"I'm good," I said primly, digging my phone out of my bag. "I'll call a rideshare."

"You will not. It'll take forever to find someone willing to take you out to the sticks. Plus, carpooling is better for the environment."

I gave him a dramatic eye roll.

"Come on. My mother would never forgive me if I left you here. She raised us right." He cocked a brow. "Or at least she tried to."

"She wouldn't know."

He laughed. "My mother knows everything. As does yours, by the way. They probably know we're arguing instead of driving to Lovewell right now."

It was late, and my weekend had gone to shit. I'd probably spend tomorrow working. After I hit the gym, of course. Maybe, just maybe, I should lower my weapons and accept a little help.

"Fine," I said, standing up and pushing my chair in.

His answering smile made my stomach drop. And when he put his hand on the small of my back and gently led me through the restaurant, something inside my chest fluttered. There weren't many people who could make me feel small, but his size and his presence were comforting. And *that* was unnerving.

He opened the door to his truck, and I climbed inside. It was immaculate.

I didn't know what I had expected. Maybe empty protein shakes and condom wrappers? Regardless, the person I'd eaten dinner with tonight was shockingly different from what I assumed all Heberts were like. They owned a rival timber company, and our grandfathers had had a falling out sometime in the 1950s, so I'd spent my life hating them. They were rich and entitled and thought they were better than the rest of us. While our family and others struggled to survive, the Heberts were flaunting their wealth, all while actively trying to buy out the other local timber companies.

Riding beside Finn down the lonely rural roads made me itchy and self-conscious. Maybe it was his confidence. Or maybe it was the way he carried himself. The straight military posture mixed with the bad boy tattoos and long hair.

"I've had a shit day myself," he said as I sat perfectly still, keeping my focus locked on the road ahead. "Had to drive all the way to Bangor to sign legal paperwork. My ex, Alicia, is a lawyer."

I nodded, not sure how to respond. We had grown up in the

same tiny town. I knew Alicia Walker, his ex-girlfriend and the mother of his child. Her grandmother had lived down the street from my parents. They had hooked up when he enlisted in the Navy but had never married. There was all kinds of local gossip and speculation as to why. I'd always assumed it was because she realized he was a Neanderthal. She was a smart and motivated person. No wonder she'd become a successful lawyer and had left him in the dust. These days, the rumor was that she was engaged to another lawyer. Apparently, some people could find their happily ever afters. Just not me.

"You could try to make polite conversation," he said, sounding annoyed. "Your manners leave much to be desired."

"Newsflash. I don't give a shit what you think of my manners. And being polite is overrated. Why is that the gold standard for womanly behavior? I have no interest in pretending to care about what you think of me."

He whistled. "I guess it's not a shock you got dumped, then."

"Fuck off. Your commentary about my love life is unwelcome."

"Only calling it like I see it, She-Ra."

I rolled my eyes and went back to ignoring him, studying the lane markers on the road instead. His monster of a truck was beginning to get a little too small. Finn wasn't just physically large. His booming voice and deep chuckle made his presence almost all-consuming.

I hated it. Or, more accurately, I hated how I felt around him. Off my game, on the defense, and out of my depth. No thank you.

Thankfully, he got the message, and once again, we rode in silence. Once we hit Lovewell, I busied myself directing him to my house.

He put the truck in park out front. "You live here?"

I nodded. My house was my sanctuary. A craftsman cottage on a neat acre, it had a white picket fence, a porch with rocking chairs, and my gardens in the back. It had taken years to save for and even longer to fix up, but it was mine.

I unbuckled my seat belt and reached for the door.

"We should do this again."

I shot him a look. "Good one."

"Why not? Because our families hate each other?" He cocked a challenging brow. "Who cares? We're adults."

I turned and studied his face. *In for four, out for four.* Finn Hebert already knocked me off balance. And his casual assertion that we should hang out only made me more nervous.

I leaned forward, watching as he bit down on his bottom lip.

"Because I dislike you. And, more importantly, because you couldn't handle me."

He stared at me for a long moment, the heat of his gaze making my body shiver. And then he slid his hand into my hair and gripped it tight before pulling my lips to his.

His lips were full and soft, in complete juxtaposition to his rough, strong hands. Both of which were in my hair.

He was hungry and intense yet gentle at the same time. A dizzying combination that kept me coming back for more.

A slight moan escaped my throat, and I angled closer, fisting his flannel shirt. What was hiding under this shirt was no secret. I saw this guy at the gym every day. His chest was broad and strong. Though the one mystery was whether he had chest hair, and suddenly, I was desperate to find out.

Fuck, this is bad. I hated Finn Hebert. I hated his family and everything he represented. But my body didn't care.

Instead, it ignored my brain's plea to jump out of the truck and never look back.

I pulled away long enough to breathe before diving back in, reveling in the taste and feel of him. He groaned, letting one hand slide down my neck, his rough fingers teasing my skin.

My heart nearly jumped out of my chest at the sensation. I should have stopped. This couldn't happen. I knew that, but I was already mentally figuring out how to get him into my house without my neighbors seeing. The last thing I needed was the town rumor mill kicking up.

But before I could form cogent thoughts, he pulled back and gave my hair a gentle tug, then released the strands. The glow of the dashboard illuminated his symmetrical face as I attempted to catch my breath. My heart was pounding like I'd run a marathon, and I swore my nipples had poked holes through my very expensive bra.

I looked up to find him grinning. Fucking grinning. Clearly pleased with himself that he'd almost made me orgasm on first base. As if kissing the shit out of me was somehow amusing to him. What a smug prick. I should have known he'd be like the rest of them. A taller, hotter, military version, sure. But he was no different from every other asshole I'd kissed in my life.

And then I snapped.

"What the shit?" I said, pushing against his chest so he fell back against his seat, trying to muster all the indignation I could. "Did I say you could kiss me? Or is consent optional for you?"

He continued to smirk. It was an infuriatingly sexy one at that. "Are you forgetting the part where you grabbed me and stuck your tongue down my throat? Let's not pretend you weren't kissing me back, She-Ra."

I said nothing. There was no point in denying my participation. Best to ignore it and move on.

He folded his arms over his expansive chest. The move was so distracting it took me a moment to remember why I was mad.

Damn hormones. It was my own fault. I always dated guys who were lousy lays and couldn't keep up with my libido.

Not that Finn would have a problem. No, that kiss alone proved he'd be thorough, attentive, and just wild enough to satisfy me.

I squeezed my eyes shut. I was supposed to be mad. No, furious. This cocky Viking thought he could do whatever he wanted.

I sat up straight, grabbed my purse, and reached for the door handle.

"Thanks for the ride home," I said primly.

"Anytime." He was still grinning at me.

"Maybe next time, keep your mouth to yourself."

I opened the door, ready to step out, but before I could, he leaned over the console, his broad shoulders crowding me.

He lowered his gaze to my chest, where my nipples were likely acting like traitorous whores desperate for attention. "Maybe next time I'll use it on other parts of your delicious body."

And then he winked. *Winked.* The audacity.

I opened the door, jumped out, and strode to my front door without looking back.

On the way, I rummaged around in my giant purse, praying I'd find my keys quickly.

Of course he remained idling in the driveway, waiting for me to go inside.

With shaky hands, I finally got the door open, and I

slammed it shut the second I was safely inside, then slid down to the tile on the other side.

I tilted my head back, taking deep breaths to calm my racing heart.

Finn Motherfucking Asshole Viking Degenerate Hebert had kissed me. And I liked it.

I touched my swollen lips. This would obviously never happen again. I hated the guy. I hated his family. And I wanted nothing to do with any of them.

But on the bright side? Since he'd sat down, I hadn't thought about getting dumped once.

Acknowledgments

Thank you for taking this trip to Lovewell with me! This book would not have been possible without the help of so many talented and dedicated people. Every book starts off feeling impossible, and I'm only able to get it over the finish line with the help of some amazing people.

This book would not exist without Erica Connors Walsh. Thank you for being my friend, my cheerleader, and the best PA ever. You have been with me since Day one, and you push me to be better every day. We have cried and laughed and yelled together over the past two years, and I am a better person and writer because of you. I believe deeply that some divine cosmic power brought us together, and I'm so grateful to have you on my team.

To the incomparable Jenni Bara, you are so talented, humble, and kind. Every book I write is better because of your ideas and energy. Thank you for being a true friend and for teaching me to just roll with things.

Brittanee Nicole, you are one in a million. Thank you for finding me on Instagram two years ago and putting up with me since. You are brilliant and creative, and I love your beautiful face.

Swati M.H., you are the best thought partner and friend. Thank you for talking me off the ledge and helping me figure my shit out on a daily basis.

To my beta readers, Amarylis, Christina, Amy, and Jenni, thank you all for helping me work through Paz & Parker's journey and giving me helpful notes.

Beth, thank you for your thorough editing. I am amazed by your patience, professionalism, and kindness. I'm sorry I'm such a lazy writer and never put my quotation marks in the right place.

Lindee, thank you for the gorgeous photos. Taking photos of shirtless men is a hard job, and I'm grateful you do it.

Shannon and Brian, thank you for the amazing cover photo. You are beautiful people, inside and out, and I am honored to have you on my book.

Thank you to my mother, who always pushed me to do my best and believed in me even when I did not. I am the kind of person who decides to write books in my nonexistent free time because of you.

Thank you to my family for being hilarious and loving and silly. To my children, G & T, you push me and challenge me and surprise me every day. Thank you for never going easy on me.

And finally, thank you to my patient and devastatingly handsome husband. Thank you for the Lumbersnack inspiration and endless support. You are my original Alpha Roll.

Also by Daphne Elliot

LOVEWELL

The Lovewell Lumberjacks Series

Wood You Be Mine?

Wood You Marry Me?

Wood You Rather?

Wood Riddance

The Maine Lumberjacks Series

Caught in the Axe

Pain in the Axe

Axe-identally Married

Axe Backwards

Axe-ing for Trouble

HAVENPORT

The Quinn Brothers Series

Trusting You

Finding You

Keeping You

The Rossi Family Series

Resisting You

Holding You

Embracing You

About the Author

In High School, Daphne Elliot was voted "most likely to become a romance novelist." After spending the last decade as a corporate lawyer, she has finally embraced her destiny. Her steamy novels are filled with flirty banter, sexy hijinks, and lots and lots of heart.

Daphne is a coffee-drinking, hot-sauce loving introvert who spends her free time reading, gardening and practicing yoga. She lives in Massachusetts with her husband, two kids, two dogs, and twenty two backyard chickens.

Find Daphne At:

daphneelliot.com
daphneelliotauthor@gmail.com

Stay in touch with Daphne:

Subscribe to Daphne's Newsletter
Join Daphne's Reader Group
Follow Daphne on TikTok
Like Daphne on Facebook
Follow Daphne on Instagram
Hang with Daphne on GoodReads
Follow Daphne on Amazon

Made in the USA
Las Vegas, NV
23 April 2024

89076876R00236